the Rowantree Crop

the Rowantree Crop

A Mystery
by
Elisabeth Pollack

NORTH COUNTRY PRESS • UNITY, MAINE

Library of Congress Cataloging-in-Publication Data

Pollack, Elisabeth, 1921-
The rowantree crop / by Elisabeth Pollack.
p. cm.
ISBN 0-945980-18-3 : $15.95 (est.) — ISBN 0-945980-16-7 (pbk.) $8.95 (est.)
I. Title.
PS3566.04796R69 1989
813' .54—dc20

89-39542
CIP

Cover and book illustrations by Jeanie Munro Peraino,
Trillium Enterprises, Sugar Hill, New Hampshire.
Design & composition by Sandau Type & Design, Brunswick, Maine.
Printed in the United States of America by
The J.S. McCarthy Co., Augusta, Maine.

1 2 3 4 5 6 7 8 9 10

Dedication

"For John and Susan and Maureen."

Acknowledgements

This story is pure fiction, although there is a county called Oxford in the State of Maine and many of the town names in Maine and Connecticut are authentic. The rest is the way it might have been.

I am grateful to many people who gave me encouragement and did some reading for me "early on." You all know who you are. In particular I want to thank George and Grace Emmerton, Wini and Schuyler Mott and Terry and Mark Silber. George Morrill, my one living character, gave me permission to use his name for the auction scenes, and a dear daughter-in-law, Maureen Askew Pollack, flat on her back in British Columbia recovering from major surgery, helped me with the first editing.

And without Bill and Linn Johnson, my publishers, this might not have happened. I am ever grateful.

Characters

Lee Heaward	Co-owner of Carriage Trade Realty and owner of High Meadows Farm in Paris, Maine
Meg Bundy	Lee's partner in Carriage Trade
Reed Jamison	Chief of Police of Town of Paris
Ted and Ellen West	A young couple who works for Lee at High Meadows
Dorie Wilson	Secretary at Carriage Trade
Clipper (Jack) Cleaver	Owner of Cleaver Real Estate in Paris
Bunny Cleaver	His wife who does counted cross-stitch
Cokie Adams	A saleswoman for Cleaver Real Estate and a bit eccentric
Malcolm Bandridge	A retired clothing store owner, little theatre member, and part-time broker with Cleaver Real Estate
Elvira Bandridge Campbell	Malcolm's sister from Philadelphia
Carter Ransome	A friend of Lee's and owner of a bookshop in Salisbury, Connecticut
Hod Cole	A Maine woodsman known as "Old Poacher", who meets Lee in unusual circumstances

Dr. and Mrs. Attlebury	Summer residents who live between Lee and the Hartley place
Jim Davidson	A real estate appraiser who is hired to appraise the Hartley place
Nancy Davidson	His wife
Dot Bailey	Dispatcher at the Sheriff's Office
Mrs. Bemis	Owner of the Cottage and member of the Historic House Garden Tour
John Ridley	Planning Board Chairman
Sam Childs	Developer
Jan Howard the Patterson sisters the Ward sisters the Rhineharts	All members of the Historic House Garden Tour

Members of the planning board; the surveying crew; Meg's husband, Will, and daughter Jolie

George Morrill	Owner of Morrill's Auctions Inc., Gray, Maine
Rom	One of the Morrill auction crew

and

Kate Gordon	A Gordon setter belonging to Lee

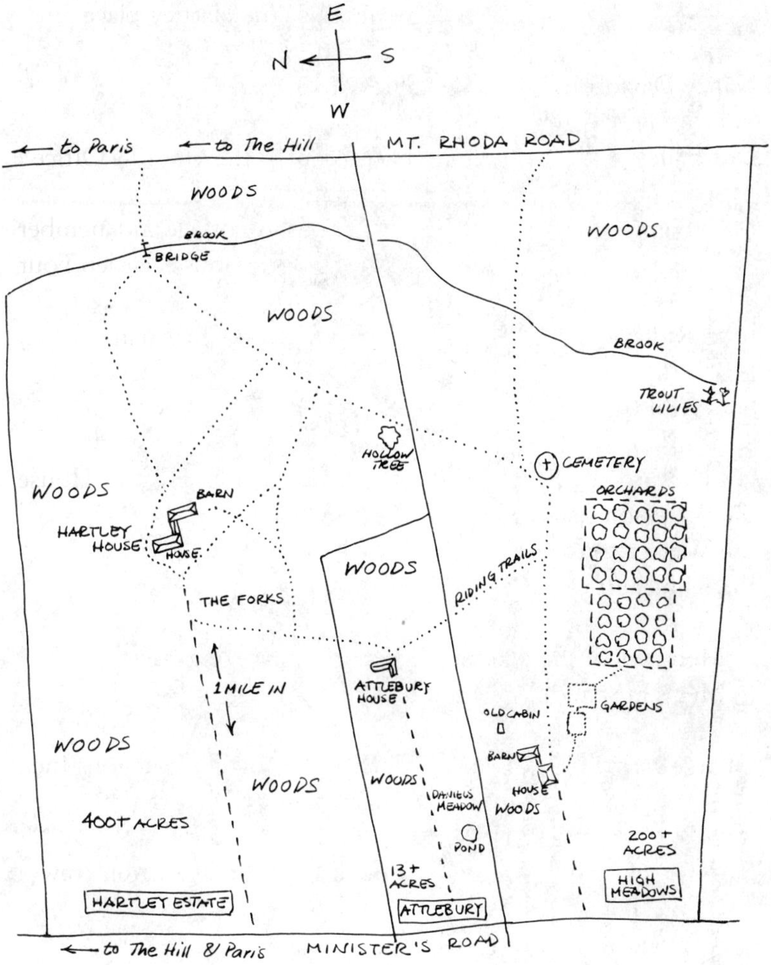
E
N
S
W
← to Paris
← to The Hill
MT. RHODA ROAD
WOODS
BROOK
BRIDGE
WOODS
WOODS
BROOK
TROUT LILIES
HOLLOW TREE
CEMETERY
ORCHARDS
WOODS
BARN
HARTLEY HOUSE
HOUSE
WOODS
RIDING TRAILS
THE FORKS
1 MILE IN
ATTLEBURY HOUSE
GARDENS
OLD CABIN
WOODS
BARN
HOUSE
WOODS
WOODS
DANIELS MEADOW
WOODS
400+ ACRES
POND
200+ ACRES
13+ ACRES
HIGH MEADOWS
HARTLEY ESTATE
ATTLEBURY
← to The Hill & Paris
MINISTER'S ROAD

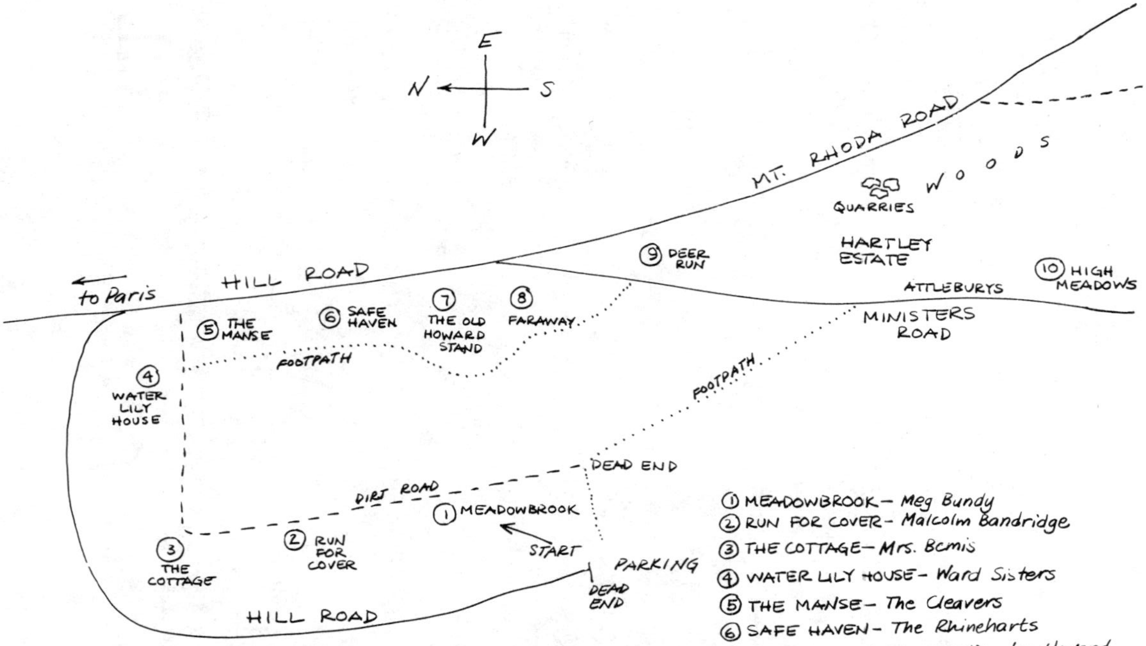

HISTORIC HOUSE GARDEN TOUR MAP

—July 11-12 —

THE HILL

1. MEADOWBROOK – *Meg Bundy*
2. RUN FOR COVER – *Malcolm Bandridge*
3. THE COTTAGE – *Mrs. Bcmis*
4. WATER LILY HOUSE – *Ward Sisters*
5. THE MANSE – *The Cleavers*
6. SAFE HAVEN – *The Rhineharts*
7. THE OLD HOWARD STAND – *Jan Howard*
8. FARAWAY – *Unoccupied Historical Site*
9. DEER RUN – *Patterson Girls*
10. HIGH MEADOWS FARM – *Lee Heaward*

Prologue

The party was almost over. The small boy, tight within the wrappings of brown paper topped with fir boughs, felt stifled. He had not won first prize as he had been promised if he would allow them to transform him into a Christmas tree.

He had been laughed at by the other children, and he had been unable to go to the bathroom because he could not free himself from this melange of paper and glue. His underpants were damp and he was angry.

He watched as the bear won the first prize, a rollicking brown bear made from his rival's mother's old fur coat, with a head of papier-mâché with glued-on fur stripes.

The small boy did win the consolation prize, but he vowed this would never happen to him again. By now, his underpants were very wet.

Nearly half a century later, in an attic room, standing in front of a large cheval mirror, a man dressed himself in a new suit.

He had designed it carefully so that in a very few seconds he might enter this creation of cloth and fakery held together by two large zippers. The top was a different matter; it had to be placed "just so" and secured with a roundabout zipper. Done properly, the suit became a second skin.

The man looked at himself, swung his arms from side to side and did a little two-step.

"You fool," he addressed himself in the mirror. "You always let them tell you what to do. This time it will be different. We'll see who wins the prize."

WINTER

ANGELICA
PARSLEY
COMFREY
BASIL
VALERIAN
CHIVES
GARLIC CHIVES

1

High Meadows Farm rode sidesaddle along the top of a ridge of land. Set back nearly a thousand feet from the main road, on a graveled lane bordered by firs, the old weathered cape with its connecting shed and barn did not invite entrance. Few people knew of its existence; those who did were natives or friends of the owner. Occasionally an out-of-stater turned into the graveled lane by mistake, seeking the Mt. Rhoda Road on the eastern boundary, but in general High Meadows kept its privacy.

Woods blocked out the road frontage to the west; open land lay to the north and east, and the large herb and vegetable gardens led into the orchards and woodland, far back from the public view.

Tonight, Friday the 13th, the night of the full Snow Moon, Lee Heaward sat in the window of the upstairs north bedroom and stared out at the snow-covered gardens. She sat deep in her great-aunt Bess's old wing chair, with an old wedding ring quilt pulled close about her shoulders as if for shelter. In two worlds, Lee was looking inside herself as well as outside the window.

Snow covered the High Meadows world. Knotted beds of thyme and oregano in the herb garden slept beneath the February drifts. The stone statue of St. Fiacre, the patron saint of gardeners, showed just the bearded head and tip of his spade. Here and there patches of hay surfaced where the wind had blown away the garden's protection against the icy gales of a Maine winter.

The outline of a path could be seen leading from the herb garden into the vegetable garden and beyond, into an opening in a double stone wall leading into the orchards. Beneath the trees were deer, up from the woods to search for the last-drop apples beneath the snow. Lee Heaward, leaning forward, watched them intently.

They fascinate me, she thought. *They are me, searching to survive. Raising their heads to listen for the enemy without, while I search myself for the enemy within.*

She gave herself a good shake. *I may be uneasy and not able to sleep, but I'm not going to end up talking to deer at three in the morning. Warm milk can cure anything!*

A warm, wet nose poked into her lap and Lee came back to reality.

"It's all right, Kate, I'm just thinking deep thoughts. Come on, let's see what we can find downstairs."

The Gordon setter whined softly and padded along behind the woman as they descended the staircase. Lee took milk from the refrigerator, warmed it and added cinnamon, and picked up a book from the living room bookcase. She trailed back up the stairs, the old book of magic in her hands. For half an hour she followed the holly and ash and oak back through time to the days of the Druids. *My rowan trees,* she thought, *my protection against harm,* and she wondered for how many generations farmers had placed pieces of the mountain ash in their animals' mangers to ward off evil spirits. She dozed for a minute, then pushed the bedcovers aside impatiently and returned to the window. The moon was low in the west by now and the shadows from the clouds traced movement through the orchard. The deer were still there, farther back than before, but still pawing through the snow's crust. The light was dimmer, but watching closely Lee could still see their movements.

Her mind moved back over the past years. At forty-five , after the tragic accident in which she had lost her husband, Lee had come to Maine to claim the inheritance of the old farm left to her by a favorite great-aunt on her father's side of the family. Aunt Bess had used High Meadows as a summer home, and every year Lee's father had driven to Maine from Connecticut to help Bess with plans to keep the farm running. The 8-year-old girl accompanied her father and sat quietly in the parlor of the old house while the three of them took tea in the late afternoon. The morning had been spent walking the farm and discussing the proper care of orchards, hayfields and timber, Lee listening to every word that passed between her father and Aunt Bess. Then, the ritual of the tea service observed, Lee was free to wander by herself for an extra hour while the adults shared a glass of sherry.

The farm, with the enchantment of the meadows and brooks and woods, fascinated the little girl—a fascination that never left her in later life. Seated between stone walls cornering in the small cemetery lot at the bottom of the old Wolf River Orchard, Lee spun dreams about those who might have shared this spot at different points in time.

Then her father called and they said goodby to Bess for another year. Lee could reach out and touch her picture of Aunt Bess with hand raised in farewell. The memory never failed her.

The family had always assumed that when Bess died High Meadows would be sold and the money split among the various nieces and nephews. Aunt Bess had other plans. She left the farm to Lee.

Along with a note, asking her to please take care of the little cemetery. And every spring to walk to the meadow brook and look at the trout lilies.

"They will be there, Lee, long after we are gone."

After years of life spent following a service husband across the world, and one year of retirement in a small Connecticut town, Lee suddenly had found herself alone. A drunken driver's moment of misjudgment had changed her life forever. Aunt Bess had died the following year, and Lee came up alone to the old farm, not quite sure of her own direction. But it was spring, and in the meadow were the trout lilies.

Lee went back to Connecticut, sold her home within a month, and moved to Maine.

Well-meaning friends were distressed.

"Don't you want to think it over more? You're moving so quickly after Ray's death. What are you going to do all alone on that old place?"

Lee sighed. Impossible to explain the trout lilies.

A year and a new septic tank later, Lee was settled in. She had found a farmer to cut hay and run the orchards. The old cape had been shored up, chimneys rebuilt, the well cleaned, and paint and paper brightened up some of the old rooms. The rest Lee did not want to change. The old sheathing, the remains of the wall murals in the front room, and the old iron stove in the kitchen were all part of Aunt Bess and resisted change.

A paddock for her horses, a start on restoring some of the old gardens that had slipped back in the last years of Bess's life—Lee felt a happiness filling her days. Besides the trout lilies she had found arbutus, pink lady's-slippers, and, deep in the pine grove, a surprisingly fragrant *Daphne meserina,* an escapee from an old garden.

Tall and attractive, with short curly brown hair and brown eyes, with an athletic build and a lifelong interest in horses, antiques and the land, Lee made friends easily. When she met Meg Bundy at an auction her first fall in Maine, it was natural that the two women should become friends. Meg, whose husband ran one of Paris's garages, and who had six children, was casting about for a job or business and Lee was becoming more and more interested in Maine land. Together they formed Carriage Trade Real Estate, their name stemming from the old stables they turned into an office.

From the beginning Carriage Trade was a class act. An antique home and an old farm were their first two listings, and after that it was natural to make these their specialties. For eight years their partnership had been lucrative.

The accessibility of southwestern Maine from Boston and New York sent dozens of buyers looking for second homes. Country living was in vogue. Sales were good. Lee and Meg found themselves in the path of success. Every listing sold and the supply was endless.

All of the East Coast had discovered Maine and Carriage Trade was in the right spot at the right moment.

Until lately. Something had changed. Small conversations had become difficult between the two women. Development was suddenly blossoming, and Meg and Lee suddenly differed on their business direction. Rather fiercely, Lee found herself in a minority position against so-called "progress", which was encouraged by most real estate brokers. She found herself linked with only a few who were far-sighted enough to want some control, some brake put on before too many of the lakes were polluted by new subdivisions and too many old farms were cut up into small lots.

The "quick buck", to use a real estate term, was fast becoming king in southwestern Maine and any one who questioned was fast becoming unpopular.

Suddenly, the phone calls. At odd hours, disguised voices telling her to tend to her own business, leave well enough alone and let people do what they wanted with their land. Maine didn't need Lee Heaward, thank you very much indeed.

At first, it seemed ridiculous. Crank calls. But now some of her own broker friends showed open disagreement. Carriage Trade had lost two listings it should have had. Open warfare was on the horizon.

Lee shivered and shook herself. The heat was down in the old cape. She had stared outward long enough just as she had stared inward. Nothing could be solved tonight. More sleep might help.

Just at that moment, a movement caught her eyes. The remaining deer had gone back to their woods, but to the left on the edge of the orchard something moved. Gliding, rather than leaping, out of the tree line and into the field to the east of the barn, moving slowly. Hard to define as cloud cover was becoming denser.

Certainly not a deer.

Straining forward, one hand on the sill, the other pulling the old quilt closer about her, Lee watched as the figure came closer, toward the side of the barn, into the shadows.

Skis, she thought, *and he's good on them, carrying something in one hand and balancing the two sticks in the other. Poles of course.*

But what's he doing out there this time of night? Can't be one of the cross country club—he'd be going out to the cabin rather than coming in. Unless he's been there already and is coming home early—that could be it.

The Gordon setter, roused again and out of her L.L. Bean bed, laid her nose in Lee's lap, sensing her feelings.

"Quiet, girl." Lee's voice was hushed.

The skier came closer to the east side of the barn where he disappeared. Lee thought quickly. She had to find out what this was about. In a moment she had slipped on shirt and pants, heavy socks and a sweater, with the moonlight making it easy to see without lights.

I wonder if he noticed my movements?

Probably not.

The figure had seemed intent on its own path and had looked straight ahead rather than up. No reason for anyone to think that the inhabitant of the house would be awake and moongazing at that time of morning.

With the dog close at her heels, Lee descended to the kitchen and put on a jacket and her barn boots. For a moment she considered taking the .22 rifle from high on the old pine shelf, but decided against it. She opened the door and stepped out into the connecting ell and woodshed. Ahead of her the Gordon dashed straight to the big door that separated the barn from the ell. She scratched impatiently, whining softly.

Lee could hear the mare whickering, a gentle insistent sound asking for an early morning snack.

Inside the large old barn, built ten years after the house in the late 1700's, the great beams stretched overhead. Pegged together by men who pitted their carpentry against the snows and winds of the hilltop, the barn still stood sturdy and strong. Sheltered in their box stalls beneath the hay loft, the horses moved restlessly, seeming a little tense at this unusually early visit. Lee gave each a loving pat and a small flake of hay to tide them over till regular feeding time. They quieted, munching contentedly.

Kate, meanwhile, worried the rear door, the door to the outside paddock and the winter wind. Lee opened it, pushing hard against the now rising blasts, and Kate shot out, running about barking loudly. Nothing flushed out. Lee's eyes saw no movement.

"Kate, come here." The dog heeled quickly and Lee mentally thanked obedience training.

"Good girl. There's no one there. Thank you." She patted the Gordon's head and looked down at the trusting eyes.

"I wonder what I would have done if there had been someone out there?"

With the door hooked securely and the lights turned off in the barn, Lee paused for a moment, feeling secure in the great old building with the horses and the dog beside her. She had never felt fear here. Local people, when she first came to High Meadows, had been bound to tell her of the woman who had hung herself in the barn in the late 1800's. Aunt Bess had never mentioned her. The woman, wife of one of the past owners, had lost two sons in the terrible diphtheria epidemic of that year, and lost her own courage. In desperation she had thrown a rope over one of the beams and jumped off to end her own life. She was supposed to haunt the barn on winter nights, but Lee had never met her.

If she is here, Lee thought, *she accepts me. She knows I love the place as she once loved it.*

Lee retraced her steps, back through the ell into the kitchen.

Noting the clock hands at four she decided there was little point in going back to bed.

Thoughtfully, measuring the cups with deliberation, she made coffee. She filled Kate's dish and got milk out for Charlie Cooncat who had not taken well to being rudely awakened by a bouncy Gordon's nose in his basket. With a cup in hand, Lee retreated upstairs to the wing chair.

She dozed and when she woke it was 6:00. Still dark outside, the moonlight had lost out to the clouds and snowflakes were falling in earnest. The wind was rising and Lee felt the makings of a storm. Her body was stiff and she wished she had gone back to bed rather than to the wing chair.

Back in the kitchen, Lee made fresh coffee, good and strong, for if a storm was in the making, she knew that Ted would be by for a cup and talk of snowplowing. From the very beginning of her stay at High Meadows, Lee had been blessed with Ted and Ellen, a couple in their late twenties who, as it was so aptly put in New England, "helped out". With no immediate family, Lee felt Ted and Ellen to be a substitute, and their relationship was of mother and children rather than employer and servants.

Thinking of all that had happened in the past few years, Lee considered oatmeal with apples and raisins, decided it to be a splendid idea, and putting the pot on the rear of the woodstove she now judged to be drawing properly, she shoved two apples in her jacket pocket and headed out to the horses. Greetings were exchanged, and noisily eating their grain, the two animals seemed in better spirits than they had been a few hours ago.

Lee opened the rear door to the wind and snow, struggled with ice on water buckets at the open faucet and looked across the tops of the trees to the mountains.

Mt. Washington was hidden this morning in the gathering storm, but smiling to herself Lee thought, *I know it's there.*

Kate raced around happily chasing snowflakes, scattering snow and bouncing in drifts. She stopped to bark at the arches under the barn stalls. The old barn, built as so many Maine barns were, into a hillside, carried its stalls on the first floor, its shelters below and the haylofts above the stalls. The ground floor shelters had dirt floors where the animals could retreat from summer heat and flies, and in the winter parts of the shelters became drops for the stalls above.

Lee called Kate but the dog would not come. Frowning, and a little surprised, she walked through the snow to the barn corner. The big beams and supports met here to form right angles and give entrance to the space beneath, now large enough for only one person to enter as it had been partially boarded over. This morning Kate lunged about in front of the opening, barking excitedly and refusing to back off.

"All right, old girl, now what's the matter? Was someone here last night?"

Scanning the ground, Lee thought she might be able to make out tracks, although the snow was falling faster than before.

One hand on the supporting beams, Lee swung herself halfway into the opening. She squinted, looking around.

In the dim light she almost missed the can.

Directly in front of her, as though someone had deliberately placed it there, sat a small can, the kind used for storing gasoline for lawnmowers or small engines. Beside it was a plastic feed bag half opened. Newspapers and sticks stuck out of the top.

Kindling! Lee's mind raced.

Kindling and paper and gas. Directly under the horse stalls.

Her hands gripped the old beams. She felt a terrible sickness in her stomach. Beside her the Gordon whined nervously. Lee heard herself whisper softly.

"My God, Kate, he was going to fire the barn!"

2

Lee felt terror. Normally solid and good in an emergency, she felt the countryman's age-old fear of fire. She breathed in deeply, exhaled and collected her thoughts. She swung her body up out of the opening, called the Gordon and hurried back through the barn and into the house to dial the sheriff's office.

Dot Bailey answered. Dispatcher for many years at the county building, Dot and Lee had begun a solid friendship when Lee helped Dot sell her parents' farm. Since then, well satisfied with Lee's sales ability, Dot had been the source of many listings and the two women had become friends. Dot belonged to the same riding club and although there was ten years' difference in their ages, Dot's forty-five to Lee's fifty-five, they shared common interests.

"I'm glad you're on, Dot. Is Reed around? I'd like him to come up if he could. Someone was wandering around the barn last night and I'm a little disturbed."

More than that Lee did not volunteer. Reed Jamison, the police chief in the town of Paris, was the one to deal with the details. Dot, the central dispatcher, would locate him and send him up, but more than this Lee did not want to talk of, even with Dot, until Reed had a chance to look at things.

"He's out on call on the old West Road. I'll contact him, Lee, he's just come on duty. Likely he'll come up as soon as he's through with that call. Where you gonna be, office or High Meadows?"

"Here at High Meadows, Dot. I'll be here all morning. In fact, I'll stay until he comes. It is rather important."

Dot, alert to voice patterns, heard the strain in Lee's tones.

"Anything missing? Know who it was?"

"No, nothing's missing. I don't know who it was. Thanks, Dot."

"Okey dokey, Lee. I'll contact him pronto." Dot tended to read westerns.

Lee's second call was to Meg. Carriage Trade would not open until nine; Meg was still at home. Lee explained briefly and Meg assured her that she and Dorie could handle the office. The storm would cancel some appointments and Saturday in the wintertime was slow anyway.

Hanging up, Lee opened the door for Ellen. Kate was happy; Ellen usually arrived with a dog bone hidden in one pocket, and they played their usual game of finders keepers. Satisfied, Kate settled in by the woodstove and the women sat down to share a cup of coffee.

"Ted just dropped me off. He'll be back up to plow bye and bye. Do you want me to do up the big room proper, Lee? You having the historic club meeting next week? They still planning the garden tour this summer?"

Lee agreed on doing up the big room and admitted to the meeting. Normally with a quiet social life, she had agreed to let the farm be part of the garden tour for the benefit of the Hill's historic buildings, and she was finding the meetings more demanding and involved than she had supposed. It seemed that every small detail had to be addressed and she could not for the life of her see any difference in whether you approached a garden clockwise or anticlockwise. But, she had agreed, and next week Friday was slated to be the first of several planning meetings for the July event. The committee members would like the big room and maybe Ellen's famous chocolate cake and coffee would placate some of them.

Half an hour later the door to the ell opened and Ted and Reed Jamison stepped inside together, shaking snow from their jackets and stomping their boots on the doormat. They joined Ellen and Lee at the old pine table by the window.

Reed noted that Lee's face looked tired and strained as she handed him his coffee cup and remembered to pour a tablespoon or so of cream into it; she was one of those few people who always knew what you took with your coffee. Ellen tended to Ted, who was laying waste to a bran muffin while shoveling sugar into his coffee.

How different they are, thought Lee.

Graduating in the same high school class, with totally different goals, the love of the Oxford Hills bound Reed and Ted together.

Tall and blond, with an intelligence both native and schooled, Reed could have done anything with his engineering degree, but he had, instead, chosen to return to the small town of Paris and take the job of chief of the police force. Ted had elected to stay close to home; mechanically minded and not too sure of the written word, he did odd jobs, worked on a farm and did some logging in season. He and Ellen had married right out of school and when Lee needed a farm worker and a once-a-week house cleaner they fell naturally into the positions, seemingly more kinfolk than hired hands.

Reed and Ted hunted and fished together and their respect and love for the woods and fields was a source of strength and joy to Lee.

Warmed by the woodfire of the old stove, seated around the pine table, and looking out on the falling snow, Lee felt tears rising close to the surface.

But there was no time for that now.

"I've kept Kate close since this morning, and the gas can and papers haven't been touched, Reed. I started to take them out from under the barn and then realized you wanted them just the way I found them. Fingerprints, maybe?"

Lee passed more muffins.

Reed had been taking notes since his arrival. He asked a few questions as to time, and what little Lee could identify of the figure in the moonlight. He respected Lee, knew her mind was sharp, and that her story would be embroidery free.

"Can you remember anything about the way he moved? I'm saying *he*, Lee, could it have been a *she*?"

"Either, I suppose. I just know there seemed to be a bundle or bag in one hand; the other had the poles. I've done that myself lots of times, carrying things. Gives you better balance. Once in a while someone from the cross country ski team goes out to the cabin, but they usually ask. When I think of it, they always ask. So that surprised me a little. I was more concerned when he didn't come straight on but took off to one side of the barn. Into the shadows. You know the rest."

Reed nodded. He had made notes and gone through the story twice. Now it was time to look. Kate was ready to join them.

"No, stay here with Ellen." Lee patted the Gordon's head, but refused to play.

"I'm the lucky one." Ellen grinned. "Come on, Kate, let's see if we can find the dust mops," and they were off to the large pantry storeroom on the far side of the kitchen.

Under the barn Reed carefully picked up the can and bag after taking photographs and looking the area over intently.

"There could be fingerprints, but I doubt it. He must have had gloves on and to identify this particular can and bag won't be easy. Everyone has a gas can; this looks used; and everyone has feed bags like this. At least three stores sell this kind of feed and the bags go the rounds with trash and all sorts of stuff in them. The kindling is the kind you get at the woodmill; every other house in Paris has some of it in the basement or woodshed. Not what I'd call the easiest stuff to trace. And no prints under here. He just dropped it in; set it in easy like. Close enough to light. The dog's barking must have scared him off. Shed of his bundle he'd move faster and he must have just skimmed out through the paddock, down the far field and into Attleburys' woods. With this new snow, the tracks are gone. That's what I'd guess."

"Me too." Ted had been looking at the ground. "Right here, the lee side of this drift, looks like it might be the trace of a track. Anyways, you're right, Reed. That's the way I'd go. Get away from the dog and into the woods. And if he knew Lee, he knew she'd call off her dog."

"If he knew me?"

"Where'd you set a fire, Lee?" asked Ted. "If you was a-going to? Had to know where the stalls was and the opening just under them. Otherwise, take him a while to choose a place. He knew if he moved as quick as you say—he come right straight up to the opening. So he had to know you and know right where the horses were."

Reed agreed.

"Ted's right, I'm afraid. Do you have any real bad enemies? I know this land development thing is getting pretty hot between some of the real estate people, but I can't see it going as far as a barn-burning. Have you had anything different happen lately? Anything you can sort of put a handle on?"

Lee, pulling her jacket about her, thought.

"Only the phone calls. I thought they were kids at first. Now I don't know."

"When?" Reed's voice was quick and he pushed his hair off his forehead. "What did they say?"

"They weren't the usual obscene type. They started about four months ago; I haven't had any lately. I thought maybe it had something to do with running off some kids from the woods cabin. Then there was a call after that. Oh, they just said 'mind your own business' and 'wouldn't walk in the oak woods alone'. Things like that. The last one said 'we don't need you around here'."

"Could you recognize the voice?"

Lee looked thoughtful. "No, it seemed different at times. Once I thought I might know, but I'm not sure. All women who live alone get their share of phone calls, but these weren't what I'd call obscene."

Reed's concern was evident. "Well, if there are more, let me know. Are you alone this weekend? Is Carter coming up, by any chance?"

Lee nodded. "Yes, he should be here this evening, unless the weather gets too bad and they close the turnpike. He's staying for a few days. Even if he wasn't coming I'd be fine. I have the dog and Ted and Ellen are right down the road. And I do have Betsy up on the shelf."

"And you leave her right there unless you're really pushed." Reed was stern. "The sheriff's office is right at the other end of the wire. Now, I want to take a good look at the can and bag back at the office. First off, though, Ted, want to come with me and look at the road coming out of the Attlebury place? I'm guessing he swung through there and came out on the main road. The patrol goes by at night. If he knew Lee's barn and the ski trails, he'd know that too. If he left a car there we might find some evidence, although the snow'll cover most everything. But we can look."

"Reed, thank you. I really appreciate it."

They walked back into the house, and for a moment Reed's hand rested lightly on Lee's shoulder. Thirty years younger—twenty-five to her fifty-five—he still felt a kinship and understanding with this woman who lived at High Meadows. Every Christmas he cut his tree back in her woods, and every Christmas he would stop by on the way out of the farm and thank Lee for his privilege. They would share a glass of sherry and maybe some cookies Lee had baked, and sometimes they would speak of what Christmas might have been when in the 1800's people lived without central heat and inside plumbing and comforts taken for granted today.

Lee would have apples strung to dry on a long rope before the old fireplace in the kitchen, and herbs from the garden hung from the ceiling. The chunky old ceiling beams, the white-washed plaster kitchen walls and the apples in bowls on the big pine table seemed to make this kitchen one of earth's chosen places.

Reed liked this woman and wanted no harm to come to her. He resolved to find out what was going on in someone's mind that would precipitate arson.

"All right, I'll see you later, Lee. I'll be in touch." Reed was off.

Ted checked in for a few words with Ellen, still cleaning the big room, and Lee went upstairs to dress for the office.

Fifteen minutes later she looked the same as many other women country brokers. Turned out in a Harris tweed jacket and corduroy skirt, with high leather boots and an English leather briefcase, a cashmere turtleneck sweater and bright scarf, Lee had a successful, organized appearance.

Clones, she thought, *that's what Dorie calls us.*

Incredibly dull at times but necessary for business.

It was almost eleven when Lee arrived at Carriage Trade. The storm, which had settled in in earnest, made traveling even the few miles into Paris difficult. The first plow was out, and she followed behind the driver. Swirls of snow came back from both sides of the truck and her vision was limited. With this weather, Lee knew the few appointments would be canceled and they would close the office early.

She felt relief when she finally swung into the horseshoe driveway, feeling her wheels slide as she turned the corner.

Inside, Meg and Dorie sat in front of the blazing fireplace. Long French windows on one side of the room looked out upon a small lawn and garden, now covered with snow.

The fireplace balanced the opposite side. Neutral wool carpeting made a background for old oriental rugs, and a large walnut partners' desk held the center of attention in the middle of the room. A few country Chippendale rush-seated chairs, two large wing chairs on either side of the fireplace, and more easy chairs with small tables alongside them completed the picture. Dorie's desk and chair took up one small corner near the entrance.

A few country watercolors, one English landscape oil, pots of blooming gloxinias; this was a country office that made you welcome with its warmth.

As Meg and Lee had intended. A class act.

For months they had searched for the furnishings at antique

shops and auctions. They had bought orientals from the old Poland Spring House, a desk from F.O. Bailey's in Portland and the chairs at one of Morrill's auctions. They had whitewashed the walls of the old building, stained the old brown beams and made the line of horse stalls down the rear into four separate offices.

Lee liked this transformation; she and Meg had put their hearts into it, but the turn in the direction of the real estate market was beginning to drive a wedge into their dream.

Dorie brought some coffee and juice in on a tray and Lee drew up another chair and told them briefly about the happenings at High Meadows.

Meg's face whitened when Lee described the gas can, and she leaned over and touched her hand.

"I'm afraid for you. That is a terrible thing. You could have lost the barn, the horses and even the house. Have you any idea who it was?"

Lee shook her head.

"It's hard to believe anyone hates me that much. I have to think an arsonist. Reed is checking but I don't think he's going to find any clues. I'll just have to live with this thought that someone doesn't like me and be careful. Let's forget it for the moment. I need to get my mind regeared. We need to talk about our direction and today's a good day. It's bound to be quiet. Dorie, will you check the mail and get the phone while Meg and I talk?"

Meg placed a small maple log on the fire and the two women pulled their chairs closer.

"Listen, Lee, we've got to talk this development thing out. Up to now it's been enough to do antique homes and farms. We list them; we sell them. I always thought it was enough but now all the rest of the brokers are development-oriented. We need to go after more land listings, do more advertising on lots and maybe even buy some pieces to develop ourselves. We could back a division:

five-acre parcels for quality homes. There's a lot of money in that direction. A bundle. I think we ought to change our image."

Meg finished her speech in a rush, knowing she was treading on Lee's innermost thoughts.

"You didn't used to think that way, Meg."

Meg sighed. "I didn't have children ready for college and a husband with a long recovery period from a heart attack."

"I know." Lee's voice softened. "But we both had such a commitment to the land when we started. Such a commitment to Maine. We didn't want to do development sales. Meg, when the land goes, it's gone. You know what happened to the Doughty farm. All little three-acre lots with houses. And it was some of the area's most beautiful crop-land. The woods all stripped. I hate so to see that."

"I hate so to see the balance in my checkbook." Meg sounded exasperated. "You try to tell any Mainer that there is a shortage of woods. Lee, we've done well with this office. But you have to change and the money is right there in front of us. You can't stop progress."

"Progress." Lee almost spat the word.

"Think about it," Meg almost begged. "Let's give it a week or two. If we can't agree we can always one buy the other out. I'm sorry, we've pulled together like two draft horses in team."

Lee smiled. "Like the ones that used to be in the stalls. You're right, Meg, that's what hurts so, you're right. The extra money would be helpful. It seems as though I'm forever painting and patching High Meadows. It's just that part of me wants to go ahead and part wants to go back. I'm having a hard time with what's happening in Maine real estate." She was silent for a moment. Then she said it. "If we were to invest in a piece of land, do you have one in mind?"

Meg nodded. "The old Brown farm, for example. Or a piece

that's near you, the old Hartley estate. That's about four hundred acres, nice views, woods, a mixture of all types of land. We probably couldn't afford it, but that would be ideal."

Lee put down her cup and stared at Meg. "My God, that's right next to me. Only the Attleburys' small place in between. The riding-club trail goes across both of them. You remember, Meg, we rode out that way last fall. The Moss Path is on that land, there's nothing else like it in the area. It would be a shame to change that land. But it won't happen for years anyway—Mrs. Hartley is in a sanitarium somewhere in Arizona."

Dorie's voice interrupted. "Not any more. Not according to this letter I just opened from an estate lawyer in Scottsdale. She died last week and the heirs are considering sale. The lawyer wants you to call him collect as soon as you can. He wants you to go look at the property. It looks as though you two might be making your minds up sooner than you thought!"

3

The storm lasted for three days; very little traffic moved in the small town of Paris and several offices closed completely. Carriage Trade made an effort; Dorie, who lived close by in town, came in for the mail and a little floor duty. Meg, who lived on the Hill, stayed away as did Lee. All appointments were cancelled; no one wanted to look at property and all the real estate offices in town were closed down completely. Even the banks had a hard time staying open with skeleton crews.

Mainers are used to this kind of weather. They simply settle themselves in and wait out the storms. The old homes with connecting ells and barns are made for New England winters. People cope; they are famous for their coping and the books and knitting and whittling come out by the woodstoves and by candlelight when the electricity goes off.

Lee, in her soul, welcomed blizzards. Carter could not get up from Connecticut; the turnpike was closed for two days and he and Lee agreed over the phone that it was foolish to drive six hours or more through a storm.

Carter's quiet, steady voice over the phone calmed her; the events of the past few days seemed diminished and she realized how much she had come to depend on him during the past few years. Widowed himself, without children, he spent most of his time running a small bookshop in the Salisbury area. He had gone to school with her when they were both children in Connecticut. On one of her trips back to her old home, Lee and Carter had renewed acquaintance when she stopped to look for a garden book at his shop.

The friendship had slowly blossomed into what Lee called "an unexpected treasure" at this time in their lives, and they since had spent whatever hours they could manage at one or the other of their places. This evening, on the other end of the phone, Carter's voice was reassuring.

"It's snowing like blazes down here, Lee. Sorry about our weekend plans—you just curl up with a book, have a large glass of sherry for me and we'll make up for the delay in two weeks when I have time off from the shop."

Lee, one hand absently touching the Gordon, smiled. "The book's a sad substitute but it will have to do. I'm fine, really. I have a fire going and Kate and I will just cozy-in this evening. I have seed catalogues, herb books and plans for this spring's garden. I'd rather be sharing sherry with you, but you know what they say about our age group—we're patient. I can wait."

Carter laughed. "Good girl. Be careful. I know how much you like living alone, but don't take chances. Everything you've told me says that someone has a real problem up there. Keep in close touch with Ted and Ellen."

"Don't worry. Ted comes through with the plow three times a

day during a storm. And they're right at the other end of the phone. Kate hears every sound. I'm beginning to think that the person who tried to fire the barn was an arsonist and doesn't really have a grudge against me. Reed's still looking into it. I told you about the letter from the Hartley family lawyer. Meg and I will be skiing in to look at the house. I'll call you back soon. Goodnight, love."

Kate's tail thumped as Lee hung up the phone.

"Heard his voice, old girl? I like him too, Kate."

The phone rang a second time. This time it was Reed Jamison.

"Lee, how are you up there?" The police chief's voice sounded anxious.

"I'm fine. Has anything developed?"

"Sort of and sort of not. No prints really on that can or the bag—everything just smudged or wiped off; he must have had gloves on. Gasoline was the regular kind you'd use in a lawnmower—nothing unusual, and the can was so old it could have come from anyplace. The papers were a mixture of Lewiston and Portland—no names or labels and nothing unusual —you can't tell what store they came from. They were about three weeks old. The only thing different—one of the crossword puzzles in the Portland paper was partly worked—just a few words. Printed in pencil—pretty hard to match that up until we have a suspect. But if the papers belonged to whoever planned to fire the barn, he did crossword puzzles. That's a long shot; you could get papers anywhere. They might not have been his own."

Lee frowned.

"A lot of people do puzzles. But that is something to think about. Look, did you notice the words?"

"I tried to get a picture, Lee."

"Can you remember any?"

"Not offhand. I don't do puzzles much. I'll look, and bring it up next time I see you. Don't say too much about all of this. Just in case."

"I won't. Thanks, Reed. Keep in touch."

She hung up thoughtfully, considering the situation.

"I wonder how many arsonists do crossword puzzles?"

Kate's whine made her realize she had spoken out loud. Lee sighed. Somehow the picture did not fit. Some detail nagged at the back of her mind, but she could not pinpoint it—who did she know who did crossword puzzles?

The storm blew out by Wednesday morning and business was back to normal in Paris. Drifts lined the back roads and going was difficult, even through the main streets of the town. Carriage Trade had three calls for appointments and an offer came in on a property. Meg and Lee made plans to ski into the Hartley house on Friday morning, for the lawyer's letter with the key enclosed had followed the phone call.

Friday evening was also scheduled for the Historic House Garden Tour committee meeting at High Meadows and Ellen was busy turning out chocolate cake for the committee members.

"Who all ought to be going on diets, if you ask me," Ellen informed Kate testily as the Gordon sat hopefully waiting to lick the batter bowl.

"And you're not to tell a soul."

Friday morning, Meg called in with what Mainers would call a "wicked cold".

"Lee, I'm miserable. We'll just have to put the ski trip off until next week. I'm going to bed for the day. I'm sorry, but I'm not up to it."

"No problem. It's beautiful out; maybe I can get someone to go in with me. Or maybe I'll just go by myself. I know every inch of that trail anyway; we ride it during the summer. I'll talk with you tomorrow, Meg. The meeting is tonight and I'll let you know what happens. Take care of yourself."

It was a beautiful morning—a February day that pretended it might be April and a day that made the whole of the oak woods look like a cathedral. Lee skied gently—almost reluctant to make tracks on the untouched trail. Oak, beech, and maple gave way to fir and hemlock. The land rose and dipped and then rose again. There was no sound, only the soft swish of the skis' glide/kick, and once the scream of a jay disturbed by the woman's presence. Lee felt she was finding her own balance inside, and she was glad she had decided to come alone.

Strange, she thought, *being two people. Part of me a business woman with an analytical mind, part a naturalist with a love and commitment to the land. There is simply no compromise.*

Around one more bend of the trail and the house came in sight—an old Federal one room deep; chimneys and roof ridge still solid and straight. A long ell, connecting the house to the barn, seemed sturdy. The barn was in the worst shape. Yearly the estate hired workmen from the nearby town, details all arranged by letter, to enter the house, shore up where shoring up was needed, repair floorboards, air it out, close it back up and take care of repairs in general. During the summer, a caretaker cleaned it periodically in case a member of the Hartley family should visit, but no one ever did, and year after year the old house stood alone.

It had been broken into only once; an elaborate alarm system was installed after that one attempt, and it was so far in from the main road that the logistics of hauling anything out seemed to deter would-be thieves. There was also a legend of sorts that the Hartley house was haunted and old man Hartley was said to have rigged gun traps. So where it would ordinarily have been vandalized, it was pretty much left alone—only hunters, a few snowmobilers and the riding club came anywhere near it during the year.

Dr. and Mrs. Attlebury, the owners of the property between High Meadows and the Hartley estate, spent time in the oak woods during the summers they stayed at their cottage, for they were moss collectors, among other things, and the Hartley estate was the site of the famous Moss Walk.

Lee, skiing steadily along toward the house, suddenly realized that she had told Reed that she and Meg were going together. The alarm system had been explained so she knew how to turn it off after opening the door. She had her flashlight and a pad and pencil along with a Thermos of coffee in her backpack. Although she was familiar with the riding trails, she did not know the inside of this house.

Today would be mostly looking at the interior, measuring and taking some photographs if light would allow. Lee always made a bet with herself that she could guess the square footage of a building and she was anxious to see if this Federal was of a classic size.

She finally reached the front steps, which were covered with a drift of snow, and as she took off her skis a red squirrel skittered along the porch railing. He dove underneath, chattering angrily, surprised at this intrusion upon his preserve.

Lee could still hear him as she opened the door and carefully followed instructions, reaching to the left and turning off the switch controlling the security system. Waving her hand before her, she scanned the hall with her flashlight. Trees surrounded the outside of the house making the light coming through the closed shutters dim.

Thank goodness I remembered the flashlight.

Directly in front of her the ship's staircase reached to the second floor; a whale-backed ceiling rose above the staircase. On either side lay one room and Lee elected to enter the right-hand one first. The air inside the house was chilly; she suddenly felt the chill and drew her jacket collar up about her neck.

Why is it that an empty house with no heat always feels so much colder than outside? Like a tomb.

The right-hand room was a parlor and the paneling around the old fireplace appeared to be of the period. The floor was wide pine; the windows still held much original glass; protected by shutters, they still were much as they had been in the beginning. A few scatter rugs, mostly hooked, covered the floor and most of the furniture, to Lee's surprise, was Victorian rather than the earlier primitive and Federal she had expected. The room to the left seemed almost a duplicate of the first and climbing the stairs, Lee found two bedrooms, one on either side. Both held cottage sets and chests of drawers, a few rag rugs here and there, and bowl and pitcher sets on washstands. No sign of any bathroom, but a door leading from one of the bedrooms continued out into the shed chambers over the ell—probably servants' rooms.

Walking through the first of the chambers towards the second, Lee found a padlocked door. She remembered the lawyer's comment that some of the furnishings were in a locked room. Certainly the furniture she had seen so far was not valuable enough to warrant the elaborate security system—the locked room must contain the good pieces.

Descending the stairs and holding on to the shaky rail, Lee again felt the chilly air and thought for a moment that she could hear a noise. *Squirrels in the downstairs ell; if they ever get into the main house they will damage it.* She flashed the light before her and opened the door from the parlor into the rear ell where the kitchen was situated. This would be the main kitchen, she was sure, the summer kitchen would be beyond.

Again, moving back in time, she saw the details of a kitchen that had changed little since Civil War days. In the corner was the old soapstone sink with its wooden pipe above which furnished the water—probably gravity feed. The pipe was dry now, but had still been used when the Hartley family was last in residence. The great old brick fireplace with a chestnut beam across the front housed a boiling cauldron set in brick on one side—Lee had only seen three of these in all her years in real estate and she knew they were rare now in this part of Maine. The old wide pine floorboards were scrubbed almost white and a large braided rug, well worn, lay under the kitchen table and plank-seated chairs.

And still the noise, a chattering sound Lee felt sure was squirrels. Then, suddenly a thump like the slamming of a door, not in the main part of the house. Lee hesitated, then, pulling her jacket even closer, proceeded through the summer kitchen which seemed to serve as a storeroom, and into the ell leading to the barn.

She walked gingerly along the side of the woodshed, feeling the rough wood of the wall under her fingertips. For one moment she paused, considering that she had broken the cardinal rule of brokers and was in an empty house by herself a long way from help if something unpleasant happened.

But what could happen? Lee did not believe in ghosts and she had faced many squirrels, porcupines, bats and raccoons in her travels. Very little else inhabited old houses. This one was fairly well kept except for the barn area and all she had to do was take a quick look at that and she was finished for today. She would save the cellar, undoubtedly dark and dirt-floored, until Meg came with her or the caretaker returned from Florida.

Lee walked forward, giving her shoulders a resolute shake. Straight ahead was the door to the necessary, so called, and off to one side, the entrance to the barn. A hook held the necessary door shut.

Flashing her light before her, Lee undid the hook and swung open the door, shining the beam directly into a surprised face.

A man, pants dropped below his knees, sat on the worn pine boards attending to nature.

Hooded eyes, rather amused, looked directly into Lee's startled face.

"Can't a man have a little privacy?"

•4•

The worn wooden door slammed in Hod Cole's face. Smiling to himself and methodically hitching up his pants, he had to admit it was an amusing situation.

Which ain't to be taken lightly; I probably scared the living beJesus out of her. Although she don't look like she scares easy.

"Be out in a whipstitch," Hod called. "Just don't go 'way. Seems like with this introduction we at least ought to get acquainted."

Lee, gathering herself together, had to admit it was a funny situation. The last person she'd thought to see was Hod and she was relieved it had not been a dead body. She had never run into Hod Cole before, but she'd heard other brokers speak of him. An old Mainer—land trader—horse thief probably, and hunter and poacher bar none—his reputation was county-wide. He probably owned some of the largest pieces of timber in the county and got a considerable amount of pleasure sitting in brokers' offices ruminating on the possible value of a piece of land in case he ever got around to selling it. That is, if he could lay his hands on where he'd hid the deed.

Hod spun a good yarn, got several of the younger brokers all excited about the possibility of selling some of his acreage and then led them gently upcreek by the nose like a young horse, until they learned, as had the older and wiser among them, that Hod had no intention of parting with one acre of his holdings.

As Clipper Cleaver observed, "He's planning on building a bridge back from wherever he's going in case he wants to return and haunt the forest."

The door opened and Hod stepped forth, extending a hand to Lee.

"Hod Cole. Sorry if I scared you. Used the outside door to old man Hartley's necessary. Always did think he had the best ideas in Oxford County. You'd be Lee Heaward, I reckon?"

"How did you know?"

"Seen your picture in the paper. Real estate news. Listing this place, are you? They finally selling?"

"Mrs. Hartley just died and I'm looking at the house for the estate lawyer. It appears they will be selling and my firm will represent the property. More than that I can't say at the moment."

Lee felt herself using real estate terms, not wanting to say too much nor too little. Never turn down a potential customer, and Hod was rumored to be able to find backing to buy land any time he wanted. He was a puzzling man and Lee was finding she liked him.

The light was dim in the ell. Turning, Lee retreated into the kitchen and back through the house to the big front porch where she had left her skis. Hod followed along behind her. They sat down on the top of the steps and appraised each other.

Hod liked her instinctively. Her brown hair was stuffed up under a yellow knitted cap, and her brown eyes bespoke an honesty one needn't be bedeviled by, thought Hod. Yellow Windbreaker and pants and a small backpack made up her outfit. *Looks kind of like a daffodil out of place in the spring snow.*

Hod grinned, dug deep into one pocket and offered up a squashed sandwich. Lee opened her Thermos and now, in the good light of day, took a long look at him.

A man whose age you will never know.

Weathered, lined face, hooded eyes that held faint amusement, a rather small hooked nose in a face that could have seen anywhere from forty to sixty summers. Lee had seen men like this before and knew they were often the best hunters and woodsmen. Quiet, relaxed men who walked slowly, methodically through the woods, not missing a board foot of timber or a deer's tracks, or the arbutus hidden under the dried leaves on the banks of the woods road.

She remembered a line of poetry from when she had been in high school:

"Wherever he walks it shall be through this forest."

Hod, she thought, *to a T.*

Lee offered coffee, pouring from the small Thermos into its round cup, and Hod took it quietly, saying "Thankee."

Almost Elizabethan, she thought, recalling that here and there in pockets of the county, men spoke in out-of-the-ordinary ways because of their heritage.

"You must have come in the back way; I didn't see any tracks. Isn't this kind of out of the way for you and a long way in the snow? I thought you were from Sumner?"

"Well," Hod stopped a minute to take out a pipe and tobacco and go through the process of tamping in the tobacco and finding a match.

"This time of year, late winter, ain't much good for anything sometimes. Stopped woodcutting; it's almost too warm for skiddering and twitching out, so I thought I'd just take a day off and mosey around looking for some oak stands. Haven't been by this way in a long while, so I just left the car on the Mt. Rhoda road and snowshoed in the back way along the old wood trails. Everything kind of stark and still on a day like today and you can see the trees good. Just stopped by to use old man Hartley's outhouse; remembered he had one of the only two in the county with an outside door. And then you know the rest. Happen we kind of met unexpected-like, you might say."

This was a long speech for Hod. Lee had been listening intently noting the change of pronunciation and language, as he talked. She was curious.

"What happened to 'ain't?'"

Hod grinned. "Oh, that's just to keep the out-of-staters happy. They kind of expect a lack of niceties. Don't do to let them think I'm too smart."

Lee laughed. "You must know a lot of the county."

"You might say I do. Probably hunted most every piece of land and every stand of woods for miles. Two ways."

"Two ways?" Lee was puzzled.

"Legal and illegal—but the latter only when necessary."

"So you've been through most of these woods, then? We ride the trails during three seasons. That is, our horseback-riding club does."

"Best not to in hunting season," Hod grunted. "No one goes out then. Suicide."

"I gather you don't hunt." Hod grinned.

"Let's just say I tolerate it. My late husband did and I went along for a while, but I guess as I get older I just want to see the animals rather than hunt them. With you I suppose it's the meat."

Hod shook his head thoughtfully. "Partly the meat but mostly the hunt. And then, sometimes sitting on a stone wall, waiting, I get to thinking, it isn't either one. It's just being there—outside in the woods with the leaves turning all colors and the air smelling like apples and the mountains up there watching over me; well, I guess it's just my season. Something special in the air, if you know what I mean."

Lee nodded. "I know what you mean. It's where my strength comes from—this land. How many years have you been here?"

"Longer than I'd care to think. Mother was a schoolteacher. Raised us on granddad's place after dad died. Two sisters, a brother and me. Four mouths to feed. I finished high school and went one year up to Orono and then came back to go to work in the woods. Every cent I could save I'd get a little piece of land. Back then it was cheap—why one man over Sweden way even had a sign saying he'd give it away, but his was mostly alder swamp. I tried to find him once, but he'd moved away. Anyway, I kept adding on chunks of land here and there and logging off a little now and then and I began to get ahead. Working the woods and guiding—guess that's what my life's been so far. And sometimes I just take a day off and walk through the woods—like today. Only today I got lucky I guess. Pleased to meet you, Miss Lee Heaward."

"And I'm pleased to meet you, Mr. Hod Cole. You're a legend, you know. Thanks for sharing lunch."

"You're welcome. You got to lock up this shebang? My snowshoes are around in back."

They stood up. Lee tucked the Thermos away in the backpack; Hod drew on his gloves and they walked through the house to the ell. Hod opened the outhouse door and showed Lee the secret of the hidden outside entrance, a small wooden button at the top of the door.

"I'm buttoning the outside now," he said, "so she's tight, and I'll take off around the back to the Mt. Rhoda road. You let me know when you have the price. I might be able to meet it. Or at least dicker it down."

Lee nodded, said goodby, and went back through the house, locking doors as she had found them. She reset the security system just inside the front door and secured the large front entrance. Putting on her skis, she thought about Hod and their strange meeting and the sudden empathy between them.

Slowly, she skied around the perimeter of the old house, taking measurements and recording them on the small pad she took from her backpack. She added a few comments on the interior while it was still fresh in her mind, then put the pad back and took out her small 35 mm camera to snap front and back pictures. She could do no more today; the cellar and interior room measurement could wait for her second visit.

She turned and started down the trail suddenly remembering that the Historic House Garden Tour committee would be meeting at High Meadows that evening. Dusk came early in February and there were still several jobs left for her to do. Horse stalls needed mucking out and Kate needed a quick run through the snow of the back fields. With luck she herself could find time for a chamomile soak in the large old bathtub and a moment to lie down to soothe the gathering headache brought on, no doubt, by the thought of the committee meeting. She needed to call Meg and Dorie and then she could relax.

Three hours later, with the house in order and chores accomplished, Lee, dressed in a simple red wool dress and low-heeled loafers, lit the fire in the big room and sipped a cup of Ellen's famous chicken soup.

Kate, turning around several times to be sure she had just the perfect spot, cozied up to the large old fire screen. Lee's hand traced the top of the black-and-gold-feathered setter.

"You may stay if you're good. But no fighting Mrs. Bemis for her cake, or away to the bedroom you go. You nearly gave her convulsions the last time she was here, and I'm not going through that scene again. So behave and you can stay. OK?"

Kate thumped her tail and her eyes promised she would try.

"What you have," said Lee, "is a wicked way."

Sherry was traditional for the Hill club committees. Lee set out the old blown-glass decanter and the small glasses on a large silver tray. Adams china cups and saucers came out of the setback kitchen cupboard and Ellen's chocolate cake was already on a plate surrounded by smaller plates, forks and napkins ready for service. She filled the coffeepot and put it aside; she would start it just before the first members arrived. Everything attended to, she added a log to the fire and turned on the outside lanterns, lighting the brick pathway. Ted had widened it this morning, pushing back the receding snow banks even more.

Lee settled down before the fire. The headache had left and she blessed Ellen's soup, which was not a timid one.

My strength comes in two ways: the land and Ellen's cooking. What would I do without either?

The bell rang, Kate barked, and the committee members arrived—six women and two men, shaking snow off their coats amid a flurry of conversation and greetings. They hung their gear in the mud room and followed Lee through the kitchen into the big room. Hands were warmed by the glowing fire, Kate was greeted and admired, and Lee passed sherry while people settled in chairs and the large comfortable old couches on either side of the fireplace.

"Do let's get started," dowdy Mrs. Bemis squeaked, giving the impression of a fat gray mouse. "Meg can't be here, so she's asked me to take charge. Therefore, I call this meeting to order immediately. Malcolm, take notes even if it is just a committee meeting and not the whole membership."

Malcolm Bandridge rolled his eyes heavenward and winked at Lee, who smiled back at him. A long-time friend from many auctions, Lee liked this man who seemed at times an enigma. Malcolm was a retired men's clothing store owner whose family had long owned one of the Hill's choicest homes, Run for Cover. A bachelor, Malcolm lived there alone year-round now except for a sister, Elvira, who visited him in the summertime. He had become interested in real estate and worked as a part-time broker for Clipper Cleaver. He dabbled in art and antiques, was part of the town's little theatre group, and often accompanied Lee to auctions.

In fact, Lee had felt last summer that Malcolm might be getting a little too friendly toward her, and it had been necessary to talk it out with him. Surprisingly, she had felt his anger, but that had quickly disappeared and their friendship now seemed firmer because of their talk.

Tonight he greeted her with a hug and a kiss on the cheek along with an invitation to an April auction at Morrill's. The flea market would open in March and they had also planned a Saturday browsing through the stands.

Having opened the meeting, Mrs. Bemis placed a hand-drawn map up on a large easel she had brought with her.

"Now, here are the ten homes." She pointed with a pencil. "We'll start here at Meadowbrook and go straight down the street through the others. Deer Run will be the last house on the street and then we'll go to High Meadows. There will be numbers on all the houses and on the map and an insert in the program telling the history of the buildings and the gardens."

"Isn't it rather early for planning?" Jan Howard's voice was querulous.

The troops are rebelling already, thought Lee.

"Not really." Although Mrs. Bemis looked like a small gray mouse, she had the heart of a red-tailed hawk. "Not really. We have to make arrangements for the advertising early, and the map of the homes makes a good logo. Tonight we'll plan the map and the dates. Details can wait for a few months. But we have to think ahead and chart our direction."

"Do we have a direction?" Only Malcolm would dare say that to Mrs. Bemis.

Mrs. Bemis smiled. She had been delighted when Meg had called to ask her to substitute and chair tonight's meeting. As a matter of fact, Mrs. Bemis had felt rather left out when Meg had been made chairman by the president of the group. Tonight she had a chance to show her abilities and she did not intend to let things get out of hand. Having put Jan in her place, she concentrated on Malcolm.

She pushed back her fading red hair with one hand, pushed down her sensible gray tweed skirt with the other and took a strong draught of her sherry.

Turning toward Malcolm, she spoke firmly. "You can see the map I've made. They will start at Meadowbrook, Malcolm, so Run for Cover is number two. All we have to do tonight is see if the direction of flow suits everyone and then we can have the map ready for the advertisement. How about having Lee and Clipper write the ad? That's their field. Just one-quarter- or one-half-page size with the map in the middle. Date, time, price. Do we have enough in the treasury for ads in *Down East, Yankee* and the special section of the *Globe?* Bunny, what's our balance?"

Bunny Cleaver could have been christened Barbie; in fact her parents had debated on that choice of a name. Willowy, well turned out, well-versed in almost any subject, as far as one could tell, she was a perfect mate for her raucous hustler of a husband.

She had always been content to stay home with her two children, and be the patient, understanding wife of a real estate broker who kept odd hours but who made a large sum of money keeping them.

Needlework and flowers were Bunny's hobbies and when Clipper had decided this past year to buy a house on the Hill and move up, Bunny never questioned the decision. Tonight, perfect in her gray flannel slacks and turtleneck cashmere sweater, working on a piece of needlepoint for one of her dining-room chairs, Bunny was learning about the garden-club members. Bunny Cleaver learned fast. She was quiet, with an eye for details and when old Mrs. Hannigan, the former treasurer, died, Bunny was a natural for the job.

"Take it, hon. We'll make it on the Hill with you in the garden club. Good for business."

"Actually, it's good for the children too, Clipper. That's one reason we moved. The other street was getting really run-down. I don't mind being the treasurer; it's a small account. Although why they don't use Malcolm I don't know. He takes the minutes as the secretary and most small groups have the two combined. Anyway, I'll do it because it won't take much time and besides I'm going to learn more about getting our grounds in shape. These women know what the old gardens used to look like and I can learn a lot from them."

Bunny was smart. Bunny watched. It was only four or five years ago that she'd learned real was better than plastic when it came to flowers.

Tonight Bunny reported prompty and efficiently that the treasury had sixteen hundred dollars of which they could certainly spare a good amount for advertising. All that was really needed was ticket money and advertising money. Everything else would be donated and if one thousand people came through at five dollars a ticket they stood to make a neat five thousand less expenses. That should be a very nice addition to their treasury.

In addition, individual homes always sold extras like wool for knitting and country-type dolls and carvings and baskets and special fudge cookies and cider with half of the moneys going back into the club. So, all in all, they could certainly plan some decent advertising. The tour would be in July and unless they had a hurricane or the weather turned cold, it was bound to be a success.

The vote was taken, eight hundred dollars allowed for advertising and tickets, and Mrs. Bemis banged her gavel and brought the meeting to a close.

Lee rose and started for the kitchen, Clipper and Malcolm behind her.

"Lunch next week, Lee?" Clipper reached for the coffee and poured two cups for Bunny and himself. "I hear you and Meg are listing the Hartley place. It'd make a good subdivision. I could be real interested. You got a price yet?"

"No, not yet. Jim Davidson has to do the appraisal. Mr. Cameron, the Hartley lawyer, says he wants to be sure of the title himself at the beginning rather than hold up the sale at the end. He's having a Portland law firm do the work. We do have the signed listing with the agreement the price will match the appraised value and that title be solved subject to Mr. Cameron's approval. So we can't start to show until he says so—or plan advertising."

"Little unusual, isn't it?" Clipper looked at her.

"Yes, it is. But I can understand his concern. We aren't making appointments to show yet, unless clients understand we don't have all details. Davidson can't look right away, he's so busy. I suppose it *would* make a good subdivision, but I really hope it doesn't sell that way." Lee paused thoughtfully.

Clipper snorted. "You got a problem with that, huh?"

She shrugged her shoulders. "Don't you ever get tired of dividing up Maine, Clipper?"

"Hell, no. Not while I'm making money doing it. If I don't someone else will. Listen, you're too damned goody-goody for this business. Your conscience bothers you too much. Take the money and run, I say. If I don't, you can bet the next broker will."

"Exactly." Lee's voice was sour.

"Don't knock it. What did you think real estate was, anyway, when you and Meg started your business? A historic house tour? If you're going to play with the big boys you'd better play by their rules."

With this Clipper helped himself to Ellen's chocolate cake and fixed a plate for Bunny.

Lee stifled the impulse to push the cake in his face. Yet she knew what he said was true. If she was going to play the game she'd better stick to the rules.

Or else get out of the business for good.

SPRING

ANGELICA
PARSLEY
COMFREY
VALERIAN
GARLIC CHIVES
CHIVES
BASIL

·5·

February melted into March and an early spring was forecast. The winds whipped around High Meadows; the old barn creaked in the gales and the horses stomped about in their stalls on days when it was impossible for them to romp about in the shrinking snowbanks.

Lee let Musette and Nat out on the polished old boards of the barn floor, and the two horses munched on piles of hay still smelling of last summer. They discarded the dried daisies, vetch and milkweed, but they loved the still-green clover. Heads down, with the cold winter's light streaming down from the hayloft windows, they shared their barn with the spirits of horses and cattle who had gone before.

Lee felt a contentment from the continuity of life within this great sheltering structure.

Let me never forget what is important in my life.

The warmth of the horses, the smell of the stalls, the sense of time and comfort seemed to give Lee strength for the days that loomed ahead. There had been no further phone calls, and Reed had not turned up anything new on the threat to the barn.

She was not afraid, but she had begun to be extra careful and, at Reed's suggestion, she had installed a large security light for nighttime vigilance.

The Gordon, waiting patiently in the corner of the barn floor, whined softly, and Lee's thoughts returned to the present. She finished mucking out and walked the horses back into their stalls, now neat and clean. In each manger she placed a stick of rowan tree—the mountain ash—taken from a branch she had trimmed from the larger trees near the herb garden.

I'll use all my magic to guard the barn.

"Rowan ash and red thread
Keep the devils from their speed."

The woman and the setter walked back through the ell to the house.

Dressing for work, Lee felt today would be busy at Carriage Trade. Mr. Cameron had given them information for the appraisal of the Hartley place. Preliminary work had to be done on advertising. Meg and Lee had planned to spend the entire morning discussing the estate, with Dorie running interference on the office phone and the mail.

Meg Bundy had spent a difficult past month. Her need for ready cash was twofold: college and hospital bills had piled up and the Hartley estate promised an exceptionally large commission. Although Lee had almost given in to Meg's way of thinking, the direction of advertising on the estate presented a difficult hurdle. This morning, Meg, dressed in a blue sweater and gray slacks, with a great deal of pseudo-gold jewelry, put out her hand to touch Lee's shoulder.

"We've done so much together. This is an opportunity for both of us. We have to advertise this as being great developable property...."

Lee interrupted. "You're right. I have to agree even though I don't want to. Our first duty is to the seller. We have no choice. And that means the very best advertising campaign we can mount. Which means we have to point out its development potential along with other attributes. That's clear. I hate it, but it's clear. We can also show other uses: it could be a gentleman's farm, or a green area someone could buy and give to the town, although that's such a remote possibility there's little chance on that angle; a camping area; or the type of division with just three or four very large and very expensive homes. I'd give anything to be able to afford it myself. But I know the price will be way too high for my pocket."

"Thank God we agree momentarily." Meg was relieved as she had expected Lee to be difficult to deal with on the estate. She knew Lee's love of land and how deeply she felt on the subject.

"By the way, when can Jim Davidson go in? Are you going with him, or shall I go? Maybe you'd better; you know more about the place than I do."

"On Monday; I've planned to meet him there in the late morning," Lee answered. "The snow is going fast; the thaw's taken it off faster than usual this spring, so we may not be able to ski, but we'll mush through with our boots. Monday's the sixteenth. I can go alone, Meg; we have an appointment with the Travers' that day, and the Harrison house is just right for them. Why don't you take them out; we'll switch floor days, and I'll meet Jim and show him the Hartley place. I have all the measurements and the last bits of information on the spring and the cesspool. The exercise will do me good."

Meg agreed; plans were made and on Monday, March 16, one day after the full moon, Lee and Jim were scheduled to meet at the Hartley estate.

Thinking back on it afterwards, Lee saw the pattern beginning with the February full moon.

Dressing that Monday morning after finishing the horses and mushing with Kate in the orchard, Lee found her mind going through the list of Indian names for the full moons. The northern Indian tribes had called this March moon the Crow Moon, for the sight of crows wheeling in the sky, cawing loudly, had meant the beginning of spring and the end of the long winter months. In some of the New England states it was called the Sap Moon, for the maple trees began their gift of syrup. It had even been called the Worm Moon, for the frost began to leave the ground and worms stirred beneath the ground's surface.

"Crow Moon for me," said Lee aloud, and bidding Kate and Ellen goodbye, she set off for the Hartley place.

Lee's appointment with Jim was for eleven o'clock. Ordinarily she would have driven, but the woods roads were opening up now in the spring weather and it was good to walk. The morning was bright with the feeling of early spring, although snow still lay underfoot in patches. It became deeper as she entered the woods on the Attlebury property and crossed what was still called the Daniels Meadow, an open spot close to the road into the Attleburys'. She sighted the house through the trees. Soon the Attleburys would return from Massachusetts and Lee would renew a friendship she cherished.

The old white cape, with a foursquare frame attachment, was set far back in from the road and had been built, it was believed, by the same person who had built Lee's house; the original owners had been brothers on side by side farms and the Daniels

Meadow still carried their name.

Today, most of the snow had melted from around the house, and in one spot a stand of early yellow crocuses could be seen peeping up through the snow. The old herb garden behind the house was nearly clear of winter and Lee could see the outlines of the tiny fishpond.

Skirting the house, she followed the woods road back until it reached a stone wall with an opening large enough for a horse or a man to use, and stepped into the woods of the Hartley property. This was the trail the riding club used and it was well known to Lee. She was approaching the house from the southwest.

In the woods, at a turn called the Forks, she headed due north for the house. There were fox tracks across the trail ahead of her; the fox dens were deep in the beech woods and she had often watched the kits at play.

Fox tracks usually ran in a straight line, purposeful tracks with a sense of direction; one foot in front of the other, searching for food; circling trees in the orchard for mice to bring to their young. The kits would be born in late February or March and their mother would be out through the woods, over the fields and into the orchards.

And I will share with you, thought Lee.

A good orchardist welcomes foxes. Constant mousers, they will rarely bother domestic animals, other than chickens, unless they are really hungry. A cat walking the top of a stone wall in a remote area and meeting a fox might also meet his maker, but it would be a rare occurence unless the fox was hungry.

Fishers now, that's another story.

She was coming close to the main trail. At the branch of the two roads were tracks: Jim Davidson's, no doubt, coming in from Minister's Road. Jim had said he would meet her directly at the house; he wanted to look at the land coming up from the road and would walk in.

In fact, at quarter to eleven that morning, Jim Davidson had left his car parked on the side of Minister's Road, and changing into his old woods jacket and boots, taking his briefcase and a flashlight, he had set off up the trail to meet Lee.

Jim was sixty, tall, well-kept on the outside, but harboring a heart that made him stop periodically to rest and look at the topography. With a well-established appraisal business and more clients than he needed, Jim still had been happy to receive the request from the Hartley lawyer. Mr. Cameron had sent on the deeds with lines drawn under any areas he had considered possible problems. He had indicated he expected to pay a good solid fee for an appraisal of that size and detail. This was the type of work Jim liked to do. Today he would inspect the house with Lee, for Carriage Trade would be the brokers. He was glad that Lee and Meg had been chosen, for some brokers seemed to have no idea of what their listings entailed and furthermore, didn't seem to care. Carriage Trade did their spadework and this would, in turn, help Jim. Lee was fun to be with; they both liked horses and skiing and Jim looked forward to sharing lunch in a country setting on this springlike day.

For spring was here. It promised things to come and Jim, looking upward at the blue sky between treetops, saw a crow circling overhead, cawing loudly.

Far above it wheeled, circling, calling to other crows out of Jim's sight, but within his hearing. He watched for a moment, waiting for signs of the others, but saw only the one.

One crow, sorrow; two crows, joy.

Oh well, they're up there! Smiling to himself, he rounded the corner of the house, thinking, *On such a day, how could there be sorrow?*

He took out his tape measure, hooking it on a handy corner

board, and decided he would start while awaiting Lee.

A true Federal; he could see that already. And in just the state an antiques buff would look for if he were buying a country house. The caretaker had done a good job; the clapboards seemed free of rot and the roof line was still straight. Taking notes and hooking on his measure wherever he found a handy spot, Jim proceeded along the side of the main structure and the ell, until he reached the barn. The snow had receded along the southern edge of the buildings but on the northern side it was deeper and Jim's boots sank into the drifts. On the lawn, grassy spots showed in places, but some snowbanks were still a foot deep. This was the time of year with one foot in winter and one foot in spring.

Jim cornered the house to meet Lee coming into the yard at just about half-past eleven.

"Good morning. Say this is quite a place. You'd never know it was here if you weren't familiar with these woods. This certainly is a choice listing from what little I've seen so far. It's good to see you. How's business?"

Lee sat on the front porch, shaking snow from her boots.

"Business seems good. We're delighted with this listing. Although part of my heart is having a hard time with the thought that these four hundred acres might turn into a subdivision. But business stays good, even though I was booed at the planning board meeting the other night. I asked them to consider more controls. Guess I'm just having a bad time with my conscience."

Jim nodded.

"I understand. Once I didn't care either. Now I begin to feel torn every time I'm called to do an appraisal on a large land area. The money is great; the seasons are great; it's just what's happening to the lakes and farms that begins to haunt me. Maybe you have to grow old in order to appreciate the fragility of the countryside, Lee. Or maybe we're born outside our time. I don't know. We see what's happening, but some of the others, I don't think they ever will. And after a while, I just draw inward and give up. I'm leaving the business in another six months. After this summer. Going up to my cottage on Howard Pond and vegetate and write mysteries. Something I've wanted to do for years. My heart just isn't in this business anymore."

Lee took a long look at Jim Davidson. From the beginning there had always been an easy understanding between them, a respect sometimes never found between broker and appraiser. Where sometimes it seemed a battle between two opposing forces, with Lee and Jim there had always been regard and mutual understanding. Lee did her homework; Jim did his and it generally agreed. There was no guile, no hidden detail Lee couldn't or wouldn't tell Jim, and the two worked quietly together with efficiency. Jim welcomed an account that involved Carriage Trade; no one would try to influence his thinking and that he appreciated.

"I wish you well. Mysteries, huh? You're so methodical and you're great at puzzles. Listen, tell me your opinion," and Lee recited in swift, concise detail the story of the phone calls, the February skier and the attempted arson.

"Crossword puzzles?" Jim mused. "I do a lot myself. Has Reed found anything new to go on?"

"No, he says sometimes it can be a year before an actual solution can be found for a crime. He's been investigating quietly but so far nothing has turned up. It just all seems to be a dead end."

"Phone calls stopped?"

"No more. It's as though the whole thing never happened. Not a clue. But somehow I'm waiting for the other shoe to drop." Lee sighed.

"Well, keep on looking around you while you're waiting. And keep right on going ahead. Best to keep busy when things happen you don't understand."

Lee agreed. "I am busy. Carriage Trade is doing well, even though I thought my stand on development might hurt us—it did for a while but we're pulling up again. I'm looking forward to spring's trail rides and I'm going to work on my herb garden. I'm still a little uneasy, though. Fire terrifies me."

Jim agreed and changed the subject. "Has Carter been up recently?"

"No, we planned for him to come a couple of weekends ago but then a family friend died and Carter couldn't get away. Now we're planning on sometime around the twenty-first—I admit I have missed him, Jim."

"Is this an affair of the heart? Are you two serious?"

"I'm not sure. I like him a lot, maybe love him a little. There is a special feeling between us, but I want to stay here and Carter likes where he lives in Connecticut. He enjoys running his bookshop. So we can't seem to arrive at a decision."

"He's a lucky man, Lee." Jim touched her hand briefly. "If I weren't already taken, I'd give him a run for his money."

Lee smiled.

"And I'd take you up on it."

For a moment their hands touched and the solid friendship between them needed no extra words. The best word for friendship is simply friendship.

"All right, let's go to it." Lee rose and led the way, opening the door, turning off the security system, and Jim began his work within the house.

A *hulloo* from outside was heard and Lee backtracked to the porch to face Clipper Cleaver and Bunny, wading through the snow to the porch.

"Thought I'd come look at the place while it was open." Clipper beamed at Lee. "Meg told me you were here. Bunny and I just put our boots right on and came out to join you. Knew you wouldn't mind, Lee. You might just sell me the place before you even get it on the open market."

"Jim's doing the appraisal this morning, Clipper. You can look through with me, but I can't quote any price yet until the estate lawyer gets his report and decides on the price. But come on in."

The person, thought Lee, *I'd least likely wish to spend the rest of my life with. The worst type of a broker. Please, God,* she prayed, *don't let me have too many Cleavers to deal with.*

Bunny was having trouble with her boots; her usually immaculate exterior was a bit rumpled and she looked as if she would much rather be at home doing cross-stitch.

"He just had to come," she told Lee. "I said, wait a bit at least until it's priced, but, no, he had to see it right away the moment he knew you and Jim were out here. It's cold," she shivered, "and dark too."

Clipper, scurrying in all directions at once, reminded Lee of a rambling muskrat. He knocked on walls, opened closet doors, almost fell over a rag rug, and when they reached the kitchen and he saw the boiling cauldron, he let out a yell: "Look at that damned lobster pot! What a party we could have here, hey, Bun?"

For the first time Bunny rebelled.

"There is no way, Clipper, absolutely no way, I'm ever going to live here. You can build all the houses you want and buy all the land you want, but I am never going to live in this house. It's cold as a tomb and I don't like it. What's more I'm going outside and sit on the porch where it's warmer."

"Don't know what's got into her—been like that all morning," Clipper confided to Lee. "Just told her Malcolm and me and a couple of doctors were considering going in on a deal to buy the whole shebang and maybe one of us live in the house and fix it up, and she just got so ugly. I mean, I know we like the new house on the Hill and it's great for the kids, but there's money to be made here and this place would fix up real nice with some wall-to-wall and some new windows."

Lee sighed and blessed Bunny. Maybe the house would at least get into the hands of someone other than Cleaver.

"Malcolm is on his way up, too," Clipper continued. "Got his broker's license, you know."

"I didn't know that." Lee was a bit surprised; Malcolm had decided to be a part-time salesman and was interested in the investment end of real estate but had never shown enough ambition to aspire to be a broker.

"I always thought he would be content with just a dabbling in real estate the same as his antiques and the little theatre group. I never thought he'd want all the stress. But he will make a good broker, Clipper, I'm sure."

"Yes, I think so too. Where's this go?" The door to the long ell leading into the barn opened under Clipper's forceful hands.

"Out in back to the barn and the outhouse. That's all in rather bad shape in the barn area." Lee found herself following him.

"Outhouse, huh? Kind of a cute place."

Lee decided not to tell him of her experience with Hod Cole and the outside entrance. She was wishing more and more that the Hartley buyer would not be Cleaver Real Estate.

"Here's the barn, Clipper. I doubt it can be restored. But you might take some of the boards and beams and make a smaller building. It has sort of a half cellar, built into the hillside. Horses stood underneath."

Then Lee drew a quick breath. "Clipper, be careful!"

Clipper pawed his way through debris until Lee warned him again that it might not be wise to go any farther into the center of the barn floor.

"That carrying timber is out of its slot. I'd really be more careful. When I'm showing a place I feel responsible for the clients and I wouldn't let anyone mill around in a place like this. It's too dangerous. Do be careful."

Clipper waved his arms cheerfully. "Never seen a place I can't get through—spent time in 'Nam, you know. You're too damn conservative, Lee."

Nervously, Lee watched Clipper pick his way over the partially open floor, and finally satisfied, he rejoined her.

"Just let me look in this door, will you?" and Clipper went off through the tie-ups to look at what had once been the old milkhouse.

Lee, standing alone in one corner and looking up at the old beams, felt uneasy. The light was poor; she had left her flashlight in the main house. She could hear Clipper walking about in the tie-up area. Suddenly, out of the corner of her eyes, she thought she saw movement.

"Clipper?"

No answer and no sound from the tie-ups.

My imagination. Probably a raccoon or rat. Still, she was sure there had been some movement in the corner near the outside wall. She stepped back out of the dim light so that she was protected by the shadows, and looking intently into the corner thought for one wild moment that she saw a large furry creature slide between stable openings and disappear downward.

Lee stifled a scream, took hold of herself and decided it was impossible that she could have seen what she thought she'd seen.

A bear? At this time of year?

It could be, but it's early for one to be out of hibernation and certainly it shouldn't be walking upright on a barn floor.

"Hey, I'm back." Clipper crashed cheerfully through a demolished doorway.

"Some setup, Lee. Regular workshop in there. Nails sorted in all sizes in jars and bottles neat as a pin. Kind of like looking back in someone's life. My grandfather, I haven't thought about him in years; he had things all sorted out like that. And then he died and my grandmother, she just pitched them all out or gave them away. Took him years to collect that many bottles and jars. You know, Lee, once in a while I see how you feel about these old places. That old man Hartley, he had labels on everything. He even had burlap bags all sorted into piles. Must have been some old coot, huh?"

Lee nodded. *Was it possible, just possible, that Clipper had a soul?*

She was glad to see him back safely, and decided imagination had gotten the better of her eyesight. Together, they retraced their steps back through the barn into the ell and then into the old kitchen.

"Jim," Lee called. "He ought to be almost finished by now."

There was no answer.

"Think he's done? I'd like to know what he's come up with on a price." Clipper was eager.

"Well, he won't tell us today. He has to see some of the land first and then work it all up. It will be a week or so until his report is in. And he won't even hazard a guess. Jim's as ethical as they come, Clipper."

Clipper snorted. "You just don't know how to work it, Lee. You just watch the old Clipper."

"Jim," Lee called again.

Still no answer.

"We better check the front rooms." Lee was beginning to feel uneasy.

"Maybe he's with Bun. Don't know where she went to."

Lee, following Clipper, said, "Bunny wanted to stay outside in the sunshine."

Moving ahead, Clipper opened the door from the front room into the hallway at the front of the house. He stumbled, gasped and pushed Lee backwards with his hands all at the same moment.

"My God, Jim. Lee, don't look."

But Lee pushed past and stood looking down at the appraiser.

Jim Davidson was crumpled on his side, the remains of the second-floor railing spread about on the floor around him. His head and neck were twisted into an awkward position and on his face was an expression of surprise and fright.

Almost in tandem, Lee and Clipper moved swiftly but within a minute they knew there was nothing first aid could do to save him.

"We can't move him. It looks as though his neck is broken." Clipper was kneeling now close to the body.

Lee, on the other side, whispered, "There's no pulse. He had a bad heart. Look at his face, Clipper. Something must have scared him and he fell or backed into the railing and it let go. CPR won't help with his neck like that. We'd do more harm. I don't think there's anything we can do but go get help. I feel sick."

Clipper rose, guiding her by the arm and trying to open the front door at the same time.

"Get outside. Get some air. Where the hell is Bun?"

Lee, almost crying, felt as though she could not carry on more conversation without throwing up. She knew the railing had been shaky; she had mentioned it to Jim. She also knew that he was a very careful man, used to old houses, and that he was never, never one to take chances. Something had happened to make him back into the railing, break through it and drop to the hallway floor below.

Lee could only guess: *a massive heart attack? Maybe. But, from the look on his face, something scared him terribly.*

Something or someone?

In the sky above the Hartley house, a lone crow wheeled, cawing.

Cawing and cawing.

• 6 •

Bunny Cleaver was screaming and screaming. She had walked back along the path to the house after exploring the dooryard while she waited for Clipper and Lee. The cold house was not to Bunny's liking; she wanted warmth and outside air. Coming back she found Lee on the porch just at the doorway, and Clipper, leaning over Jim's body.

Bunny fell to pieces.

Clipper grasped her, wheeled her away from the body, shaking her at the same time. Malcolm came running up to the porch and for a moment the four people were caught up in total confusion.

"What's going on? My God, Jim." Malcolm stood still staring down at the body.

Bunny simply kept screaming.

"All right, now, Bun, shut up. Shut up or I'm going to have to slap you. Come on, Bun, settle down." Clipper was desperate.

"Bunny, stop screaming." Lee's voice was suddenly authoritative. "You must help now, one of us has to go call for an ambulance and the sheriff's department. Someone has to stay here. Clipper, should we look upstairs?"

"Good idea." Clipper, having finally calmed Bunny, began to feel someone had better take charge and he elected himself for the job.

"Malcolm, go up there and see if you see anything that might have scared Jim. Bun, walk back down to the car and phone into the sheriff's department and tell them Jim's dead and have them hurry. Tell them where we are and stay down there to bring them back up the trail. Lee, you stay here with me. Go on, Bun, hurry."

"No, I'm not going anywhere alone. I'm afraid in these woods now. If something scared Jim it could still be around. Don't make me go alone, Clipper, please."

Clipper felt his hold slipping. Not an insensitive man, although he appeared otherwise most of the time, he was more shaken than he appeared. He knew Bunny could fall apart again and he was not too sure of Malcolm. Lee he could depend on. He elected to send Malcolm and Bunny off together and keep Lee with him.

Malcolm, back from a fruitless search upstairs, put one arm around Bunny and started back to the car phone.

Lee, still feeling ill, appealed to Clipper.

"Can't we at least cover his face?"

"Take my jacket, and there's a blanket on that couch in the front room." Clipper was feeling queasy himself. "You all right now, Lee? You look a little green."

"Yes, I'm all right. I could stand some coffee—there's some left in my Thermos. Do you want some, Clipper?"

"Might help us both. Lee, what could have happened?"

Lee shook her head. "All I can think of is either he had a massive heart attack and stumbled backward out of the room or something scared him so he backed out and hit the railing and fell. I've known Jim for years. He knew old houses. He never would have depended on that shaky railing. In fact, we both spoke of how it needed repair." She hesitated. "There's something terrifying here, Clipper. For a moment—in the barn...."

"In the barn?"

"When you were off in the tie-ups and the toolshed. I had a feeling I saw something in the shadows."

"What something?" Clipper looked at Lee intently.

"I don't know. Something large. I'm not sure. I've been in this house and barn before. I never had that feeling before. I can't describe it. Like something evil was sliding by."

"Your imagination, Lee."

"I wonder. Well, Reed can sort it out. There isn't that feeling now. I just feel sick. Clipper, Jim was such a good man." Tears rolled down Lee's cheeks.

"Hey, Lee, I know. Here, drink some more coffee. I'm sorry too." He patted her hand awkwardly.

They settled in to wait, that tired silence between them that sometimes comforts in its very being. Together, yet apart, their thoughts strayed in different directions.

Clipper broke their silence. "How much of a difference is this going to make in putting it on the market? The sheriff's office or the state police will probably put it off limits until they search the place and see if they can find any clues. How long do you suppose that will take?"

"I don't know, Clipper," Lee answered slowly. "I can't even think about it right now. I'll call Mr. Cameron as soon as I can pull myself together. There will still have to be an appraisal. Jim's notebook and papers must be upstairs. I guess we shouldn't touch anything."

"Do you want to walk back down to the road, Lee? It's

probably going to be a long wait."

"No," Lee's voice was tired but steady. "I'll stay here. I feel a responsibility to this house. And to Jim. I'll have to be sure who's going to be in charge of shutting it up. I guess the state police will do that. And, oh, my God, Clipper. Who's going to have to tell Nancy? I don't want that job. But I'll have to go up to see her."

In the Jeep below, at the end of the trail where it joined Minister's Road, Bunny and Malcolm waited. Malcolm's car was parked alongside the Cleavers', but Malcolm sat now with Bunny who was still crying. They had phoned the message into the sheriff's office, and Dot had said help would be on the way directly. Reed Jamison, the police chief of Paris, would be coming in from the north end of town; the state police were called and the sheriff's office was sending men. Dot had called the medical examiner, Dr. Burton, and he would be along with the ambulance. Bunny had only said there had been an accident and a death, as Clipper had instructed her, but the hysteria in her voice alerted Dot, an old pro, that this time might be out of the ordinary. She put the team together in her usual efficient manner, and within forty-five minutes they were moving toward Minister's Road.

Sitting in the Jeep, Malcolm questioned Bunny, who seemed to be crying harder by the minute.

"What happened? Have you any idea? Where were you—where were Clipper and Lee? I heard you screaming while I was walking up the trail. My God, you were loud. How did Jim fall?"

"They don't know." Bunny shuddered. "I heard Clipper say something about his face, and that his neck could be broken. He must have gone through the railing."

"Well, Jim had heart trouble. Don't you suppose he might have had an attack?" Malcolm patted Bunny's arm. "Stop crying now, your nose is all red. I'm sure it must have been a heart attack."

Bunny shook her head. "I heard Lee say something about seeing something strange. Scary. Like Jim might have been scared by something upstairs. I'll never go in that house again. And Clipper was thinking of buying it."

"We both were." Malcolm found a Kleenex and handed it to Bunny. "Blow."

"Thank you. I just feel miserable."

"That house could be fixed up nicely and the land would make a high class subdivision," Malcolm continued. "We were talking about it this morning. In fact, the house has the same type of paneling as I have in Run for Cover. Noticed it right away. I wanted to take a good look around myself, but I guess I'll have to wait now. That's the first time I'd been inside it, Bunny, although we've ridden by several times on trail rides with the club."

"Listen, do you hear cars?" Bunny put her hand up to her ear.

Reed and two members of the sheriff's department plus a state trooper pulled up on the side of the road. Behind them came the ambulance and, behind it, Dr. Burton's old Ford station wagon. They parked as far up the trail as cars could go, which wasn't far because of a late snowbank blocking the road. Overhead, crows made great, swooping circles as they shrilled out their raucuous cries.

Reed listened intently as Malcolm gave a brief report, the state trooper asked a few terse questions, and the group slogged up the trail to the Hartley house, Reed leading the way.

Bunny wanted to go home, but Reed said quietly, "Mrs. Cleaver, they'll need your statement so you must come back up with us. You can stay outside on the porch and we'll try to let you go as soon as we can, but the state police are going to need your version of events."

He turned to one of the medics, saying, "John, do you have

some aspirin for Mrs. Cleaver, she's pretty upset. OK, Doc?"

Doctor Burton nodded and Bunny at least felt that her feelings were being considered, which was exactly what Reed had in mind.

The medics picked up the stretcher they had put down to get Bunny's aspirin, and the party continued up the trail. They reached the house within a few minutes. With the state trooper in charge and Reed, who knew everyone, keeping things calm, with Doctor Burton and the medics in the front hallway with Jim's body, with the rest marshalled onto the front porch for questioning, the terror within the Harley house seemed somewhat diminished.

The wind was brisker now—the chill of a March not yet sure of its nature. Clipper pulled on his down jacket. Malcolm shivered in his light-weight tweed. Lee pulled her scarf closer about her neck and even Reed and the state trooper stomped their feet on the old worn porch floor.

"All right, let's go over it." Reed was puzzled. It looked like an accident, in which case the state police would not be involved, but the expression on Jim's face didn't tally. Something didn't fit.

In turn, Clipper, Bunny, Malcolm and Lee told their stories. Lee and Bunny thought they might have heard a noise which could have been Jim falling. Malcolm, who said he must have been at the beginning of the trail, knew nothing until he reached the house and found the other three. Clipper, deep in the recesses of the barn, had heard nothing. He and Lee, returning from the barn through the ell, had found the body when Jim didn't answer. Bunny, outside seeking sunlight, had gone for a short walk and on returning, found Lee in the doorway and Clipper inside bending over the body. Bunny's screaming had been heard by Malcolm as he drew closer to the house.

When it comes down to it, thought Reed, *none of them can back up his story. They were, each one, alone.*

"I just kept screaming, that's all I can remember," said Bunny. "I couldn't look at him with his head bent that way."

Clipper agreed. "I knew when I saw Jim's neck that he was dead. Lee and I both said CPR the moment we reached him, but it was all over. His neck had to be broken. We didn't dare move him, even with both of us having training. I covered his face because he looked so horrid. I wouldn't want anyone to see me like that."

"Did you touch anything else?" Both Reed and the state trooper were taking notes.

"Nothing." Clipper shook his head. "Malcolm went upstairs to look around, but there was no one there."

Malcolm agreed. "I don't know what I was looking for. Just furniture in that room. Jim's stuff was scattered on the floor—his pen and clipboard. I didn't touch anything."

"Good." Reed turned aside to talk with the sheriff's men, who had gone through the ell into the barn and returned.

"We'll have to put the house off limits, Lee, until there's a chance to make a more thorough search. Do you have all the keys?"

"All but to the locked room. There are supposed to be some antiques in there. The security system is off. We'd just begun to talk of advertising. We were waiting for Jim's report and the price for the lawyer."

"Well, you'll have to call him and explain the situation. Tell him it will be at least a week, maybe two, until we can let you back in again. Meanwhile, we'll be responsible for the property. We'll set up a guard at the end of the trail in, and one in the house until we get a chance to look at all the rooms. I don't know who'll be in charge; depends on whether it was accidental or not—Attorney General's office will be if it wasn't. You can all go now, but Lee, I want to talk with you a few minutes longer."

Reed and the state trooper conferred. Within an hour the body was removed and Dr. Burton slogged down the trail to arrange autopsy details. There was no question Jim's neck was broken, but why he fell was another story. A deputy from the sheriff's office was dispatched to inform Jim's widow and contact the family minister. Clipper helped a distraught Bunny into their Jeep and Malcolm volunteered to wait for Lee while Reed spoke with her inside.

The remaining deputy handed Reed the briefcase that had been found on the lower hall floor under Jim's body. Reed prowled through the upper bedroom, noting the furnishings, looking for any signs of a struggle, and any clue that might shed light on what had happened. Finally, he called Lee to come upstairs.

"Take a look at this room. Anything seem out of order? You know what it looked like better than anyone else here. Anything different?" Reed looked at her, noting the shadows under her eyes, knowing that she was strung pretty tight and that there was only a little space left before she went to pieces.

Lee shook her head. "I can't see anything different. Maybe this little basket of flowers on the mantel. It might have been moved—there's a thin film of dust if you look closely, and the basket looks to have been moved to the left. That's all. I really could have moved it myself—I admired it when I went through the house in the beginning."

The tiny basket, filled with dried wormwood and moonshine, or pearly everlasting, sat on the mantel over the fireplace. The flowers were faded; it had probably been there for several years. Only a discerning eye could note the pattern of dust beneath the basket.

Reed, pacing about the room, bent down to pick up the clipboard and pen.

"He must have dropped these when he backed away. It looks

like it anyway. Unless he just stood in the doorway and threw them at something."

Reed looked at them thoughtfully. A usual appraisal form, the type demanded by banks, an ordinary clipboard, Clipped to the form was a small piece of lined yellow paper, part of a legal pad sheet. Jim always used this for extra comments made when there was no space for them on the appraisal form.

Jim was famous for his addendas—comments on the style and feeling of a house. A small sketch of the rooms with their approximate dimensions was required, but Jim went one step further. Woodwork, architecture, detail were in his reports. Although he filled in the required blanks on a form, he had a discerning eye and a bank officer reading one of Jim's appraisals had a better than average knowledge of a property he was going to back financially. For this reason, Jim was one of Oxford County's best appraisers. His mind had housed an encyclopedia of both antique and modern detail.

Reed was looking at the piece of yellow lined paper.

"Lee, look here. This last bit after 'mantel has dentil work'. It looks as though he started to write something and then the pen went off the paper. An initial? What does this look like to you?"

Lee scrutinized the paper.

"An 'R' maybe? No, a 'B'. I've no idea. He must have started to write something, then dropped the board and backed out and into the railing. You know he always said he would write mysteries when he retired. Maybe he was trying to leave some sort of a clue."

"If he was threatened. And he had only a moment to think. Jim was quick. That could be." Reed wrinkled his forehead and brushed back his blond hair.

"How about 'B', Lee? Could it be that rather than 'R' ?"

"Yes, it could be. It could be. And that fits somehow."

Reed looked at her. "What do you mean, it fits?"

Slowly, Lee spoke almost as if she did not believe what she was saying. "'B' is possible. It could be what he thought he saw. Because that's what I thought happened to me in the barn. Only it wasn't possible. At least I didn't think it was possible. Now I'm not so sure."

"Care to tell me what you're talking about?" Reed felt a slight chill. The house was very cold, although the sun was bright outside.

"When I was in the barn waiting for Clipper, I thought I saw a shadow slipping through the recess in the rear. A shadow, a movement, something in the corner. Then it was gone. Up until now I thought it was just imagination and the dark and the cold. The barn is scary. Not like my own barn. Not a comfortable sort of barn. And it was gone in a moment—I can't be really sure."

"How large?" Reed looked at Lee. "Show me with your hands. How large was this thing?"

"As large as a person. Or an animal."

"An animal?" Reed's hands stopped in midair.

"There was sort of a smell. I can't explain it." Lee paused.

Reed very gently took her by the elbow and they sat down on the stairway.

"OK. Now you and I have known each other for some time. If it was Bunny, I'd discount the whole thing. You I want to hear more from. What do you think this was, if you did see something?"

"That's the problem. It couldn't have been. Not in a barn and not generally in March. And certainly not to end up in an upstairs bedroom. It's not possible."

Reed sighed. "Trivia question. What are you talking about?"

For a moment Lee closed her eyes as though gathering strength to say what she wanted to say.

"Well, I think what Jim wrote was a 'B', Reed. And I think what I saw in the barn was a bear. A large, shaggy, black bear. And maybe that's what Jim saw too. Or thought he saw. In an upstairs bedroom. Where no bear could possibly be—ever."

7

For a long moment, Reed reflected on Lee's story. Although he was young for a town police chief, he was wise in the ways of the country. Maine people knew bears, gave them a wide berth except for the hunters who pursued them with dogs during the season. Bears met in a berry patch, possibly separated from cubs, were let strictly alone. Bears met on a horseback ride meant you wheeled your mount and took off in the opposite direction. Horses were spooked by bears; the two seldom mixed. You never went at a bear, you went away. Rarely was anyone hurt by a bear; natives knew enough to respect them and these were the smaller black bears and not the western grizzlies. They were a nuisance around the camping areas of the state parks, but here in the Oxford County woods they were not a major threat. They had increased recently, some sheep had been attacked, but they were not particularly interested in humans and the feeling was mutual.

For Lee to see a bear this early in the spring was possible but for her to see one inside a barn was highly unlikely. For a bear to be in an upstairs room of the Hartley house was the height of fantasy, and beyond logic. Bears climbed trees, not stairs.

Yet Lee had seen something. Jim Davidson might have seen something. Whatever it was, it might have caused his death in a combination of possible heart attack and fall.

"All right." Reed spoke slowly. "Let's say you did actually see something. For right now, let's keep this between us. You can't show this property for at least two weeks. You and Malcolm are free to go now, and I'll deal with the security system. I don't know yet exactly who will be handling this until we get the autopsy report and the cause of death. It won't be in probably for a day or two. You did right to let him lie there and not touch him, Lee. So don't fault yourself on that part. Doctor Burton said his neck was broken."

"Poor Jim."

"Um—well, I'll talk with his wife. Somehow I don't feel he was meant to be killed. Most likely he came on something and his fall was an accident." Reed sighed, again pushing back his hair. "I need a haircut."

Lee rose. "I have to call Meg. We'll plan to go to the funeral. Everyone in real estate liked Jim. He was a good man."

She joined Malcolm who still waited outside talking with the second deputy. The state trooper had left, and the house was cordoned off at the end of the trail.

Together, Malcolm and Lee walked back to Minister's Road, sobered by the past few hours. Even Malcolm, talkative as he usually was, seemed jumpy.

"I didn't really know him well, you know. I talked with him a few times when he came in the office. You and Clipper knew him well—what was he doing upstairs, anyway? I thought he was outside." Malcolm's voice was whiney.

"His appraisal, Malcolm. You have to do every room in the house. You've been in the business long enough to know that by now. For some reason, he must have just backed out of the room and fallen through the railing. Oh, I've talked about it so much, Mal, I just don't want to anymore."

Malcolm persisted. "Does Reed have any idea what might have happened? Any of the deputies an idea?"

Lee sighed. "Reed didn't say. They have to wait until the autopsy results come in—even then they may not be sure."

"Well, it might have been his heart just gave out and he wasn't scared at all. Such a fuss." Malcolm was the perfect irritated bachelor. His day had been upset; he didn't like upset and his lack of feeling was noticeable. He had wanted to talk more with Clipper on the possibility of a subdivision and a group purchase. Now everything would be stalled. Bunny was not going to let Clipper have his way and the delay in sales time might let her pressure him into giving up on the whole idea. She had made up her mind she hated the house. She would never live there. Bunny alone could destroy the conception of "Hartley Heights" as Malcolm and Clipper had secretly christened it.

Malcolm Bandridge was not a good loser.

"Look, Mal, I'll talk with you later. I'm going back to the office after I check in with Ellen at the farm." Lee was tired and needed to be alone.

But Malcolm continued, "Don't forget the flea market opens this weekend, and the first auction Saturday evening. Are you planning to go?"

"I'm going to try. Carter may be up and I'm going to need to take time off. Maybe we'll see you there. I have showings all this week, and I'll have to go to Bethel to see Nancy Davidson. I haven't much heart to make plans right this minute. I don't want to talk anymore now, Mal, please."

Lee turned away, refusing Malcolm's offer of a ride and walked down the road toward High Meadows. On either side of the entrance to the Attleburys', giant pussy willows exploded their March greetings. Rowan trees lined the stone walls of the Daniels Meadow and the ice was gone at last from the little pond hidden in one corner. Redwings would return soon and spring would officially begin with the bright flash of their wings above the heights of High Meadows.

For years Lee had kept a diary and knew that, like the barn swallows, the red-winged blackbirds seemed to return on a certain date. Her eyes searched the reeds and small bushes along the pond shore, but, so far, there was no sign of the birds.

Only the crows, cawing and circling high overhead.

It was late afternoon before Lee left High Meadows to drive the three miles to Paris. Ellen had fixed a sandwich and a pot of tea, but the food tasted dry and Lee had little appetite. Even a short walk with Kate was not the usual happy jaunt and when Lee brought the horses inside after their day in the spring sunshine, she felt tears in her eyes as she thought of Jim.

I have to keep going, she thought, and calling the Gordon to her, she decided to take her to town.

"You must learn town manners soon, Kate," said Lee, remembering the English setter who had gone before and had been such a gentleman.

"But I love you and you're trying. Steady now, girl." Lee snuggled the Gordon's face for a moment as she snapped on her leash.

Meg and Dorie had heard the news. Meg's face showed signs of tears and gently Lee filled her in on as many details as she dared. Remembering Reed's advice, she did not talk of anything in the barn's shadows or in the upstairs room.

Only the bare bones of Jim's death.

Dorie, meanwhile, placed a call to Mr. Cameron. It was early afternoon in Arizona and the lawyer, used to almost any problem when it came to estate settlement, talked at length with Meg.

"Well, we have plenty of time, and the estate still has the stock portfolio to dissolve and several other personal items to sell out here, so it doesn't matter if your timetable in Maine is delayed. Too bad about Mr. Davidson; he seemed a good man. You girls just find another appraiser to do the job, and send me whatever Davidson's bill would be. I'll write out a check for his widow. Have the upstairs railing repaired as soon as the police turn the house back to you. Send the bills on to me as we agreed in the beginning."

"He really is a good person. How many lawyers would have thought of Jim's bill and his widow?" Meg had hung up.

"I know," Lee replied. "I'm constantly impressed by the way he handles details. He wants everything just right and he's certainly not the usual estate lawyer. How many of them would be concerned with title at the beginning of a sale rather than leaving it to the end?"

Meg nodded. "We'll have to go up together to the funeral, Lee. Are you going to see Nancy?"

"Yes, tonight." Jim's wife often came to real estate meetings with him and although she was a quiet woman everyone liked her. The real estate community in the Oxford hills was large and ever growing and some members were respected more than others. Jim and Nancy Davidson ranked among the best with both brokers and appraisers.

Lee felt the tears rising again. "I hate it, but I'm going to drive up tonight. Ellen's making a cake for me to take. Meg, do you want to find another appraiser? I don't know if I can face that right now."

"I'll get Reisman and Hughes from Lewiston; Dorie can set it up tentatively for two weeks from now. And I'll talk with Reed to see if he thinks that's a reasonable time lapse. Just don't think about it, Lee." Meg was beginning to realize how deeply Lee had been hit by Jim's death.

Meg, herself, was tired. Her husband, Will, was still not making the recovery they had expected after his heart attack. The daily routine of being a part-time nurse, wife and mother, along with showing property, was beginning to be difficult for Meg and she, who had leaned on Lee, found herself having to be the comforting partner.

This is not, thought Lee, *a good time to talk of taking a few days off.* Carter was due this weekend and, for the past few hours, Lee had been considering returning with him to Connecticut. Spring would be two weeks ahead in Salisbury, and perhaps she might be able to gather her forces. Like a road running beside a river, thoughts of Carter had been running parallel to the sadness of the past hours. A separate part of her mind let Lee think of two things at once and gave her the ability to deal with the real world while she put her own feelings temporarily aside.

Now, bending down to stroke Kate, who was lying quietly in front of the fireplace, Lee turned to Dorie.

"What's the schedule for the next few days?"

"Showings tomorrow." Dorie consulted the calendar. "Ads are all set up for the next two weeks. Two closings at the end of the month; I have all the data ready for you to deliver to the banks. Three calls today to have you go look at property for possible listing. Two calls on the Hartley place to see if it was ready to show. One from Malcolm Bandridge; did he find you?"

"Yes, he did. So much happened, I forgot to tell you. He came up late, right after Clipper and I found Jim's body, and just after

Bunny came in from the porch. As a matter of fact I walked back down to Minister's Road with him. Did he tell you, Dorie, that he and Clipper and a few others have been thinking of purchase for a subdivision—Hartley Heights they were calling it. Clipper said he was interested, but he hadn't told me all the details. Malcolm filled me in." Lee paused and sighed deeply.

"I'm sure they could raise the money." Meg was eager. "I know you wouldn't like it, Lee, but if they make an offer or meet the price, it would be a good, quick sale."

"Well, price we aren't sure of yet and now we're two weeks more not sure, but you're right, Meg, much as I hate to admit it." Lee's voice was strained. "Look, I'm going to take Kate back to the farm, collect Ellen's cake, have a cup of tea and drive up to see Nancy. I'll be in early to take the first two showings if you want, Meg. Tell Will I hope he feels better. And, Dorie, what would we do without you?"

Bending over, Lee gave Meg and Dorie both hugs. *Women can show how much they care.*

Two hours later, in the gathering March dusk, Lee drove the road to Bethel. Mountains rose on either side as Route 26 wound through the valley of West Paris and Woodstock. Patches of snow still glimmered in the woods, but the promise of spring sang in the brooks running fast and the faint sign of color in the tree trunks. Lights were beginning to glow in the farmhouse windows.

I have been in at least half of the kitchens in those houses. Up and down the valley, back on dirt roads running like narrow ribbons through woods of pine and hemlock and maple and beech and oak, back in on dirt roads with no electricity or directional signs; I have been in half the kitchens in the county and shared coffee at table and listened to people tell me they have finally decided to sell their homeplace. Old men and old women have said, "Guess it's time to sell our land" and "What do you think this place is worth?"

How many times have I asked, "Isn't there someone in the family who wants it?" and how many times has the answer been "No."?

Lee felt the weight of despair. *This beautiful valley, with its woods and meadows and little lakes and hayfields and apple orchards. How long will it be before it too is discovered for development?*

This business I am in; it can break your heart.

And make you wealthy at the same time.

Clipper's right, she thought. *If you can't stand it, get out of it.*

Nancy and Jim Davidson had lived in a new ranch house in the Paradise region of Bethel. Beautifully built and only about five years old, the house showed Jim's capable carpentry, but it was really Nancy's dream. Jim's heart lay in the old camp on Howard Pond, inherited from his father, a country doctor, and as long as Lee had known Jim she had known his wish to retire there. He had worked longer than he'd planned, for he and Nancy took in foster children, but this summer would have been his last in the business.

Nancy's eyes were red, but her voice was steady as she put her arms around Lee and accepted Ellen's cake. The old country tradition of food for the family gave comfort and purpose to the mourners. It was more than a cake they would share.

"Thank you for coming," Nancy whispered. "And thank you for being there with him. They haven't released the body yet. Doctor Burton, the medical examiner, called, and said it would be a while before the autopsy is finished. He wouldn't tell me anything more. What do you know, Lee?"

Holding Nancy's hands between her own, Lee told her briefly of the happenings of only a few hours ago. She spoke of finding Jim, knowing immediately that he was dead, knowing that first aid would not help. She did not speak of the look on Jim's face or the suspicion that something had caused Jim's fall from the second-floor hallway. She knew Nancy would learn more eventually from the sheriff's department, but she felt that, at this point, Nancy did not need any more pain. They talked quietly, two women whose lives had often touched and who both knew Jim's hope that this would be his last summer in the appraisal business.

"The funeral will probably be Friday, Lee. Doctor Burton called our minister and said we might arrange for then. The funeral home will bring him back and I guess we'll use the little family church at Rumford Center. Jim's parents always took him there when he was a boy. I think he would have wanted it that way."

"Will you be all right, Nancy?" Lee's voice was low.

"Yes, he had a small insurance policy, and we have this house and the camp on Howard Pond he loved so much. He never was one of those who got rich off the industry. We put three foster children through school. But we were very happy. You know how he was."

"I do, and you were a lucky woman. Meg and I will be up for the funeral. Nancy, can I do anything? Your minister...?"

"He was here a while ago, and he's coming back this evening later. Two of the children are coming in from Boston. I'm fine, Lee." Nancy hugged her and struggled with tears.

"You were one of the brokers he trusted. It's hard for me right now, but we've known about his heart for several years. I always hoped that if I wasn't with him when it happened, there would be someone there he knew. I'm glad it was you."

Listening to Nancy, Lee suddenly realized that she thought it had been only a heart attack. Best to leave it that way for the moment.

Half an hour later, she took leave of Nancy and set her course thoughtfully back through the dark to High Meadows. The lights from the oncoming traffic seemed to act as punctuation marks between the happenings of the past hours. Something didn't seem to fit. She wondered what Reed had found out, what the autopsy would show, whether the Attorney General's office would come into the picture if it was not an accidental death, and what had really happened to Jim. She decided to call Reed as soon as she reached home.

Driving up the lane she saw the house ablaze with light and a Connecticut car parked before the barn. Carter had arrived.

"I took care of the horses." Carter, turning away from the stove, carefully covered a simmering concoction, and put his arms about Lee. Kate was bouncing up and down joyfully; Carter was one of her favorite people, and even though there were long weeks between visits, she greeted him with great joy every time he came to the farm.

For a long moment Lee and Carter stood together in the middle of the old kitchen. Holding his head between her hands, Lee looked at this man who was so dear to her. Brown hair, threaded with gray, a lined skin and clear blue eyes, a pleasant, patrician New England face, wise and comforting, gentle yet sensual, a face to be trusted and loved with the depths of friends who had become lovers and are the better for having been friends in the beginning.

"I missed you. I've so much to tell you."

Carter touched her eyebrows gently, drawing a line on the side of her face near his lips. "A new line here. The last few weeks must have been grim for you. We have to do some serious talking."

"Thank you for feeding the horses. I've been with Nancy Davidson, Jim's wife. Did Ellen tell you what has happened?"

"Yes, she was here when I arrived. There are several messages she left by the hall phone. The horses are bedded down; Kate and I drew water for them. Now, you come sit by the fire while I open this bottle of Chianti I've brought up and we'll eat in front of the fireplace. Ransome's special spaghetti is in the works. Your time to rest; my time to wait on you. Tomorrow you can make breakfast."

Lee laughed. "That's why I love you so. You know just when I need taking care of."

Carter grinned and opened the wine.

"Trouble is, you don't need taking care of too often."

He poured the Chianti into antique glasses, set them on the low table in front of the fireplace and added a small pot of paté and rye bread from a brown paper bag. Together, Lee and Carter touched glasses. Kate, sitting properly to one side, thumped her tail in anticipation of a possible treat.

They talked, as friends talk, having been apart for too long a stretch of their lives; Lee bringing Carter up to date on the events at the Hartley place and Carter bringing Lee up to date on his plans for a used-book section in his shop and his intention to stop in Portland at O'Brien's to search for some costume brochures he'd had a call to find.

"I'll stay through Sunday, Lee. I was rather hoping you could take a week to come back down with me. If you have to go to the funeral on Friday I can go to Portland then and on Saturday we could do the flea market and auction. Spring's way ahead home and my crocuses are almost past; daffodils are blossoming now. Come for a week; it will do you good and get you away from the stress up here. Besides, if what you say holds, you'll not be able to market Hartley Heights for a few weeks, anyway."

"Carter, don't say Hartley Heights, please!"

"Sorry. But, Lee, think about what I suggest."

"I'll talk with Meg; this might not be such a bad time to take a week after all. She and Dorie really can manage the showings. Contracts aren't due till the first of April and we have two closings then and I'll be back in time." Lee rearranged her mind.

"Good." Carter refilled their glasses. "We can take Kate with us."

Lee, patting the gold and black Gordon, said finally, "All right. Now, I'm starved—did you mention food?"

"Sit still." Carter's hand touched her shoulder gently as he rose to walk to the stove. "Relax and I'll serve."

Two minutes later, spaghetti Ransome filled two large old ironstone plates, fragrance steaming upward. Lee, enjoying herself and sopping juices with the crusty rye bread, said, "Carter, you're a wonderful chef. It almost makes me want to leave High Meadows and live with you in Connecticut forever just for your cooking!"

"Promises. Shall I propose again?" Carter smiled.

"No, but I'm beginning to bend a little. You are very special to me. There's no one else."

They sat looking at each other; then Carter stood, refilled the glasses and held his high in a silent toast. The kitchen doorbell clanged, and Reed's voice called, "Anyone home?"

"Come in, Reed. Have you eaten? Would you like coffee or wine, or are you on duty? I'm about to make a fresh pot of coffee." Carter, who knew Reed from former visits, made him welcome.

"Coffee's fine, thanks. I'm off duty but wanted to see Lee. Some things on my mind since this morning. Do you know all about what happened up at the Hartley place, Carter?"

Carter nodded. Reed settled himself in a low armchair. He accepted paté and rye bread and munched slowly, stretching his boots out toward the burning logs. He brushed his blond hair back and, turning toward Lee, spoke slowly.

"Will you go over exactly what happened from the time you left Jim in the house until the time when you and Clipper found him? Think carefully, now. As close as you can recall exactly what happened."

Slowly, Lee recited the story again. Leaving Jim, going with Clipper through the house into the ell and into the barn. Clipper going off by himself into the tie-ups and the old toolshed. Her own sense of some presence in the shadows of the barn. This was the part that bothered.

"I just can't be sure, Reed. There was a presence. Animal-like. Movement. A smell."

"A smell—what was it like?" Reed pounced on this.

"Musty—an odor; it's hard to put into words. Like meat hung too long, old and decayed. Then it was gone and I thought I'd imagined it."

"Could the movement have been Clipper coming back the other way? And it was unexpected and scared you?"

"No, Reed. I heard him stumbling around in the tie-ups, I think I did anyway. Everything in that barn creaks. It didn't seem like a person. It was like a shadow, moving. A presence. It sounds as if I'm getting squirrelly."

"No." Reed spoke gently. "If you sensed something, there could have been something. And you said before...?"

"A bear," Lee answered. "A large blackish bear. It had a furry sense. I know it's hardly possible. Unless it had hibernated over the winter under the barn floor and then woke up with all our noise. Reed, you know the old Mainers would say I 'needed a keeper.' It upsets me just to think back on it."

Carter, listening intently, said to Reed, "Lee doesn't usually hallucinate."

And the police chief agreed. "I know that. It's the reason I keep going back over this. Whatever it was, if it existed, it surprised Lee. I'm wondering if it surprised Jim. And scared him so he backed out of that room, into the railing, and it broke and he fell to his death. I just got the autopsy results before I came up here. Massive coronary and broken neck. Accidental death supposedly."

Reed sat quietly, thinking, and Carter refilled his coffee cup and placed a large piece of lemon meringue pie on the table before him. Carter collected plates, removed the spaghetti's remains to Kate's dish in the kitchen, fixed coffee and pie for himself and Lee and finally came to rest by her on a chair facing Reed.

"Oh, my, you've done it again." Lee savoured pie and smiled at Carter.

Reed, fork halfway to his mouth, laughed and said to her, "Why don't you marry him before someone else catches him? This man cooks like a dream, drives six hours to see you and even feeds your horses. I'm beginning to doubt your intelligence. I'd give him a run for his money if I was twenty years older, but I can't beat his pie. He's a keeper, Lee, if I ever saw one!"

Lee, laughing, reached across the table to take Carter's hand. "Kate thinks so too."

"Reed," Lee continued, "I'm thinking of going back to Connecticut with Carter on Sunday. Would that be all right with the police department?"

Reed nodded agreement. "Yes. We'll have to keep the house out of bounds for some time to go over the ground thoroughly. Jim's body will be released tomorrow—funeral's Friday—I guess you know that. Getting back to the front hallway—when you and Clipper found Jim—exactly what happened? I know you've been through this more than once. But think back again—every little thing. Forgotten anything?"

"No, like I told you, he was lying on his back with his neck all crooked and angled around. We knew it had to be broken. Clipper felt for a pulse and I listened for a heartbeat. Nothing. We had both said CPR the moment we saw him but then when we really saw the way he was all crooked with his neck at that angle we knew it was useless and unthinkable to move him at all. He was gone, Reed. His face had a horrid expression. I remember I felt sick. And, one other thing, I'd forgotten till this minute. On his forehead, to one side, it looked as though he'd scratched himself. Just a couple of lines. Then Bunny came and started screaming. Clipper took off his own jacket and covered Jim's face." Lee paused.

"OK." Reed leaned forward. "That's just as before, except you remembered the scratches. The medical examiner noticed them too. The clipboard was upstairs—notes in the blocks of the appraisal form. Notes on the small yellow ledger-pad sheet attached. He had writen down 'dentil molding, corner cupboard, paneling'."

"Anything else?" Carter knew Reed was leading up to something.

"A letter—looks like he started to write a word." Reed spoke deliberately, "And it looked like a 'B'."

"'B' for 'Bear'," whispered Lee.

"It could have been anything," Reed continued. "Maybe he meant to write 'board floors' or 'bedroom'—but Lee, I have to entertain the thought he tried to leave a clue. And if that's what the 'B' meant then something scared him enough to give him a heart attack, cause him to back out of the room and fall through the railing."

"It doesn't look as though you could prove it." Carter had been following Reed closely. He filled his cup now and watched the young, blond police chief study this problem. This was no ordinary cut-and-dried affair.

And Lee, looking into the fire as if to seek the answer to the question, said softly, "I thought I saw a bear. Jim did see something. And there is something evil in that house."

8

Reed and Carter finished the pot of coffee and Lee brewed more. Slowly and deliberately, for this was his way, Reed recreated the events starting with the February full moon and, as he did so, it became evident that Lee seemed to be the catalyst.

"One thing," Reed said, "mysteries don't always get solved in a week or two like in the books. In real life the police sometimes take years. And some go unsolved forever. I can't seem to fit anything together yet. But I have a suspicion there's a pattern. And you're right in the middle, Lee."

"You think the full moon means something? When is the next one?" Carter was listening to Reed intently.

"April fourteenth," answered Lee. "I keep a diary type of notebook, sort of a nature diary. It helps me to plant the garden, tells me the dates to expect bloom in the orchards, and the time the swallows and redwings return from the south. Both due this week, by the way."

Reed rose to go. "I have to go over statements with Malcolm and the Cleavers to see if they can recall anything else. Best what we talked of tonight we keep between us for right now. Are you going to the flea market and auction this weekend?"

"We expect to. I'll plan on going to Connecticut with Carter then, Reed. Ted and Ellen will stay at the farm, I'm sure." Lee walked to the door with the police chief.

"You need some time by yourself. Look, I'll see you later. Thanks for the good food, Carter. Remember what I said, Lee. Hang on to him."

With that Reed left. Carter and Lee walked through the ell into the main barn.

"I can't ever seem to sleep unless I'm sure they are safe." Lee sounded tired. "We could ride tomorrow morning early. If I can get a good night's rest. So much has been happening."

"Sounds like a good idea." Carter nodded.

"They don't have shoes on yet, but the woods roads still have snow patches we could skirt around, and we might take Minister's Road over to Mt. Rhoda Road and then branch off on the Thatcher road to get in just a few miles. It will be their first time out so we don't want to push too hard." She stroked a velvet nose. The mare whickered softly, inviting a flake of hay and Carter obliged.

Ordinarily she was Lee's mount, but sometimes Carter rode her as she stood taller than the gelding, Nat. Once a showhorse, Musette's eyes were still bright, her step still jaunty, and riding her was like riding a cloud.

A beautiful lady, Carter thought. *Like her owner.*

Sometime later, lying beside Lee in the upstairs north bedroom, Carter determined to ask her if she would seriously consider a life with him in Connecticut. *Probably not. Probably I'll* have to compromise and spend part of each year in Maine. He considered the size of his cottage on Lincoln Farm Road. Perfect for one person, a bit crowded for two and a Gordon setter to boot. Which led his thoughts on to the expression "to boot" and where it began and this led into fishing and finally into sleep.

When he woke, Lee was already up and the aroma of coffee wafted up the stairs—followed minutes later by Lee with a breakfast tray.

"Don't get into the habit, but I thought it might be nice this morning." Lee offered pineapple juice and coffee and fresh blueberry coffee cake made from Streaked Mountain berries picked the summer before. The old bamboo tray, bought at one of Morrill's auctions, fitted neatly over Carter's knees.

Spreading butter on his coffee cake with obvious delight, Carter mouthed, "Do you still want to ride?"

"Oh, yes." Lee's short brown curls shone in the sunlight coming through the window. "It's frosty but beautiful out and I think it's going to be quite warm according to the weather forecast. All your gear is in the closet."

Half an hour later they were riding down the lane, Carter ahead on Musette and Lee on Nat. Kate, under protest, had been left with Ellen who'd arrived as they were saddling up the horses. Ellen's pockets promised bones, and the Gordon stayed at home.

There was no traffic on the Mt. Rhoda road. Lee knew that later there would be locals and a logging truck or two but, in general, this was a quiet road.

"Look, there's a redwing, Carter. It's such a good feeling to see one. They are just like the swallows when they return. They're so brave and they fly thousands of miles. The world wouldn't be right if I didn't see them in springtime. It's too early for our arbutus, but there are some late pussy willows over to your left. I have to say I'm ready for warm weather." Lee rode happily, her hands patting Nat's neck gently every so often and telling the gelding how happy she was that they were riding again.

"Wait until you see Salisbury. We're a month ahead of you."

"How about a short trot to the end of the road?" Lee could feel Nat's pent-up energy and she decided to let him out for a short distance.

Carter nodded, and they were off, letting the horses stretch their legs this first time out, but holding them back from a full gallop until they were in better condition.

The Thatcher road was dirt, a dead-end that had once been a county road leading from Mt. Rhoda to the Buckfield area. Woods had closed in over the years. Few cars, and those only four-wheel drives, drove in here and horseback riders had come to value its wilderness and seclusion. One old cape at the end of the road—the so-called "turning point"—belonged to summer people who came only for three months; the rest of the year it remained closed.

Thus was Lee's first spring ride about to be disrupted as they turned the corner to face a truck unloading surveying equipment.

A blond, burly giant was shuffling papers from his briefcase as Lee drew Nat to a halt.

"What's going on?"

"Getting ready to survey lots. Leastways, that's my orders."

"Here?" Lee sounded indignant. "This is the Crossen property."

"Right, lady, that's what it says on this paper. We're supposed to be marking off ten lots."

Lee was puzzled. "I didn't know they were selling."

"You got me, lady. I just do the surveying. Long as I get paid, I don't ask questions. Mine not to reason...."

"I know the rest." Lee's voice was testy. "Has the planning board okayed this?"

"I imagine so. The subdivision application at least." The blond giant mentioned the name of an area developer who specialized in lots, and Lee, noting the name, decided she would go to the planning board meeting that evening.

"There's a deer yard in here," she said to Carter as they turned to ride back through the woods. "And a brook runs through and empties into Stony Brook and that runs into the river. I would think sewerage would have to be looked at carefully before any okay is given by the board. There are so many alders at the south end that this land can't be good for septic systems."

Carter felt Lee's dismay. "You go to the meeting. I've books to work on for a few hours. I brought them up and I'll take Kate out for a run while you're in the office this afternoon."

Back at High Meadows, horses cooled off and settled into the paddock, stalls cleaned and an extra pot of coffee brewed, Lee showered, changed clothes and drove into Paris.

"Dorie, did you know the Crossen land was being divided?" Lee was hardly over the threshold before she asked the question.

"I just heard it yesterday," Dorie replied. "In fact, Meg just came in and said she met Sam Childs in the store this morning and he was excited about his new development. He's going to call it the Old Crossen Farm Stand. Meg's in the rear office, Lee."

Lee walked down the hall, found Meg and told her of the morning's encounter with the survey crew.

"See, Lee, I told you there's money to be made in subdivisions. Trust Sam Childs, he won't even bother to list it with brokers, probably. I think he's taking the site plan to the board tonight."

"After the fact." Lee frowned. "I suppose there is little chance of changing his mind, when he's gone this far. It's one of the best deer yards in the area, and the bridle path runs along the perimeter. Now there will be traffic and the whole ecology of the region will be changed. Meg, am I so wrong on all of this?"

Meg, pushing back at least six bracelets on her left arm, thinking of children's school bills and Will's illness, thinking of mortgage payments and car payments, thinking of her credit-card bills and mounting debt, shook her head against her will. "No, Lee, in one way you're not wrong. You're idealistic, that's the trouble. You should have given that up after your college days. Few people can afford to be the way you are. I can't. What's more important? People need housing. They want a rural setting. You want an undisturbed bridle path. Lee, you can't beat development, no matter how hard you try."

Lee felt deflated. "I suppose not. But I'm going to keep trying for a bit more control. Enough of this. Carter's here; we're going to have a happy weekend. Dorie has me lined up for three showings today, and I feel a sale. I'll see you later."

The day was long and unproductive, even though Lee had felt one piece of land in the Harrison area was surely sold. By the time she arrived at the planning board meeting that evening, her patience and understanding of real estate had worn thin.

The planning board met the third week of each month in the town office. Unpaid, genuinely caring men and women, they listened stoically to the ideas of individuals ranging from mobile-home owners wanting to shift positions of their modest homes, to developers with dollar signs in their eyes. Zoning was a dirty word to Mainers; the old Yankee "You can't tell me what to do with my land" attitude was unbeatable.

As a result there was almost no control and if a plan from a developer fell within the small perimeters of the board, it was bound to be allowed. Tonight Sam Childs presented his Old Crossen Farm Stand ideas and the three men and two women listened guardedly.

Lee, when the presentation was done and the public allowed

questions, inquired about the deer yard. Sam admitted to knowing one was there, but suggested the deer ought to be able to move into another area with all the available woodland surrounding his development.

"There is hemlock on the Crossen land, Sam. You know how the deer depend on that for food. The other land is higher and belongs to a lumber company that could strip it at any time. I'm concerned about what you are doing. It's the total impact on the area that will count in the long run."

"You're always concerned." Sam's voice was acid.

"That's enough. Public has a right to voice concern." John Ridley, head of the board, took his pipe from his mouth and leaned forward. "Soil tests, Sam?"

Sam handed over the papers, and the man beside him, the soil scientist, according to his letterhead, described the land and the fact that he thought most of it *could* be made suitable to take septic tanks, if enough fill was added.

Lee, trying again, spoke of the small brook running down the center of the acreage.

"We don't feel this is a problem." Don Harris, the soil expert, had met Lee at meetings before.

"Um, well, let's look at this further." Ridley spread papers out on the long table and huddled with the other board members. Meanwhile two abutting owners had arrived and were gathering forces to object to the heavier traffic on the narrow dirt road.

"Gathering the troops, I see." Sam glanced at Lee. "Why in hell don't you just quit real estate altogether and stop showing up at these planning board meetings? You're getting mighty unpopular, I can tell you that."

Lee's eyes snapped. "As long as there is a you, there's going to be a me. There are two reasons this plan of yours ought to be reconsidered. The deer yard and the sewerage. You ought to be able to find another acreage to develop that wouldn't be so questionable."

John Ridley sighed. He knew Lee; liked her and sympathized with her feelings, but he also knew he had very little control over what was happening to the town's land. When usage changed, it had to come before the board, but if the owner or developer could show he was within the rules, the board had no choice but approval. Ridley was saddened and bothered by what had happened so swiftly within the past two years. He was about to give up his chairmanship out of sheer frustration, but on the surface he had to appear to be the impartial member carrying out his duties.

"Sam, we need a little more information on this before we can give you the go-ahead. I suggest we get a fish and game warden in here on the deer yard, Lee, and suggest you do a little more research on the sewerage situation, Don. It does look as though there could be a problem with the brook."

"And if we can satisfy you?" Sam had only begun to fight.

"Then we'll give you the approval. Those seem to be the main objections." John knew the words too well.

Sam and his soil man rolled up the plans and walked out. "We'll be back next month."

Lee rose to leave and touched Ridley's shoulder on her way out. Stoking his pipe, he looked up at her. "He'll win, Lee."

"I know, John, but I have to try."

"Any more threats?" Ridley had heard of Lee's problems.

"No. Did you hear about Jim Davidson's death?"

Ridley nodded. "Yes, I'm going up to the funeral. He was a good man, a credit to your industry. So are you, Lee. Don't get discouraged. There are some developers who care. And then others—like tonight. It's probably been this way since the first piece of real estate ever sold. Think about the 1920's. You couldn't give land away."

"I guess I'm beginning to be tired of fighting, and I'm a little scared. I feel threatened. Thanks, though. You make me feel better." Lee patted his shoulder.

"By the way—" Suddenly John Ridley remembered something he had meant to tell her. "You know Hod Cole? He's an authority on deer stands. He'd know as much if not more than any game warden. If you could get him to do a little research and come to next month's meeting, his word on wildlife is respected. Might even be better than a game warden. I understand Augusta has consulted with him several times."

"Hod Cole? I never thought of him. I'll talk with him before the next session. But—I've heard they call him 'Old Poacher'."

"That's so. I think he's saved more game than killed it, though. He's pretty highly thought of by all the woodsmen."

Lee drove back to the farm thinking that Hod was beginning to occupy one small corner of her mind.

The following Friday, gray and cheerless, was Jim Davidson's funeral. Meg and Lee, driving up the valley together, joined most of the real estate community honoring Jim. Seated with the Cleavers and Malcolm and Cokie Adams, the six of them drove back to the house to pay their respects to Nancy after the graveside service at the little church at Rumford Point. The tiny churchyard stood on the banks of the Androscoggin River. Arborvitae trees lined the winding pathways; old lilacs and the remains of rose beds stood between slanting slate gravestones. Snow patches, still on the ground, were rapidly giving way to green grass, but the wind was bitter and overhead were the crows, circling and relentlessly cawing and cawing.

Lee, feeling tears close to the surface, watched a red-winged blackbird perch for a moment on one of the old gravestones. She drew her coat around her shoulders, shivering in the sharp spring air. *Jim—he was so close to Howard Pond. How close am I to what comes next? How much is my own life worth?*

Back at the house, Clipper Cleaver hefted a cup of coffee in Nancy's front parlor and turned to speak with Lee. "I heard you were at the planning board meeting. I just heard about the Old Crossen Farm Stand development myself."

Lee nodded. "I'm opposing it. Too close to the brook for septic tanks. And there is a deer yard."

Clipper, making inroads on a piece of sponge cake, agreed. "Have to say you're right this time. Sam Childs usually wins, though. He asked me about going in on Hartley Heights, but I don't want him in our group. Malcolm and I can handle it just dandy by ourselves—maybe one or two others."

"So you've pretty well decided on a bid, Clipper?" Lee was curious.

"I'm not sure yet. We might throw in an offer—when you settle on the price." Clipper was hesitant.

"I may be away next week." Lee was watching him closely.

"If we do bid, I can deal with Meg. Got to do some talking among ourselves, but we're interested. We won't bid top dollar. But we'll bid a fair price." Clipper seemed to be thinking it out as he ate.

"Well, Meg and I will be phoning each other. So if you have any ideas, tell her. But until the new appraisers come up with a figure, and until Reed or the sheriff's office releases the property and Mr. Cameron approves everything we're right back at square one."

"The old Clipper'll just wait, then, Lee. You leaving so soon?" as Lee rose to depart.

"Yes, when I say goodby to Nancy. Hello, Cokie, how are you? How was the vacation?" Lee turned toward the young woman who had joined them.

Cokie Adams always looked outrageous—everything a successful New England broker aspired not to be. Long dangly earrings, pseudo-diamond studded, swung beneath strands of carrot-colored hair that was not due to L'Oreal. Cokie's clothing was numerous and sweeping, layer upon layer of various colors, usually orange and blue and green without any apparent direction or design other than to clash one layer upon the other. Today she was in black and pink, all of it belted together with a large black suede belt with a rhinestone buckle, complemented by black suede ankle-strap, three-inch-heeled sandals and a tiny black cloth hat. The whole effect was one of wild disarray.

Cokie generally unnerved any real estate buyer, but Cokie sold a lot of real estate. When at first she distracted, within a half hour into a showing she attracted, for most women customers became maternal and started to help her. Keys had to be turned in locks, spec sheets had to be found in Cokie's trunk-like handbag, and most men then offered to help carry her scattered belongings.

Showings ended with Cokie being fed a cup of coffee and a sandwich while the customers made an offer. This strange quality, this strange attraction Cokie had for the general public was nothing she cultivated. It just happened.

In fact, looking at Cokie, you got the feeling *she* just happened. Surely no modeling school (which she was supposed to have once attended) could have turned out this product.

Lee knew better. Inside of this product was a smart lady not to be underestimated. Cokie had pulled many a sale together, saved many a negotiation. She never said too much; in fact she said very little other than to breathe *oh's* and *ah's* at whatever features a property had to offer. To show a house with Cokie was to attend theatricals, but Cokie sold a lot of houses. Details of the contracts were settled in Cleaver's office; Cokie brought the prospects back there and Clipper took over. Cokie was his most valuable broker.

"The trip was wonderful, Lee. I could live in Spain forever.

Now I have to get selling to pay for the next vacation. Are you leaving? I don't want to stay any longer, myself. I hate funerals. I wouldn't have come to this one only Clipper and Malcolm insisted. Are you going to the flea market tomorrow?"

"Yes, I'll probably see you there." Lee turned to take leave of Nancy.

Driving back to Paris, Meg did not hesitate. "Lee, Clipper said he might put in a bid on the Hartley place."

"I know, he told me that too. He seems to be hesitating a little."

"Well," Meg continued, "you go ahead and go with Carter next week. If Clipper does anything, we can talk on the phone. He always negotiates property right into the ground. Take your week, you need it, and I'll take mine in the summer."

"Meg, you're a good lady. This is one time I'm glad we are partners."

Later, in front of the fireplace, Lee and Carter compared their days. Carter had spent hours at O'Brien's in Portland and come away with a book on fishing lures and two costume brochures he'd been searching for. Quietly, over dinner, with the candlelight forming shadows on the walls of the kitchen and the great ceiling beams, a depth of calmness and contentment soothed Lee's spirits. The old house, the firelight, the odor of good food and the comfort of companionship brought a pause in the strain she had been under for the past two months.

Across the table hands touched.

"Carter. Thanks for being here."

"My pleasure."

On Saturday, the 21st of March, the first flea market of the spring season opened its doors. The huge old Victorian barns, sprawling spiderlike upon the land, wore Chinese hats in the form of giant cupolas, their turrets flying banners proclaiming opening day. An antiques dealer had purchased this complex several years previous, recognized its future appeal to the summer tourist trade, and divided the interior into open booths within the old stalls and tie-ups. He had installed a large hot-air furnace barely adequate to heat the buildings, but with heat enough to take the frost out of the air, and, besides, customers moved about with coats on, anyway.

Because the owner loved plants, the main floor overflowed with spring flowers in every available redware pot, stoneware jug, wooden dough box, dry sink, flower pot or wooden barrel. Pansies and tulips and primroses forced you to believe spring was really here and the sharp March air was forgotten. Today was the first day of the season. Tonight would be the first auction.

Carter and Lee browsed. Lee looked for small primitives, Carter for his dearly loved fishing equipment. Rods and reels, lures and creels; show him a Thomas rod and he was happy for weeks. The market was getting a bit rich for his pocketbook but Carter was a shrewd buyer and he had amassed quite a good, if small, collection.

Lee held up a candle box in the old red, priced at nearly two hundred dollars, when Malcolm tapped her on the shoulder.

"Looking, or buying?" Malcolm's knowledge was wide and he and Lee often had attended auctions together in the past.

"Just looking. What do you think of this?"

"Too much; dicker if you want it." Malcolm sounded sour. "Where's Carter?" he continued. "Or are you minus boyfriend today?"

"He's over there. Why that tone of voice, Mal?" Lee looked at him inquiringly.

Malcolm shrugged. "Jealous I guess. Rather it was me instead of Carter. I'm just kidding, Lee. Sour grapes."

"Well you are snappish. But you're always my good friend. Do you think I could get this box for less?"

Malcolm nodded. "That dealer will always reduce his price. Make an offer. I'm looking for material, anything to make costumes. The school play has tryouts soon; Cokie and I are on the costume committee. Anything we see that fits, we collect ahead of time: old beaded fabric, velvets, brocades, satins, fake furs. Anything. By the way, if you have any old felt hats we could stand a donation."

Malcolm picked up a piece of brown velvet and held it to Lee's face.

"Too dark for you. Just right for Cokie. Listen, I'll see you later. I have to check all the booths."

Carter and Lee spent most of the morning browsing, took a long walk in the afternoon, a short nap, and that evening attended the first auction of the year: the contents of an old cape removed to the gallery floor of the flea market.

Spread over large tables, small items of tinware and dishes were mixed with Larkin desks, oak tables and, here and there, a small primitive with possibly a Shaker identity. Nothing of great value with the exception of a Hoadley grandfather clock with the original stenciling; this whetted the dealers' appetites and unleashed some spirited bidding at the beginning of the evening. After that, things settled down and reason prevailed.

Most of the real estate crowd sat together. Carter and Lee had come early; Malcolm and Cokie joined them and Bunny Cleaver came in late. She had recently shown an interest in antiques and was learning fast. They all settled in to watch the bidding; Bunny took out her needlepoint and slotted that into one portion of her mind.

Malcolm was restless. He bid on several articles, missed most, urged Lee to try for others, fussed with Cokie because she talked too much and, in general, seemed preoccupied.

Finally he took orders for hot dogs from the group, rose and walked into the small food stand to buy them along with soda and returned to his seat.

"Here, have some ort." He passed hot dogs and soda down the line.

"What are you talking about?" Bunny asked. "I thought they were Jordan's long red dogs."

"He means food." Cokie handed napkins down the line. "Here's your diet soda, Bunny."

At that moment Malcolm hushed them as he bid on a small Paris Manufacturing Company child's sled. Again, he was outbid and his mood was not a good one.

"Damn," he exploded, "rejection seems to be a way of life for me. What I need is a charm to change my luck."

• 9 •

"Did you see what Malcolm was buying?" Lee asked Carter as they loaded luggage into his car trunk. "He certainly does love fabrics. He and Cokie are doing the costumes for the school play. Elvira, his sister, told me once that he loved to make up plays when he was little, and they always were sure he'd end up on the stage."

"Which he appears to have done," said Carter, lifting in his bundle of books.

"In a small town, anyway," Lee laughed. "But he's spent most of his life running that men's clothing store and dabbling in antiques. Cokie's parents were minor actors, I understand, and that's why she and Malcolm get along so well. I'm glad he has someone; he seems so lonely at times."

"I'm afraid his life style and all those fabrics don't interest me. I've been looking for that old fishing tackle brochure; have you seen it?"

"Didn't you leave it upstairs? By the way, do I need any particularly good clothes?"

"No—country things. At the most we'll go one night to the White Hart, or maybe drive over to the Beekman Arms in Rhinebeck. You don't have to be too fancy. Bring your riding gear; the stables are open and we can go across some of the back roads, maybe up to the Riga Lakes if we take our time."

"That's steep, Carter."

"It's not too bad. And there is little traffic in springtime."

"It will be like old times when I rode over Belgo." Lee smiled at the memory. "I always thought that if I went back that's the area where I'd like to settle."

"If you ever come back you're going to live on Lincoln Farm Road with me, lady. If I can ever convince you that the joint state is better than the single."

"We'll see. I have to talk with Ellen for a few minutes and then I'll be ready." Lee, with Kate following, disappeared into the house, accepted coffee from Ellen and a packed lunch that Kate inspected minutely.

"Bones for Kate on that side," Ellen pointed. "Two sandwiches each for you and Carter, Thermos of coffee and some fruit. Ought to take you to Connecticut."

"Thanks, Ellen. I hadn't realized how few times I've left this place since I moved here. Now, you and Ted are all set, aren't you? Here's the phone number if you need me. All the other important numbers are on the wall of the den."

"Ted and I will be right here. I'm going to turn out the upstairs bedrooms while you're gone. Wash some curtains; Ted's going to look at the fences. Can't think of any reason there'd be a need to call. We'll keep a sharp eye on the horses."

"Good. Ellen, I can't find one of my favorite silk blouses—the light-blue one. I haven't worn it in a while, but I wanted it to wear with my gray skirt and jacket for dinner. Have you seen it?"

Ellen shook her head. "I'll look when you're gone. Maybe it's double hung. You going to call halfway through the week?"

Lee gave her a quick hug. "Probably. Ellen, what would I ever do without you and Ted?"

Ellen hugged in return, and Lee held the younger woman close for a moment, grateful for her friendship.

Carter blew the horn; Lee ran out with the lunch and Ted helped put Kate in the rear seat. Ellen waved and they were finally on their way.

"You'd think," laughed Lee, "I was going to Europe."

"That's not such a bad idea—maybe we can honeymoon in England." Carter, seeing an opening, took it.

"That tempts me. But I don't want to talk about it now. I only want to think small thoughts. Ellen packed us a lunch, Carter, she was determined we not be hungry."

"All right, that gives us a chance to run Kate. You know, Lee, when our family traveled, we always used to run our dogs in local cemeteries. No one was there to bother us, we kids would search out old graves and Dad would let the dogs work off steam. We did it all over the country. Let's see if we can find one off the pike for Kate when it's lunch-time."

Lee touched his hand. "I'm always surprised by you. A lot of old New Englanders wouldn't like that idea. Are you a witch in disguise?"

"Maybe a good one." His hand covered hers.

Kate, curled up in the rear seat, sighed mightily. She did not like long auto rides but she could do nothing except suffer it out. Lee petted her absently, thinking, *I'm so country set in my ways I'm not sure I want to leave High Meadows even for a week. I can't let Carter know how I feel, but every mile tells me I belong back in Maine.*

Spring proceeded down the turnpike; the greens became greener as they moved the three hundred miles south, the grass taller and spring flowers bloomed around country houses. The long stretch over the mountains through Becket showed the season to be at least three weeks ahead of Oxford County's, and by the time they swung into Lincoln Farm Road in Salisbury, tulips were in full bloom beneath magnolia trees.

"I always forget how neat and trim it all is." Lee's eyes admired the stately old homes with their well-kept grounds, like little old ladies retaining some of their girlish beauty. "None of the shagginess or rawness of Maine. It's so different."

Like Carter, she thought, *Connecticut was a well-turned-out identity that showed control. Would that we had some of that in Maine.*

Carter's little Victorian house, nestled among trees on the height of Lincoln Farm Hill, overlooked Lakeville Lake, Lake Wononscopomuc its Indian name.

Below slept the valley, rolling hills and mountains beyond. This late spring afternoon, the sun made tiny specks of light upon the waters of the lake, not unlike a Monet painting. Shades of green ranging from light to dark gave a tranquil feeling to the valley floor. A whip-poor-will called. And Lee, even with her great love for Maine, felt the peace and harmony in this beautiful spot.

There is order here. I could live here with no fears, no pressures. All would be arranged. I'm not sure this is what I want, but it is tempting.

"Thoughts?" Carter, carrying in bags and bundles, headed for the small kitchen.

"I don't know," Lee murmured. Kate, at her side, whined softly. "Come on, we'll check out the yard." Outside, Kate sniffed new surroundings while Lee stood gazing down at the lake. Kate had been here before as a small puppy.

Perhaps she remembers just as I do.

"You can never go back, at least that's what they say." The Gordon wagged her tail, looked up and seemed to agree. "I'll stay, but only as long as you stay."

"A week, old girl, a week. I have to try this out."

Carter called, Lee went back inside the small house and, sometime later, they sat down to one of Carter's cheese quiches, taken from his freezer, and a small green salad.

Carter was happy on Lincoln Farm Hill. He had lived alone here for the past ten years, ever since his wife had died and he had sold the larger house on Belgo Road. This small cottage was late 1800's, a one-story Victorian cottage with Gothic overtones. Carter enjoyed his small kitchen and pantry, his living room with the bookshelves he had built on either side of the marble-faced fireplace, and his tiny dining room and two bedrooms, one of which had room for a large Victorian walnut bed and two matching chests of drawers. The bathroom had an old-fashioned claw-legged tub with a ring shower, and off one of the bedrooms was a room called the Bamboo Room because of its wallpaper. Here Carter had created his study, and here he spent hours among his books ranged upon three walls. Windows, long and opening to the outside, looked down upon the lake, and a tiny stone terrace joined the larger brick terrace fronting off the living room. Living in this house was totally oriented to the rear where the view reached out to the lake, and the front of the house was shielded from the roadway by a high picket fence. A small cottage garden and Lombardy poplar trees completed the picture, one that could have been drawn by Andrew Jackson Downing.

At the bottom of the field, stretching away from the terraces, was a small wood, called by Carter the "wild wood". Here deer made their home, and an occasional bobcat. This small pocket of land remained wild. Two large farms abutted Carter's land and then one passed woodland for almost a mile before coming to another house. The Lincoln Farm road was little known except to natives. It concealed an English feeling of visual rural beauty not easily duplicated.

Lee had always loved this spot; it was the only one tempting her to leave Maine, but each time she visited it she ended up back in Paris with her heart closer than ever to High Meadows.

The pull between us is difficult to resolve.

That night, looking at the lights coming on far down in the valley, and with the last of the sun's rays touching the waters of Wononscopomuc, Lee felt the tug of nostalgia.

"My uncle caught one of the largest trout ever taken from that lake. I used to swim there when I was a girl. And sail boats. It had some of the clearest, deepest waters for miles around. None of the other lakes were half as good."

Carter agreed. "We ice-skated there, right near the Lakeville shore. The town had a rink every winter. And remember the basketball games, Lee?"

"I remember the bus we rode to the night games. And the driver, old man Miles, trying to keep us from being too boisterous and trying to collect us all after a game to get us home on time. That all seems so far in the past, Carter. It was all country here then. Down on the main road it looks like the town and the countryside are all one solid mass. Wall-to-wall homes all the way across the state line to Millerton. What's happened in forty years?"

"Lee, you're doing it again—can't you leave it alone for one week?" Carter offered more quiche.

Lee knew he was right. She had come to get away from stress but she had brought it with her; somehow there had to be a compromise.

She held her plate up for Carter's offering. "You're right, as you most always are. Your quiche is grand, Carter. How many cheeses?"

"Four. With thyme and savory and whatever I could find that day." He poured Lee a glass of good Washington State wine and looked at her for a long, thoughtful moment.

"Lee, I'm at peace here. Are you sure you don't want to share it?"

"Let me have this week to consider. I want to ride tomorrow morning—I want to go back in time. I'm not trying to be difficult, Carter. I just don't know. Can you understand?"

"I guess I have to. I'll call the stable." Carter rose and went into the Bamboo Room for the phone. Kate rested her nose on Lee's lap and looked at her wistfully.

"Manners—later, girl." Lee heard her own voice as she sipped her wine and looked at the lights below, now tiny marcasites on a background of the black velvet night.

Tomorrow. Tomorrow I will ride over Belgo. Tomorrow I will go back to the way it was. She remembered a day in England, when, by luck, she'd been able to hire a horse and ride below Bredan Hill in Housman country. The British bridle paths, the gates opening to present new fields, the ascending hill road, and, finally near the top, the exhilaration of being there—finally there. The same feeling she had known as a girl riding the lower Taconic Mountains and the Belgo area.

Tomorrow. Tomorrow I will ride over Belgo.

Carter returned, touched Lee's head fondly, and said, "We're all set. Ten o'clock. How about Belgo?"

Lee smiled. "You read my thoughts. Where else?"

Later that evening, side by side in the big Victorian bed, with moonlight streaming through the long windows, Lee and Carter talked quietly together, only to be interrupted by the phone.

"Who at this hour?" Carter stretched out one arm and pulled the phone to his ear. "It's for you, Lee, it's Ellen...?"

"Ellen? What's happened this late?"

"I tried before, but all the circuits were busy. I'm upset, Lee, there's something you should know. I found your blue silk blouse."

"Where?" Lee had heard the anxiety in Ellen's voice.

"At the bottom of the closet. Stuffed in one of your winter boots. And, Lee, it was ripped to shreds. Like someone took a knife to it. It's scary."

Lee sat up straight. "Ellen, don't panic. Where are you right now?"

"At the farm. Ted's here; everything seems all right. But, Lee, it wasn't there the last time I checked that closet. I mean, in the boot. That was just before the committee meeting. I remember because I put ironed clothes back in the closet that day and I did up the big room downstairs for the meeting."

"All right, Ellen. I'll be back in a week. Have Ted call Reed and tell him about this. Don't talk with anyone else. Whoever did it must be really twisted, so you just take care of yourselves and the horses. Has anyone called?"

"Meg and Clipper and Malcolm. They know you're away. Just the regular real estate messages. That's all."

"Well, if anything else develops call me tomorrow night." Worriedly, Lee replaced the phone, reaching across Carter. He took her hands, saying quietly, "What was it?"

Lee condensed the story of the blouse into a few words. Both considered this new puzzle.

Finally Carter said, "Do you want to call Reed yourself, tonight?"

"No, Ellen or Ted will tomorrow. I'll talk with him when I get back. Carter, who would do that? Someone hates me; that's a nasty thing to do. It's one threat after another. I'm almost getting afraid of living there alone."

"Maybe that is just what someone is trying to do—drive you away." Carter spoke slowly.

"I just didn't want to believe that at first. That's a lot of hate. And now I'm not so sure it has to do with real estate. Maybe I need a private detective."

"Who's he going to watch?" Carter sat up and looked at her, trying to make light of the situation.

"The farm—oh I don't know. Someone had to get into the house and my closet. They certainly didn't slash that blouse outside."

Carter sighed. "From what you told me, the whole garden-tour committee was there that week and lots of times Ellen and Ted must have been outside and anyone could walk in."

"Well," Lee kissed him gently, "go to sleep. It's not your worry."

"You're wrong. I worry for you. Down here you seem to be safe. Up there I'm not sure. As long as I care about you, it's my worry too. Lee, even though I kidded you a moment ago, this is not a small matter." Carter was showing his concern.

"I know." Lee lay close within the circle of his arms. "This almost destroys my week, but I won't let it. I don't think Ellen and Ted are in any danger. I seem to be the target."

Carter slept well; Lee slept fitfully, dreaming sometimes that she was running in a woods followed by a creature with no face and, when she turned back toward it, it became a bear. She woke, trembling, bathed in perspiration, and took a long while getting back to sleep. In the morning her head ached and it was a while before the crispness of the spring day cleared her dreams away. With Kate left in the house, Lee and Carter drove to the stable and finally began the day's ride toward Belgo Hill.

Carter, sitting a dapple-gray, swung up the pathway from the stable onto the winding blacktop road's edge. Lee, riding behind him on a small, old-fashioned Morgan, sat easily while looking at all the recent new homes. Edifices of glass and cement and brick and stone, along with older, restored homes surrounded by flower gardens and wide green lawns. Here a cape with a cottage garden, there a new saltbox built on the foundation of an older house, but with a stand of crown imperial not yet opened, on the path to one side. Seldom seen in New England gardens now, this plant once bloomed in almost every colonial garden. Daffodils and tulips decorated the borders in front of homes, every flower in full bloom, and reminded Lee of the crocheted borders of old-fashioned blankets.

All this building, thought Lee. *A whole new village within these woods. Once I rode through maple and beech and oak, now I ride past houses.* Few of the great old trees remained; those that did had been allowed to stand to blend in with so-called "natural landscaping". Deer and bobcat and fox had lived here; now they were shunted back into the woods further still, or driven to their deaths by encroaching civilization. As neat and tidy and acceptable as the homes stood in the spring sunlight, so much more appealing had been the forests of her childhood. She shook her head, urging the Morgan forward to catch up with Carter who had lengthened the distance between them.

"I'm saddened. I belong in another time. I admit it's all good design, but it's still development and all your control couldn't stop it."

"Lee," Carter spoke wearily, "some people like this type of living. Most people in fact. They don't remember the mountains as you remember them. All they want is a little bit of country surrounding an expensive country home with other homes nearby. No shacks, no trailers, no cheap housing, no junked cars. Everything posh and acceptable. In a rural setting without too much maintenance."

"I suppose." Lee knew it was a losing battle. "Carter, look. There used to be a trail here. It went over the mountain to the Upper Dam. That's what we called the little lake on top of the mountain. The trail ended there and we used to swim the horses across the lake to the opposite side and ride downhill through thick forest to the old Maltby ore-bed on the New York side. Then we'd join up with the Belgo road again and ride back over to Lakeville. It was almost an all-day trip with a stop for lunch. No houses for miles and miles. The trail must have led across the end of that lawn. No entrance there now."

They wheeled the horses, rode for another few minutes in silence, and retraced the road back down to the stable. Talking with the groom as she dismounted, Lee found that she had gone to school with his mother.

"I heard you were quite a rider," he said shyly. "Things must look different to you; my mum says she rode when it was all woods for miles and miles. Every year they build more houses. Did you see that one hung on the mountainside over New York way? Don't know how they ever hauled the lumber up there. Let alone put in a septic system."

Lee patted her horse. "I sell real estate in Maine. I've found out people will build anywhere."

"Food," Carter called from the car. "We can picnic on the back terrace; it's warm enough."

Back at the house and with Kate between them, they rested on the rear terrace, eating their lunch slowly, savouring the spring day, watching the play of light on the lake below, and recalling their ride. Kate, happy to have them back with her, sat at attention waiting for any stray scrap that might sail through the air into her waiting mouth. The serenity of a perfect spring day surrounded the two people and the dog.

The phone rang.

"Should I answer?" Carter looked hopefully at Lee. "I'm afraid it's for you, after Ellen's call last night."

The phone kept ringing, insistently.

"All right." Carter resignedly went inside and in a moment called for Lee. "I should have been a detective. I knew it was for you. It's Reed."

Reed's voice, quiet and authoritative, spoke at the other end. "A new development, Lee. I thought you ought to know. Young fellow in jail told another prisoner who told me. Seems someone sent letters cut out of newspaper to this fellow asking him to make phone calls to a certain number and say certain words. Everything was all laid out for him. All he had to do was read off what was written at a certain time. He didn't know who he was calling; he just knew the number. Every time he got instructions he got a fifty-dollar bill in the letter; the writer said he'd know if the fellow had followed instructions. If he did the first call right, he'd get a second one. So he made the calls. He was sort of a boozer and needed the money. Lives in the Silvertown area and he's not too smart. Anyway, he had five letters in all, each with fifty dollars. He burned the letters afterwards, like he was told. Said the last one said he'd be killed if he didn't do everything just right. Then it stopped. He got put in jail for drunken driving and got to talking one night with his cellmate and told the story to him. The cellmate told me. The thing is, Lee, he remembered the number he called; it was the same every time—although the words were always different."

"My God," said Lee, "you don't mean...."

"Afraid I do. It was your number."

Lee, during Reed's story, had motioned Carter to pick up the extension in the bedroom. Carter, now listening intently, said, "Reed, could he have been the same person attempting to fire the barn?"

"No, I asked him and he doesn't ski, doesn't know the farm, and he doesn't know who he made the calls for. I can't connect him to the barn attempt at all. It just looks as though someone picked him out to do a job and he did it. He's really scared the person who sent the letters will find out he's told us. I've assured him we'll keep it quiet. If he ever gets any more letters he'll come straightaway to us."

"Do I know him?" Lee wondered.

"I doubt it. He's just one of those Silvertown rowdies and probably will be all his life if he doesn't drink himself to death."

"I'll be back at the end of the week." Lee was tired, the whole day seemed thick with intrigue again, and the sunshine of the day was tainted.

"Sounds as though our mystery person has a plan, Reed." Carter was still on the phone.

"That's what's worrying me. This isn't just happenstance. Make Lee rest down there, Carter. I'll talk with you later." Reed was gone.

Lee, hanging up, stared through the window at the field and the "wild wood". *Waiting, like my own woods wait at High Meadows. And somewhere, on the face of this earth, someone or something waits for me in my woods. Waits and waits.*

Beside her chair, the Gordon whined softly. And Lee shivered, not knowing why.

• 10 •

At the end of the week, heading into April, Carter drove Lee and Kate back north. He stayed long enough to talk with Reed, who came up to the farm the next morning. Privately, without Lee's hearing them, they agreed that about all she could do was to be extra vigilant and to let someone know when she was alone for any length of time. Kate was a good watchdog; Ellen and Ted were at the farm much of the time and it would not do for Lee to become so frightened that she became paranoid.

Publicly and to Lee, they spoke simply of her taking average care and Reed expressed his views that the case might never be solved. The blouse worried him. One detective from the sheriff's department had been assigned to the case and he was following every lead but so far everything was a dead end.

Carter left with a feeling of frustration. There were problems still to sort out and it would take a while.

He gave Lee a long hug. "You know how much I care for you."

"And I you." Lee fought back the tears.

April finally arrived. Kestrels and robins flew the air above the fields, the apple crew pruned trees in the lower orchard, and Lee saw a fisher one morning early as she walked with Kate. Like quicksilver its brown body melted over the top of a stone wall and into the woods beyond, even before Kate, running low to the ground through the beginning growth of grass, noticed its scent.

Go and good riddance, Lee thought, for fishers are known to be a cat's enemy and several cats had been lost in the past few years. Charlie Cooncat stayed close to home and his security basket; he was an old man and his days of roaming stone walls were long gone.

April and the Attleburys arrived together. Lee saw the smoke from their kitchen chimney and remembered that Ted had mentioned they had called him last week to ready the house for them, turn on the water and fill up the kitchen woodbox. Ellen had done a general cleanup of the few rooms they used and when Lee, driving to work one morning, saw the smoke, a warm feeling stirred within her. They were special friends.

Dr. and Mrs. Attlebury always seemed to give the impression that they were about to leave for someplace rather important and a goodly distance away. Lee could never recall seeing Mrs. Attlebury without her hat on—"just in case"—she would say. The Attleburys were old, but still young; in their late seventies they had the same quick minds they had been blessed with in their forties.

Life to them consisted of the world of nature. Birds, bugs, mosses, trees, animals, the stars above and the earth below, they had studied it all in their lifetime. They knew every inch of their land, Lee's land, and the Hartley estate. Dr. Attlebury had once taught at a boy's secondary school in New England, but that was years past, and their present life pattern took them to England for walking tours, to France for canal trips, and to Maine to spend summers in their cottage near High Meadows. They knew all the woodland trails and it was from Mrs. Attlebury that Lee had learned of the famous Moss Path and the old springhouse hidden in the Hartley estate woods.

The Maine waters had been famous at the turn of the century, and the Hartley land had once housed a sanatorium, so-called, where city folks came to board for a few weeks and drink the waters from the woodland spring. Just as some city dwellers came to spend their summers in Maine at the famous Poland Spring House, so did many do the same "taking of the waters" at smaller spas deep in the Maine countryside—the Summit Hill House in Harrison, the spa on Allen Hill in Otisfield, and the old Oakfield house deep in the Hartley woods.

They, the Attleburys, had old brochures dating as far back as 1890 advertising a stay of a week at Oakfield for $25, which included all three meals and taking the waters twice a day.

The Attleburys came yearly for tea at High Meadows; they refused to socialize with most of the Hill folk, but they had become great friends when Lee and Mrs. Attlebury had discovered a mutual love for Harvey's Shooting Sherry.

"We could cut our wrists and swear eternal friendship, dear, but I do think toasting it in sherry is better, don't you?"

Lee hated being called "dear", but from Mrs. Attlebury it seemed quite proper.

Today the couple was dressed, as usual, in what looked like safari clothing: bush jackets and long knickers of khaki, long gauze scarves wound about their necks and, this morning, Mrs. Attlebury affected a jungle helmet which she wore while stirring muffin batter.

Dr. Attlebury was busy unpacking a case of books they had brought up from their Massachusetts home. Mrs. Attlebury hugged Lee, offered her a cup of coffee and settled her into the old Shaker rocker insisting that she spend a half hour with them.

Dr. Attlebury showed Lee a copy of Gene Stratton Porter's *Girl of the Limberlost* he had brought for summer reading, and the conversation took up almost where it had left off the past fall. Lee told them of the spring's happenings: the potential sale of the Hartley property, and Jim Davidson's death.

Belle Attlebury, sipping coffee, sighed, "What will happen to the Hartley place, Lee? It is hard for me to envision that woods being broken up into lots. I don't like change. I've always enjoyed walking the paths on that property. I guess I never really thought about where the lines begin and end on the three places. Now it could all become so different. I don't like it. I guess this is the first time I've felt old. And I don't like that either."

Dr. Attlebury, slowly turning the pages of a Wilkie Collins novel, nodded, "We're just past our time, Belle. I'm going in and have my nap now."

"But it's still morning, Frederick. We haven't had lunch yet. I was going to heat up the soup and I'm making those walnut muffins you like. I was going to ask Lee to stay and eat with us."

"Yes, I'll take my nap now." Dr. Attlebury shuffled out of the kitchen into the little borning room behind the pantry, closing the door softly behind him.

"I can't stay; I just stopped for a few minutes to welcome you back. I have two showings today. But I thought perhaps you'd like to come up to the farm for sherry and a light supper tomorrow evening. Sort of a celebration of your arrival along with springtime. Mrs. Attlebury, what is it?" Lee saw tears welling up in the old woman's eyes. Her face, still beautiful, although covered with a network of deeply etched lines, quivered and for one difficult moment Mrs. Attlebury almost lost control.

"What is it? Did I say something?" Lee was anxious for her friend.

"No, dear, it's not you. It's Frederick." Mrs. Attlebury always called her husband by his full name. In sixty years he had not become Fred.

"He's getting forgetful. Like mixing up morning and afternoon just now. He forgets where he is sometimes. It's become more noticeable over this past winter and it won't get better. I think it is Alzheimer's disease, dear. I'm having one of the doctors up here look at him. I guess I'm a little scared, Lee. I haven't told anyone this, so please keep it to yourself."

"Does he know?" Lee felt helpless.

"He's too intelligent not to know. But I don't know how often he thinks of his situation. We will come up tomorrow evening. And there is something else I've been thinking about all winter and I want to talk with you. Now, more than ever, when you've told me about the Hartley sale. Can we plan a few hours together next week if you have time?"

"You sound mysterious," Lee answered. "I'll help you in any way I can. Do you want to talk about it now? I run by appointment, but I could call in and see if Dorie would take my place for the first showing."

Mrs. Attlebury shook her head. "No, next week will do. How about the ninth, that's a Thursday? I always liked Thursdays. Almost the end of the week and they were long weeks with all those schoolboys and only being able to see Frederick at mealtimes. Thursdays were what I called a "saving grace" day. I'll just note it here on the calendar. See, Lee, I've all horse pictures this year."

She marked Thursday's date. "What time is good for you? Is

ten o'clock all right? You can stay for lunch and we'll finish in the afternoon if need be."

Lee hugged her. "You're being very mysterious. Don't forget—tomorrow evening at High Meadows. About six. Do you want me to drive over for you?"

Mrs. Attlebury smiled. "No, no, Frederick might forget his destination if I wasn't with him, but he still likes to drive his own car. We will be there on time."

"Would you like to see Malcolm?" Lee had a thought. "The garden club is planning a historic house garden tour in July. We've had one meeting already to make plans. I think they want to ask you to put the herb garden on the tour, but no one has dared mention it."

"Precious afraid of me, aren't they? Well, I won't put it on this year; you'll see why later. But I would like to see Malcolm and formally meet that peculiar Mrs. Bemis, if you wish. I think I'll enjoy watching those two trying to outdo each other. We'll see you tomorrow, then." And for the second time she hugged Lee and patted her head.

Lee, backing her car down the driveway, noted that Mrs. Attlebury's hand, raised in farewell, reminded her of Aunt Bess's years before.

I must go see if the trout lilies are out.

Duty called today, however, and fresh from her time in Connecticut, Lee took showings this morning. It was Meg's turn now to be away from Carriage Trade, and Lee sold both properties she showed, one a shore lot at Bryant Pond and one a woodlot in Woodstock. Luckily both pieces of land were near each other and she was able to book one directly after the other without too many road miles in between. Two other contracts had been signed while Lee was away, and those needed to be checked and consultation done with banks and appraisers. This was going to be a busy week. Little time for riding or long walks with the Gordon.

The following evening the Attleburys arrived at six sharp. They were never late, and Lee, upstairs showering and changing, was glad Malcolm had arrived early and could entertain them. He arranged sherry glasses and biscuits and was delighted to have the chance of the Attleburys alone. He filled glasses, settled them into the couches by the fire and brought in some herb cheese from the kitchen. Mrs. Bemis knocked at the door just as Lee, in a blue knit dress, came down the staircase.

Introductions were in order as Mrs. Bemis had not formally met the Attleburys. She wasted little time for she had decided before coming that she would ask Mrs. Attlebury for the use of her herb garden for the July tour.

"Oh, I do love sherry so, and I see you do also. And I understand you have an interesting herb garden. Roman wormwood I've heard, and someone once said your garden had the first *Daphne meserina* in the area. I've never seen it, you know, but Jan Howard told me. And aren't there some large woad plants, the ones used for wool dying when the old farms had sheep? And...." Mrs. Bemis was off and running.

"For heaven's sakes, Ellie, let her get a breath. This isn't a committee meeting; we're here to welcome the Attleburys back this spring. You're not even acquainted yet. Maybe Mrs. Attlebury doesn't want to make the herb garden public."

Malcolm interrupted and Mrs. Bemis, when he finished the last sentence, bristled.

"Don't you tell me how to act, Malcolm Bandridge. I guess my social graces are as good as yours any day. My family goes right back to the Battle of Monmouth in New Jersey and when did yours arrive, I'd like to know? Not until the Civil War, anyway, and then from the South. So you just keep your tongue quiet. I'll talk as I please. And don't be so stingy with those biscuits."

Lee and Belle Attlebury exchanged glances over their sherry glasses. Dr. Attlebury did not even seem to hear the conversation; he rose and wandered to the bookcases, choosing a town history of Paris to leaf through. Kate came into the room, picked a spot by the fireplace and noted that Mrs. Bemis, her old friend, was eating biscuits and cheese. Kate started forward but Lee's hand caught her collar in time.

"I'll have to banish you upstairs, old girl, if you do that again. Mrs. Bemis doesn't appreciate you."

Mrs. Attlebury's hand touched the gold and black setter. She liked dogs and missed their golden labrador who had died several years before. "Come sit by me, Kate," she whispered. And the Gordon obeyed instantly.

"My herb garden does have several unusual plants, Mrs. Bemis." Mrs. Attlebury took up the conversation. "But I'd really rather not put it on tour this year, if that's what you have in mind. I've some other plans and we wish to have a quiet summer. Perhaps the next time, though, if you ask me again I'll try not to refuse."

Mrs. Bemis was impressed, as Belle Attlebury knew she would be. She hadn't won, but she hadn't lost either and it would be a plum to be able to tell the committee that she was sure of the legendary herb garden for the next time.

Mrs. Bemis nodded, smoothed down her knit skirt and sipped her sherry. This promised to be a productive evening, in spite of Malcolm Bandridge.

Lee ushered them into the kitchen and indicated places at the pine table. Jonquils and pussy willows in an old pewter pitcher made a bright spot in the center, and the white ironstone plates held herbed chicken, rice, and some of the last of the freezer's green beans from Lee's garden. Another plate of biscuits came hot from the oven of the old Atlantic range and a small green salad completed this "simple supper".

Mrs. Bemis and Belle Attlebury, having come to a truce over the garden tour, decided that they liked each other in spite of everything, and they chatted happily about types of hedgerow plants native to the area.

Malcolm listened, putting a word in now and then, but he felt a bit left out of the conversation he had intended to control. Lee kept their plates full and discussed Wilkie Collins with Dr. Attlebury.

"His books have terrified me at times," she said. "I don't like them."

"*The Moonstone*, now there's a story. I never tire of rereading it." Dr. Attlebury savoured his chicken slowly.

Malcolm, having tried unsuccessfully to get Mrs. Attlebury's full attention, turned to her husband. "Magic—it seems to me Collins is tame alongside today's books."

The doctor considered.

"Perhaps, but such style. Science fiction is sometimes just trash, and half of what I read today is unbelievable."

"Plus half of what happens in daily life." Lee joined in.

"You, of course, are a nonbeliever," Malcolm scoffed. "There are a lot of things happening in the everyday world you couldn't conceive of. Events can be made to happen, you know."

Lee raised her eyebrows.

"Are you on speaking acquaintance with witches? Or are you just making conversation?" Lee could hardly keep her face straight.

Malcolm's eyes snapped. "Don't disparage what you don't know about, Lee. Nonbelievers are the first to suffer."

Lee was beginning to be exasperated. "Malcolm, I don't believe you. This is supposed to be a friendly conversation. It's not as though any of this were true."

She suddenly realized Malcolm was very angry.

Dr. Attlebury, certainly for this moment aware of the turn in conversation, directed his attention to Malcolm. "There are seemingly unexplainable happenings one could attribute to the unknown. Generally they turn out to have some basis in fact." His eyes twinkled. "As I'm a Druid myself, I tend to take everything seriously in the woodlands and the countryside. So you may both be correct."

Malcolm seemed momentarily placated. Lee was silent, hoping the talk would turn in another direction. Her mind relived her own experiences and the feeling she had had at Carter's that something waited for her in her "wild wood". To think that both Dr. Attlebury and Malcolm had some belief in magic and unexplained events did not add to her comfort.

How did we ever get on this subject?

Supper finally over, with guests gone, Lee climbed the stairs to hexr north bedroom and stood for a moment looking across the valley. The light from the old Collins farm on the hillside shone through the darkness, a beacon for Lee as long as she had lived at High Meadows. Once, meeting the elderly Collins couple in town, they had talked of their lights and how each felt the other's presence across the valley. Tonight the light shone brightly—*a beacon to count on as long as I live*, thought Lee.

Then, for a moment, it went out. Came on again. Went out for a second time.

The deer. The deer are passing. The first time she had seen this happen, she had not known their pattern. Now she knew that nightly, spring and summer and fall, they would pass from the woods, through the hayfields and into the orchards. Only in winter, when the drifts were too deep for this pathway, would they keep to their forest deer yard. When they passed directly in front of the beam of light, it was blocked out for anyone looking out of the window at High Meadows.

Go, and in good health.

She slept well that night, dreaming only of deer deep under the forest hemlock. One took an apple from her outstretched hand, and one, a small fawn, stood silently as she stroked its spotted fur. Then she woke to sunshine and a warm April morning.

The next Thursday morning Lee knocked on the Attleburys' front door. Mrs. Attlebury, carrying a straw basket of massive size, answered cheerfully.

"I'm so glad it's sunny today, Lee. I was afraid we might not be able to see properly if it was raining. No electricity in that part of the house, you know."

Lee was puzzled, but she followed behind Belle Attlebury through the old cape to the door at the end of the small borning room off the kitchen. Here the cape joined the older, larger house and here the older woman produced keys from her basket and opened the heavy Christian cross door.

"We never use these rooms. Since Mother and Father died we've just kept them locked. I go in sometimes in the spring to clean a bit. I did have to set some mouse bait in here last fall when we left Maine. Come this way after me, please." Lee followed, through the first room which seemed to contain dining-room furniture of unknown ancestry, into the hallway and then into a larger parlor on the end of the house.

Mrs. Attlebury opened inside blinds, so often erroneously called "Indian shutters", and light flooded into the room, spreading dancing specks of dust before their eyes. Boxes and barrels were stacked in one corner. Two rugs were rolled up, a long church type of bench stood at one end of the room, and at the other, an old blanket chest with traces of red paint and snipe hinges stood in the same spot it had occupied for nearly seventy-five years.

"Those are things that had always been in the little house—we just moved them in here to get them out of the way. Grandmother brought back what I want to show you. In these crates." And Mrs. Attlebury produced a miniature crowbar and hammer from her basket, handing them to Lee. "Now, we'll need these to open some of the box frames."

Lee looked about the room. Plaster walls still held traces of stenciling, still fairly legible in spots. Giant weeping willows shaded men and women strolling on the banks of a river. The Androscoggin? Here a small boat, almost a raft, held a man and a boy fishing with several fish laid behind them on the river bank. Two men and a woman, riding sidesaddle, were crossing a crude bridge. Deep mustards, old reds and blues and the green shades of the willows still were evident on the plaster walls. Rufus Porter? He was known to have worked in the Oxford County area. Looking closer, as her eyes became accustomed to the light, Lee knew these were among the best wall murals she had ever seen. There had been one antique home she'd sold several years ago that had two rooms with murals, mostly willow and elm trees, but none were as detailed as these. And, could it be—surely that was an Indian standing by the trees to the left of the bridge. And there, another.

"Mrs. Attlebury, I'd no idea these were here. I'm amazed."

"Well, the blinds are always shut and I think they've been preserved as they have because of the lack of sunlight. Mother never used this room and it's been closed since I was little. We just called it Grandmother's box room." Mrs. Attlebury removed her khaki jacket to reveal an old knit sweater underneath, and she put one hand on the nearest crate. "Let's start here, Lee."

Together, crate by crate and box by box, they moved back in time to the days of the great European travel experience before the turn of the century. They had little trouble exposing the treasures; the boxes had been nailed back lightly after their move and whole sides lifted off with ease when the proper fastenings were pulled away.

Lee was speechless.

Two armoires, one an English dark oak and the other a greenish-blue painted Austrian type, saw the light of day for the first time in nearly one hundred years. Several gold and white Louis XIV chairs appeared. An English oak dining table, a French provincial sideboard with table and chairs, a group of Welsh type of chairs with rounded turnings, several Continental curio cabinets, what appeared to be authentic Chinese Chippendale chairs. Finally, a highboy and behind that, two sheet-covered crates with boxed ends.

"Paintings," said Mrs. Attlebury. "She dearly loved English paintings."

Carefully, Lee used the little crowbar, and together they lifted up and out an oil, framed in an old deep-gold frame, and leaned it against the highboy.

"She loved horses," said Mrs. Attlebury. "Did I ever tell you she was quite a good rider, Lee?"

And there they were—the horses, set for a moment in time in the English countryside, ready for the hunt with the men atop, the hounds below, the landscape behind and great oak trees towering to one side. Far in the distance was a manor house, close beside them were the stables. Grooms, hunters, dogs, horses of bay and white and chestnut, some with hooves upturned, some poised to move the moment the horns were sounded. Beautiful in repose, painted probably for one of the riders to hang above his fireplace and feel the pride of possession that comes with land and family.

But the horses—the beautiful horses!

Lee felt her blood quicken, her senses tingle; tears filled her eyes. Softly, as though still not believing, she spoke one word. "Stubbs!"

"Stubbs?" Mrs. Attlebury looked at her.

"George Stubbs. He was an English painter; I think he lived from about 1724 to the very early 1800's. He was what they called a set-piece painter, Mrs. Attlebury; he painted objects standing still rather than in motion. In particular, he painted horses for the nobility, and scenes from homes on the lands of the owners. He also did paintings of exotic animals. And enamel paintings. He is enjoying quite a revival right now; he's been written up in two antique magazines and some of his work is at the Tate. I don't know if there's a complete inventory of all he painted. But he is very famous and brings big prices." Lee paused for breath, then continued.

"I can't believe this is happening. A real Stubbs. There's the signature. It will have to be authenticated. But I know you, Mrs. Attlebury, and I *know* these came back with your grandmother. Is the other by the same hand?"

Mrs. Attlebury nodded. "Mother said Grandmother bought two oils by the same painter. She never said who. Are they worth a great deal, Lee?"

"Yes, they are. But what is all this leading to?" Lee could no longer contain her curiosity.

Belle Attlebury lowered herself onto the floor and stretched her legs out before her, getting comfortable. The old khaki jacket doubled as a cushion.

"I want to sell them all, Lee. Everything in this room. I need to either have an auction or find a private buyer. I can't deal with all of this alone any more, and you can see what is happening with Frederick. He may need more care as time goes by, and I'm not getting any younger. Up until now I never gave any of this more than a thought every year when we came up to Maine. I always thought tomorrow would be time enough. Now tomorrow is here. If you could help me arrange for the disposal of all this, Lee, life would be simpler and I'd have a bit more money in my pocket. You know a lot of people and I trust you. Who would you recommend?"

Lee, having joined Mrs. Attlebury on the floor, sat raptly before the horses. She thought for a moment.

"If I were going to have an auction I'd have George Morrill. I know we could ship all this to Sotheby's or a city auction room, but somehow I think you could do very well right here. The auction could be in the Daniels Meadow. Art buyers come from all over; they like country auctions and Morrill has connections all over the United States. I could call him and have him come here to see you. I'll stay right here that day. I never dreamed you had anything like this."

Mrs. Attlebury smiled. "I'd forgotten some of the things. Grandmother did like to collect. And she had some good friends in Europe and especially in England. I guess she had plenty of money in those days too. We're an old family. Only when she returned home she began the long, downhill decline in health and so half the things she'd bought weren't unpacked; they sent them up here from Boston and stored them in this room. Mother didn't need them, she said they didn't fit in the cape, and so they stayed in boxes, and then Mother died shortly after Grandmother. Frederick and I just used this for our summer place, and Frederick made enough at school so we didn't need any extra income. Once in a while I'd dust off the boxes in the summer, but I never used anything. We lead a simple life. After a while I just forgot about this room. That happens, you know. So, if it is all sold, I'll never miss it. I say, though, he really could paint horses, couldn't he?"

Lee touched the frame of the painting reverently. "Yes, he could. In my wildest dreams I never thought I would sit on the floor in front of an honest-to-goodness George Stubbs."

"Is he really worth all that much?"

"He is," said Lee softly, "worth so much it takes my breath away!"

• 11 •

George Morrill came and looked at the Stubbs and agreed. Agreed as he partook of Mrs. Attlebury's oatmeal cookies and fresh-brewed coffee and walked through the two joined old houses admiring the stenciling and the antiques and taking time to talk of Wilkie Collins with Dr. Attlebury.

Agreed as he strolled the Daniels Meadow with Lee and Belle Attlebury, and chose the place the tent would be pitched in August and the place where the little portable outhouses would be hidden behind the great sprawling oaks and looked at where the ladies of the historical society might like to place their small catering booth with the best of the Hill's pies and cakes and lobster rolls and herbed ice tea.

Agreed as he too sat on the floor of the large dusty box room and admired the Stubbs.

And agreed, most of all, that this auction would be among the most, if not *the most,* elegant sale of the summer in the Oxford Hills. Together Lee and George and Belle Attlebury spoke softly as they discussed details of the August auction and feasted their eyes on the horses. The incredibly beautiful horses.

"I think," mused George, "that we will have to deal with the sale as a bit out of the ordinary. The month before we'll put a guard on the house for you, Mrs. Attlebury, so you won't be bothered with strangers coming to the door. We'll make it as easy as we can and we'll shield the doctor from the public."

Mrs. Attlebury nodded. "Work through Lee, if you will. I trust her and I know that the two of you will help me with Doctor Attlebury. I'd like to keep the public out of the herb garden. I might want to go down to the meadow when you sell the Stubbs, but for most of the auction I won't leave the house."

George agreed. "No problem. We'll rope off the private areas and the meadow is partway up off the road to the house so we will rope it off above the parking entrance. I'll have the ads and flyers worked up and things should go smoothly. August is the perfect month and we have plenty of time to schedule."

So, with an extra cookie in his hand, George left. Lee walked him to his car and saying goodby, she knew that by the end of August Mrs. Attlebury would have cleaned out her box room and increased the balance in her savings account.

Lee walked back through the herb garden, just beginning to awaken from its winter slumber. Mrs. Attlebury was bending over some lavender bushes that had suffered from the snow and ice. "Lee, I meant to tell you, I saw a bear a few days ago. I was walking up by the Hartley place thinking of early dandelions and there he was right at the side of the barn, sort of bending over. I backed out of there. But something was strange. Maybe I ought to talk with Reed, what do you think? He didn't act the way a bear acts after the winter."

So you saw one too. And close to the Hartley barn. "I'll call Reed and have him come up to see you." With this she bid Mrs. Attlebury goodby and walked back through the woods to High Meadows. The maples were showing red buds and, high above, she heard the sound of geese going north. A surge of spring touched her spirit as she glimpsed them through the treetops, and somehow the day seemed brighter and happier. She thought of their age-old journey back to Hudson Bay, and knew that somewhere the swallows were gathering to start their long flight back to the rafters of High Meadows barn. Nearing the horse paddock, she heard the song of the white-throated sparrow, and finally her eyes found him seesawing on the paddock fence.

Musette and Nat moved slowly in the soft air of springtime, and the faint, sweet smell of stable filled the air.

Is there any better place to live? Why did Jim die and who hates me so much as to cause me to fear these beautiful woods?

Carriage Trade was busy, and after putting in a call to Reed for Mrs. Attlebury, Lee changed and drove in to the office for the rest of the day. The troubles with the Crossen land at the planning board meeting had deepened the division between Lee and some members of the real estate community, but it had also begun to lead to support from realtors who were beginning to see Lee's point of view. Stiffer rules had to be made for the planning board or a moratorium on development had to be called. Several area towns were already considering these ideas. One thing balanced another and Carriage Trade had actually gained new listings from the dispute.

Meg, moreover, was coming around to Lee's point of view.

The Lewiston appraisers had looked at the Hartley estate, given their estimate to Mr. Cameron, and he had decided on the price.

"Five hundred thousand. Half a million. I sort of expected

that." Meg had talked with Lee the day the authorization came in. "Now we can begin advertising. I think we should call those New York clients who wanted a large acreage."

Lee nodded and smiled. "I guess we ought to tell Cleaver the price too. I'm sure he and Malcolm are still talking Hartley Heights, although I'll wager Bunny will put her foot down on moving to that house."

"I feel queer about showing the place." Meg was hesitant. "Maybe you and I should go up there together and go all over it again to get our information straight before we really start showings. And, Dorie, we'll need more camera film. Will you check that, please?"

Dorie, coming in from the small kitchenette with a pot of Earl Grey tea and cups, set the tray down in front of the women.

"I'll start in on the spec sheets. By the way, Lee, what was in that locked room when Reed got the key from Mr. Cameron?"

"Very little," said Lee, sipping tea. "That room is at the end of the bedroom ell and has a fireplace, up over the kitchen fireplace, and some old wide board sheathing on the walls, but it's sort of queer, there wasn't anything in that room. I can't understand why the Hartleys had it locked. Mr. Cameron said he didn't know; he thought it was furniture. The Hartleys are dead and the heirs haven't been in Maine for years. The caretaker died over the winter in Florida, and Mr. Cameron said he'd never been in the room anyway, the caretaker, that is, as far as he knew. So it's a puzzle why the house has such a special security system. Reed left the room unlocked after he looked at it."

While she spoke, Lee thought of Mrs. Attlebury's cache of fine antiques, undisturbed for years in an unused room. It was certainly possible that the Hartleys had once stored items in that room of theirs. Maybe over the years they kept thinking the room still held the furniture, even when it had been removed. Mrs.

Attlebury said people "get used to things." She had forgotten what she had stored away; maybe the Hartleys had forgotten they'd removed the contents. Was that possible? Or had someone else removed the contents without the Hartleys knowing? So all they had protected was an empty room. Was that possible?

Lee finished her tea and rose to leave. "There's a planning board meeting tonight and I've asked Hod Cole to come by and talk a little about the effect of developments on the area's deer yards."

"You were actually able to get him to talk with the planning board on the Crossen property? That's quite a plum, Lee, he rarely talks with anyone on anything. He's known to be close-mouthed and difficult." Meg was impressed.

Lee smiled, thinking of the conversation she had had with Hod at the Hartley place, and the circumstances of their meeting. *Maybe there are two men here, and I know the hidden one. I rather like him.*

Aloud, she said to Meg, "I'm on my way. How about lunch at Mariah's soon? Clipper and Malcolm might want to talk about the Hartley place and that might be a good way to hear what they have in mind."

Meg agreed. "I'll call them—how about one o'clock tomorrow? How about Cokie? She's selling a lot of property for Clipper and he's quite proud of her. Malcolm's working just as hard, but I hear he's not doing as well as she is."

"One o'clock it is. You know," Lee continued, "Malcolm has rather a cynical turn of mind and sometimes buyers sense that. He knows his land and his house values, but sometimes he doesn't understand his people. He has a lot of out-of-state contacts, though, so Clipper says in the long run he'll be valuable to the firm."

On the way home over Minister's Road, at the end of the day, Lee passed Reed Jamison, who, for the past hour, had been talking with Belle Attlebury. Reed liked the Attleburys; he always stopped to see them several times during their seasonal stay at the cottage. Belle Attlebury baked something special every time she knew Reed was due, and this afternoon, after asking Lee to tell Reed that she, Belle, wanted to see him, she had made sure there were fresh cookies to accompany his coffee. While the doctor napped, she clearly and briefly told Reed what was bothering her. Belle's mind was sharp; what she'd seen puzzled her and she could not guess the meaning, but she knew Reed might. She was proud of him, knew that he might well have been other than a small-town chief of police, and she thought of him as the grandson she lacked. Today, she went directly to the point.

She had been looking for early dandelions in the old Hartley house barnyard. She and Frederick had been at the cottage a short while; she had settled him that day in the kitchen with a cup of tea and a case of books, and decided to take a walk up through the trails onto the Hartley land.

"I needed some fresh air after Massachusetts smoke, and I'd been thinking dandelion greens all winter. I knew it might be early for them, but I just had to see. I was leaning over, looking at the ground, when I straightened up and saw this bear. Walking upright, he was. He disappeared around the corner of the barn, then reappeared and just stood there. First I thought he must see me, but he didn't appear to, and I just stood very still and kept low to the ground. You know, Reed, I'm never afraid in the woods; I've come across bears plenty of times when I was berrying and always gave them plenty of space. I'd just fade away sort of—they never bothered me. So I just slowly crouched down in that old barnyard. The grass was ragged spring grass and there wasn't much cover but I kept still. I don't know what bothered me so except this bear wasn't like any I'd ever seen."

"How so?" Reed spoke softly.

"Well, he kept standing up. He never got down on all fours. He stood upright, took a few steps forward, a few steps backward, like he was dancing. Swung his arms out a few times. He was fooling around. I felt like I was watching circus practice. Then he ambled away—I say ambled because it seemed as though he did a certain type of swaying walk and an amble is the closest I can come to what it was like." Belle paused.

"That's all?" Reed had finished his coffee and set his cup down carefully. There seemed to be no sense to what Belle had seen.

"That's all." Belle echoed his words. "I picked up my dandelion knife and my basket and got out of there, but not on the trail. I kept to the trees at the edge. I didn't feel like I wanted to meet him. You see, Reed, I don't think it was a bear."

"You mean you think it was a person?" Reed was relieved that Belle echoed his own thoughts.

"Exactly. Pretending to be a bear. Although that's a strange place to be doing an impersonation."

"What did the fur look like?" Reed was listening intently.

"Kind of scruffy—like a bear coming out of winter hibernation. Spotty in places. Black—furry. The head looked a little small; in fact when I think about it, he was a little out of proportion. Sort of a small bear. The kind we have in the woods. But they usually travel with all of their feet on the ground, Reed. This one kept standing up. The other thing is, I was uneasy. I might have spoken right up, you know, just come right out and said, 'What are you doing, practicing for some circus?' But I was afraid, so I got out of there as fast as I could. The doctor and I talked about it when I got home, and I asked Lee to call you today. It seemed so silly, I almost didn't mention it. Who would be around the old Hartley barn, pretending to be a bear?" Belle looked at Reed as though he knew the answer.

Who indeed? Reed shook his head and sketched bears in various positions. "I don't know, Belle, wish I did. There is something going on around here I don't like. It's an evil feeling; you were right about that. Lee thinks she might have seen a bear in the barn the day Jim Davidson died. There is a slim possibility Jim saw a bear and it caused him to fall, although his death was called accidental. Then you think you saw a bear. I don't know how it all connects. But it centers around the Hartley house and besides that, Lee's had threats. I'm going to tell you what I told her. Be on your guard—be extra careful."

Belle Attlebury looked thoughtfully at Reed. "I've roamed these woods alone or with the doctor for more years than I can remember. I never feared anything. It's sad that times have changed. But, I will be careful, Reed. I promise."

Reed hugged her as he rose to leave. "I'll be back soon, Belle. You're looking well, by the way. Has Hod been in to see you?"

"Yes, not long after we arrived. I do like that man. He is a strange one, but you know I think he may be coming out of his shell. I believe he likes Lee Heaward—met her up on the Hartley land. He asked me if she was 'attached'—that's the way he put it. He and Lee'd make a good pair. They both love the land so much."

Reed smiled. "They are both mighty independent people. Guess we'll have to wait and see, Belle. Take care of yourself and the doctor, now."

Lee, back at the farm after her talk with Meg and Dorie at Carriage Trade, took Kate for a short ramble in the orchards where the trees were beginning to show the pink shading on their trunks as their season began. Kate bounced about happily smelling for mice, and Lee waited patiently for the Gordon to get her exercise. Coming back up the hill, she heard Ellen calling from the house, "Lee—phone call."

Hod Cole was on the other end. "What time tonight, Lee?"

"Eight o'clock. Can you make that? I really appreciate your doing this."

"Yep. I'll be there. How long do you think it will take?"

"A couple of hours," Lee answered. "It depends on when we are scheduled. It shouldn't be more than two hours."

Hod chuckled. "Good, that's about all I can stand of the real world. Maybe I can buy you a cup of coffee afterward?" His voice was hesitant.

"That would be nice." Lee hung up and walked thoughtfully to the barn. This was a strange man, mysterious in a way, certainly not the man Meg had described as being closemouthed and difficult. *I don't even know how old he is. Or whether he is married. I'm not sure I even want to know.*

She fed the horses and returned to the house to draw the bathtub full of hot water for a long chamomile soak. *Better to be in good shape when I face the planning board and Sam Childs. And maybe, just maybe, have a cup of coffee afterward with a man I am beginning to be very interested in.*

A few hours later, Lee walked in the door of the town office to face Sam Childs on the Old Crossen Farm Stand subdivision. Hod was already there, looking quite different in a white button-down oxford-cloth shirt worn without a tie, chino pants and an old tweed jacket with neat chamois patches on the elbows. He sat quietly on the end of one of the long benches, and rose when Lee came in the door.

The planning board members were all seated, looking over the evening's agenda, and Sam Childs, backed by his soil scientist and the surveyor, was unfolding his plot plan and tacking it up on the board at the front of the room.

After disposing of the matter of two trailers located on grandfathered plots of ground, the board turned to the Crossen property. Again the two abuttors objected to the runoff, with the soil scientist arguing this was no problem, but there was no guarantee forthcoming. Then it was Hod's turn, and he rose slowly to talk about the impact of the subdivision on the ecological systems of the area.

Lee was impressed.

Hod spoke slowly, with a minimum of words, and came directly to the point. He never said "could be", he said "is", he backed all of his facts with almost undisputed information, and his quiet voice filled the room with authority.

"The deer," said Hod, "need all the help they can get. They're being slowly crowded out by people, and now they have a new enemy, the coyotes. Every year deer lose their cedar and hemlock trees, their winter feed and their yards. Woods are cut faster than woods are replaced. Cedar's a favorite deer food. You put a lot of houses in there, even if you save the middle for a common area, the deer don't know that. If they get to be a nuisance, they'll be shot. Nobody told them about the balance of nature. Or how to move to another deer yard. They just have to hunt for food in a different place in a hard winter. That land's had a deer yard for years. It's also swampy in some spots. Water stands on it even in a dry summer." And Hod had several written statements from the warden attesting to the fact of the deer yard location.

He spoke for three minutes, made his point and sat down. Lee smiled across at him, grateful for his help and surprised at this new Hod Cole.

The planning board faced a difficult situation as they had so many times in the past. Sam Childs usually had his way; he had won in two nearby towns, and he simply kept coming back. Time and time again he stood in front of a board and finally overcame his opposition. He wasn't going to let the Old Crossen Farm Stand go easily; he had paid more for this land than he had intended and he needed to get these lots on the market soon. Lee Heaward was a fly in his ointment and he was getting tired of seeing her pop up at meetings. Hod was something new, something he hadn't counted on and wasn't quite sure how to handle. Sam Childs was definitely not pleased with the direction of this meeting.

"We can make the lots larger," he informed John Ridley. "I have a back-up plan for making them two acres instead of one. And I'm willing to make the common area larger. Cut no more trees than necessary. Unless you can prove that our drainage and septic plans are really going to affect the abbutors, I don't see on what grounds you can turn this down. We've done everything according to plan and I'm getting a little tired of this opposition."

Ridley, although in his heart on Lee's side, had to agree with Sam. The impact of the development on the wildlife was the only possible reason to put the decision off once more. The board decided to table the request until more information came in on this factor. Hod agreed to get a member of the fish and game department down for the next board meeting, and have them walk the land before meeting night. Childs agreed to make a new plot plan with larger lot sizes. It was a stand-off with no winner yet declared, but Lee knew the delay was only tentative.

"Can I buy you some coffee?" Hod followed Lee out of the town office.

"That sounds good, but would you rather come back up to the farm? Would iced tea sound better? It was so warm in there."

"Glad to." He followed her car up the road; Ellen had left the big security light on and Kate was at the door to greet them. Lee introduced her to Hod, who said it had been a long while since he'd seen a Gordon.

They inspected the horses and Hod reached over gently to stroke Musette. "She must be all of twenty-five."

Lee was surprised. "Few people know that. I didn't know you liked horses. Do you ride?"

"Used to, a little; when my wife and I were first married we rode out on the woods trails quite a bit. Haven't now for years. Just walk." Hod spoke quietly.

"You're married?" Lee held her breath.

"Was. She died five years after we were wed. Childbirth. Lost both of them. I haven't been connected up since. Took a long while getting over."

Lee was taken aback. Whatever she had anticipated, it wasn't that answer. "I am sorry, Hod."

"It's all right now. Thirty years ago, Lee. It took me a while. I had a friend some years later, but it never came to anything. So I guess I'm an old bachelor. You travel faster that way, they say. Did you say something about iced tea?"

They walked back through the ell into the big old kitchen, Hod admiring the beams and the big fireplace. Lee poured tea, set out some of Ellen's peanut butter cookies on an old Peruvian Horse Hunt plate and they faced each other from either side of the old pine table.

"Ever look to see if you had a smokeroom behind that old fireplace?" Hod asked, munching on a cookie.

"No. I rebuilt the old chimneys in this house and, as far as we could tell, there was no hidden area. There could have been a little room in the living room under the stairs because there was a space with a brick floor right behind the chimney area. The room didn't lead anywhere, but I thought it might have had a trapdoor to drop down into the cellar years ago. I've seen one or two of those setups in houses I've sold, Hod. But there was nothing like that here. I have wondered about the old Hartley place."

"Actually," said Hod, reaching for another cookie, "it does have a secret passage. In the second floor bedroom and it leads down to the cellar. I think it used to go into the barn area through some kind of a tunnel. Old man Hartley showed it to me once; he was right proud of it. That dated way back. I think he spoke of a second passageway, too, but I don't recall his showing me. He said the place was a regular rabbit warren. Old man Hartley kind of got a kick out of those ways in and out. Said he could escape from his wife that way!"

"Hod, listen." Lee leaned forward and rapidly told him the complete story of Jim Davidson's death, the look on his face, the scratches, the feeling she had had in the barn and seeing a bear. Then she took a long breath and told him everything that had happened at High Meadows since February including the phone calls, the threat to the barn and the slashed blouse.

Hod listened intently, interrupting only once to ask more about Reed's information from a prisoner at the jail. His eyes narrowed when Lee spoke of the gas can under the horse stalls. "Lee, when you thought you saw something in the Hartley barn; was there any odor?"

"I think there was—yes—I'm sure there was. I can't describe it. Even now it all seems my imagination. But there was a queer smell."

"The phone calls," Hod continued, "what were the voices like? Was there more than one?"

"I told all that to Reed. And I just told you what the prisoner said—he was hired to do it by letter with a payment each time. The voice on the phone was rough—Reed said the man had a low, gutteral voice. Reed's at a dead end on that—all the letters were burned. All along I thought it was my stand against development, but now I'm not sure."

Hod was still thinking, slowly and methodically, trying to

puzzle it out. "You don't think the barn attempt is connected to the calls?"

"Reed doesn't think so. And it makes no sense to me."

"Whoever skied up to the barn had to know your land. If he was the phone caller, he had to have some pretty detailed instructions to pull that off. Those boys down at Silvertown will do most anything for money, but trying to fire a barn in a strange place on skis on a winter's night isn't exactly easy money. Lee, here's another thought. Maybe he just wanted to scare you, not really burn the barn down."

"He scared me all right. Reed mentioned that idea too. I'm glad we talked about this—I feel a little better. I'm just determined I am not going to let anyone drive me out of here." Lee's voice was emphatic.

Hod laughed. "I wouldn't want anything to happen to you just when we're getting acquainted. Keep an eye out, though. Keep that dog with you. I'll bet she wouldn't let anyone touch you if it came down to the wire."

Kate's nose touched Hod's hand and she wagged her tail.

"You take care of her, hear?" He patted the Gordon's velvet head. "Well, I have to go. I'll see what I can do in Augusta. Thanks for the iced tea. I'm real glad to see you again, Miss Lee Heaward."

Lee walked out with Hod to his Jeep. The sky seemed close: a dancer's skirt of black velvet with diamond sequins hanging low over the farm and woods. A whisper of spring was in the night air, too early for the hyla's song but the promise was whispered. Promise not to be lost.

"I'd like to see that passageway in Hartley's if you can locate it, Hod. Meg and I will be up there next week; if I call you will you come and show it to us?"

"Sure. Glad to. I'm afraid the price will be too high for me so

I'll just set on that one, but I'll come join you. By the way, Lee, the Attleburys are back." Hod, too, seemed to want not to end the conversation.

"I didn't know you knew them." Lee was surprised.

"I have for years. Always stop by to see Belle. She's a special lady. Likes dandelion greens and fiddleheads. She knows more about these woods than most anyone." Hod's love of Belle Attlebury was evident.

"They're my friends, too, ever since I moved up here. Hod, the Hartley price is half a million and I don't think the estate is going to lower it much, according to Mr. Cameron. Meg tried to call you. We wanted to tell you right in the beginning."

"Like I said, that's more than I can pay. But I'll keep thinking on it. Goodnight. Thanks again."

Lee stood under the comforting security light, watching Hod open his Jeep door, start the motor, and then sit still for a brief moment before he reopened the door. He walked back to where she stood.

"Listen, Lee, in a week or two I have to go over to Fryeburg to look at a piece of river land. Canoe a bit on the Saco—land runs along it for a piece. Do you want to go with me—maybe take a lunch?"

He stood quietly, waiting for his answer. Lee, looking at Hod's lined, tanned face saw a man trying on something for size, something he hadn't done in a long while, something he was still unsure of.

She heard herself say, "I'd like that."

"All right. I'll call you. Take care of yourself." He was gone.

What just happened here, thought Lee, *is something that could be very special.*

12

The following day, lunch had been scheduled at Mariah's, but Meg and Lee had unexpected clients who wanted to look at a Bethel property, and Clipper phoned to say that one of his closings had been moved up so he could not come. It was a full week later, towards the end of April, when Meg, Lee, Clipper, Malcolm and Cokie gathered for lunch.

Working her way through a chef's salad, Cokie was putting questions to Meg. "Any bites on the Hartley property yet?"

"No; in a way, that's why we are here. To talk about it. Clipper," Meg said turning to him, "at half a million, what are your thoughts?"

"Dark." Clipper replied promptly. "Isn't that what they say in the books? Bun's been reading some of those English novels lately. Dark. That's a stiff price. Too high for development potential; that's what I think."

Malcolm spooned Mariah's famous fish chowder into his mouth and wiped his lips daintily with his napkin. "Two or three parties could still go in on it."

"Yeah, I've been thinking of that, Mal. The four hundred acres ought to be divided into at least thirty lots with a common area and it could make a right nice high-class development, but it's still a stiff price." Clipper ate food the same way he sold real estate—with gusto. "And," he continued, "I wouldn't sell anything under two hundred thousand; that's house and land together. No cracker-box architecture. Real class, Lee."

"Who are you figuring on selling that price range to, Clipper?" Lee, eating Mariah's quiche abundant with fragrant cheeses, paused with her fork in the air.

"Well, there's some new blood coming into the hospital—hey, I made a joke!" Clipper grinned, pleased with his wit.

Malcolm rolled his eyes upward, looking at Lee. They both had heard Clipper destroy the English language too many times to condone it.

Clipper continued, "We're beginning to have a bedroom-community mentality when it comes to Portland. I don't think we'll have any trouble selling those houses."

Lee sighed. "Here comes the dessert wagon. None for me today, thanks, Mariah. The quiche was wonderful."

Mariah's dark face shone with pleasure. The brokers ate here often and had been among her best customers since she had opened her restaurant. Bringing in clients, lunching together or separately, they'd supported her for her first few months. Lee had been among the first to eat here, and she was one of Mariah's favorites.

"I don't have to watch *my* weight." Cokie chose the Black Forest cake.

The others made their choices and the cart rolled on to the next table. Malcolm, watching Clipper eat fudge pie, said pointedly, "You'd better watch your weight if you intend to be with us on the next trail ride. Ten miles up and down a mountain is going to be tough on you the first time out this year. Soon as the weather's good we're going to plan a day."

Clipper waved his hands. "No problem. I'm looking forward to it. I'm going to brush up at Callahan's stable and it'll be a snap. I have clients coming this summer who ride and are looking to buy a horse farm. I need to be able to talk horse with them."

Dear God, thought Lee, *give me strength. It isn't enough I have to watch this man ride, I am going to have to listen to him "talk horse".* Grudgingly, Lee had to admire Clipper. Their values were far apart, but he did try hard to relate to his customers, and any new subject that surfaced more than twice in a conversation sent Clipper off to study up on it for the next time around. More and more area residents owned horses and Callahan's stable did a good business with both children and adults who were learning to ride or brushing up on forgotten skills.

Malcolm, finished with dessert, turned to Cokie. "I'm going out on the lake road to look at a house. A man is thinking of listing it. Do you want to come along?"

Clipper, pushing back his chair, nodded at Cokie. "Go along with him; you need to see this listing. Good practice for both of you."

Meg, watching them leave, said suddenly, "I hadn't noticed before how well Cokie gets on with Malcolm. They make a handsome pair."

Clipper agreed. "Cokie peps Malcolm up; he gets discouraged easily. And he's a bit stuffy at times. I got to say that girl can sell real estate. She just seems to be a natural. Malcolm has some sort of a problem; I can't figure it out. Needs to go to a Dale Carnegie school. He gets almost to the sale and then it falls apart. Do him good to spend more time with Cokie."

"They do little theatre together, Clipper. But I know what you mean. However, people sometimes sell in spite of themselves. Malcolm probably will do well in the long run. You may find he's better on development than outright sales. Now, what about Hartley, Clipper? Are you talking or are you buying?" Meg could be brisk at times.

"I'm going to wait a while. Don't think you'll sell it right off at that price. I'll just ruminate on it."

Lee grinned. "That's cows, Clipper. Chewing cuds."

Clipper looked at her severely. "Just what I said. Chew it up till I'm done with it. Bunny got me a word calendar, you know, a word a day. Well that's today—I've been waiting for a way to work it in. Ruminate." Clipper rose. "Goodbye, ladies, duty calls. See you all later." He left, stopping by a table on the way out to shake hands with possible clients.

Meg looked at Lee and laughed. "He simply doesn't miss a trick. A word a day. I'll bet Bunny makes him use it in a sentence every night at dinner, too. You can't help but admire his attitude."

Lee, smiling back, said softly, "I don't think attitude is the word, Meg. I think it's hustle."

The next week was busy. The Hartley place was shown to out-of-state buyers, but no one made an offer. Three smaller properties sold, and two lake-front cottages on Lake Thompson were listed. Will Bundy was better and Meg seemed less frantic about money. Lee settled into the routine of spring at High Meadows and work at the office. She was careful to let someone know of her schedules and she avoided the deep woods alone. Reed came up twice to talk of Jim Davidson's death. The autopsy said accidental death probably caused by the broken neck in the fall after the heart attack. Reed, secretly, thought otherwise.

Nothing new surfaced; it was as though the case was suspended in time with no answers. Reed felt uneasy. There was more to come, and he did not know where to look. How could he warn Lee without knowing where the danger would develop?

On this morning, the first week of May, Lee, at Carriage Trade, talked with John Ridley, the head of the planning board. John had phoned and their conversation was lengthy.

"We're going to have to approve Sam Childs, Lee. He's making the lots larger and he's going to have an oversized common area. There's no way we can delay him further or turn him down. Even though there's a deer yard, Sam has a lot of pull. His soil scientist says his sewerage system won't harm the abuttors; the state can't stop it. One of the abuttors withdrew his objections; wouldn't be surprised if Sam got to him some way. He might have swapped him a piece of land to sweeten the deal. Even with the help Hod gave you, we can't do anything to stop him. Sometimes I don't like my job. I'm sorry, Lee."

Lee thanked John and put down the phone. For a while she sat, thinking, *Another one gone, another setback. There's a war going on here, and all I can come up with is a delaying action.*

Dorie, laying papers on Lee's desk, put her hand on her shoulder. "You tried. That's better than nothing. It's all you can do, Lee."

"Dorie, I didn't realize it meant so much to you, too."

"'Course it does. It didn't at first, but now I'm beginning to see what's happening. I'm old Maine, Lee. Like Hod Cole. Maybe your standing up will cause a few of the old places to be saved. Here, I'll get you a cup of tea." Dorie patted her shoulder.

Lee gave her a quick hug. "You always think a cup of tea can fix anything."

"Can't it?" Dorie laughed. "I'd rather work for you and Meg

than that Cleaver outfit. I don't believe he even drinks tea."

Lee smiled. "I'll have to call Hod Cole and thank him for what he did. I understand the state fish and game department sent a letter to the board."

Hod's quiet voice answered after several rings.

"I wanted to thank you for all the work you did on the Old Crossen Farm Stand. I hear we lost, but I do appreciate your help. I'm ever grateful, Hod. And Meg and I do want you to come to the Hartley house with us soon." Lee's voice was warm.

"You're welcome for the help. I was just about to call you. I'm going over to the Saco next week to look at that land. Wednesday. Like to go? There'll be a slew of black flies maybe, but a little Muskol'll fix them."

"I'd like to go." Lee for a moment felt like a schoolgirl accepting her first date. "I'll fix a lunch."

"Good. I'll pick you up about eight—it'll take an hour to drive there, and we'll be back by dusk. I'm looking forward to it." Hod rang off.

And so, thought Lee, *am I.*

Wednesday morning came quickly, and Hod arrived on the dot. Like the Attleburys, Lee was to find that he was seldom late. Canoe atop his Jeep, Hod drove up the lane just as Lee finished pouring coffee in a Thermos and packing the lunch. Ellen, eyes twinkling, watched Lee's preparations with amusement. "If I didn't know better, I'd think you might have a new beau."

Lee looked at her long and hard. "Ellen, you know me too well. This is uncharted territory—I don't know the man yet. I'm not sure I want to. But I'm tempted. And that's not being disloyal to Carter. We're having our difficulties right now so maybe I need a breath of fresh air."

Ellen was almost laughing. "Well, Hod Cole's a breath of fresh air if ever I saw one. Don't fall in the river, now."

Lee, laughing also, took a swipe at Ellen with a dish towel. "You just take care of Kate and the horses. I'll tend to the river. And don't you dare start laughing when you wave goodby!"

It was a May day like a jewel—clean and crisp with the promise of summer to come—and with a gentle breeze blowing away the flies from their stated business of annihilating humans. The river was flowing up to its banks with the height of the spring waters. Hod, used to rivers, made short work of launching the almost antique Old Town canoe, wooden, beautifully kept and shining like the treasure it was—a collector's item in the antiques market and seldom seen in use anymore on Maine rivers. Hod loaded the gear, maps, lunch, extra jacket, life jackets, and finally helped Lee into her bow seat, taking his position in the rear.

The Saco, on this spring day, was a benign river. Although high in the early spring, it was not overflowing or flooding on this day, and the water, at least in this part of the river, was easy for a canoe. Banks rose on either side and farms could be seen, set a way back from the water, with large barns giving forth the scent of manure being hauled out after a long winter to be spread on the intervale along the river. Sometimes the view was of the old farms, sometimes long stretches of woodland, sometimes sand pits and small islands and marshlands; Lee watched them all in silence as they glided by.

Hod matched his paddling to her strokes, steering expertly and with apparent ease. There was little conversation. They passed a camping area and another large farm.

Hod grinned. "Hope you don't mind a good, clean smell."

"Not a bit. You forgot I have horses." Lee turned her head for an instant and smiled at him.

They paddled along quietly, neither making a great effort, as though they had wordlessly agreed to prolong this day.

Finally, Hod pointed out a piece of woodland on the left that was his goal, and beaching on a low sandy area, they pulled up the canoe and walked inland across an open scrub area into the woods. Here oak and beech mingled with a small amount of dark growth. The woods were old; they had not been cut in many years.

"I've owned this about twenty years. Haven't done anything but let it grow. Had two offers from New Yorkers a few years back, but I'm not ready to sell. Kind of like these woods. Look, Lee, deer sign."

Lee stood beside him, looking down. "These are beautiful woods. I wouldn't sell them unless I really needed the money."

They walked for a while, following a small trail leading through the woods to an open field beyond, then turning back and retracing their steps to the river. Hod spread out an old plaid blanket and Lee opened their lunch. They shared food, thoughts, and each other's company. Hod lay back, putting his arms behind his head, and said, rather shyly, "My ten minute nap."

"You take one too." Lee was surprised. "I thought I was the only one in the area. None of the other real estate people take time out. My nap keeps me going. So, I'll join you."

Waking, Lee met Hod's eyes watching her.

"Didn't mean to offend you. It's been a long time since I really looked at a woman. I'm kind of out of practice." Hod was apologetic.

"You didn't offend me. I'm comfortable with you. And if your eyes are asking me a question, I have no final commitment. I have been—I am—seeing Carter Ransome. But I'm not totally attached yet. Does that help your thoughts any?"

"Makes them more confused." Very gently, Hod touched her face and traced her lips with his fingers. "I have to think on this; I've been a long while alone. I'm not a wham-banger, Lee. I tend to take things seriously."

"I'm as confused as you are. And, I understand, Hod. Thank you for being you." The moment was met, and dealt with. Lee felt better.

They packed up, Hod stowed away the blanket and picnic basket, and they pushed off again into the river. Slowly they proceeded downstream toward the bridge that was their destination. Hod pointed out two more of his properties; they stopped at each and walked inland and over the trails. He did not touch or move toward Lee again, other than to help her over a rock or a fallen log in the pathway. It was as though their conversation had not happened; he tucked it away in the back of his mind to pull out later and consider. Around them herons rose; spring's bird population had come back to the river and, almost out of context, sea gulls cried out from the manured fields of the farms.

Finally, at the bridge, they beached the canoe and the man Hod had hired to pick them up packed them and the canoe into his red pickup truck and took them back upriver to their starting point.

"Have a good day?" inquired the man of Lee.

"Very." Lee's eyes met Hod's.

For the hour's drive back to High Meadows, they spoke little. Once, Hod repeated the question, "Have a good day?" and Lee, placing her hand over his, replied quietly, "One of the best in a long time."

"Me too." Hod swung up the driveway to High Meadows, stopped the Jeep and came around to open the door for Lee, who stepped down into his arms. For one moment, the magic between them leaped strong and hard.

Just for that one moment, he held her, and then, stepping back, said quietly, "Lee, like I said, I tend to take things seriously."

Lee's voice was low. "Let me think a little."

"All the time in the world." He bent low, brushed her forehead, and strode around to the driver's side of the Jeep. "I'll call you soon." The tanned, lined face was gone.

Lee shook herself, gathered the picnic basket and the Thermos, and went inside to meet a happy Kate and Ellen, who had received a phone message from Mrs. Bemis saying the next garden tour committee meeting would be on the 13th and they would like to meet again at High Meadows if that suited Lee.

Lee nodded. "I'll call her right back. I might as well get this over with. We're bound to have two or three more of these meetings before July. It suits me, Ellen, it suits me just fine."

Ellen, sensing Lee's mood, laughed. "Looks to me like everything suits you fine today. How was it?"

Lee, running upstairs to change, looked back at Ellen. "Unusual, Ellen. Hard to explain. I like this man. Very much."

Sometime later, Lee returned Mrs. Bemis's call and confirmed the date. Ellen agreed to make biscuits. Mrs. Bemis had members bringing cheese. Malcolm and Lee would supply the sherry. "I hate to part with my Shooting Sherry, Ellen. It's not easy to find. Let's get Bristol Cream; everyone likes that." The week progressed. Meg and Lee found themselves using the Maine expression "right out straight" to describe their days. Land and lake-front prices were rising. A price of five years ago was now quadrupled and on some lakes frontage was becoming difficult to list.

Good, thought Lee. *I'm too busy to consider Hod or Carter or even the "wild woods". Just work and mucking out stalls and walking Kate and falling into bed at night. No decisions to make. As if I could.*

Carter called twice; he planned to come up in apple-blossom season which meant the end of May. His bookstore started its seasonal business after Memorial Day and he wanted to see Lee before summer.

"Are you considering Lincoln Farm Road, Lee?"

"I've been too busy to think. Maine pulls me right now, Carter.

Come up here and we'll ride and discuss it some more. Stay at least for a few days. You know how it is with me at apple-blossom time—my heart's in the orchards. We need to talk, Carter."

"Something serious? Has Reed found anything more about the threats or the blouse?"

"No. I meant us, Carter. Just come; we'll ride and talk. I do miss you." Lee found it hard to convey her mixed feelings over the phone.

Going to the barn one night to bed down the horses, Lee, with Kate beside her, looked up to the North Star far above the peak of the barn roof. The Big Dipper rode high, upside down with the two pointer stars directing her eyes to the North Star.

A *good sign. Take care of us here at High Meadows; let no evil touch this farm.*

Lee shivered for a moment, touched the Gordon's head and went inside to dream that she was riding Musette through the woods and that a bear lurked in the shadows behind the oak trees. The horse sensed its presence and turned, carrying Lee to safety. She struggled up from the dream with difficulty and relived it for an hour afterward as she drank warm milk to return to sleep and some sense of composure.

Dreams; do they portend the future?

The night of the 13th of May, clear and cold, and with a touch of winter's return, arrived. *Full moon*, thought Lee, dressing in a warm sweater and tweed skirt. *Maybe the charm is broken. Maybe there will be no more threats.*

The committee arrived, hugging their sweaters around their shoulders and glad for the warmth of the old fireplace. They filed into the big room, settling into the couches in front of the fire, and discussed, as Mainers do, the weather.

"Cold for this late in the spring," boomed Clipper. "Hope you don't lose your apple crop, Lee."

"I hope so, too, Clipper. The blossoms are coming early this year. I don't think they are quite far out enough for frost to hurt them, but it is colder than I want."

Mrs. Bemis, sipping her first glass of sherry, joined the conversation. "I say, the violets along your brick path are beautiful, Lee. The white ones with the yellow throats are gorgeous."

"They're old plants; they've been there for a long time. The primroses in the herb garden are almost in bloom. They are in a sheltered spot in front of the valerian along the stone wall. We can take a flashlight and I'll show them to you later, if you like." Lee felt generous toward Mrs. Bemis tonight.

Malcolm, meanwhile, fixed biscuits and cheese contributions and brought them in on a large tray to the table in front of the fireplace. He placed it in front of Bunny and returned to the kitchen to open another bottle of sherry. Cokie followed him.

"This is a beautiful house," said Cokie, polishing off Stilton cheese spread on one of Ellen's biscuits. "Lee must be rich."

"You eat too fast. And Lee worked hard to restore this place. She did a lot of the work herself. She does have an independent income besides her real estate earnings: she's a service widow. But she's not what you'd call rich." Malcolm sounded impatient.

"Well, you missed the boat, old dear. I heard that you and Lee used to go about together quite often," Cokie teased. "Think how easy life would have been for you if you'd married Lee. I heard she threw you over."

Malcolm did not like the turn of the conversation. "What's the matter with you, Cokie? Lee and I were never more than friends. Now you and I; I'm sure we could come to an arrangement."

Cokie giggled. "Don't you think I'm too young for you? And how do you know I even want an arrangement as you put it? I'm happy by myself. Quite satisfied, thank you, old dear."

The conversation was definitely out of hand. Malcolm did not want to be made fun of—especially by Cokie. He poured coffee hurriedly into one of Lee's best Adams Lowestoft cups and offered it to Cokie.

"Would you like some?"

Cokie, sensing a truce of sorts, accepted with thanks.

Together, they returned to the large room. Mrs. Bemis called the meeting to order and Bunny gave her report on the advertising plans, the tickets and the dates which would be July 11th and 12th. Mrs. Bemis was in her element, Meg having decided to let her chair all committee meetings in her place; and she was determined to do a "bang-up" job, as she called it. Discussion turned to prospective hostesses and hosts for the house gardens, although they would not need the close surveillance that the interiors of the homes had needed on Christmas tours. With all the questions that would be asked it was decided that any garden owner might ask for an extra hostess. At the end of the second day there would be the usual potluck supper to recap the tour and share stories. Bunny suggested selling tickets in Meadowbrook's gazebo and the talk turned to the maps and the names of the houses. By now, sherry was flowing freely and the tray of biscuits and cheeses went back in the kitchen for a refill.

"Malcolm, why is your place called 'Run for Cover'?" Cokie asked as Malcolm was reappearing from the kitchen with a second tray of food. "I'm curious; that's a strange name."

"We think it had something to do with the Underground Railroad in New England during Civil War days. There's always been talk of tunnels running from my place to one of the others on the Hill. I've never found anything. There was talk of secret passages in some of the Hill houses, too."

Lee, listening to Malcolm, remembered what Hod had said

about the Hartley place. Hod knew about one set of passages. Malcolm had heard of some. Who else knew?

Jan Howard, who seldom spoke, leaned forward and touched Malcolm's knee. "Do you know, my father once told me there were houses with secret passages. He said one was yours, Malcolm, and he thought there were some in the old Hartley place. I can't recall any others. Lee, you have the Hartley place for sale. Have you found any passages there?"

"Not yet. Someone did mention it. Meg and I are going to take a good look, but so far I haven't seen any indications of anything unusual. I must admit I'm curious."

Jan looked at Lee. "Don't be too curious. Remember what happened to the cat."

Mrs. Bemis banged her hand on the small table alongside her chair. "Really, we are getting off the subject. Let's finish. What else do we need to discuss? Bunny, you've gone over everything on my list. Are there any questions or new business?"

No one had any questions and the meeting was declared over. Lee warmed her hands by the fire for a moment and then went back into the kitchen. She filled her sherry glass from the bottle of Shooting Sherry in the corner cupboard, considered her private, very-hard-to-get stock known only to a few. At that moment the phone rang and without replacing the bottle, now only one quarter full, she went to answer. Mrs. Bemis, having closed the meeting, went to the upstairs bathroom and came back into the kitchen looking for Lee, who had promised to show her the primroses. Lee was still on the phone, talking with Meg, who had a child ill, but who had received an offer from a client by phone and needed to talk with Lee for a moment. It developed into a long conversation; when Lee finally put down the phone and replaced the bottle in the corner cupboard, she had no way of knowing that the quarter left was now an eighth for Mrs. Bemis, alone in that part of the kitchen, had spotted the Shooting Sherry and helped herself.

A few minutes later the two women, with flashlights in hand, bent over the primrose bed in front of the old stone wall at the edge of the yard. The soft yellows and pinks and mauves of the large plants were just surfacing and the bed would be in full bloom within a week.

"I've never seen a bed like this on the Hill," said Mrs. Bemis. "They aren't easy to winter over. I have a few plants, but not like these. Look at their size. They must be quite old."

"They are. Aunt Bess took good care of them and she told me they were here before her time. They reseed and I put a little fertilizer on them once a year."

"Well, it's a treat to see them. Lee, let's go back inside; I feel a little dizzy. My head seems to be going around. Oh, my!" Mrs. Bemis stumbled and almost fell.

Lee, suddenly feeling a little weird herself, supported the chubby little woman and they made it to the kitchen, where within minutes Mrs. Bemis was violently ill.

Lee's head was splitting and Clipper packed them both into his car to speed to the emergency room of the hospital.

Full moon, thought Lee, as she held her whirling head in her hands and they roared through the streets of Paris.

Full moon. And something's happening again.

•13•

It took Lee a few days until she felt completely better and until the terrible headache receded. Mrs. Bemis spent two days in the hospital. By the time Reed knew the story it was the afternoon of the following day—Clipper had simply taken the two women to the emergency room and they had been treated for food poisoning. No one thought to tell the police chief; food poisoning was not uncommon. It was Ellen, after being called by Clipper to come spend the night with Lee after she returned from the hospital, who did up the dishes and glasses and put away the cheeses and the sherry—it was Ellen, who, the next morning, ministering to a very weak Lee, called in to Reed to come by the farm.

And it was that afternoon before Reed, on his day off, finally arrived and sorted it out.

It took him a while. To smell the cheeses, look at the clean sherry glasses, talk with Lee and ascertain that she alone had drunk Shooting Sherry. He went away, taking the cheeses and thanking Ellen for not having thrown them out, and with the bottle of Shooting Sherry from the cupboard.

It was the next morning before he could talk with Mrs. Bemis and find out that she had helped herself to the sherry. And the next afternoon, late in the day, when the laboratory report told him that the cheeses, although strong indeed, could do no harm. But the Shooting Sherry could. It was laced heavily with ground-up valerian root.

"Valerian?" Lee, with her head on pillows piled up on the big-room couch, echoed Reed's words. "Valerian? It's in all of the gardens—almost all—and it's even gone wild in this area; you can find it anywhere. The woods roads are bordered with it—it grows up and down Minister's Road. I knew the root could be used, ground up to make a concoction, but I didn't know it could be that dangerous. How did it get in the bottle?"

"Not how—who," said Reed. "Who put it in there? It's definitely poisonous in large dosages—read the herbals. That's what I've been doing for the past hour. It excites the cerebrospinal system, causes headaches and agitation, I quote directly. A large-enough dose could kill. Lee, how long since you had a drink from that bottle? Before the meeting, I mean."

"I think the night the Attleburys were here." Lee was not sure.

"Well, someone certainly wanted to make you feel ill. The sherry is strong enough to mask the taste of the valerian and with the cheese added I doubt you'd notice. It had to be meant for you. Mrs. Bemis was a mistake. Who helped you serving?"

"I guess several people. Malcolm. Clipper. Bunny sat in the big room and Malcolm put the tray in front of her to help people. The sherry bottle is dark glass; I wouldn't notice any sediment when I poured it out. I didn't put it back in the corner cupboard when

Meg called."

"Actually," Reed said, "anyone who came in and out of the kitchen could have placed the drug in the bottle at any time. They would have to know you; that only you would touch the bottle. Unless they sneaked a drink, like Mrs. Bemis. Who's been in and out?"

"Hod Cole. Ellen, Ted. Malcolm and Mrs. Bemis were both here the night the Attleburys came. Mrs. Bemis surely wouldn't place valerian in a bottle and make herself sick." Lee shivered. "And not Ellen or Ted. Never. And not Hod Cole, no, Reed, not him."

Reed smiled. "I hope not. But someone had to, Lee."

Lee sat straight up. "Listen, valerian's not even in bloom yet. The plants are just beginning. Mrs. Bemis and I talked about them when we went out to look at the primroses. Whoever had ground-up root kept it from last year. You grind it, boil it in water and give it in tea. That's what the herbals say. A very small amount. You have to know what you are doing. So someone gave this a lot of thought. And that means, Reed...."

"That means someone planned it beforehand. Full moon, threaten Lee, make a statement. This time he came close. We are not dealing with a prankster or a spur-of-the-moment person. We're dealing with evil and a precise plan. I've gone over and over all this and I can't put the puzzle together. That bothers me. I haven't a clue." Reed rose to leave, then stopped.

"Lee, the threads run through you. Just keep that in mind. I can't put a guard on you. All I can do is say what I've said before. Be careful; watch what you eat and drink and where you go. I'm going to solve this yet and God help the man or woman when I find him—or her."

"I know all these people." Lee looked up at Reed. "They are friends and business associates. I can't believe any of them planned this. You're right, Reed, it *was* full moon again."

Reed nodded. "I know. That's what bothers me so. Because now I'm almost sure there's an element of witchcraft in these plans. That's why I'm afraid."

Alone, after Reed's departure, Lee took a shower and put on old jeans and a heavy turtlenecked sweater. She brushed her short, curly brown hair and put on some pink lipstick to make herself feel better and face the mirror's image that looked so taut and drawn out. She moved slowly, still feeling a little dizzy, and realized she had not had food since yesterday.

Kate and Ellen greeted her in the kitchen and Ted, just in from fencing to get some coffee, joined them. Ellen put out cups and saucers and a loaf of new whole-wheat bread.

"Lee, you look better. You aren't going to try to go in to the office today, are you?" Ellen was anxious.

"No, I'll try tomorrow. I'm over it now, just a bit weak." Lee tried an orange and accepted a slice of bread spread with butter and jelly.

"Do they know what it was yet?" Ellen was curious.

Lee realized that Reed had not released the news of the poisoning. She wondered just exactly how much she should tell these young people.

"It was some sort of sediment in the sherry, Ellen. Mrs. Bemis had some from my bottle, and it affected her along with me."

"As long as it wasn't anything I cooked. That was the first thing I thought of. You know I use everything fresh. I was kind of worried it might have been something in the biscuits. Then you all had that outlandish cheese. Could have been any one of those cheeses!"

Lee made a decision. "Ellen, it wasn't the biscuits. Or the cheeses. It was in the sherry bottle, my Shooting Sherry. It was an herbal poison called valerian."

Ted's cup stopped halfway to his lips. "Someone's at it again?"

"It looks that way," Lee answered. "I don't want this to be common gossip. Don't you two discuss it outside. Reed is trying his best to puzzle it out. Everything seems to lead back to High Meadows. So we have to be extra vigilant."

"Whatever that means. I'd be careful, anyways." Ted reinforced himself with a second cup of coffee and spread a thick slice of bread with a heavy coating of jam. "Ellen, don't never worry about your cooking. It's the best in the world."

Lee rose, patted Ellen's shoulder and said warmly, "I agree."

The phone rang and Meg, at the other end, spoke briskly. Meg had been told only the bare details and it would be much later when she learned of the sherry bottle and the valerian. At this moment, she had a message for Lee. "Hod Cole called. He wanted to talk with you and said he would go up to the Hartley house with us whenever we were ready and see if he could find that panel and the passageway. I told him you had the day off, so he wouldn't call and bother you if you were resting. How are you feeling now?"

"Better. I'll be in late tomorrow morning. How about we go to the Hartley place then if I can get Hod? We could ride up together."

"Fine; will you call him then?"

"I will." Lee welcomed the chance and reason to call. There had been no contact since the river trip. *Perhaps he's forgotten.* Lee wondered how it would feel to see him face to face again.

"Hod, it's Lee. Meg said you called. Would tomorrow morning be a good time for you? About eleven?"

"Sounds fine; I'll meet you there at the house." His words were short and clipped.

For a moment Lee felt rebuffed. She hesitated, then took a deep breath and asked, "Would you have lunch with me at High Meadows when we are finished?" and waited, feeling this was some kind of a test.

"Thankee. I'll see you tomorrow." The conversation was finished. *Why is he so short—or is this just the other Hod Cole, the one I'm not sure I like. The one Meg had heard about. The hermit. Not a word about the Saco.* Lee felt lost.

May 18th, Meg, Lee and Hod met at the Hartley place, Hod sitting on the front porch waiting for the women. By now the woods road was passable; the lawyer had arranged for extra loads of gravel to fill the deepest of the winter's ruts. Ted had smoothed things down a bit with his skidder. Cars, driven carefully, could now make it to the end of the road. Hod's Jeep had an easy trip; Meg's low-slung Chevy kept bumping on the bottom. She drew a breath of relief when they reached the dooryard. Ted had removed remainders of the winter's branches that had blown down and had cleaned up around the house and barn. The place looked trim. He had done a better job than the original caretaker who had died in Florida during the winter. Mr. Cameron had asked Lee to suggest a substitute and Ted, always looking for a little extra change "in pocket", as he put it, seemed right for the job.

Today the grounds looked better than they ever had; daffodils blossomed in great naturalized clumps close to towering old arborvitae trees; a forsythia bush, a tangle of unrestricted growth, gave forth showers of golden stars, and somewhere, high above, a white-throated sparrow poured his heart out in song. Lee opened the door, turned off the system as she had so often, and they walked upstairs to the room Jim had last been in when he was surprised. The railing in the hallway had been rebuilt.

It never changed for Lee. Every time she entered she saw Jim's body; every time she showed the house she felt tears close to the surface. Only a strict control gave her the strength to go into the house today. One day out from her own illness, one day out from the now certain fact that someone was trying to harm her; today was almost too much to deal with.

Hod suddenly took her elbow and steered her to the corner of the upstairs room. So quickly that she almost thought she imagined it, his head bent close to hers and he said softly, "I'm here. Just hang on."

Meg, behind them, did not hear his soft words.

Lee was grateful. When she had least expected it, he showed his caring. She stood quietly, listening to him, now in a completely different tone of voice, explain the paneling.

Carefully, Hod's hands searched along the surface of the fireplace molding. He pressed down in several spots, but nothing happened. "Can I take down this board that's closing up the fireplace?"

"Go ahead," said the women in unison. Dirt, dust, dried leaves and a dead bird fell as Hod removed the board.

"I'll get a broom and clean it up later." Lee watched Hod peer up the chimney. Soot particles fell on his plaid shirt; her hand reached out and brushed them off as he backed out of the opening. For one moment their eyes met and she again felt a tug at her heart.

"Nothing I can see, except years of soot. There ought to be a place where you press and the panel to the left of the fireplace swings open. There was an opening, large enough for a man to stand in as I recall. Then there is supposed to be stairs and a passageway ending up downstairs or maybe in the cellar. Old man Hartley was explaining it to me and we were going down through it when Mrs. Hartley came in the room and wanted to know what we were doing. So I never got any farther. I thought I could remember just where he placed his hands, but I don't seem able to. Sorry. Guess I led you on a wild goose chase." He showed his own disappointment.

"No; the very fact you know there is a panel helps. Lee told me about the outhouse. Keep trying, Hod." Meg liked this sort of mystery and was storing it up to tell her family at the dinner table. Hod kept trying, but with no success. After fifteen minutes more of press, push and touch, he finally had to give up. He simply could not find the proper place. "Look, I've gone all up and down the side of the fireplace and over the wall and I can't find it. There's a deacon's cupboard up here above the mantel but I don't recall Hartley touching it. Sometimes those cupboards had false backings; guess it was so a man could keep a bottle there. But I never did know old man Hartley to be a drinker. He was pretty elderly when I knew him. Might be he was reformed. But if he said there was a passageway, there was a passageway."

The women both tried their luck, pressing and touching in several places. Finally Lee went downstairs, took a broom and dustpan from the kitchen corner and came back upstairs to clean up the mess. Hod replaced the board closing the chimney. They left the house, resetting the security system.

"Anyone looking at the place?" Hod asked.

"Several parties including Cleaver Real Estate. Some of the out-of-staters will be here in June. Development people. But, so far, no offers. Malcolm and Clipper need more people to go in with them. Bunny hates the place. The lawyer has given notice he wants no dickering—it's a firm price. At least during this summer." Meg knew Hod as a possible buyer and filled him in on details.

"Well, then there's no use my trying to dicker, is there?" Hod grinned, and turning to Lee said, "You say something about lunch?"

"Meg, would you like a sandwich and some iced tea?" Lee wasn't sure what answer she wanted, but it seemed polite to ask.

"No, thanks. I have to go back to the house. But, listen Hod, don't be afraid to make an offer. We all know prices can change." Meg was a good broker and never gave up on a possible buyer. Hod Cole was rumored, among other things, to have a bit of money.

Hod laughed. "All right, Mrs. Bundy; if I get in a dickering mood I'll make an offer. Afraid it's too rich for me now, but never know what'll happen. Besides, I'll get to see you ladies a bit more if I dicker, won't I?"

Meg, getting into her car, turned to Lee. "I've heard all sorts of things about that man, but he is nice, isn't he? He likes you; I can see it in his face."

"It's mutual. And a little disturbing. We canoed on the Saco to look at his land and I found I wanted to know more about him. But you know I've been seeing Carter Ransome for years. He'll be up at the end of this month."

"You're too conservative. Go have your lunch and see what happens."

"You surprise me, Meg. You with a husband and four children."

"Lee," Meg put her hand on her partner's arm, "what you see is me, now, with the husband and children. What you don't see is me a long time ago. I should have taken some chances. I never did. You still have a choice. Go on, now. Enjoy your lunch."

Meg swung down the woods road; Hod and Lee followed in his Jeep. Ellen had left a note with lunch and after washing up, Hod and Lee sat at the old pine table with a plate of sandwiches and a pitcher of herbed ice tea before them.

"We could eat out on the barn bench, if you'd like. The sun is strong this noon and it's good to be outside after the winter. Do you want to?" Lee gestured toward the barn.

"Any place you say." He opened the door and they carried their lunch to the old blue bench to the left of the barn door. A stone wall ran along behind the bench, and over the wall grew purple clematis and red rambler roses that were old, established plants. Today, only the leaves were out, but the promise of bloom showed in the sturdy canes. The old blue bench spent winters in the barn but, come May, went outside in the sunshine to stay until apple harvest was over. Lee did not know its age, but it carried the memory of Aunt Bess and this was one of her favorite spots.

"You've got a quiet bench." Hod sat down happily.

"A quiet bench?"

"You know, where you sit quietly and sort of ponder a bit and don't talk much. Every old farm used to have one. Farmers sat out for a piece right after the noon meal and had their quiet time."

"That's a name I didn't know. You're right—it is my quiet bench."

Hod poured tea into the heavy Ashburton glasses and chose a sandwich. "Did you make these or did Ellen?"

"I did—those are roast beef. Hers are egg salad."

Hod munched quietly on his roast beef. The sun shone gently on the farm, on the orchards beginning to unfurl their pink and white blossoms, on the hayfields clovering out in the first spurt of growth, on the violets and primroses and daffodils, and on the tulips beginning to open their cups along the stone walls. Native bees hummed; the grass grew tall enough to begin to think of cutting and the two horses dozed in the sunshine. Kate lay quietly at Hod's feet.

For ten minutes there was no conversation.

"See what I mean?" Hod broke the silence.

Lee nodded. "I do, indeed. I feel so comfortable here with you.

Not afraid of anything. I have to spoil it. I have to tell you what has just happened." In a few short sentences she spoke of the valerian poisoning and the conversation she had had with Reed.

Hod looked at her sharply. "Do you feel all right today? Maybe you shouldn't have gone up to Hartley's. I wouldn't have been so long there if I'd known you'd been ill. Has Reed talked with everyone there at the committee meeting?"

"He said he planned to—I haven't heard the report from him yet. Anyone could have put the ground-up herb in the bottle. Anyone. They all have some knowledge of plants—even the Cleavers are becoming interested in gardens since this tour idea. But, these are everyday people I know—none of them would do this. I can't believe they would, anyway."

Hod leaned his hand on her knee for a moment. "I maybe didn't make it clear. You're important to me, Lee. I care about you."

Before Lee could reply there was the sound of a car ascending the driveway. Mrs. Attlebury, driving an Oldsmobile of questionable vintage, and handling it as one would a horse, swooped up to a jarring stop and exclaimed "whoa." Her driving was "in fits and starts" to quote Aunt Bess and very few people, having taken passage with her once, would do it the second time.

"How are you, Lee? Reed called me and said you'd recovered. Hello, Hod, I'm glad to see you."

"I'm much better. Have you heard anything from George Morrill?" Lee hugged Belle Attlebury who, in turn, shook hands with Hod.

Pulling off white cotton work gloves and hitching up her long khaki skirt, Mrs. Attlebury removed her bush helmet and sat down between them. "Just why I'm here. George is bringing a man from a Boston museum up tomorrow and I wondered if you'd come over while they are there. They want to authenticate the Stubbs, of course. Do you feel up to it, Lee?"

"I'll be glad to—it will be exciting, Belle."

Lee retired to the house to replenish the pitcher of iced tea and Mrs. Attlebury turned briskly to Hod. "If you want her, young man, you've got to get to work. It won't just happen."

Hod grinned at Belle Attlebury. "And how do you know so much?"

"It's written all over your face. I'm betting you two are made for each other. Besides, it's time somebody figured out what's going on around here. Reed is trying but he's not getting ahead very fast. Carter's down in Connecticut and I don't know what good he can do down there. I tell you frankly, Hod, I'm concerned for Lee. I don't think I saw a bear; I think I saw someone *pretending* to be a bear. And no one in his right mind is going to do that for long in our woods. That's what worries me."

Hod was thoughtful as he listened to the words spill out of Belle. "There's getting to be more sightings," he said. "Building new houses and this dry spring seems to be moving them around. The pretend bear is liable to meet up with a real bear and that ain't going to be funny. He keeps popping up around the same place. What's that tell you, Belle? Guess we better put our heads together and see if we can figure this out."

Lee reappeared with a second pitcher of iced tea. The three sat quietly for a few minutes watching a hummingbird at one of the violets.

Mrs. Attlebury broke the silence. "When is Carter coming to Maine?"

"In apple-blossom time—next week I think. At least that's his plan. It could end up later. I have a raft of appointments and he opens his bookshop after Memorial Day. So I'm not positive."

Hod rose to leave, said goodby to Mrs. Attlebury and thanked Lee for lunch. "Walk to the car with me, Lee?" They stood by the

Jeep, Hod holding her hands for a moment. "I'm planning on seeing you again."

"I'd like that. I enjoyed the day on the Saco. I thought perhaps you'd forgotten."

"No." Hod shook his head. "Guess I was just thinking on it. Take care of yourself, now. Call me if ever you need me." He was gone, the Jeep sliding noiselessly down the driveway, as silently as he could walk through the woods.

"Wherever he walks it shall be through this forest." Lee's mind quoted the poem. She sat down by Mrs. Attlebury on the quiet bench. "Have you known him long?" Lee was almost afraid to ask.

"Since before you came to High Meadows. He always stops by in the springtime to bring us fiddleheads. He's a good man, Lee; he closed off his life from the outside world after his wife died. He just stayed at his woods cabin, hunted, fished, dealt in timber. Men's dealings you might say."

"I'm in a confused state. I've been happy seeing Carter but we can't agree on where to live—Maine or Connecticut. And he wants a much more social life. The last time I was in Salisbury I was homesick for Maine. Only three hundred miles apart, but it seems a world away. I'm beginning to think of Carter more as a friend than a lover. In all your worldly wisdom, Mrs. Attlebury, what do you think?"

Belle Attlebury, sitting with feet spread apart, in her old garden moccasins, with dirt streaked across the front of an old navy blouse, with khaki skirt hiked up over her knees exposing white cotton stockings and helmet pushed far back on her head, looked like the last person to be asked such a question. Worldly? Hardly. Yet Belle Attlebury carried knowledge in her head that is given to few people, and she was gifted with a common sense outlook on life that should be given to more.

"My dear, follow your heart. That's exactly what I would do, and have done. Do what you want, with the man you want, in the place you want. It's a simple solution, not an easy one sometimes. Most people do what they don't want half the time. Lee, you'll know. No better advice can I give you."

Lee leaned over and hugged her.

"I have to get back to Frederick. Your phone is ringing, Lee."

Carter was at the other end. "I have to put it off again, Lee. I won't be up until almost the second week of June. How are you and how is everything up there?"

"Oh, Carter, I'm all right." She did not say what a relief his news was at this moment. At the end of their conversation and when he turned away from his phone, Carter was up to date on all of the happenings in Lee's life with one exception—Hod Cole.

Mid-afternoon of the following day, Lee and Belle Attlebury stood in the box room watching George Morrill and the museum expert examine the Stubbs oils. The sun shone gently on the two paintings: one the large hunt scene Lee and Belle had so greatly admired, the other a portrait of a gentleman on his hunter with his manor home and family in the background. Even the art expert, with his wide knowledge and experience, felt awe at the discovery of the paintings in this old Maine cottage.

"There is no doubt—the signature is genuine." And George and the expert retired to the steps outside the kitchen door to bask in the sunshine and discuss art. Mrs. Attlebury brought out cookies and tea and the four moved to benches in the herb garden.

"You may want to remove them someplace for safekeeping." The museum man, used to a totally different pace of life, was a little dubious about Mrs. Attlebury's box room.

"No, I'd rather not—I'd rather they stay right where they are until the auction," replied Belle. "Do you agree, George?"

George nodded. "You're probably safe enough. The advertisements pinpointing the auction location won't come out until early July. Then I'll put a guard on the property for you—one of my staff. He'll have a small travel trailer to sleep in and he'll be close by all the time up until the auction day. Reed Jamison will have all this information; we'll need men from the police department for the auction and I think they'll be safe."

The museum expert rose to leave, assuring Mrs. Attlebury that he would be at the auction himself. George left soon after and Lee and Mrs. Attlebury sat alone among the scents of early spring herbs.

Belle Attlebury had a question. "Lee, how much is the price on the Hartley property?"

"Half a million. I doubt it will go for much less. Cleaver is trying to get financing together to buy it, but he hasn't gotten his act together yet. I wish I could buy it myself and just keep it in a trust for a green area for the Hill. But I don't have that kind of money." Lee sighed.

Mrs. Attlebury shook some dirt out of her moccasin. She looked long and hard at Lee.

"Wait until after the auction. Maybe I will."

SUMMER

ANGELICA
PARSLEY
COMFREY
VALERIAN
GARLIC CHIVES
CHIVES
BASIL

·14·

June and Carter arrived together. Finally having settled matters in his bookshop by hiring a clerk to help him, Carter decided to spend two weeks at High Meadows and settle matters with Lee. He had been having ambivalant feelings. He loved her and probably always would, but he resented the fact that she could not seem to make a decision on their relationship. Besides that, he was beginning to enjoy luncheons with a woman who ran a gourmet food shop in his building, and this new relationship held promise.

Today, near the end of the second week in June, Malcolm and Cokie had come to High Meadows for lunch. With Lee and Carter, they sat at the picnic table on the edge of the herb garden sampling Ellen's curried cold summer soup. Ted was busy at the end of the garden, fixing the old wooden fence that ran atop part of the surrounding stone wall. The early June sun was hot; rabbit-foot clover was leafing out along the driveway up to the farm; the dogwood trees lining the stone walls of the near fields were in late blossom. A light breeze kept the black flies out of range, and there was peace and simple pleasure eating on the edge of the plantings of aromatic plants.

To use a real estate term, thought Lee, *this is a place of "quiet enjoyment."*

Malcolm, however, had come to talk with Lee about real estate and himself, and he was loath to just eat and drink in the quiet beauty of the farm. Before he could start conversation, however, Cokie began to chatter.

"I always liked all those little herb things; I just don't know much about their names. Your garden is going to be beautiful for the tour, Lee. Did you plant all of these yourself or were they here? What's that one?" Cokie pointed.

"That's rosemary," Lee answered, looking at a large garden urn filled with the fragrant topiary plant. "I have to replace that yearly. It won't winter over out here for me—too much wind and ice. Over there is valerian—it will bloom soon—and that's foxglove and monkshood or aconite. That's a patch of sage; it's had a hard time over the winter. I may have to replace it. I do most of the planting. Mrs. Attlebury gives me advice and Ted does the heavy work. I like this herb garden the best of all the beds I have."

"Valerian? That's what Reed said was in the sherry that made you so sick. You never did find how it got in there, did you? Reed certainly asked us enough questions. Bunny said maybe you put it in there yourself by mistake because you do keep ground herbs." Cokie chattered on.

"Yes, I do." Lee was puzzled that Cokie had brought the subject up. "We don't know how it got in the bottle. I never use valerian for teas, Cokie. Comfrey and some of the others, yes. But not valerian, which, by the way, most books call garden heliotrope."

Cokie did not pursue the subject. Malcolm said nothing. Carter called Ted over to join them for iced tea.

"Are you going to look at the back fields before you leave, Ted, and see how they look for haying?" Lee knew from now on she and Ted would be discussing hay weather daily.

"Thought I would, but not today. Want to get this fence finished first." Ted drained his glass and returned to his job.

Cokie, meanwhile, asked to see the horses, and Carter took her off to the paddock.

Cokie patted noses. "I don't know much about horses. Are you and Lee riding today?"

"Later this afternoon, we're going out by the Moss Path. Lee usually rides about four o'clock if she's home. That's the best time of day and she has this afternoon off." Carter showed Cokie the tack, the feed room and the small room to one side that Lee had hopes of rearranging into a larger tack room. They walked around the barn, Carter pointing out the path to the old cabin and rather enjoying playing host to this odd, but attractive, young woman.

Malcolm, taking advantage of their absence, bent forward to touch Lee's hand. "I never see much of you. You're getting so involved with Carter, you're neglecting me." Malcolm had not yet heard about Hod.

"Carter's a good friend, Mal, that's all." She did not like this turn in the conversation. A private life was a private life.

"As I wanted to be." Malcolm frowned.

"Malcolm, you are a good friend. Cokie's much better for you. Younger. Sportier. You both like the theatre and antiques and real estate. Things are going well for you, aren't they?" Lee hoped to shift the subject.

Malcolm shrugged. "I'd like to sell more. People just don't seem to know good buys when they are shown them. Clipper doesn't always match me up with the right buyers. I'm sure I could do better. I don't feel appreciated. You know what I mean, Lee."

"In real estate we have to deal with all sorts of people. You can't be a snob, Mal. Whoever you get on a certain day, you have to work with that person. Every property isn't for the wealthy buyer. There are lots of cheap properties you have to sell just as hard as the expensive ones."

"I hate," said Malcolm flicking a fly from his plate, "trying to sell to people with no money."

"Well, it's a neat trick if you can do it." Lee felt she had been enough of a lecturer.

"Anyway, I wanted to ask you if you want to go with me to next week's auction? Or is Carter still going to be here?" Malcolm was not going to give up.

"I'm not sure how long he can stay. If he's here we could all go together. We're riding this afternoon; I'll ask him."

Malcolm, even in his late fifties, could pout. "That wasn't what I had in mind. I mean us. Alone."

"I don't think so—another time, Mal." Lee was beginning to feel uncomfortable and she did not like the feeling. Malcolm was pushing more than usual and he seemed to be getting out of hand. She rose as a way of ending the conversation and started off to join Carter and Cokie at the barn.

Ted, at the fence, gave no sign of having heard the exchange. As Lee walked by, he said, "Decided I'm going to get this finished even if it takes all day."

"It looks fine, Ted. Just like the old walls used to look with the fences on top. Do you want some dessert with us?" Lee patted Ted's shoulder.

"No, guess I'll just try to get this finished up."

Cokie and Carter returned, the four finished off Ellen's

brownies and, in a rather surly mood, Malcolm left with Cokie. Carter and Lee lingered over coffee.

"I have to call Meg and plan tomorrow; I have a client from Connecticut looking at a Harrison farm. If you're going to take a nap, Carter, I'll make that call right now. I want to walk Kate a bit; then we can ride."

"Agreed." Carter gathered up dishes and silver; Lee brought along the red-checkered tablecloth, and they crossed the lawn to the house. Ellen, inside at the sink, was finishing washing the coffee pot.

"Ellen, it was superb as usual. When are you leaving?"

"Guess we'll go about three or four, when Ted finishes." Ellen placed dishes on the shelf. "Reed's coming over tonight with a new girlfriend; we haven't met her. So it's sort of a get-together." Ellen wiped her hands on her apron.

Carter nodded and went upstairs. Lee located Kate, who was in the pantry checking out the remainder of the brownies—rescue came just in time. The brownies were stashed safely on a high shelf and the woman and the Gordon walked together toward the pond.

Ted, meanwhile, made one of his sudden decisions and gave up mending fence to head for the back hayfields and see how close they were to cutting. He ambled slowly down the wagon road past the Cortland orchard, past the MacIntosh orchard, over the little farm bridge and up through the hayfields: sixty acres of timothy and alfalfa interspersed with patches of blue vetch and daisies.

Don't want to see too much of that vetch, thought Ted, *it'll snap the baling twine.*

The fields rippled gently in the afternoon breeze; meadowlarks and bobolinks rode the tops of the grasses like small boys riding pogo sticks. Ted, sticking a bit of grass between his teeth, decided that they could start to hay as soon as the weather began a long dry spell. Hay was early this year; it was nearly topped out, and Lee liked to have the first cutting done while the hay held its full protein content. Lee pushed hard on first-cut hay; Ted would have taken his own time but he respected her and was willing to cut it her way.

Everything, in Ted's life, arrived in due time. "Hurry" was not in his vocabulary and "slow" was a way of life. Hulking big—"wicked big", Ellen called him—nevertheless Ted was one of the best all-around farm hands in the hills and counting both natives and those from away, one of the best hunters. Haying for Lee meant the privilege of hunting her woods in the fall and being able to bring a few close friends in with him. Deer meant freezer meat for Ted and Ellen, just as it did for Hod, and with both of them the hooded eyes and slow gait belied the swiftness with a gun when it came to deer season.

Now, standing almost waist deep in the hay fields, Ted's thoughts were walking through the forest.

"Better start thinking about equipment," he said aloud, and turned and started back up the wagon road. On the curve, set back from the fields and the orchards, protected by the woods in that one corner, the small family cemetery showed an open gate. Ted, bending to tie his shoelace, noticed it as he straightened up.

"That shouldn't be open." Again aloud. He started forward to close the gate and at that moment the door of the tomb opened slowly and a bear backed out. There was no sound, no squeaking of the old iron hinges, no movement other than that of a small, blackish-brown bear coming backward out of the receiving tomb, which, as far as Ted knew, hadn't been opened in years.

The bear stood upright.

One paw reached out to close the tomb door while the bear, turning sideways, looked directly at Ted, who stood still, fairly paralyzed. Generally nothing scared him; he was used to all the woods creatures. His mind was slow-moving and for one moment he did not realize the full impact of what he saw.

For one moment he just looked, trying to make some sense of what his eyes were seeing.

The bear moved fast. It vaulted the low iron fence, moved toward Ted, and let out a low growl.

Then Ted laughed. "Oh, you're just fooling me. What you doing with that getup on? Lee don't like nobody around that old cemetery. She finds out you been fooling around that tomb, you're gonna be in trouble. You just being funny or what...." On that one last word Ted suddenly realized the bear was too close. He was alone, weaponless, and something was not working out properly. Suddenly, Ted was afraid. In that last moment of awareness he raised one arm to shield his face as the bear swung hard at him with what seemed to be a great front paw.

"Hey, wait a minute...." were the last words Ted uttered.

The bear grunted, turned and walked back toward the cemetery fence. He was angry; he had been caught out for he hadn't planned on Ted's being in the hayfield. He opened the tomb door, took out what appeared to be a coil of wire and closed the door again. He had almost forgotten his plan; he did not like interruptions. The fur was hot and the bear, making his way across the fields to the shelter of the woods, was cross.

The hayfield was still now; the breeze had lessened; the birds were quiet. Beneath Ted's big body lay three broken white daisies. On a blade of grass a bobolink swung to and fro. A bobolink that did not sing.

The bear continued through the woods. He had planned this very carefully, very carefully indeed, and his plans had not included Ted being in the hayfield when he was supposed to be fixing fence.

A bit later in the afternoon, Carter and Lee rode through the Hartley woods along the Moss Path. They rode single file, rarely speaking, just sitting their mounts easily as is often the way of country riders. The filtered green light of the woods swept all the problems from Lee's mind. Oak and beech branches touched her shoulders gently and once a cloud of yellow sulpher butterflies rose from the path. The mosses showed shades of green and gray; natural in their growth, they had covered nearly a quarter of a mile of this trail for so long that no one could recall their first discovery.

Off to one side of the trail, reached by a small pathway, was a perfect circle of reindeer moss and gray lichen, bordered by small, stunted birches, twisted and bent low to the ground. No one knew what had caused the circle, but it was a magic spot and Lee felt this magic whenever she entered the circle. She thought of it today as she rode past the small, almost hidden, entrance path.

I need all the good magic of these woods. I need help from all the creatures that live here. Protect me from whatever or whoever stalks me. Protect me and I will try to protect you.

The chestnut mare plodded down the trail, moving as one with her rider. Musette and Lee trusted each other completely, with a sensitivity a horse may know and a human may give. They had taken this path often. Although Musette was old, she was sure-footed and had great stamina of heart. Once she had been a showhorse but now she spent her last years on High Meadows' pastures. Lee knew little of the mare's history; she had descended to being used as a camp horse when Lee bought her. The moment Lee had seen Musette's great, velvet eyes, she knew she would buy the horse. Musette was asking for help—Lee gave it without question of price. It was Lee or the knacker man. Musette's soft whicker was thanks enough.

"Carter, do you want a short gallop?" Lee turned in her saddle to look back where Carter and Nat ambled along, each thinking separate thoughts yet moving as one unit.

"Right." Carter came out of daydreams and smiled at Lee.

She touched the mare tentatively with her crop and a gentle pressure in her legs, and the mare moved forward into her rocking-horse gallop. It was hardly necessary to even use the aids; Musette knew instinctively what was in Lee's mind. The trail curved now, bent to the left, and then straightened. Lee, enjoying the ride and the woods around her, almost missed seeing the wire. Stretched across the trail it was just high enough to catch the mare's chest and stop her. There was barely time to pull Musette up, even though at the same moment the mare sensed danger and tried to turn.

It was close—too close.

Together, as one, they veered to the right into an opening between two pine trees, and skidded to a halt. Lee's kneecap caught on a pine branch, but she did not feel the pain because of the pounding of her heart. Her riding crop, wedged between branches, broke.

Behind her, Carter and Nat had more time, although they did not fully understand the danger.

"It's all right, old girl, it's all right." The words came automatically as Lee patted the mare and slipped down from the saddle. *It's not all right—this is no accident.* The mare, trembling, obeyed as she was backed out and tied with a small lead rope to one of the oak trees. Carter had dismounted and, coming forward leading Nat, saw the wire.

"Hell, Lee, that's barbed wire. Right across the trail. Who in the name of God would do that?" Rarely was Carter upset to the point of swearing.

Together, they took a good look. The wire had been hooked neatly to small pines on either side. It had been wound twice around and then twisted. It was no worn-out old rusty wire. It was fairly new and had been clipped with wire cutters. It was a piece of wire cut and fitted for a specific use in a specific place. Not a piece used in a hurry. A piece used with intention.

Here, along the trail where they always galloped, in an overhung area where light filtered in dimly, it was hard to see. Only the instincts of the mare and the woman who rode her had saved them. Lee felt sick, knowing what might have happened.

This is not a nice person. Phone calls, threats, terrorizing I can deal with. My horses—that is another matter. Lee felt anger as she had not felt it in years. *It's taken me so long to deal with my temper. So long to learn to deal logically with problems. Now, I simply want to kill someone. Whoever it is—I simply want to kill him—or her.*

Carter took the wire down from the two trees and formed a coil. "I don't want to carry it horseback, Lee. I'll hang it here. Let's get back to the farm and call Reed."

Lee nodded. She was thinking rapidly now. Someone had to know of her practice of riding that trail afternoons. Moreover, they had to know she was inclined to gallop at that spot. Not a nice person. For, had she not stopped, the wire would have bitten deeply into the mare's chest. And she, Lee, would have almost certainly been thrown from an animal screaming in pain.

It would have been a disaster.

They turned back, out of the woods and along a field toward the house and barn. Musette was still quivering; Carter's face was stern and Lee still felt sick. Her knee ached. She wanted to get to the phone; Carter was thinking methodically of who would have known they were riding there at that time. He was also considering the outside chance that it might have been happenstance, some neurotic placing a wire there to catch someone, as a new landowner had once done when snowmobilers had used his land against his wishes. His wire, stretched in the same manner, had decapitated a trespasser speeding over a woods road after a snowstorm. But this was summer and on the Hartley land with no one trying to ward off trespassers and on a trail that horseback riders were known to have used for years.

No. Not happenstance. This was an evil mind and that brought Carter's thoughts crashing back to combat tactics. He had spent his service time stateside at an office desk, but he knew well what barbed wire meant in training. Whoever stretched that wire knew what it could do. Reed would have no chance of finding fingerprints. Carter knew that was almost impossible. Little chance of finding who did this. Which was exactly what Reed said later. When he finally went back to find it. And it was gone.

They had reached the barn by now; Carter took the horses and Lee hurried into the house. She dialed the sheriff's office with shaking fingers. Dot's voice answered and Lee had just started to speak when she heard the keening.

Out of the kitchen window she could see Carter, holding Ellen, who was crying and screaming.

"Dot, I need Reed, but something else has just happened. Hold on, hold on."

Ellen burst into the kitchen, Carter trying desperately to understand her. "Ted, he's hurt, he's in the back field. I couldn't drag him, he's too heavy, there's blood all over his face and head. I don't know if he's dead. Help me, Lee, help me. Carter, please, come back with me."

Lee's voice on the phone suddenly sounded frantic to Dot. "Just send an ambulance, quick, and Reed if you can find him. Ted's been hurt, Dot. Ellen says it's bad. I have to go. Please, Dot, quick."

Carter, in one motion, grabbed dish towels from the rack and pantry shelf. He took the Land Rover key from its hook and, with Ellen and Lee, was in the car within a minute. The wagon track to the back field was bumpy but, driving carefully, he swung along by the orchards, over the farm bridge and into the fields. Ted's body lay across the path, face up, eyes open with a horrified look and giant scratches across his temple. His hair was matted with blood and the top of his shirt was covered with blood. His cap, torn, lay on the ground beside him and just the flower of one white daisy lay crushed beside the cap.

Carter's hand searched for a pulse while Lee tried hard to control a sobbing Ellen who was determined to take Ted's head in her arms.

"Is he dead?" Lee felt her own faintness.

"I think he's still alive. Hold these towels here, Lee, maybe we can stop some of the bleeding. This is a bad head wound. God, I don't know where to start." Carter and Lee worked together, Lee with her knee still painful, knelt on the ground beside Ted, holding the towels against what seemed to be the major wound. Ellen was still crying softly, holding Ted's hand and trying to get an answer from the man she was so devoted to.

"Carter, how will the ambulance know where to come?" Lee looked up at the grim face.

"Either you or Ellen will have to go back to tell them. Which one of you wants...."

"I don't want to leave Ted." Ellen was gradually regaining her balance but the tears were still flowing.

"I'll take the Land Rover and drive back. We didn't lock the house; anyway Kate won't let even Reed in without me. They should be here soon, so I'll go." Lee rose, handing Ellen the remainder of the towels, and got into the car to drive back to the house.

Carter and Ellen, left bending over Ted, tried to do what they could in what they both knew was the short amount of time that Ted could have remaining. Lee met the ambulance as she drove into the yard. Reed was right behind it. Pointing down the wagon track and shouting to Reed at the same time, the thought came to Lee to check the horses who had been thrown into their stalls without cooling off or removal of their saddles. She made short work of this, and locked the house after giving Kate a biscuit and telling her to be a guard dog. Then Lee turned and limped back down the wagon track, knowing that to drive the car only meant cutting off the ambulance on its way out.

For at least an hour people came and went. The ambulance left with Ted, Ellen at his side. Reed's car phone summoned two men from the sheriff's department. Lee and Carter told their story of the woods ride and the wire and what had transpired since they returned to the farm. The sheriff's men searched through the grass where Ted had dropped. It was late that day, almost dusk, before anyone thought that the cemetery might be involved. It was the next day before it was discovered that the old iron hinges to the receiving tomb had been oiled recently and that someone or something had been inside.

It was the next day before Reed learned for sure that Ted's wounds were similar to Jim Davidson's. The scratches were in the same general area. Jim had died although not from a blow—he had died from his heart attack and the fall. Ted was in a coma—on the edge of death. It would be some time until he could talk.

Meanwhile, Reed and the sheriff's department could only guess at what had happened. Reed was good at guessing. He called in the state police, for he was pretty sure, by now, that Ted had met the bear in the hayfield.

The bear who was not a bear.

•15•

During the next two weeks, Lee went almost daily with Ellen to see Ted in the hospital. There was little change; he did not totally regain consciousness and he could not communicate. His eyes looked straight through Ellen and Reed, who came daily. There was little movement in his body. Grave injury had been done to that great, strong man who so loved the fields and woods. Ellen brought wild flowers, the ones he took special pleasure in, and spoke their names to him but there was no sign of recognition.

Lee made new arrangements for haying, trying not to let Ellen know how hopeless Ted's condition appeared.

She tried to comfort Ellen. "Your place is here forever and Ted can take up where he left off as soon as he is well. Don't think of anything but just being with him, Ellen."

Reed, as much as any of them, felt the loss, and spent hours sitting beside Ted in the hospital, talking of fall hunting. Reed was tired, concerned, and more than a little jumpy. His old trick of brushing his blond hair back from his forehead seemed to need repeating every ten minutes. Two people he cared about deeply and he couldn't seem to protect either of them. Reed Jamison was a frustrated policeman.

Lee's days were divided between real estate, farm chores, and walking with Kate, who was now left daily to guard the house. Carter had returned to Salisbury with their relationship unsolved and delegated to the back corners of their minds for the present.

The first three weeks of June were ones of change and sorrow. Haying season was nearly over; the garden tour committee had met again, this time at Mrs. Bemis's, and Lee had sold five properties and taken an offer that was rejected on the Hartley estate.

The week of June 22nd, Hod Cole called Reed. "You have time to run over to my camp? I've been trying to puzzle things out and I think I've found some new angles. I've put some of these pieces of yours together."

Hod had been among the few allowed to see Ted in the hospital. He had seen Lee twice, stopping by Carriage Trade, but the talk had been more of Ted than themselves. Hod had been the one to help Lee find a farmer to cut her hay. Unbeknownst to Lee, Hod had swung around by High Meadows several times to check on the horses while they were alone. Kate's great rolling barks from the security of the house had pleased him. In his own way, Hod kept watch over the farm and over a woman he had discovered he cared for deeply. Reed and Hod had talked by phone several times and Hod, by now, had about all the information the police had.

Except for one thing. Hod was beginning to believe he might know what was going on. True hunter that he was, he could transfer himself into the minds of the hunted. He knew the ways of every forest creature.

He knew the bear was not a bear.

What is more, he thought he was beginning to know why.

Hod, today, sat with elbows on the tabletop, looking directly at Reed Jamison. He judged Reed to have a fair amount of imagination and imagination was heavy on Hod Cole's mind. For the past two weeks he had been puzzling over what he secretly called "Lee Heaward's problem." Since their first meeting he had become more and more aware of this woman. The afternoon spent on the Saco had been a turning point. For the first time in almost twenty years he found himself seriously thinking about a woman. Only problem was, this woman had an enemy. Hod had spent several hours trying to figure it all out—"puzzle it," as he called thought processes.

To begin with, Hod liked puzzles. Thirty years of living by himself had given him plenty of time to read, to build things with his hands, to spend hours alone in the woods and to do quite a bit of dreaming. He found he liked all sorts of books; he learned how to build anything from a raft to a root cellar to a rotating windmill for wind power.

Many men, alone after a family tragedy, would have taken to letting themselves go, as the country people called it; hard drinking and womanizing would have been their solace. He had no such inclinations. After the first few lonely years, he began to enjoy his own company, and he spent hours of the winter evenings reading up on whatever he had chosen to study, for Hod was a planner and he blocked time out by hours of the day. As a result, he was a walking encyclopedia of information. Magic, witchcraft, herbs and the occult had taken up evenings during the winter of one year, and to Hod's way of thinking, Lee's problem was possibly deep-rooted in these factors. Everything had a solution in Hod's world, and he had set himself to solve this. It was not only the puzzle—it was Lee who drove him forward to ferret out the answer.

Today, facing Reed, he wondered how much imagination this young police chief had; would he believe what Hod was almost dead certain was true?

Well—might's well try the waters. Hod shrugged his shoulders and started. "Reed, when was Lee's barn threatened? Remember the date?"

Reed pondered. "It was a Friday. Friday the thirteenth as a matter of fact. Yeah, I remember that because I thought about bad luck."

Hod continued. "And when did she have the phone calls?"

"Let's see. Right around the second week of January—no, the third week for the last ones. The others about a month before that."

"All right." Hod made marks on the large calendar he had laid out on the table in front of them. "Now, when did Jim Davidson die?"

"Hum, sixteenth of March. A Monday."

"And when did Mrs. Attlebury think she saw that bear up around the Hartley place?" The older man was making notes.

"I guess that would be around the third week of April."

Reed watched Hod's pencil make another small circle.

"Now, what date was the Historic House Garden Tour committee meeting Lee and Mrs. Bemis were sick after?"

The police chief leaned forward. "That was another thirteenth, middle of May. What are you getting at?"

"Well, according to my calendar, every one of those happenings comes on or shortly before a full moon. So I kept thinking—why? Full moon's supposed to affect a lot of things. Lots of people run by the full moon. I got to thinking about that, and then I calculated when the next time might be if my theory was correct. That would be around June eleventh. And I was right. Carter and Lee almost ran through the barbed wire on the trail. Ted had a bad accident—if it was an accident—I'm betting he saw the same thing that Jim Davidson saw. The blouse was slashed the night of the first committee meeting, but everything else fits. Now, I feel like I'm getting close. Whoever does all these things likes to do them at full moon time. So, now, where am I?" He stopped and looked at Reed, then continued, "You aren't going to like the way I answered myself. I don't think this is a set of coincidences and odds and ends. I think it's a thought-out plan, excepting maybe Jim's death, which probably was an accident and maybe meant to be Lee. I think whoever is doing this dabbles in witchcraft. Maybe he—or she—has a big ego and a kind of character defect. Sort of doesn't really care about right or wrong. Magic covers this up; kind of lets him—or her—have an excuse. So this person decides to be a woods creature. A bear."

Reed brushed back his hair. "Maybe I'll surprise you. I've been thinking along the same lines. Only it all seems a little crazy."

Hod leaned over and picked up the short riding crop he had been working on as a gift for Lee. A small piece of deer horn formed the handle; the wood was mountain ash—the rowan tree. Polishing the wood in long, gentle strokes, he sighed, "I think, Reed, you've got it—it's more than a little crazy. It's evil—and that's the worst of it."

Reed rose and helped himself to coffee from the old pot on the back of the small woodstove, now nearly out. "Is that mountain ash?"

Hod nodded. "I'm making it to ward off any evil spirits. I'm crafting it for Lee. Because I can't think of anything else to do. And I'm scared, Reed, I admit I'm scared."

Reed looked at the older man. "Go on; you evidently have

thought this all out to a conclusion. I want to hear every angle."

"All right." Again Hod traced a circle on the calendar. "Whoever this is, his or her plans run along full moon time. Maybe he's a moon worshiper, or some kind of animal worshiper, thus the bear symbol. Certainly some type of witchcraft. We have two bear sightings—Lee and Mrs. Attlebury. We have scratches on Jim and Ted. We have a herb used for poisoning—valerian. And what did Jim scribble on his pad? B... for what do you suppose? Now, follow me, 'cause this gets real strange. I said someone wasn't playing with a full deck. So follow close."

Reed took out a pencil and pad and sat ready to make notes and follow the thought train of this man, face now becoming grimmer, who sat opposite him.

"First thing," said Hod, "is the phone calls. If you used one word to describe them, what would it be?"

Reed shook his head. "I don't know. Threats, maybe?"

"How about *Beware.*" Hod drew a capital B on his pad.

"All right," said Reed. "*Beware.* I don't follow you."

"Just hang on. You'll see. The calls—I'd say *Beware*, maybe even *Back off*. Now, what's the starting letter?"

"*B.*" Reed stared at Hod.

"Exactly. *B.* Now, when the barn was threatened. What word? What letter?"

"*Barn*, of course. And I see what you're getting at. *Burn. Barn* and *Burn.*" Reed was getting warm; beginning to follow. "And, *Bear* when Jim died—and *Bear* with Lee and Mrs. Attlebury. And then—the poison in the sherry. That doesn't fit, Hod. Valerian, poison, sherry. No *B's* there, Hod."

Hod looked at him. "How about *Bottle?*"

"My God." Reed's voice was low. "I don't like this; I don't like this at all. He runs by the full moon and has some sort of a master design?"

"*Barbed wire,*" Hod's voice went on. "*Bear*—Ted's attack. And even the blouse—*Blue,* wasn't it? That worries me the most. Nasty things, both of them. Nasty person. And, you know what, Reed, I think a person who thinks he can't be caught. So he plays games, like kids play games. Like 'Catch me if you can, only you can't, I'm smarter than you are'. Well, people grow up and they don't play those games anymore—unless, like I said a while back—something's wrong in their mind." Hod stopped talking.

They both sat still, thinking of what they faced. Finally, Hod stood up, paced back and forth on the worn floorboards of the kitchen and stopped in front of Reed.

"I don't know the proper title for a person who thinks this way. A psychiatrist would know. I think you'd call them a psychotic. Somebody smarter than I am knows all the terms. But I think the person we're looking for is very, very cagey. He seems to like the idea of being a bear and he likes to do harm starting with a *B* and he runs by the full moon most of the time. And he certainly has created a bundle of mischief since he started. I think he might have meant it just to be threats—he certainly doesn't like Lee. Could be jealousy of some type. But I think the threats got out of hand; I don't believe he meant to kill Jim Davidson. On the surface Jim's death seems natural—heart attack and broken neck from the fall. But we think something scared him into that heart attack. Now, what comes next? We're getting into July; full moon's around the eleventh. Anything slated for then?"

"The garden tour," Reed answered. "The Historic House Garden Tour on the Hill. Lee's place is the last on the list. There's usually a thousand or more people who come through on either the Christmas or the garden tour. You think that's the next place, huh?"

Hod nodded. "That's right. I was figuring it would be about that time. If this person follows the pattern it'll be just about then."

The police chief by now was impressed and filled with foreboding at what Hod had shown him. Reed felt he could handle an ordinary criminal, but the unknown was something else. He was determined to solve this but he felt defenseless. This was like no other case and the presence of an unbalanced mind was not something he relished. The one thing he was sure of was having Hod Cole as an ally. About now, Reed Jamison needed a sure thing.

"I got to wondering," continued the older man, "what kind of person this is—tried to figure out his characteristics. Has to have an interest in witchcraft and herbs; he knows the forest well; he skis; back up a minute—he has more than a passing interest in herbs for he used valerian. If I was going to kill outright I'd use foxglove or monkshood."

"That's exactly what Mrs. Attlebury said," Reed agreed. "So it looks like he's a threatener rather than a killer, doesn't it? But Hod, women are the majority of poisoners. Where does that lead us?"

"Could have been a woman." Hod was thinking. "But, I tell you, Reed, here's how I see it. Say I'm this person. I'm laughing all the way home 'cause I've tricked people—and I've laid clues right in their faces—so let's try poison and that will confuse things even more. Here's a person who likes the full moon and the letter *B*. And he is devious, Reed, devious. Person like that would try poison just to put us off."

Reed sighed. "I have to agree. What I'm afraid of is threats aren't going to be threats anymore. He got a taste of blood with Ted. That is, if the bear was what attacked Ted. Scratches are what I'm going by. Police report says attack by persons unknown. And the barbed wire—whoever tangled with that would have been a bloody mess. So he's braver now. And meaner."

"I've thought of all the same things. Will you have police on duty the day of the tour, Reed? Could there be a man at High Meadows?"

"I have to spread them around—I only have a couple of men. I might be able to work with the sheriff's department. But there probably will be only three or four of us. I'm going to talk with Lee again. This time I better make it clear we have an opponent who's not rowing with both oars in the water."

"She's a sensible woman." Hod smiled to himself. "Tell her as much as you want her to know. But make sure she realizes this is a very dangerous person."

Reed nodded. "I'm going to be talking with Ellen and Lee tomorrow. I think Carter is due up soon. Why don't you come over with me and explain your theory?"

"I don't know whether it'll come better from you or from me, Reed. You're the police chief."

Reed rose to go. "And you're part of the brains behind me. If you can, I think you'd better show up at High Meadows. She's quite a lady, you know, Hod. I don't think she's totally committed to Carter. I noticed you seem kind of interested in her."

"I didn't think it showed."

"Well, it does, a little. You won't know until you've tried, Hod." Reed placed his hands on the older man's shoulders. "I'm in your corner."

"Guess I'm out of practice. I may be too much of a woodsman for her."

"Don't sell yourself short. I have an idea you are exactly the kind of man Lee Heaward could be happy with. You made this house comfortable, Hod. I haven't been over here for a while. I'd forgotten." Reed, looking around him, was impressed and he realized again, as he had so many times, that Hod was many different men.

One of whom could be the right choice for Lee Heaward.

•16•

It was the afternoon of the following day when Reed collected everyone at High Meadows. Carter had arrived the night before, and he joined Lee and Ellen in the kitchen. Ellen had decided to work a few hours daily during the time she was not sitting at Ted's bedside. It helped them financially and it helped her emotionally to keep busy. Hod was on time and settled into one of the chairs by the pine table, accepting a cup of coffee from Ellen.

Reed, with swiftness, went through the calendar of events Hod had drawn up, stilling the exclamations until he had finished. Lee looked intently at the diagram.

"You did this. You thought it all out. You must have spent hours." She looked at Hod.

"I had the time and it was like a puzzle I had once when I was a kid. I couldn't work it out, then all of a sudden it fell into place.

I'm still not sure I understand why but there's a pattern here, I'm sure of it."

Ellen was quick to see. "Then we have to think about the garden tour, don't we? That's July eleventh—full moon."

"I can't really take High Meadows off the tour now—the committee's counting on it. Besides, what could I tell them? That I'm afraid of a full moon? That there's a pretend bear on the loose? Only a few people know I've been threatened." Lee spoke with sadness.

"Of course not. You'll just have to continue with your plans. Remember, too, that whoever this person is, he may not know—probably doesn't know we've even figured out his scheme this far. Take one or two of the offered helpers from the committee; you stay right here all those two days and I'll have one of my men directing traffic near the road—he can check in every few hours. I don't think a bear is going to appear in the middle of all those tourists. But watch what you eat and drink and keep the big security light on at night. If we get through the full moon period we will have done the hardest part. Ellen, will you be here part of the time? How is Ted today?" Reed turned to her, seeing the sorrow in her eyes.

"I go every day mornings, then work up here for a few hours and go back to be with him again late afternoons and some evenings. He just seems to sleep a lot; the doctor says he's not in a true coma, but he doesn't talk. It's trauma, the doctor says. He squeezes my hand when I ask if he hears me, but he can't talk. I can't even get through to him with a pencil and pad. Nothing works." Ellen put her hands up to her face.

Reed patted her. "I'm going in to see him tonight. We hope he'll be able to talk soon and tell us what happened. I'm having the hospital staff check his room often. I don't want anyone to try again."

Reed rose to leave and Hod and Carter walked with him to the cruiser.

"Does it seem now that whoever is doing this has changed from being just threatening to wanting to kill? Is this what you're saying?" Carter looked at Reed with tired eyes. "Are you saying there's a greater danger here than you suspected in the beginning? That this is an unbalanced mind?"

Reed nodded in the affirmative. "That's what Hod and I are afraid of, Carter. This person is devious and a planner. He thinks he can't be caught and I think he is more than a little unbalanced. I think he's way off his rocker and very strong. The unbalanced mind has great bodily strength. Ted's a big man; it had to be a massive blow to floor him. And he never tried to fight back."

"Do you think he knew who struck him? Or should I say what struck him?" Carter's face was like granite.

Hod answered the question. "I'd say it was likely. What's more, it's likely that whenever he leaves the hospital the person could try again. That is, if Ted regains his senses."

Reed started the motor. "Yeh, that's what worries me. It's not only going to be Lee we have to keep an eye on. Now it's Ted as well."

Hod and Carter, standing together in the yard, seemed suddenly to have made a truce. A woman, a man and a farm they both cared for would be silently watched over during the coming days. Whatever feelings they may have shared, both courting the same woman, these feelings were pushed to the background by the present crisis. Friends are made in strange circumstances. None were stranger than those of the past months.

The weekend of July 11th and 12th arrived with no more incidents along the way. Saturday, the 11th, was ordered especially for the garden tour. Little white clouds speckled the china blue sky, and a soft breeze blew across the Hill. Every garden sparkled; purple and red bergamot, delphiniums, shasta daisies, poppies and nasturtiums along with lilies of all descriptions filled the garden beds; they crowded against the birdbaths and sundials and sculptures. Clumps of white alyssum and blue ageratum overflowed the brick and cobblestone paths leading through the old gardens. Bees vied with people for the flowers, birdbaths tucked here and there along the paths called to sparrows and finches, and hummingbirds darted about looking for red-hued flowers. Early pastel foxgloves and deep blue monkshood, along with pink and white valerian, formed the background for many of the perennial beds and over and over, through it all, were hundreds and hundreds of golden marguerites, the mainstay flower of several of the older stands.

It was a perfect day. Before ten o'clock in the morning, the Historic House Garden Tour committee had an advance sale of two hundred tickets and a line was already forming in front of the Meadowbrook gazebo.

Meg's daughters sold admission tickets. At High Meadows, on the other end of the tour, Ellen set out paper cups and plates for the herbed ice tea and cookies that would be given gratis to the end-of-the-line visitors. The old herb garden gave forth scents of lavender and lemon balm. Oregano and sage filled small knotted beds and the urn of rosemary sported tiny blue blossoms. St. Fiacre had been scrubbed clean, and Charlie Cooncat wandered along the brick path looking for his favorite stand of catnip just coming into bloom. On an ordinary day Charlie would roll once or twice in the leaves and then curl up in the shade beneath the huge plants; today he would retire to the haymow when the visitors arrived.

At Run for Cover, the second house on the tour map, Malcolm tied up straggling lilies and valerian and ran the hose over the thyme-covered brick terrace that led from his kitchen door to the cutting garden. Going inside, he poured coffee he had made earlier in his European pot and gave thought to the fact that tomorrow evening he would see Lee and Cokie at the party following the tour's close. The first of the visitors came through the gate into the main garden. Malcolm put his cup on the rear of the kitchen counter and walked across the terrace into the garden to greet them.

On one side of the brick path stood a cast-iron bench, painted light green. The back showed a pattern of three children entwined, depicting the seasons. On the long iron seat was a fat green and white striped awning-cloth cushion that Malcolm had sewn. One lady, sitting down and taking off her shoes, said to her companion, "My feet hurt already and it's only my second garden."

"I told you not to wear those shoes, Sophie." The elderly second lady, complete with large round straw hat trimmed with roses, noted Malcolm approaching, and boomed, "Oh, Mr. Bandridge, we do so admire your garden. How do you manage so many blooms all at once? My garden doesn't look like this; of course it's been a dry summer so far and my plants aren't as settled in as yours, but I can't get my marguerites to look like yours. What is your secret?"

Malcolm winced and muttered a four-letter word under his breath. But he smiled sweetly and said obligingly, "Fertilizer, my dears, fertilizer. The very best cow and sheep, you know. I make tea of it and the little plants spring right up."

"Imagine." The lady took out a pencil from her voluminous handbag; a small pad of paper appeared and she wrote carefully—"fertilizer tea." "I must remember that."

Malcolm sighed, but he had agreed to do this so he became the perfect tour guide, showing them the large Canterbury bells he was so proud of behind a clump of daisies. He ushered them through his stand and off down the small lane leading to the next house, which was the cottage owned by Mrs. Bemis.

And good luck to her, he thought, as he returned to the kitchen and cold coffee. His thoughts backtracked to Lee; once he had great hopes for this relationship but nothing had developed; in fact when he tried to tell her how he felt she had been quick to say she only wanted friendship. Malcolm had felt rejected; he spent much time attending auctions with her and he had been sure she returned his feelings, but it had all come to nothing. *The story of my life.* Swallowing his pride was hard, but lately he had begun to have a relationship with Cokie and he was beginning to feel they might become lovers. Malcolm had only one relative, his sister Elvira, who came up to the Hill in the summer. In fact, she was due this evening from Philadelphia, and would go with him tomorrow to the party at High Meadows. Malcolm was a lonely man, not an unfriendly man, but one who had turned inward too much during his lifetime. He had never found the right person to share his life with and, whenever he had been on the brink of discovery, something always ended the relationship.

Walkers were beginning to come through at the proper clip now and Malcolm, carrying fresh coffee, returned to the main garden to sit on the seasons bench and talk small talk with the sightseers.

Next door, at the cottage, Mrs. Bemis, in a bit of a snit, was trying to do duty in all four corners of her garden, her helper not having arrived. The Cottage had long been noted for its topiary display; old yew hedges trimmed in the forms of ducks and geometric designs formed borders for the garden which held large clumps of lilies, daisies and delphiniums. Hosta and impatiens grew in dark corners under maples and along the edge of a little brick terrace shaded with sweet olive trees. Mrs. Bemis's garden was rather like Mrs. Bemis—an old stand worn and tattered but still making a brave show.

Mrs. Bemis had dressed for the day. She was resplendent in a voluminous skirt of Liberty print with a cream-colored low-necked blouse, sandals, and a wide Panama hat that harkened back to the Victorian era. It was an outfit that would have looked delightful on Cokie Adams; it gave Mrs. Bemis the appearance of a large colored mushroom.

However, Mrs. Bemis was greatly at home in her garden, more so than almost anyone else on the tour. She knew more of herbs, simples, tisanes, specifics, and other properties of roots and leaves, than did anyone on the Hill with the exception of old Mrs. Attlebury. Malcolm, himself, had a large collection of old herbals in his library, but even he did not have Mrs. Bemis's knowledge. If the truth were known, Malcolm did not care much for Mrs. Bemis, and they waged a perpetual battle within the confines of the garden club.

Today, Mrs. Bemis yoo-hooed over the length of the short lane joining the two stands. Malcolm recoiled from her ladylike yoohoos, but finally, in desperation, yoohooed back, which satisfied her and stopped the noise.

He waved; she returned the wave, and the walkers continued on through number two to number three on their maps, little knowing that the two owners were not on the best of terms.

At the Water Lily House, number four on the map, the Ward sisters, summer occupants only, greeted their guests with a quiet simplicity. Both sisters were in their late sixties; the Ward girls as they were always called, came up only in the three seasonal months of June, July and August, opened their small inherited home, and cleaned out the three small ponds on the grounds. The ponds had been on the Water Lily property as long as memory served on the Hill, and yearly the sisters cleaned them, sank new barrels with lilies, reset the old barrels with the roots that had wintered over in Mrs. Bemis's cellar, and replaced the golden carp that might have died over the winter. The large garden, which took up most of the stand's acreage, was simple, almost Japanese in style, with its stone paths connecting the ponds and the clumps of Siberian iris set along the pathways. The water lilies themselves were glorious pinks and whites with a few old deep reds that had bloomed for years. The quiet setting of lawn, ponds, lilies and iris, interspersed with arrangements of white cast-iron garden furniture, was one of the most restful spots on the garden tour.

Today, the sisters sat together on a long garden bench of Lutyens design and greeted their guests with simple elegance.

Alice and Alycia were their names, and when Lee had first met them she had wanted to say "and where is Edith with the golden hair?"

Cokie Adams, who never did anything according to tradition, opened the side gate to the Ward sisters' garden, and darted toward them. "I simply must sit down," she gasped. "My car had a flat tire this morning and everything has gone wrong and I'm late getting here to help with the food booth and Bunny's going to be cross with me. It's simply not my day."

"Sit down and rest a minute." Alice Ward's voice had a kindly quality. She moved over on the bench to make room for Cokie.

"Thanks. I know I ought to start off with the first house, but I haven't time to see them all before I have to help with lunch. So I'm just going to peek here and there. My, aren't those large goldfish!"

"They are Chinese carp—the good-luck fish—at least they are called that by some people," replied Alice. "We take a few out every year and put them back when we come up the next season. Some of them, the big ones, can live in the mud at the bottom through the winter. Mrs. Bemis keeps the ones we take out in her cellar, along with the barrels of lily roots. You can't be sure what will winter over, so we do it that way. The carp came from the quarries. Those live up there year-round, it's so deep. Some of the older ones must weigh a pound by now."

Cokie leaned over. "Aren't they pretty. What do they eat?"

Alycia Ward smiled. "Themselves at times. They're cannibalistic. But we feed them fish food and bread. They'll eat baby frogs."

Cokie shook her head. "Oh dear, baby frogs. But the carp are beautiful. And all those lilies. I love water. Except I can't swim; I never learned. I just sit on the beach and sun. I just returned from Spain—look at the pendant I bought. It's supposed to be sapphires set in real silver, but I suppose it's a fake. Most things are. I bought it because I love sapphires; they are supposed to protect you from harm."

"It's lovely." The Ward sisters bent their heads in unison and inspected the pendant.

"It looks right for you, Cokie." Alycia's voice was kind.

"Thanks, well, I'm rested enough and I'll do one or two more gardens and then off to the food booth. I think your garden is beautiful. Thank you for letting me rest." With that she left Alice and Alycia.

"She's a bit peculiar, but I do like her, Sister," said Alice. "I understand she does well in real estate."

"That," replied Alycia, smoothing down her blue denim skirt and tidying her gray-blonde hair, "is because whoever brought her up taught her to say 'please' and 'thank you.' Two necessary words in today's world."

Alice frowned thoughtfully. "I rarely disagree, dear Sister. But I think you mean to say 'yesterday's world'."

At the Manse, number five on the map, small tables and folding chairs had been set out on the lawn. Bunny Cleaver, with the aid of several of the Hill ladies, was busy cutting pies and cakes and stopping every so often to stir the cold summer squash soup that would be served in tiny bowls and topped with yogurt and paprika. Lee had given Bunny her recipe and it had been adapted for today's lunch, as being exactly what would be appropriate for a hot summer's day. It would also look elegant on the long buffet tables set lengthwise across the kitchen garden.

This was Bunny's first tour and she was determined to do a good job, for Clipper's sake if not her own. Cokie was overdue already; she had a bad habit of always being late and Bunny worried that there would not be enough people to help with the luncheon. Jan Howard, from the Old Howard Stand, two houses down the small connecting lane, came rapidly through the garden, bearing two covered platters with breads, and the Rhineharts, new owners of Safe Haven, the house next door to the Cleavers' Manse, brought additional biscuits, crackers and breads to go with the soup.

"Isn't Cokie helping you?" Jan looked about at Bunny's few assistants. "You're going to need more than this when it gets to be twelve o'clock. There's going to be a crowd; Meg's daughter just called from Meadowbrook and said to tell you to expect more people than we'd planned on. She couldn't get you on the phone."

"That's because I've been out here. I didn't hear it ring." Bunny was a little cross. She straightened the long tablecloths, set out the little plastic spoons in a big tureen and picked a dead flower from one of the large arrangements. "I don't know where Cokie is and I could throttle her for being late. She always is and Clipper puts up with it."

"Well, I hear she's his best saleswoman." Jan looked keenly at Bunny. "She really is a bit much at times. I should think you'd put your foot down. How can you trust Clipper with her?"

Bunny's eyes hardened. "That's none of your business, Jan Howard. Besides, Clipper never wanders. I don't want to hear any more of that. Here's Cokie now."

"I'm sorry I'm late. The car had a flat; I came in the wrong way and I thought I had time to see some of the gardens. I really am sorry, Bunny. I meant to be on time."

"Never mind. There's an apron on the back of the kitchen door. Put it on and come help with the change basket. The girls have coffee on in the kitchen; the pies and cakes are cut and I think we're nearly ready. You better brush back your hair or tie it with a ribbon or something. It might get in the soup."

Cokie's wild red hair, blown by the breeze in all directions, spilled over her shoulders and down the front of her peach, lemon and cream outfit: a tight, knitted tank top and a flowing pongee skirt. Long, dangly earrings of silver and the silver and sapphire pendant completed her costume. There were several bracelets on her arms and two on her ankles clanking above her rather shabby sandals. *Thank God,* thought Bunny, *she'll at least be sitting still when she makes change. Why Clipper couldn't take on an average everyday broker I'll never know.*

Clipper had told her why several times, when she had objected, although she never would have admitted this to Jan Howard.

"Cokie sells one hell of a lot of real estate, and that's the bottom line. Shut up, Bun, will you?" And Bunny had shut up.

Walkers began to straggle in to the food tables. A steady stream of enthusiastic gardeners developed, discussing the houses, the gardens, the ponds and the Hill's history. Like swarms of colored butterflies, women settled on the folding chairs by the tables that were set about the lawn. A small marble statue of Diana stood in the center of the Manse garden—Diana, the goddess of the hunt and of the woods. How she had ever settled there in the middle of a Puritan New England garden was not known, although one minister who had lived at the Manse in the early 1800's had traveled for a year in the Golden Isles, and sometime later a box containing Diana had arrived at the Manse's door. The minister, so the story went, had said it was a gift and it was some time before it actually made an appearance in the garden. A bit of an unsolved mystery, which the Hill loved, but it was never made clear, since the minister died of typhoid and another took his place. Diana, shrouded in her bed of lilies, became an everyday figure on the Hill.

Gradually the pace of the tour picked up. The first walkers began to flow through the Old Howard Stand, then through Faraway and Deer Run and finally filtered down to High Meadows. A few had started in the opposite direction at the beginning, in order to have more of the gardens to themselves, and at the noon hour the Manse kitchen garden was crowded. By five o'clock that afternoon, at least seven hundred people had walked the gardens. The owners were tired, the helpers were tired from answering questions over and over, and several flower beds had been trampled.

Walkers had asked "Why is it called 'Run for Cover' and 'Faraway'" and heard the explanation that both houses had been part of the Underground Railroad during the Civil War. These two houses had similar architecture and it was rumored there were secret exits and entrances, although both owners denied seeing them. Rumor, especially that concerning the distant past, always ran rampant on the Hill.

Elvira Campbell, Malcolm's sister, arrived at six that evening, having driven up from Philadelphia in her BMW. Elvira, as usual, was impeccably dressed in a madras shirtwaist dress with matching hat. Her stacked-heeled polished Italian pumps looked a bit out of place on the terrace of Run for Cover, but she quickly changed into a sleeveless cotton blouse, Bermudas and sneakers.

Malcolm mixed their drinks and together they relaxed as they watched the sun low over the far New Hampshire mountains. Being Elvira, she wasted no time before digging into her brother's life.

"Now, dear, do tell me what's been going on since Christmas. We only had a short time together in Boston. I'm surprised you spent this whole winter alone up here when you could have been traveling or going to plays in New York. Or at least visiting me in Philadelphia. By the way, when I changed upstairs I noticed the old dome box of mother's had been moved off the chest of drawers in my old room. I always liked that box. I hope nothing's happened to it."

"I had to rearrange a few things." Malcolm sipped his drink slowly. "I've sold a few pieces. It costs so to live today, you know."

Elvira started to remonstrate and then bit her tongue. She knew she had no right—they were Malcolm's things. He had inherited Run for Cover and its contents plus a very small sum of money from his mother. The Bandridge family had once been quite wealthy—they had dealt in cutlery at one time, and surprisingly enough, had once owned a factory in the Connecticut area that Carter Ransome came from. They had also owned the Hill house and three or four generations past had moved up to Maine for good. There had been a rumor of a male family member having ill health and needing country air, and the presence of the old sanatorium nearby, the one on the Hartley property, helped the Bandridge family make their decision to move.

What other reasons there were, were mere rumor and had never been proven.

When the last Mrs. Bandridge died, Malcolm had received the Maine home and Elvira, who had married well, as the saying goes, had received a few selected items, some stock shares of little value and a modest amount of money. Elvira had not taken offense at this; she knew her brother well and knew that he was not a good businessman. The shop he kept in Paris did fairly well, but times were changing and people were shopping in Portland and Lewiston-Auburn and the malls took business away from the smaller, older shops. At least, that's what Malcolm said made him close his doors. He seemed to have lost interest, but Elvira knew he had lost clients through his own attitude at times. He had expensive tastes; he bought the best gin, the best food, and gave lively small parties to the little theatre group. He contributed to worthy causes and on the surface appeared to be a well-fixed retired businessman. He dealt in antiques and everyone felt Malcom had made some good investments with his mother's money.

Elvira had, for some time, hoped Malcolm would marry, but it hadn't happened. Someone like Lee Heaward would have suited her. Mal's sister, knowing the family history, worried over him as they grew up, but no signs of the so-called family "nervousness" surfaced, other than the time he tried to strangle a boy who was hitting Elvira. However, a brother has a duty to protect his sister and usually Malcolm was normal and charming.

This evening, watching the collage of the sun and mountains, brother and sister sat sipping gin and tonics and discussing the garden tour.

"There's to be a gathering at Lee's, tomorrow when we are finished, El," Malcolm said. "You're invited, of course. Lee said to be sure to tell you. We just have a minor amount of business—Meg will give a speech thanking everyone and tell us how much money we made. Then we'll be finished with the bloody thing. It's potluck, by the way. I bought fixings for a big pasta salad and maybe you'll help me put it together?"

"Delighted." Elvira stretched back in the 1920's wooden deck chair and sipped her drink slowly and with relish. "My, it's nice to be up here, Malcolm. You've created such a lovely garden from the old one. You just need a lady to keep you company. I thought you and Lee were quite chummy once."

"She's really not all she seems, Sis." Malcolm sounded a little tense. "She has rather common tastes at times, actually makes friends with some of the woodsmen, and besides I think she sleeps around. Really couldn't have that, you know."

Elvira sat up straight. "For heaven's sakes, Mal, I thought you liked her. Sleeps around. For the Lord's sake, at age fifty-five and with her business and the farm, how much sleeping around is she going to do? I know she's had a friendship with Carter for a long while, but I thought you could outdistance him. They only see each other once in a while. You sound like sour grapes to me. Remember me, Elvira? Your sister? I know all your secrets, so don't tell me that stuff. Sleeps around, indeed!"

Malcolm shrugged his shoulders. "Have it your way. But Lee wouldn't do at all. I did like her, but she didn't live up to my expectations."

Elvira frowned. *I thought he might have outgrown that.* She changed the subject, mixed herself another drink and returned to talk of Philadelphia and her forthcoming trip to the Continent next winter.

"Would you like to go with me, Mal? It would be good for you to spend the winter somewhere else. It must be depressing at times here with all the snow."

"I can't really afford it, Sis. This place costs so much to keep up, and besides I'm up for president of the little theatre group this coming year. Duty and all that—I couldn't leave."

"Well, at least consider it," Elvira continued. "This place is lovely but it would get on my nerves in the winter. I know you love to ski but there must be some days you can't even do that. A change would be good. The little theatre would be waiting when you returned."

Malcolm's voice changed, rose, and became peevish. "I said no, didn't I? Didn't you hear me? I have some things I need to finish. Then I'll consider a trip. Listen, El, I wanted to tell you there's to be a big auction next month, right nearby. The Attleburys are cleaning out their box room of the contents they've had since her grandmother's time. I understand there are two oils—priceless, I hear. And all sorts of antiques—it will be the event of the year. Why don't you stay for that?"

Elvira agreed. "I'll try to. It sounds like just what I'd enjoy. Mal, are you fixing something here for dinner or are we going to Mariah's?"

"Here. I put some wine in the fridge and I have a small chicken. I'll just pop it in the oven. El, I'll get you the wire basket and you get some greens from the salad garden when you finish that drink. Whatever you see for salad."

Malcolm disappeared inside for the basket, brought it out and handed it to Elvira. *Mother's old wire basket, still in use. Strange,* she thought, *we are still all bound together.*

Malcolm disappeared again to fix the chicken, and Elvira, draining her glass, walked back into the area beyond the latticed drying yard. Here Malcolm grew several varieties of lettuces. Hidden behind the lattice fence were rows of Bibb, red-leaf and oak-leaf lettuces, parsley, salad burnet and arugula. The rows were interspersed with flowers. *A rather strange selection of produce,* thought Elvira, looking around carefully. In one corner of this small garden, against a stone wall, grew valerian. In another corner stood monkshood: aconite, with blue-capped flowers spilling over. Endive took up a rear row, and foxgloves bloomed on one side, cream and rose and lavender, larger blooms than Elvira had ever seen. Along one edge of the wall was a tangle of suspicious-looking weeds—*What are they doing here?* Looking closer, Elvira picked out the deadly nightshade plants covering parts of the stone wall. *These ought to be pulled out.* Two small black alder trees would later be covered with the red berries Malcolm used in Christmas arrangements. The trees stood on either side of the rear entrance to the garden, but the entrance now was blocked off by a stone pillar. In front of the pillar grew a large stand of moonwort or pearly everlasting—not yet in blossom.

Elvira knew her plants. Her mother had not only left her an inheritance of material things, but she had left her with a rare knowledge of growing things. Elvira's mother and Mrs. Attlebury's mother had been friends years before. Most of the Hill people had more than a passing knowledge of herbs and gardens. She gathered the greens and then sat quietly for a moment on the small rustic bench in front of the lattice work. She was puzzled. Most salad and herb gardens contained more traditional plants. There was no rosemary, no sage or oregano. No stands of comfrey or angelica. All the other Hill houses had stands of these two herbs. No marigolds, usually planted between rows of vegetables.

Strange.

No angelica.

·17·

Elvira sat still. She remembered when her mother died, holding Elvira's hand in a claw-like grasp.

Her whisper, softly. "Take care of Malcolm."

Elvira had agreed. Knowing in the back of her mind that a promise to a dying person may be made but may never be fulfilled. As the years sped by, she and Malcolm saw little of each other except for the traditional summer and winter visits. They exchanged letters, never satisfying to Elvira.

She had been happy when Malcolm seemed settled in on the Hill; he seldom visited her in Philadelphia. After her husband died, she made an out-of-season visit to Maine with the thought that she and Malcolm might join forces, as he was still unmarried, but two weeks with his demands showed her this would never work. She had returned to the city and made a good life there with old friends, wondering how she could ever have entertained the idea that brother and sister might live out their years together. Almost all her worries about Malcolm had retreated to the back of her mind. Now, she pulled them out and took a good look.

What was bothering her was the angelica.

Malcolm called for lettuce, and she rose and walked back into the kitchen with the basket of greens. Dumping the contents into the old slate scullery sink, she said, "Malcolm, I'm going up to the bathroom for a minute."

Malcolm, trimming his platter with parsley for the chicken, nodded. "There's a new little oil in the hall, El. I picked it up at auction. Strawberries. Take a look at it."

Elvira mounted the stairs, took a quick look at the oil, which she instantly admired, and proceeded up to the third floor. The attic door was directly in front of her. On previous visits she had sometimes found it locked; today it opened at the lift of the latch. She entered into a long room lighted by a full window on either end. Down the middle of the room ran her mother's old sewing table, and Malcolm's machine stood at one end. Fabrics of all types and colors covered parts of the table, large and small piles awaiting transformation into costumes for the little theatre. Two dress forms, early 1900's types, stood at one end. One had a partially finished costume draped upon its body.

There was nothing unusual about this attic sewing room; it remained much as it had been in her mother's time. Malcolm had learned his sewing abilities at her side. A large part of his life had entertained this hobby, not as strange for a man today as it might have been fifty years ago. There had even been the time when his mother had the secret hope he would become a designer, in one of her flights of fancy that mothers have about their children's futures.

As enthusiastic as Malcolm could become about a project, just as quickly could he lose enthusiasm. He had never felt appreciated, he was sure his designs would be too expensive and besides, it took such dedication to the work. So that, along with other ideas he'd considered, had come to nothing. The interest in little theatre costumes was enough. He had done tailoring and alterations when he'd owned the men's shop, but in time he'd lost interest there too and people complained he had not measured them properly.

Elvira stood a moment, thinking of all this past history. Finally she turned and started down the stairs, remembering to stop at the bathroom, which had been her original goal. The attic did not hold the answer to her questions. Perhaps tomorrow evening at Lee's after-tour gathering she might gain some insight into what was happening in Malcolm's life.

When she finally met Cokie, she felt part of the puzzle was solved.

The second day of the tour was as busy as the first. Elvira helped Malcolm at Run for Cover and all up and down the small lane people filled the gardens. Lee and Meg closed Carriage Trade for the day; Dorie came to help with the food booth. Clipper even closed Cleaver Real Estate; Cokie was helping as a tour guide at High Meadows and Malcolm was at his own stand, so Clipper turned on his answering machine for the first time in a long while, and trusted he would not lose too much business. The public relations part of the garden tour took precedence over keeping the office open, even though it was a Sunday in July. The advertisements for the tour in *Down East* and the *Antique Digest* had mentioned both Carriage Trade and Cleaver Real Estate serving as patrons and Clipper knew good advertising when he saw it. He was willing to do his share, although he would never before now have thought of being a patron as a way to advertise.

At six o'clock, after the last walker left the last garden, after tickets were counted and money estimated, the members of the Historic House Garden Tour committee slowly straggled into High Meadows for their potluck gathering. Lee had set up a bar of mixers, ice and soft drinks—anyone wanting other than that brought his own bottle, which was a Hill tradition. Ellen had baked a ham and there were leftover cookies plus a cooler of herbed ice tea. Lee spread tablecloths on picnic tables and rearranged the folding chairs that had spent the two days of the tour on the edges of the herb garden.

Meg and Will and their daughter Jolie, who had helped sell tickets at the gazebo, arrived first, then Malcolm with Elvira and Cokie and last of all Clipper dragging a tired but proud Bunny. Ten minutes later the Ward girls, Jan Howard, Mrs. Bemis, the Rhineharts and the Patterson sisters completed the group, as far as the owners and committee members, and another dozen tour helpers arrived after them, as anyone who had stood duty was welcome. With few exceptions, all lived on the Hill.

"Mercy," said Mrs. Bemis, "I'm glad that's over. How much did we make, Meg?"

Meg, with the aid of a calculator, did rapid addition and subtraction and said, "Unless I've forgotten something, it looks to be in the neighborhood of six thousand dollars. More than we expected. I'm terribly pleased. We may not have to do another garden walk or Christmas open house for at least two or three years."

"Thank God for that," Malcolm stated. "I am absolutely fed up with the public. Kept asking me what I used on my flowers. You know what I felt like saying. But I didn't. I held myself in check."

Elvira, seated by Lee, and happy to be renewing an old acquaintance, said quietly, "I miss you. Last year you were often with Malcolm. Didn't it work out?"

Lee was a little surprised. Elvira usually kept her thoughts to herself and did not pry. However, she liked Elvira, so she answered candidly, "I don't think we were meant for each other. We do like a lot of the same things, but friends is all we are, El. No spark, I guess. If you know what I mean. I see Carter from time to time. Malcolm seems to be with Cokie quite often these days. No hard feelings."

No hard feelings. Not on Lee's part, maybe. Malcolm was another matter. Elvira thought about this before she continued. "I've known Carter a long while, too. Our families started out near each other in Connecticut according to family history. His stayed in Salisbury; the Bandridges came up to the Hill. I like him, Lee."

"I do too, but I'm not sure where we're going. He wants to stay in Salisbury with his bookshop. I want to live in Maine. Although, lately, so much has been happening, I'm almost of two minds."

Cokie, joining them, was formally introduced to Elvira. She picked up the thread of the conversation and addressed Lee. "What did you mean when you said 'so much has been happening'?"

Lee suddenly realized that only a very few people were aware of the occurrences at High Meadows and the Hartley place. Reed and the men from the sheriff's department were low-key and close-mouthed as far as giving out public information. The newspapers had said only that Ted West had suffered an accident, hurt by an unknown assailant. Only Ellen and Lee and Reed and Hod thought otherwise. Jim Davidson's death had been treated as accidental—a combination of heart attack and broken neck from the fall. Even though Malcolm and Clipper and Bunny had been there with Lee, they knew little of what Reed felt was someone's terrorizing Jim so that he had reacted in that fashion. Lee and Mrs.

Attlebury's bear sightings—if it was a bear—only Reed and Hod knew. The slashing of the blue blouse was under police investigation—it was not public knowledge. The phone threats—the barn threat—the barbed wire—only the police and Ted and Ellen and Hod knew. Carter, of course, knew it all; what he hadn't witnessed, Lee had told him. Mrs. Attlebury knew the whole story.

That left the valerian poisoning, and to the public it had been treated as accidental food poisoning. So, as far as the general public's knowledge, it was almost nil.

The one person who, confident that he could never be touched, knew everything that had happened, and more importantly, knew why it had happened, was, of course, the bear.

Lee made a decision. Later she wished with all her heart she had not. She told Cokie and Elvira about some of the happenings.

Elvira, leaning forward, looked intently at Lee. Once or twice she started to interrupt, thought better of it, and waited until Lee finished. Then she spoke, "You mean the scratches across Ted's face were the same, only deeper and uglier, than the ones across Jim's temple?"

"Yes. Ted's were worse. He was hit sideways and with a harder blow." Lee was already wishing she hadn't talked so much.

Cokie looked at Lee. She had been quiet throughout the whole story. Now she spoke. "You're sure you saw a bear? Little, big? What color?"

"Not too large. About the size of a man. Brownish-black. It's hard to tell exact shading. We weren't that close. According to Mrs. Attlebury it walked upright and kind of ambled. I just had a quick glance. Mrs. Attlebury said it didn't act the way a bear should act."

"You mean it might not be a bear? It might have been a person pretending to be a bear? Like on Halloween?" Cokie stayed with her train of thought.

"That's kind of an insane thing to do." Elvira heard her own voice.

"Exactly." Lee sounded tired. "Exactly. That's what is scary. Anyway, it's being investigated. I shouldn't have told you both about it. Please don't say anything."

"No, I'm glad you did tell us. I always take a woods walk when I'm up on the Hill. I'll be careful where I go, now." Elvira rose to make herself another drink.

Cokie remained with Lee. "That's why you wanted one or two people along with you every time you showed the Hartley place. I understand now. Did you notice the fur, Lee?"

"It was just blackish-brown. I wasn't close enough, Cokie. I'm still not very sure—it was dark in the barn. Mrs. Attlebury said he looked scruffy."

"Scruffy?"

"Worn in spots. Of course, he'd be just out of hibernation if it was a true bear. Mrs. Attlebury watched him—she had a good view. Listen, Cokie, this really has to be kept quiet."

"I understand." Cokie nodded. "Scruffy, huh? Lee, I'm going to get some food. I'll come back to talk with you." Cokie rose and drifted to the big table covered with casseroles and desserts.

The evening waned; tired people, well satisfied with their accomplishments, left for home and bed. Paper plates and plastic cups went into the garbage pail alongside the table, and the residue inside to the kitchen. Ellen left. She had put in long hours between High Meadows and visits to Ted.

Carter held Lee in his arms and then packed for Connecticut. Tired after two days of the tour, he had to open his bookshop by noon the next day.

Reed, the last to leave, talked briefly with Lee. He walked with her to say goodnight to the horses and cautioned her to lock the doors. "We've come this far through full moon and nothing's happened so maybe he's going to skip this one. I'll be on duty tonight, Lee, so call Dot and she can get me if anything happens out of the ordinary. Keep Kate right with you."

Lee agreed and with Kate close at her heels, gathered up the last of the paper tablecloths and closed the doors. "Good girl, you were really good, Kate." Lee patted her. "Too many people for you, old girl. We'll go to bed early and have a long walk in the morning."

The security light flooded the big yard and Lee left two of the downstairs lights burning when she climbed the stairs and without even showering, drew on an old pair of pajamas, and stretched out on the bed. *My God, I'm tired.*

Kate, on the floor at the foot of the bed, whined softly in agreement.

The shadows lengthened over the herb garden, the vegetable garden and the path leading through the stone walls into the apple orchards. It had been a long, successful day and Lee, still awake, was glad it was over. As much as the Hill had the tradition of sharing its houses and gardens with the public, so did it also have the hidebound New England trait of closing the doors of the homes and the gates of the old gardens, girding itself against the public and preserving its own privacy. The Hill had shared, but it had shared on its own terms, and now it was time to return to its own small world, a circled world of summer cocktail parties, winter teas, and selected tennis and golf games. Summer and winter residents mixed, attended the historic Hill club together, with ownership of Hill property the glue of their common bond, rather than money. Now the gardens and houses would be closed for a few years, and only those few tourists who walked the little lanes and the horseback riders who rode the old bridle paths would peek over the walls and into the gardens.

The Historic House Garden Tour had ended. Lee lay awake pondering these facts and finally, she slept.

On the Hill, at Run for Cover, Elvira bade Malcolm goodnight and went upstairs to her old room to sleep. She read for a while, plowing her way through two chapters of a new novel and then turned off the light on her bedside table. She lay awake for a few minutes, thinking back over the day, Malcolm's garden, Cokie and Lee's problems. Finally, with a sigh, Elvira slept.

She did not know when she heard a door close. She came up out of a dream of her mother, dressing the brother and sister for a Halloween party. She felt a chill; she had opened the window before getting into bed and the warm July weather was turning cool and windy. The smell of rain hung in the air. Somewhere a door banged shut. Elvira put her navy-blue terry robe about her shoulders and, sliding her feet into scuffs that matched the robe, she softly descended the stairs. No lights had been left on; the front door was unlocked and the cause of the noise was the outer screen door which had not caught on its latch. Elvira, putting out a hand to close it, saw a figure at the end of the garden. Malcolm, no doubt, out for a breath of the night air, as they had so often done as children. Elvira closed the door carefully after her and walked out to join him. Something stopped her halfway across the garden. A feeling of sorts, a sensation that all was not as perceived. In front of her, Malcolm walked rapidly away and entered the lane connecting the Hill houses. Elvira, chilly, drew her robe about her and realized belatedly that Malcolm was not just taking the night air, but that he had a destination.

And, also, that he did not want to be seen.

Elvira had a choice—to go back or to follow him. She elected to follow, taking great care that he did not see her.

It did not take long. Malcolm followed the narrow lane, probably having taken this path many times. This time of night there was little chance he would meet another Hill resident, and he had only a short distance to go. The Manse garden was his objective. More than that, the statue of Diana. Elvira knew by now what would take place.

Diana, set in her bed of lilies, was in shadow. *Malcolm would know that.* If someone had looked out of the Manse windows directly at the statue they would have seen a figure kneeling before it, but in the Manse the occupants were asleep. It is doubtful that had any of the Cleavers seen Malcolm they would have understood what was in his mind.

Elvira, on the other hand, knew. And sorrowed, knowing that the boy her mother had asked her to take care of, could only come, as the story books foretold, to a bad end.

Elvira turned and walked back through the darkness to Run for Cover. *Now I know why the Bandridges gave it that name.* As she slid into bed and pulled the covers up under her chin, she knew that in the days to come she might have to finally keep her promise to her mother.

At High Meadows, nearly an hour after Elvira had returned to her bed, Lee woke. A breeze stirred her bedroom curtains and light raindrops spattered the grass below the windows. The security light outlined the room and Lee sat up in bed. Kate was curled up tightly, dreaming, and Lee decided it must have been the rain that caused her to wake. Slipping out of bed, she walked to the windows and placed her hands on the sills to see if they were wet. The breeze was light, and there was as yet no need to close the sashes.

Across the valley the light from the old Collins farm shone through the mist and the rain. Lee smiled, sensing its security and then stiffened as it went out, on again, out again.

Of course. The deer are passing. Over the ridge of the field, over the crest of the small hill, they moved across the track well established for generations.

"Go in peace," she whispered, remembering the time she had spent a night watch in the field investigating the mystery of the light, until the sound of their hooves and the swish of their bodies passing close to her hiding place in the dark had given her the answer.

"Go in peace."

She turned back toward the bed, but a movement below caught her eye. Remembering the February skier, she looked long and hard at the orchard, now misted with rain.

On the edge of the orchard, just beyond the stone wall entrance, stood a figure.

Lee strained forward, trying to see if it was human or beast, and as she did it moved slowly toward the buildings.

It was a bear.

Kate woke at that instant. Putting her head on the open windowsill as she joined Lee, she saw the movement below, and her great, rolling bark rang out into the night. It thundered across the fields and the gardens and the orchards, echoing to the mountains beyond. Anyone would have been exceedingly brave to face this large dog who guarded High Meadows.

The bear turned and retreated to disappear among the orchard trees. For a moment, for just one defiant moment, he looked back and raised a paw above his head. Lee held the dog back, although she pleaded to be released. By now, Lee knew the strength of that great raised paw, and Kate could be hurt. The security light shone down on the yard, the rain increased in volume, and Lee checked all the outside doors. Then she called Reed Jamison, as she had promised.

The full moon was hidden behind clouds and rain. And the bear had come again.

·18·

Reed did not stay long. When he left, after looking over the grounds and the barn to be sure there was no one or no thing hidden, he knew for sure that the call of the moon and the seasons had more than a little to do with the puzzle. Lee knew Reed would call Hod that next day and consult with him. Reed knew that Lee was about as safe as it was possible to be with Kate, who had developed into a guard dog. Nothing could yet be proven, but the germ of a solution was beginning to formulate in the police chief's mind.

Hod, after hearing Reed later in the day, felt the same way. He, too, was beginning to put the story together.

On the Hill, drinking morning coffee with her brother at Run for Cover, Elvira decided to stay through until the August auction.

Nearly a week passed. The few days of rain after the tour were beneficial for the gardens and the little ponds. Now the late July sun shone hot on Elvira stretched out full length in her deck chair on the terrace of Run for Cover. She was doing a crossword puzzle and stopping occasionally to think of the Hill and its people. It was time to renew old acquaintanceships—she had been delighted to take tea with the Wards and the Pattersons; now she wanted to get to know Cokie. If there was any chance that Cokie might become a member of the family, this was a good time for Elvira to chat with her. If Lee had been the one, Elvira would have felt on more stable ground, but Cokie was an unknown.

It was beginning to be hot. Elvira knew this was a day she would do as little as possible and perhaps not even go off the Hill. She was dressed in a halter and shorts of pale yellow, with her gray-blonde hair twisted atop her head. Her feet were comfortable in leather sandals. Elvira personified the picture of old New England aristocracy in summer garb. Her almost unlined face was the result of years of creams and lotions and the help of one face lift; the faintest hint of eyeliner circled her blue eyes and the delicate cut of her jawbone showed the breeding that Boston and Philadelphia are famous for. Over half a century had passed in Elvira's life, and she had the stamina for another. The women in her family were famous for their long-livedness.

What of the men? she mused.

Malcolm appeared with fresh croissants and coffee on a tray. The doorbell rang and he placed his offering on the stand by Elvira and walked to the door. Cokie, Bunny and Lee appeared; for a second Elvira wondered if they were a committee, but evidently they were on their way to a showing and Bunny was dropping off a folder for Clipper. Offering coffee, Malcolm motioned to more deck chairs, and the three women sat down. He disappeared for more croissants and Elvira passed around the Indian Tree cups stacked on the tray.

"Elvira, Malcolm said you're staying up for the auction. I'm glad." Lee reached for cream to hand to Cokie who was making motions.

"I'm glad too. I'll get to know you better," Cokie joined in, as she pushed back her red hair and spread her croissant with butter and apricot jam. "I like auctions and Clipper's going to let me have the day off for this one."

"Cokie, don't you ever think about your figure?" Bunny sounded cross as she watched Cokie take a second croissant.

"No, I can eat anything. My metabolism takes care of my figure. Good genes too, I guess." Cokie giggled.

Elvira saw her chance. "Where did you move from, Cokie? I didn't meet you last year."

Lee wasn't sure that Cokie would answer all of Elvira's questions. And Cokie didn't. She simply changed the subject. "You're doing a crossword puzzle. I'm learning how to do those. That's for my self-improvement course. What word do you need?"

"Well," said Elvira looking at her paper. "How about a three-letter word for food?"

"Pie?" Cokie frowned.

"Bun?" said Bunny laughing.

"Ort," Malcolm sounded from the doorway where he had been passing in and out with food and coffee during the last several minutes of conversation.

"That's it, 'ort'." Lee agreed.

Elvira nodded. "It fits here nicely. Thanks." She penciled it in and added, "Actually, it means leftover food. But it's right, I needed a 'T' at the end."

"Well, if you ladies are here for the morning, I have work to do in the garden. I'm going to get the paper first, though. Anyone want a ride to town? Cokie?" Malcom seemed a bit fussed by the presence of the four women.

"I'll go with you if you'll drop me off at the office. My car is being repaired again. I seem to have so much trouble with it lately. Aren't you working today, Mal?"

"No, nothing to go in for and tomorrow is my floor day. The last people I showed property to weren't really interested—they were just doing a museum tour—it was a colossal waste of time." Malcolm sighed.

By now they were in Malcolm's car driving toward Paris. Cokie seemed to be thinking. Suddenly she tapped Malcolm on the knee. "You know, Mal, you don't do it right when you show property. You talk too much. You...."

Malcolm almost drove into a ditch. Turning on Cokie, angrier than she had ever seen him, he shouted, "How I run my showings is none of your business. Sure you can sell; you offer yourself as a door prize. I know your type."

Cokie stared. "What's wrong with you? You know better than that. I'd never do that. I was only trying to help. Just let me out right now. I'll walk the rest of the way."

Malcolm backtracked. "I'm sorry, I didn't mean all that. It's just so hot today already and I'm a bit tired and Elvira is here and I'm not used to having her with me. Look, Cokie, I'm really sorry. You know how important you are to me. Forgive me?"

"Sure." Cokie placed her hand over his on the wheel. "I fly off the handle every once in a while myself. Right now is a real stressful time in real estate, we're so busy. How are you and Clipper doing on that Hartley idea?"

"It's kind of bogged down. We want it, but the estate won't come down in price, at least that's what Carriage Trade says. Clipper won't make an offer until we're sure who's coming in with us, and he hates to tie up that much money. So he wants to wait and see if they'll reduce the price by the end of the summer. Lee's making such a stink over new subdivisions and developments that Clipper has two sales tied up over that, and the planning board is looking carefully at anything new. They say Sam Childs was pretty mad when Lee opposed the Old Crossen Farm Stand development. Anyway, to make it short, we're on the fence about the Hartley place. I could use some extra money, myself."

"You?" Cokie looked at him. "I thought you Bandridges had plenty of money. Listen, Malcolm, let's change the subject. We have to start on those costumes pretty soon."

"You're right. Why don't we look over what's in the attic and then we'll see what we can pick up at the flea market on Saturday?" Reaching the office, Malcolm stopped his car and let Cokie out, then, backing out of the driveway, he drove to a small new store on the corner. *Might as well pick up some pastry here for us; it's getting too hot to bake.* He continued on his way, thinking that he'd be glad to have his house back to himself when Elvira left after the auction.

Back on the Hill, Elvira, Lee and Bunny talked of New England traditions and the fact that the Historic House Garden Tour had done so well. Bunny, new to this world, but eager to learn, listened rather than talked. She found in Elvira a great deal of information on the Bandridge's background.

"I was surprised when I found Malcolm had gone into real estate," Elvira said. "I didn't think he liked the public that much. He seemed content just dabbling in antiques and doing little theatre, after he closed the men's store. And then, when he got his license, I was surprised he didn't work with you, Lee."

"I think he feels more development-oriented and we really don't do much of that. We're mostly cottages, antique homes and farms. He doesn't get along well with Meg, either. We might have had a problem turning him down, El, but he'd already decided he'd go with Clipper. So there was no decision to make."

Bunny, who had been listening while she ate the last croissant, entered the conversation. "I think Clipper is pleased. Malcolm lends class to the office."

That's certainly true, thought Lee. *Smart of Clipper to see that facet of Malcolm.*

"Although," Bunny continued, "he doesn't sell very much."

"Why not, do you suppose?" Elvira was interested in finding out about Malcolm's lifestyle here in Maine.

"Well, Clipper says he's too opinionated and if he disagrees with a buyer, he doesn't know when to shut up. That puts them off."

"That would do it." Lee bit her tongue.

"Malcolm always wanted his own way. When he was little, if you didn't do things his way, he would start a fistfight. You never wanted to cross him, Mother used to say. Just try to get along with him. It's good training for life, she would say. She said he took after Great-uncle James." Elvira paused.

"What happened to James?" Bunny was enjoying the family history.

"Well, he couldn't have his own way on a couple of timber deals so he just lay in wait for his two wouldn't-be-buyers and hung them on the very trees they'd looked at. Then he hung himself later on when he was in jail."

"Heavens," gasped Bunny, "it's a good thing people don't do things like that today."

"Oh, but they do," answered Elvira, "only it never happens to people like us."

"And on that note, it's time to leave." Lee rose. "Are you coming with me, Bunny?"

"No, I guess I'll go back to the house. I'll take my own car to town. I have this file for Clipper, but I forgot something. I'll see you both later. Thank you for the coffee, Elvira."

Lee and Elvira carried the tray back to the scullery. "I always loved this little room with the slate sink," said Lee. "All the glass jars of herbs and spices; Malcolm has such a beautiful sense of design and arrangement. This is a lovely old house, El. Do you miss it?"

"Sometimes." Elvira stood quietly. "Sometimes I feel I ought to be here. But most of the time I have a good life. You know, it's strange, I haven't thought about Great-uncle James in years. Now I recall what else Mother said. He was a tree worshiper. A Druid I guess you call it. At least that's what he called himself. He felt he had to protect the forest."

Lee laughed. "I guess I'm that myself, in a way. But I'm not planning on hanging anyone. Although there are times I'd like to, I admit. He sounds a little weird, El."

"I think there's always been a weird streak in the family. Sometimes I worry about Malcolm and myself." Elvira frowned and ran her hands over the edge of the slate.

"I think," said Lee thoughtfully, stacking up cups, "that many of the old families had skeletons. I have an ancestor—I can't remember how far back—an aunt who smoked an opium pipe. It's all in the family history. That doesn't mean our generation are meant to be dope smokers. It's just part of our New England heritage. El, lots of the old families had queer ones. Too many long, cold winters snowbound, too much being alone."

Elvira shivered and shook her shoulders. "I guess you're right. Well, I'm going back to the sunshine. I'll see you on Saturday."

They parted, and Elvira, stretching long and lazily in the sunshine, thought of Lee's words.

Over and over.

Carriage Trade had appointments almost every hour for the rest of the week. July and August are traditionally busy months in real estate. Meg and Lee worked together on the floor and began to wish they had another broker. Dorie did her best with the phone and the mail, but sometimes Lee's day started at seven and ran until eight that night. Ellen's time was divided between Ted and High Meadows. Ted was nearly recovered, but he would not be able to do heavy work. His memory was almost completely gone—the last he could recall was looking at the hayfield, thinking about the daisies and the vetch and his baling twine. After that he drew a blank.

Reed and Hod had talked with him, carefully and gently leading him back to the hayfield, but nothing more surfaced. Whatever had happened was locked in his head, if not forever, at least for the present.

"He may never remember." Ted's doctor spoke with Reed. "Then, someday, something may trigger his memory. But I think there is a minor amount of brain damage. He will be better if he can get outside again. I recommend Ted and Ellen take advantage of Lee's offer."

Ellen had spoken with Lee at the end of Ted's hospital stay. "We have to move from our apartment soon. Ted doesn't want to be in town anymore; he feels too closed in. I'm going to have to find a rent outside, maybe a small mobile home. He can't do much around, no heavy jobs, so I guess our dream of our own place is gone. We were hoping to put a down payment on something this fall, but we can't now. Even with insurance, the hospital cost so much, and Ted won't have the extra jobs he had before."

Lee had listened to Ellen in silence, noting the sadness in her eyes and the despair in her voice. She thought a long while and then approached Ellen on the matter of the old cabin behind the horse paddock.

"It's really not in such bad shape, Ellen; we could go over and see if it could be fixed. We've been storing hay and tools there, but the roof's good; Ted and I looked at it this spring. It would need a whole new bathroom, of course, and we might have to put in a septic, but we could hook into the water from the barn. The apple pickers used to live in that cabin. You remember, it has two big rooms and a fireplace and maybe we could run a woodstove off that chimney. Do you want to walk over and look?"

Ellen's face brightened. "Lee, do you really think it could be fixed?"

"Well, I don't see why not. I've often thought of fixing it up and renting it out. If we can make it livable, you and Ted could be live-in caretakers, sort of; it would make me feel more secure and Ted would have his country place. You'd be all on one floor, which would be easier for both of you. I could get estimates on what it will cost, and then, when you're able to find a better place, I can rent it. How does that sound?"

"Wonderful. Can we go look right now?"

"Right now," Lee responded. "I have time before I go to the office."

With Kate at their heels they walked to the back paddock and the edge of the hardwoods. The path was partly overgrown, hemmed in on both sides by brambles, but it would not be difficult to clear out. The cabin was sheltered by two old basswood trees, their branches bending down as if to protect this small creature of the woods from the woods themselves. Aunt Bess had built the cabin one fall for the apple pickers coming down from Canada—it was a small cabin made from logs from these woods, and on the rear was a small lean-to. The interior, although now used for storage, was still dry, and the floor was of wide pine boards that only needed refinishing.

"It needs a good cleaning, recaulking, the chimney checked and I will have to speak with the planning board about the new bathroom and septic. That window glass is cracked, Ellen, but all in all, I think we can fix it up. You and Ted could be quite cozy here."

"I'm sure of it, Lee; we would be so happy here, but I haven't any extra money to put a bathroom in." Ellen was desperate.

"I'll do that, Ellen. It's my expense to get it in livable shape. Let me call my contractor friends and see if we can get a couple of estimates. I'll do the whole project from start to finish—it's been a good real estate year so far and I have an idea of the cost of this already—I can stand it. With Ted being snug and safe you can help me in the house and feel he's close by—he can still do small farm jobs and somehow it will all work out. I won't charge you rental—we can rearrange wages and time to suit you. How does that sound?"

Ellen hugged her, her eyes spilling over. "Lee, you're the best friend we ever had. We'd die for you."

Lee, returning the hug, thought sadly, *Ted nearly did.*

•19•

Friday morning Lee called the contractors who agreed to look at the small log cabin the next week. She spoke with John Ridley, who told her to bring her plans to the August board meeting, although he saw no problem. At the same time, he informed Lee that the board had two exploratory questions on the Hartley estate—both from developers. Cleaver Real Estate was one.

This weekend would see one of the summer's largest flea markets and Carter phoned to say he would be driving up to High Meadows. "Lee, I'm looking forward to seeing you. How about you making a trip down in September? You're too far away. I don't mind the trip once in a while, but I'm beginning to want to settle down. I feel too old for this commuting arrangement of ours. Propinquity comes into being here—I love you but you know what that word means?"

She answered softly, "I do and I understand. Just a little more time. We can talk this weekend."

Carter sighed. "All right. I have a list of book wants and I'm looking forward to the stalls. Elvira's on the Hill, I hear."

"Yes, she's staying through to the Attlebury auction. That's going along splendidly; all sorts of advertising is out."

"I've seen some," Carter replied. "I hear several museums will send buyers and two of the largest European collectors are planning to attend. I wish I could stay straight through but I'll have to make a second trip for that."

The rest of Friday, Lee showed property. She made a trip to Lake Thompson to show a year-round chalet type of shore-front home that was well over $300,000; five years before it would have been under $100,000. She made a second trip to Harrison to show a brick colonial on four acres with a price of $150,000; five years before it would have been $45,000.

Look what's happened to us, she thought, driving along the new widened highway between long stretches of woodland now invaded by small ranches and cape cods. *Moose lived here just a few short years ago in that large swamp on the left and now they are being hit in ever-increasing numbers as the cars speed along this highway. Canadian geese are making a nuisance of themselves on some of the area lakes, crowded out by civilization from nesting areas further south.* Lee felt helpless. *There is no way to stop this, and most people don't care. In another fifty years we will be a different country.*

By late afternoon the showings were over and she returned to the farm, to find salad and cheesecake in the refrigerator, accompanied by a note from Ellen. Ted was excited about the prospect of moving into the cabin and Ellen's note was signed "Bless you".

Kate had answered the door in a rush and Lee bent over to pat her dark head and give her a hug. Over the summer the Gordon had matured and was developing into a responsible watchdog. Lee felt an inner sense of security when the dog guarded the farm, and together they fed the horses and stood in the barn doorway looking out at the mountains. A faint breeze stirred and Lee pushed back her hair from her damp forehead. "Thank God we're up high, Kate, it's wicked in town." Lee showered, and cooler now in shorts, blue shirt and sneakers, poured herself iced tea and sat down to rest and wait for Carter.

The phone rang, and the voice at the other end, quiet and low, sent a shiver of delight up Lee's spine.

"I'm over at Attlebury's. Thought I might stop up and see you. Reed told me you saw a bear the last night of the tour. Anything else since?" Hod spoke gently, treading carefully with this woman who was beginning to be important in his life.

"No, nothing more. It seemed to be a silent threat if it was a threat. It could have been a real bear. I'm beginning to think maybe I can't tell the difference. I'm going to the flea market tomorrow—Carter is on his way up this evening—he's staying for a few days. Hod, I'm really sorry, I'd like to see you. Why don't you stop by, anyway, right now?"

"No, guess I won't." Hod's voice held just a shadow of disappointment. "Have to get back. There'll be another time. Maybe I'll see you at the flea market. Take care of yourself, Lee. I'll call again, I promise."

"Please. And thank you for thinking of me."

"I do that quite often." There was a hesitation in Hod's tone, a wanting to say more with the decision not to.

Lee felt something slipping through her fingers and that she must not allow this to happen. "Look, I may have to be over in Sumner next week to look at some property. Could I maybe call in and see you?"

"Yep, call me first. I'll have to give you directions. It's a ways back in. I'll show you a real nice piece of timber. I'll look forward to hearing from you."

Lee put the phone down thoughtfully. *Why do I feel so lost? Why did he have to call the very night Carter is due? Why, Kate, at my age when everything should be settled, does it all have to be so confusing?*

Carter was late in arriving, consequently they were late leaving High Meadows on Saturday morning. Lee made breakfast after taking care of the horses; Carter, tired from his drive and fighting a summer cold, slept late. It was nearly eleven when they left the farm, leaving Kate at home. Ellen was due in for part of the afternoon and Reed had called to say he would come by that evening.

The flea-market stalls were overflowing, just as they had been in April, but now even more so when the influx of summer tourists was at its height. At one entrance stall, Lee stopped to look at Indian baskets, admiring a covered Penobscot basket from the turn of the century. Trimmed with green and red, it showed the potato stamping so common to these baskets. Lee was tempted, but she decided to wait to buy until later in the day. Carter, as always, pursued books and fishing tackle.

"Lee, look at this, a brochure on horse blankets from a feed store in Buckfield. Look at the pictures. It's reasonable, too. Only five dollars. I'm going to buy this for a customer who loves anything to do with horses. I'm going to spend a while at this stall; you go ahead, if you want."

Lee nodded and strolled ahead, talking with several of the dealers she knew.

"How's real estate, Mrs. Heaward?" boomed a large overweight man with an elegant green satin waistcoat worn under an old Harris tweed jacket. "Heard you were making quite a fuss over that Old Crossen Farm Stand development. I'm on your side. Sam Childs figures he's going to divide up the whole state of Maine."

Lee smiled. "Well, I appreciate your support, Billy. I just wish it was town meeting time and you fellows would vote with me when I try to get some zoning laws through."

Billy shook his head. "I understand what you're saying, Mrs. Heaward, but ain't nobody gonna tell me what I'm gonna do with my land."

And that, thought Lee, *is the story in a nutshell.*

Across the big floor separating the stalls, Elvira looked at scrapbooks. She had come alone, for Malcolm had an appointment later, and se did not want to have to wait for him. It had not taken her long to walk from one end of the building to the other, rapidly scanning stalls for items she would return to look at later when she had decided exactly what she wanted to spend time and money on. She had an excellent knowledge of antiques, kept an eye on the market, and was a shrewd buyer. But when she was in Maine, especially in the Oxford Hills area, what she hunted was scrapbooks.

It was the Bandridge family history she sought. Notebooks and diaries had always been kept by the old families; the New England winters kept many housebound and they seemed to turn to writing for solace. Family photographs were placed in albums with long inscriptions beneath and Elvira had been fortunate in finding several items relating to Run for Cover over the past few years. Today she leafed through a scrapbook someone had pasted together on the Paris area. It included scenes from some of the old Hill homes.

"Can I help you, lady?" The dealer was one not familiar to Elvira.

"I don't know. I'm looking for scenes from the Hill, or any diaries you might have. Any kind of paper about the Bandridge family. Do you know if you have anything like that?"

"Can't tell; guess you'll just have to go through this box. I haven't been up this way in a long while—first time in some years. Going through on my way to Canada so thought I'd take a stall. Got a lot of stuff out of a house up here years ago; least my father did. So I brought some with me. That's about what's left. That box there has papers."

The man was swarthy, burned by the southern sun, and looked out of place among the New England dealers.

"A house on the Hill sold you some things?" Elvira's quick mind collected any information that came her way.

"Well, to my father. He said it was on a side road, back in the woods. He got a lot of small items out of it and a few chairs and tables. Said it was kind of a queer deal, but he didn't ask questions. It was after dark and they let some things out of a window by a rope. Man said the stairs were blocked."

"Would you know that man?" Elvira almost didn't ask the question.

"Not me—I wasn't there. Just heard Father tell about it, and he's dead now. I'm just making conversation, lady. Father could of made up the story." The man stopped talking, uneasy that he had said too much already.

Elvira, rapidly turning pages in a large book, stopped. "This one, the pictures on this page, could I buy the page? I'm not interested in the remainder of the book. What's your price for this full page?"

"Well," the man hesitated, knowing an opportunity when he saw one. "I hate to break up the book. Never like to sell just one page. Costs more that way, you know. If you've got to have it I ought to charge you fifteen dollars. How does that sound?"

And when Elvira fished a five- and a ten-dollar bill out of her handbag and laid them on the table, he wished he had asked double. She took the page carefully, putting it into another carrying bag she always took with her to shows. "Thank you. I hope you have a good show."

"Me too, lady. Tell you the truth, prices here are higher than where I come from. Guess I'll be back. You have a good day too."

Elvira continued along the line of stalls. To all appearances her mind was on their contents, but actually she was thinking of her purchase. Strange how much Malcolm looked like his father, who had looked exactly like Great-uncle James.

Cokie and Malcolm, carrying a large box overflowing with fabrics and clothing, almost ran into Lee.

"Look what we found—a whole box of velvets and taffeta for costumes. The stall upstairs has all sorts of antique clothing. There are two Persian lamb coats and a raccoon coat; wouldn't I just love that." Cokie was excited.

"Come on, let's get out of here." Malcolm was balancing the box on one knee and trying to urge Cokie on ahead of him. "I have an afternoon appointment, so move, Cokie, will you?"

Cokie tossed her head. "Don't be so bossy." But she moved a bit faster.

They finally reached the car and Malcolm drove rapidly out of the parking lot. In his hurry, he hardly noticed Cokie rummaging through the box.

"Look, a fur hat. And a cape. And there's at least four yards of that green taffeta. Must be from the 1920's or 1930's. That's a terrific buy, Mal; do you suppose the finance committee will reimburse you?"

"They better. They'll only get what we use for costumes—I'm going to keep the rest. That cape was a steal at fifteen dollars."

Cokie agreed. "It looks almost like the same fake fur you

bought a coat of last year, remember? I think we found it at the same stall."

"I don't recall." Malcolm's mind was now on his appointment. It appeared that he was running later than he'd intended.

"Whatever happened to that, Mal?"

"To what?"

"To the coat?" Cokie was becoming a nuisance. "You bought a lot of things that day. I remember now, it was a clean-out from a costume store. It had...." She suddenly dropped her purse and, in the flurry of picking it up and rearranging the contents, she stopped talking.

Malcolm's eyes flickered and narrowed. *Pity. She doesn't know when to stop.*

Clipper, holding down the office alone, was waiting impatiently for Malcolm, whose customers had arrived early. They were eager to look at the old Lyman house in Waterford. Malcolm had brought in the listing for he knew the owners from previous antiques purchases. The two old people, lonesome and rather isolated, had welcomed Malcolm into their lives, so when it was finally time to sell their house they put their trust completely in his hands. The property was an old colonial with a fairly large acreage, so the listing had been a plum for Cleaver Real Estate. The only reservation was that Malcolm had to be at every showing, so Clipper, even if Malcolm did not show up, could not go by himself to show the property.

"Why don't you sit down and have some coffee and take a look through this listing book? I know Malcolm will be along directly. He's probably been held up in summer traffic." Clipper was a master at soothing people.

"I'm coffeed-out, had it everyplace this morning. I hate to wait," Mr. Johnson boomed. "Mother might have a cup, though.

Want a cup, Mother?"

"No, and don't call me Mother." Mrs. Johnson was definitely not in the spirit for looking at houses, let alone for a salesman who seemed late. Clipper, feeling the ice in the atmosphere, pointed out gently to Mr. Johnson that his appointment had been for one o'clock and that it was only a quarter-to.

"Always be early, that's my motto," the voice boomed twice as loud, and Mrs. Johnson put one hand up to her ear. "How do you think I got to where I am today? Certainly didn't do it by being late. No sir, on time, ahead of time, that's what I say. So where the hell is that salesman? Why do we have to wait for him, anyway?"

"Why do we have to see the house, anyway?" asked Mrs. Johnson. "I told you I'm not going to live out in the woods on any broken-down old farm. So what's the sense of even looking?"

Ah, thought Clipper. *Shades of Bunny.*

"Well, I might." Mr. Johnson was irritated. "And if you're figuring on using your charge cards I suggest you better live with me. You can spend half the year in Boston and half in Maine. I always wanted a little farm to fix up. And I'm going to have it."

"Are you sure you don't want some coffee, Mrs. Johnson?" Clipper tried valiantly. The whole conversation was getting out of hand.

Mrs. Johnson looked him straight in the eye. "God damn it, I said no. Can't you hear?"

"Now, now, Nell. The man's only trying to help us. Look, I'll take some coffee. But if he isn't here by the time I finish my cup, it's goodby Charlie. And we're off up the street to another broker."

Clipper drew a breath, swore silently at Malcolm, handed coffee to Mr. Johnson, looked in the direction of Mrs. Johnson and hastily looked away as she fixed him with her stern eyes.

"Here he is. Malcolm, we're glad you made it. Car trouble? The

Johnsons are anxious." A reprieve at last.

Malcolm was breathing heavily; taking Cokie home and getting back through the traffic had been enough to start up his ulcer. He hadn't taken time out for lunch and it was evident the Johnsons were in a hurry to start. All in all, it was a bad beginning.

He was right. The whole showing was a disaster from the word go. Mr. Johnson liked the house but said it was worth only half the price. Mrs. Johnson disliked it, refused to even look at the upstairs, said it wasn't worth even one third of the price, and marched back to Malcolm's car and retired to the back seat.

"I'll wait." With that she dismissed the property.

"But, Mother, it's just what I want. I can fool with it, fix it up. It'll give me something to do on my vacation time and you know I can't sit around doing nothing. Just exactly what I want. I'll offer you half of what you're asking, Mr. Bandridge. And it'll be cash. No bank to go through or wait for. Cash on the barrel head." Mr. Johnson beamed.

"I doubt they'll take that offer. I wouldn't advise them to." Malcolm frowned. He had a good buyer but not a good offer. *First duty to my seller, but I don't want to lose this sale.* "Look, Mr. Johnson, it's really worth what we are asking. If it was all fixed up it would be worth much more. There's a big market for this type of property. Now, I can show you some others, but this seems to be just what you want. Why don't you think it over and go higher in your bid?"

Mr. Johnson snorted. "Have you asked them? How do you know they won't take it? I demand you ask them. I say we go right back to the office and I'll sign an offer and put some money down—cash money. You hear me, boy, you can just phone them right up. I bet they'll take it. Been on the market a while, hasn't it? Let's go."

Malcolm was furious. For just one moment he felt like

swinging at Mr. Johnson, but looking past him to the car, he saw the evil eye of Mrs. Johnson shining on both of them. It was evident she wasn't going along with this and perhaps they could be allies. So, stifling his impulse to flatten Mr. Johnson, he locked the house, opened the car door, and drove back to Clipper's office.

Whereupon Mrs. Johnson simply switched to her own car and refused to go inside the real estate office.

Clipper, still at his desk, just hanging up the phone, smelled trouble the minute it walked in the door. "Back already, are we?" he sang out cheerfully.

"I'm here to sign an offer. This man doesn't seem to understand business, maybe you do. This is your office, isn't it? The sign outside says 'we work hard', doesn't it? Well, work hard. Sit right down there and write up an offer. What's the price, seventy thousand? Well, I'll offer thirty-five thousand cash and let's see what they say. Get the contract made up. I'll sign right now. Put ten thousand down right this minute. I've bought property before, you know. Money talks."

Clipper had seen plenty of Mr. Johnsons. Action was needed, directly. The only way to convince this man that he wasn't going to get the Lyman place at his price was to write out the contract. Lyman would reject it and they'd get on to the next plateau. Besides, the law was specific. He had no choice but to write the offer.

So Clipper made no attempt to negotiate further. He simply turned to Malcolm, saying, "Sit right down, Mal, and write it up."

Clipper had forgotten something. In fact, he'd forgotten two things. One was that Malcolm hadn't been too long in real estate. The Mr. Johnsons he had dealt with were few, if any. And the second thing was that Malcolm didn't like to be bossed.

Malcolm walked out. "Do it yourself!" he exploded, and left.

"Well!" Mr. Johnson was amazed. "If he worked for me I'd be rid of him before I hired him."

Clipper shrugged, allowing himself to show neither anger nor suprise. "I don't think he feels well today. Come on over and sit down, Mr. Johnson. I'll have this done in a jiffy." Folksy Clipper could smooth many a ruffled feather.

So it was written. The next day the Lymans signed it, accepting the offer, and Mr. Johnson had made a purchase. Clipper had accomplished the unbelievable once-in-a-hundred sale and Malcolm was finished with Cleaver Real Estate.

• 20 •

August arrived. Carter was back in Connecticut, Malcolm had retreated to his beloved garden, Elvira spent long hours sunning and thinking, and Lee made plans on this Monday morning to drive to Sumner.

An Auburn bank was selling a country home for an estate; the house had been appraised and Carriage Trade asked to handle the sale. The morning's mail produced keys and Lee and Meg were eager to get this listing on the market. Known as a "fixer-upper", it was bound to sell quickly.

Lee called Hod early on. "I should be finished by one o'clock; may I stop by then? You'll have to give me directions." Hod obliged, telling her where he lived, off route 117. "Not bad coming in this time of year, but mud season or snow you'd need a four-wheel drive. You won't have any trouble today. Can I make you a simple lunch?"

"Thanks. I might not be right on the dot. But I'll be as close to one as possible. Can I bring anything?" She felt a warmth beginning to close about her. *Now, where will this go, I wonder?*

"Nope, you put up with my cooking. Be glad to see you and hear what's new." Hod rang off.

Lee had on cords and a simple pink shirt. The day promised a late breeze, so she packed an extra sweater and scarf along with the Bean boots already in the car. She started the day in her usual low moccasins, but the boots prepared her for any type of terrain. Next to a briefcase, no Maine broker ever left home without his boots. The house she would inspect had a small brook, and Hod's land ran to the Nezinscot river.

Lee had always liked this area. Somehow, it seemed a little less polished than the western part of Oxford County and a little more the way Maine had been at the turn of the century. There were long sweeps of woodland with no buildings, old colonials and capes in need of repair in the small towns, cornfields and hayfields along the banks of the little streams and the river. Shacks and trailers and what could be called hovels, and everywhere the signatures of the countryside—well tended gardens and whirligigs, homemade, atop every fence or woodpile.

She finished her business by one o'clock and found the turnoff to Hod's road within another ten minutes. He was right, it would certainly take a four-wheel drive to negotiate this road part of the year. Even now it was bumpy. Soon it widened, opening into a large area of grassland with a small cabin set on a hillside above one of the smaller branches of the Nezinscot. Large old maples sheltered the small log structure, built on the site of an early cape lost to fire. The front of the cabin had two large windows affording a view to the river, and attached to the rear of the cabin was a long low building evidently used as a garage and workshop. What surprised Lee was not the cabin or the workshop or the setting under the sheltering trees, but the lawn stretching down to the river. It was not mown; in fact at first glance it seemed rather to be a hayfield.

But then you saw the wildflowers.

Every wildflower Lee knew the name of, and some others besides; it was an explosion of color. Late daisies and vetch, black-eyed Susans, hawkweed, poppies, meadow lilies, wild roses, a tangle of Queen Anne's lace; they were all there. Pink and white yarrow and blue cornflowers and others Lee could not identify. One great wildflower garden let grow by a man whose heart lay in the out-of-doors.

Now I know. Now I know what really is inside this man. Kin in another world, brother, friend? Maybe, just maybe, lover.

The next hour brought another surprise. Hod produced a lunch served on wooden plates—sliced chicken on a bed of frilled red ruby lettuce, tomatoes, cucumbers from his garden, a pot of herbed butter and a small round loaf of homemade rye bread speckled with caraway seeds from his own plants. Ending with a blueberry tart and strong, hot coffee.

And quiet, serious talk from a man who had learned by winter's reading to do the things he could do. Which was just about everything.

Hod was proud of what he had created and delighted to show it to Lee. The great room in the front of the cabin with its huge fireplace, the small bedroom in the rear, the kitchen with its old-fashioned woodstove and long table, the top bleached almost white from scrubbing. Bookshelves were filled to overflowing in all of the rooms and braided rugs were islands of color on the wide pine floors. Only the bedroom had curtains, the small bathroom had a shower, and the whole cabin had a cleanliness totally unexpected from a man living alone in a remote, wooded area. On the low table in the living area, in front of an old leather couch pulled by the fireplace, a majolica pitcher with a deer on one side and a hound on the other was filled with early asters.

"Jersey pottery," Lee breathed. "I've only seen one other like it."

"Studied about early pottery all one winter. I bought it at a tag sale." Hod smiled. "I guess I kind of liked the deer."

At the end of the meal they carried their coffee out to a bench on the small front porch of the cabin. Lee smiled, remembering. "Your quiet bench?"

He nodded. "I sit here and think quite a bit." He paused. "Lee, I want to talk a minute and I want to get it all out while I have the courage. Two things. First off, Reed and I have been working on some theories. Can't say it's all together yet, but I think there's a pattern to your puzzle. We need another few pieces but I think we may have the answer soon. Meanwhile, I want you to promise me to be even more careful than you've been. Reed says Ted and Ellen are going to use your old cabin when you get it fixed. That's a great idea, the best yet. You'll have someone close by. Be patient and cautious and I think we'll find that bear yet."

Lee sat facing him, listening and nodding. "I'm grateful. I have been careful." She felt her voice hesitate. "You know, you are beginning to be important to me."

Hod leaned forward, touching her hands, looking down at her tanned skin and matching his own weathered hands against hers. "That brings me to the second thing. You're important to me, too, Lee. I don't know just how it would work out, the two of us trying to fit our lives together. But I wish you'd think on it because I think we might be able to do it."

"Are you proposing?" Lee held her breath.

"In a way. Guess I am." And when Lee started to speak, he put a finger across her lips. "No, don't answer yet. Give it a lot of thought. Like where would we live—High Meadows or here?

How do you feel about me, a man who's spent most of his life in the woods? I don't know if I'm quite up to garden club standards. I forgot one thing, guess I should have said it in the very beginning. I love you, Lee Heaward. Very much."

Lee, holding his face between her hands, kissed him gently. "And I think I do you. I have some things to sort out. Carter is one of them. Can you be a little patient?"

"Seems like I've been patient for twenty years so a little longer won't matter. Just kinda wanted you to know what was in my mind. You take your time and pretty soon we'll both see the pathway. Woods open up sometimes when you least expect it."

For a moment they sat facing each other, then Lee rose saying, "I have to go. I want to stay, Hod, but this isn't the right moment."

Hod nodded. "Imagine us saying that at nineteen? Look, I'll call soon. Don't fret now, if it's meant to be it will be."

Drinking her coffee in front of the High Meadows fireplace that evening, Lee thought of Hod and his offer. She patted Kate's head absently and fantasized on how it might be married to Hod Cole. *Life,* she thought, *is like going around corners never seeing ahead.*

The next week, before the auction, contractors started on Ellen and Ted's cabin. Lee spent time overseeing plans and Ted came out to look at the chimney and see how long it would take to clear out the path and the small yard. He spent two days lugging brush and was happier than he had been since leaving the hospital. His strength was beginning to return and he came back into the main house often to talk with Ellen about their new home. On Wednesday morning, about the time he began to think of a cup of coffee and one of Ellen's cookies, he walked up the brick path to find Lee sitting at the kitchen table talking with Malcolm

Bandridge.

"Ted, how are you doing? Good to see you up to your old self again. I hear you and Ellen are going to live in the old cabin." Malcolm shook hands with him. He had sent cards when Ted was in the hospital and gone twice to visit when it was allowed. He had always liked Ted and enjoyed talking with him about the old ways of fencing and stonecutting.

"I'm feeling real good. Can't remember anything, but guess it don't matter. Doctor says I'll be good as new in another few months. I'm glad we're going to be up here on the farm, though. Seems like some good came out of the bad." Ted accepted a cup of coffee from Ellen and joined Malcolm and Lee at the table.

"You don't remember a thing?" Malcolm shook his head. "It must have been quite a blow."

"I sure had a headache for weeks, I know that. Sometimes I still do. No, don't remember anything after looking at the hayfield and thinking about the vetch. Don't knows I really want to, neither." Ted helped himself to more cookies and looked at Lee. "It's coming along good out there. Maybe you want to walk out later with Ellen and take a look?"

Lee agreed. "Later. I have to finish talking with Malcolm first and then we'll come out." She rose and with Malcolm following, disappeared into the living room. They had been halfway through a serious discussion when Ted had entered, but she had not wanted to discourage his conversation as he was progressing so well. In fact, she had been glad for a respite from her talk with Malcolm.

For Malcolm Bandridge had come on an errand most unlike his usual self. His fiasco at Cleaver Real Estate with the Johnsons had left him a little shaken. He hadn't really thought Clipper would fire him; it had been his experience that people put up with his explosions, and he had thought Clipper would be on his side.

Now, he had come to approach Lee about working for Carriage Trade.

And Lee did not want him. She had not yet said so, but they both knew the moment Malcolm broached the subject, that she was cool to the idea. Months before, when Malcolm had first been licensed, she and Meg had agreed they were glad he'd decided to go with Clipper rather than ask them.

"It saves our having to tell him we'd rather not have him," Meg had said at the time. Lee agreed totally. As good a friend as Mal had been, she knew his business deficiencies and knew that he would only bring trouble to the good reputation they worked so hard to maintain. Malcolm had great class and a good appearance, but he had, as Meg said, a wicked bad temper. They were well out of it.

Diplomacy is needed here, thought Lee, as she tried to see how she was going to tell Malcolm "no" in words of careful content.

"Mal, if I were you I'd go back and see if I could make it up with Clipper. You've brought some good listings in to him and he will recognize that fact. And you know both you and Clipper like the development game. We don't specialize in that at Carriage Trade, and maybe you wouldn't be happy with us. Clipper has your kind of market. I'd really try to make it up before I switched to another company. You're valuable to him and he probably felt forced to do what he did, especially with that Mr. Johnson."

And Malcolm, driving away from High Meadows, went straight to see Clipper and did exactly what Lee had suggested. Clipper, having also thought it over, was predictable. He shook hands with Malcolm and they were in business again.

"Mrs. Johnson," he informed Malcolm, "still won't go any further than the first floor. So there's a good chance this sale will blow up, and the Lymans won't keep the listing without you. I'm real glad to see you, Mal."

Elvira, staying up for the Saturday auction, had spent long hours thinking in the garden. She had wandered behind the latticed fence; sat on the four seasons iron bench with its green and white striped cushions and poked about in the small building that had been her mother's old toolshed. Last Christmas she had given Malcolm a rather special gift, a trio of garden tools from Smith and Hawken, a small English hand fork, trowel and curved scratcher. She had searched for them the past week to help her in weeding, but found only two of the three. She had asked Malcolm who said he was sure it was there somewhere, but even though they both looked, they could not find the small tool that Elvira called a scratcher. Today, stretched out in the sun, Elvira had closed the book she was reading, and her thoughts were again a mixture of past and present.

What would mother have done?

For in the short time that Elvira had spent on the Hill this summer, she had gleaned a lot of information. Lee had told her about all the events since February. Her own observation of the attic and a few missing objects at Run for Cover, plus her talk with the dealer at the flea market, had shown her a few things about Malcolm that she had long suspected but still could not prove. The garden of the Manse with the statue of Diana and Malcolm's worship—if it was worship—there at night told Elvira even more. In one column of her mind were the suspicions—in the other the clues. The balance was beginning to weigh heavily on one side and it was not in Malcolm's favor.

What would Mother have done? Elvira knew. She would wait and see—maybe time would solve the problem. That is exactly what Elvira Bandridge Campbell, a woman of the world, decided to do. She would wait and see.

Later she wished she had made another choice. But, by then, it was too late.

• 21 •

As usual, George Morrill had done it up with class. For a month preceding the auction a guard lived in the Attleburys' back yard in a camper trailer. He checked in and out with them during the daytime hours, and even Mrs. Attlebury, who feared little, admitted it was nice to see the light in the camper window at night. Generally, a guard was only used in an unoccupied house with contents, and at that only for a few days prior to the auction, but from the moment the ads started to appear in the *Newtown Bee* and the *Antique Digest,* people began to estimate the value of the Stubbs. The driveway into the Attlebury property had to be roped off to keep the curious from entering before the auction, and Ted had set up a second roadblock further up the driveway to discourage anyone wanting to walk around the rope.

Lee stopped by daily; Ted stopped by on his way back to town from High Meadows. He and Ellen were not yet in the cabin; he drove their pickup slowly and sedately back and forth to Paris. He still had difficulty lifting and still could not recall exactly what had happened, but he was able to do small jobs around the farm.

Mrs. Attlebury, who disliked fuss of any kind, did not want to be watched over, but she allowed it was a necessary evil to be tolerated. Dr. Attlebury showed more signs of forgetfulness and so Belle was resigned to this new regime until the day of the auction. Sharing sherry one evening, with Dr. Attlebury safe in his bed reading his beloved Wilkie Collins, Lee and Mrs. Attlebury walked about in the small herb garden.

"Monkshood—it is past bloom now, but such a beautiful large stand." Mrs. Attlebury touched it affectionately as though she knew each splendid, caeruleus cap. "I should divide this clump. The foxgloves were especially nice this year, Lee. I'm glad I didn't let the historic garden tour use my herb garden. It's going to be a mess enough around here with the auction. Do you want some of these plants when I divide them?"

"Yes. The blue monkshood will fit nicely with my white babies'-breath and feverfew. I've always loved foxgloves and my old strain seems to be running out." Lee stopped for a moment, then continued, "Mrs. Attlebury, if you were thinking of poison, wouldn't you choose either foxglove or monkshood instead of valerian?"

"Definitely. You know, they say poison is a woman's way. Fire seems to be a man's. Could there be two people trying to harm you? Reed and I talked about that—I like that young man, Lee, he is a thinker. I'm too old not to know there are plenty of evil people in the world, but they usually follow a pattern. I wonder, are you just being threatened and not meant to actually be harmed? Everything seems to be a near miss."

"Not the wire across the path. If Musette had run into it she would have been cut deeply in the chest. That was evil, Belle. I know what you mean about two minds, though. A man and a woman? A man or a woman? A hermaphrodite?"

Mrs. Attlebury rose, retreated into the kitchen and returned with cheese, crackers and more sherry.

"Lee, I'm almost eighty years old—that does seem a bit along, doesn't it? Inside I don't feel much older than forty-five. Age is a state of mind and I don't see much difference in these past thirty years except I move a bit slower. But I've learned one thing—most people are good. However, there are evil ones. I don't mean the right out Mafia types; you know they are evil. I mean the everyday variety, pick-a-little-here, pick-a-little-there types. The ones who never got over being the children you avoided because they always pulled the wings off butterflies and stuck pins in cats. They grew up to be the same way, only now they do things in more insidious ways. They agitate and they make phone calls at night and they slash tires and are generally nasty. They don't think they can get caught out at it. They don't really intend to kill you—just to make your life miserable. So they just threaten, and have someone else do their dirty work, if it has to be done. I wonder if this could be what's happening? I wonder if someone just dislikes you enough so that being nasty satisfies his own ego?" Mrs. Attlebury paused, slowly sipping her sherry.

Lee agreed. "I've thought so, Belle; I started to believe all that some time ago. And I've tried to think who I've really offended. Half of the area's developers, at least."

"How about someone personally?"

"Mostly real estate people." Lee was thoughtful.

"Hum, well, I don't feel it's over."

"Nor do I." Lee rose. "I should go now; Carter comes tonight and I'm off from the office for three days. I'll help you tomorrow. When is George coming?"

Belle Attlebury smiled. "That man loves cookies. He should be here early in the morning, he said, to get the tent up and the signs out and start emptying the box room. Rom has been a blessing, Lee, and I've quite come to like him."

Rom appeared at that instant, a big man at least six feet tall, heavyset, swarthy, and with his one large gold earring, looking like a gypsy. He refused sherry but accepted cheese and crackers. One of his eyes was half closed from a childhood injury and both ears were mangled as he had once been a fighter of sorts, but he had come to rest helping out at auctions and doing guard duty for George at unoccupied houses. Rom had taken the Attleburys under his wing at first introduction and he walked with the doctor up and down the woods roads, sat quietly with him during his naps in the sun, and cared gently for the old man. He filled the woodbox for Mrs. Attlebury, helped her hang out her few bits of washing, and made himself close in spirit to the elderly couple. The teddy bear in Rom was close to the surface.

Today, he reassured Lee with his presence and he waved goodby to her as she left for the farm.

The next two days were frantic. Tents up, chairs arranged with reserved-seat tags, signs posted for car-parking directions, necessaries situated discreetly behind clumps of trees, the auction was beginning to fall into its structured pattern. The preview showing would be Friday afternoon and evening and the sale itself on Saturday at ten. Every motel and hotel and bed and breakfast for miles around was sold out to auction-goers, private collectors, dealers acting as agents for private collectors, museum representatives, the curious and those who simply loved to attend an auction. Anytime, anywhere.

For all these people, rich and not-so-rich, wanted to see the George W. Stubbs paintings.

Saturday morning dawned clear and crisp, a beautiful August day with just the hint of a faint breeze. For almost two miles, the length of

Minister's Road, cars were parked bumper to bumper, and the lower end of the Daniels Meadow, used for additional parking space, was filled by nine o'clock. At the end of the meadow nearest to the house stood two tents, green- and white-striped, with flags flying atop like banners over medieval battlements. The smaller tent would hold the purchased items; the larger tent held chairs and two tables to one side in front for the bookkeepers. At one end of the larger tent, and ranged around the sides, were the items to be sold. And at the front, protected by railings and lit by soft lights, were the two paintings. The old gold frames surrounded the great horses, the backgrounds, the riders, the hounds and the houses. For this moment in time nearly two thousand people saw something they might never see again. From the interior of this modest little Cape Cod on a dirt lane in Maine came the dream of a lady who had toured Europe and England in the late 1800's. The lights shone on the oils, giving them a serenity and beauty that touched the onlookers.

George W. Stubbs had painted his subjects well.

Carter and Lee walked over early from High Meadows. Ellen was taking care of Kate and the farm; Ted had arrived at the Attleburys' early to help with parking. Clipper and Bunny and Cokie and Malcolm arrived an hour before starting time to look about and choose chairs near Lee and Carter. Reed waved to Lee as she arrived; he was overseeing the parking lot and the roadway in. There was little time for small talk. Carter and Lee, having spoken to George and the crew, moved further up the road to the Attlebury house. The doctor and Belle were sitting on a bench near the herb garden.

"Mrs. Attlebury, do you want to come down? I've saved a seat for you."

"No." Belle hesitated. "Only when the paintings go up. You keep track of everything else for me, Lee. I'll only stay to see the paintings sold. I'm not up to all that excitement today."

"All right; one of the crew will be here with you all day. Either

Carter or I will come up to get you about fifteen minutes before the Stubbs come up at eleven."

Belle nodded. "I'll be ready."

Near the striped tents, under two large old oaks on the edge of the meadow, stood the Historic House Garden Tour committee tent, with a sign in large letters attesting to its occupants. A long table groaned under pies, cakes, brownies, cookies, sandwiches, all sorts of elegant foods that were the specialties of many of the Hill's hostesses. Lobster rolls and small quiches were kept fresh in a small refrigerator connected to a generator which also fed the wires leading to the coffeepots. Mrs. Bemis was wrestling with a large pot of water for tea. The ladies had done things up properly; flags flew atop their tent and large flowered sheets covered little tables. Jugs of flowers were spaced on a few tables arranged for seating, although no one was going to spend much time away from the bidding. Trash cans hid in corners, and the two necessaries were well protected by bushes. George had even used two fancy antique signs reading "Ladies" and "Gents" to mark their paths.

Everything had been properly thought out for this, the auction of auctions.

Lee and Carter found Elvira at the food booth, balancing a cup of coffee and a roll. "I don't know if Malcolm saved you a seat, El." Lee grasped a napkin sliding from Elvira's hand.

"It doesn't matter; I brought my own folding chair. I never like those stiff auction ones and I like to sit in the sun rather than under the tent. I always bring my own chair and pillow. Have you seen anything you'd like to have, Lee?" Elvira's eyes were focused on the approaching forms of Cokie and Malcolm.

"Oh, everything, but I'm not buying. My pennies are going into fixing the cabin this summer. But, oh, El, what I wouldn't give to own a Stubbs."

Carter agreed. "Wait until you see what someone does give. I'm betting it will bring seven figures."

Malcolm fetched Cokie coffee and a biscuit roll, saying, "Have a little ort."

Amply supplied with food, they all returned to their seats. Cokie, next to Lee, quietly sipped coffee.

"What a lovely necklace, Cokie." Lee admired the sapphire necklace.

"I bought it in Spain. You know sapphires are supposed to bring protection. They are also supposed to have an elevating effect and guard their wearer. It's my birthstone, too."

"Where did you learn all that?" Lee was surprised at Cokie's choice of words.

"My self-improvement course. Malcolm said it would be a good study course for me to take. I'm learning a lot."

Lee was surprised again; the relationship between Malcolm and Cokie might be deeper than she'd thought. They were together often, eating lunch at Mariah's, sharing little theatre sessions, attending flea markets.

Well, it's good for Malcolm to have someone; no one should be so totally alone as Malcolm had seemed at times during the past year.

It was nearly ten; the last buyers were taking numbers and the seats were filled. Around the fringes of the selling tent people arranged their own chairs, groups of dealers gathered for action and there was a general low hum in the air. The first ten rows of chairs had been reserved for the famous; the locals crowded in behind to look and exclaim over the offerings. This was not the type of auction that would elicit asides such as "Mother had one just like that" from the viewers. All articles were pure and genuine, authenticated by experts and known to have come from the Attleburys. A buy was a sure buy and, for most people, this was a serious auction.

One thing was sure. There had never been a George W. Stubbs

sold in Maine.

So it began with one of the smalls that had so delighted George when he'd first viewed the contents of the box room. So it continued for one hour. The prices were good, there were no bargains, and everyone sat on the edge of his chair waiting for eleven o'clock.

At quarter to eleven Carter brought Mrs. Attlebury to her chair by Lee's side.

At eleven George acknowledged Belle Attlebury's presence in the crowd, gave a quick history of her family, the pictures and their discovery.

And then he sold the Stubbs.

The larger one sold first—the landscape with the horses—and after a gasp at the initial bid the crowd was hushed. Three bidders—two museums and a private collector—emerged. It did not take long. The horses, the beautiful horses, went for a price above what Lee had thought possible. The bidder, a museum, bought the picture at a seven-figure price.

The second picture went for just a little under the first. This time the private collector won, and he announced, through George, that he would put his prize on loan to a museum.

Then, slowly at first, but swelling in intensity, came the clapping and cheering of the crowd as, in a body, they rose.

Mrs. Attlebury squeezed Lee's hand tightly and whispered, "I'm glad they will be where everyone can enjoy them." And Lee felt tears welling in her own eyes.

Within the span of a very few minutes, Belle Attlebury had arranged for Frederick's care, for the remainder of her own life, and unknown even to Lee, for the fate of the Hartley property.

The auction stretched on all day. Furniture and rugs and vases, Sevres and Haviland, Worcester and Adams, English Chippendale, Irish pine, landscapes, watercolors, oils, silver, Wedgwood; Mrs. Attlebury's grandmother had an eclectic eye.

A very tired George and crew, a very tired police force and guard trio, a very tired Lee and Carter drew long breaths when it was over. The buyers of the Stubbs had wrapped their treasures securely and driven off in their vans almost as soon as they'd made the purchases. Now, only the box lot hangers-on remained, only those looking for the bargains of the last half hour, and there were no bargains. Finally, it was finished, and George had been correct. The auction and the sale of the Stubbs would be talked about in Maine for years to come.

Ellen had taken supper over to the Attleburys. Lee and Carter talked with them for a while and George, although tired to the bone, sat on the herb garden bench with Belle, and told her that the check and the accounting would be in her hands within a few days. The figure he mentioned as a quick estimate was larger than Lee had dreamed, but Mrs. Attlebury, a lady to the end, never gave even a flicker of an eyelid when she heard it. One didn't mention money in everyday conversation!

Together, Lee and Carter walked back to High Meadows. "It's been a long day." Carter spoke as they strolled through dusk and up the road. Lee agreed. "Somehow, I feel as though someone died. I'm glad for the Attleburys, but I have this great sadness, and I don't know why."

"It's autumn," he reflected. "There's a coolness in the air. Maybe that's it. Or maybe it's us. We know our affair is coming to an end."

Lee, looking up at him, pressed his hand. "You always know my innermost feelings, don't you? I'm so sorry, Carter. I wanted it to be. But the thought of living in Connecticut just isn't right for me. And I know you don't want to leave Salisbury. We're like two old friends, and we've been all the way round the circle of friends and lovers and now we're back to friends again. We are, aren't we?"

"Yes," he agreed ruefully. "Even though we didn't want it to turn out this way. Love is like some seasons—it starts out hot and passionate and cools off along the way. I should go back tomorrow. I wanted to ask you if you'd consider a September wedding. I came up especially to ask you. Now I know marriage isn't right for us. But friends are friends forever, right?"

They stopped under the big maple at the edge of High Meadows lawn and hugged fiercely.

Finally Lee, close to tears for the second time that day, broke the spell gently and spoke. "I won't forget you."

"Nor I, you. But we had our time. Just be grateful it happened and we part friends. Be careful here, alone, Lee. I want to talk with Reed before I leave tomorrow."

In the morning Reed and George came by, to drink coffee and discuss auction prices. There was much still to be done at the Attleburys'—tents to be taken down, lawn to be raked up and the meadows cleared of debris. George had promised it would be pristine when they were finished.

Lee said goodby to Carter with sadness. She dressed for work and stopped at the Attleburys' to find Belle pulling a pan of gingerbread from the oven of the old iron kitchen stove. "George does like this," she smiled; "I'm going to miss him, Lee."

A deep feeling had sprung up between them—the old lady and the seasoned auctioneer. Lee, listening to Mrs. Attlebury, thought, *A lot of changes took place yesterday. More than I realized.*

Something else had taken place that she was not aware of. Cokie, seated at the auction, spending part of the day watching prices and talking with Malcolm and Bunny, had suddenly solved a mystery that had been bothering her.

Without a doubt, Cokie suddenly sensed who was pretending to be a bear.

Being Cokie, she acted on her knowledge. After all, she'd done this before; the word blackmail was not new to Cokie's vocabulary. She had come to Paris with a past history of opportunity funding a fat bank account. The possibility was here again; Cokie had only to act. She did. She made a phone call the morning after the auction.

And received an invitation to a picnic.

·22·

Cokie walked fast along the woods road through the Hartley property. Her goal was the quarries and she had changed from her usual high heels into tennis shoes. Her skirt was shorter than the one she usually wore, and she carried a long silk scarf and a straw purse. Today could make a great difference in her life. Cokie was an opportunist, and the gradual suspicions that had piled up in her mind for the past two weeks had finally triggered an answer. She was sure she understood the mystery.

Cokie had never been afraid of anything or anyone, for as fragile as she seemed, she was adept at taking care of herself. She held a black belt in karate, a fact she had never felt it necessary to tell the town of Paris. Her parents had been actors of a sort and Cokie had learned several magic tricks when she was a child. Cokie, if the truth were known, could be a formidable opponent.

Today, she felt, would be a piece of cake.

A picnic and a talk had been suggested, and Cokie knew that they both knew what the talk would concern. If she played her cards right she would be several hundred dollars—maybe thousands richer—after today. She might have an income for several years. She certainly could use a new car. The word "blackmail" was not new to Cokie Adams.

She climbed steadily upward. Wild asters were coming into bloom along the path, where sunshine filtered through the trees. Rabbit-foot clover grew in sandy stretches, and here and there wild clematis twined over bushes and low shrubs. Cokie, unlike Lee, knew none of the names and backgrounds of the wild plants. She knew the blooms were attractive to her eye, but as to their names she was untutored. Asters were the only flowers she could recognize.

She resolved that this could be one of the things she might study after she finished her present self-improvement course. She had begun to learn the herbs and this had certainly given her an insight into what had happened when Lee and Mrs. Bemis had drunk the Shooting Sherry. Little by little Cokie had been piecing clues together, and after the last flea market and the Attlebury auction, she had suddenly come upon what she was sure was the answer. It had surprised her, but it was a piece of luck for how she handled this could affect her whole future.

To what extent, Cokie could not imagine.

She was nearly at the top; the road veered to the left and the two quarries, the remains of the old Standard mines, were off to the left-hand side. One was a small pool covered with algae; the other was a deep pit, for these had been open pit mines in the late 1800's—quartz, feldspar, mica, and, if one was lucky, tourmaline, the signature gem of Maine. Flakes of mica covered the ground in spots, outcroppings of granite were covered with moss and, at the very top, Cokie could look down into the larger pit with its pool of emerald-green water and garnish of cattails. The water could only be reached by a narrow winding pathway, and she walked carefully downward, watching the flash of golden carp, lit by the sunbeams striking the surface of the water. Some of the carp were huge. They wintered-over well, multiplying rapidly since the year they had been placed in the quarries by a trio of small boys emptying their mother's goldfish bowl. A hundred or more of the large ones had lived for years and Cokie, bending low, scanned the water and gasped as a school of fish shot directly under her gaze.

She had put her time at noon. It was now about quarter to twelve and Cokie retraced her steps upward to the rim of the quarry, flopped down and shook out her tennis shoes. Wood grime and sand fell out. She pushed her long hair back from her forehead and wound the scarf about her head to keep the hair out of her eyes. Dragonflies filled the air, sailing high above the surface of the water, dipping low to recklessly skim the surface, green and blue in their pale iridescence. The stillness of the woods encircled the woman and the water and had you stood to one side at that moment you might have imagined you were looking at the great canvas of a French impressionist.

Cokie sat quietly, thinking of the turns the conversation might take, knowing that subtlety was of great importance. She also knew she had done this sort of thing in the past and that she could certainly do it as well again. She smiled, thinking of her advantage and of the rewards. The sun warmed the quarry rocks; it was beginning to be hot and the slender young woman took off her long-sleeved shirt to sunbathe in her tank top. Today she wore soft green shades and, for a moment, she seemed like another dragonfly poised about the surface of the quarry. Cokie closed her eyes, put her head back, and rested.

A branch snapped in the woods; her senses alerted, she opened her eyes and looked in the direction of the sound. No movement, only the soft breeze riffling the surface of the water. Cokie dozed again. Her prey would be here soon. She had only to wait. There would be food and wine and the business of the day.

She dreamed.

And awoke.

On the edge of the woods, slightly to the right of the quarries, close to the stone wall, stood a bear. A small, brownish-black bear, rather scruffy and standing upright on his hind legs.

The bear did not move; it watched Cokie.

She remained perfectly still, fully alert now, and then, careful not to make any quick movements, she rose slowly and pulled on her long-sleeved shirt.

"Go away." She waved gently in the direction of the bear, who tentatively scratched its head with one paw.

Suddenly, Cokie laughed.

"Oh, you had me fooled. You really had me fooled. I honestly thought you were a real bear. That's a great disguise; I expected it but I didn't believe you'd be that good."

The bear moved slowly toward Cokie. "OK, now, the fun's over." Again Cokie motioned the bear away. "Take off the head and let's have lunch."

The bear advanced closer.

Cokie motioned in the air.

"All right, I'll play if you want to. Let's call it the lady and the bear. A real scene. I wouldn't have believed you'd do it so well." Cokie held up one hand.

"Stop, that's close enough. Take it off and let's stop this. I'm starved and where's the lunch? You promised to bring wine."

The bear, directly in front of Cokie by now, gave no sign of understanding. Suddenly, a paw holding a steel claw took a great swipe at Cokie's face, while the other paw pushed her backward to the rim of the quarry. A growl-like sound came from the bear, a hideous, painful, angry sound of a soul tormented to the point of having to finally kill.

It was no longer a game.

Stumbling, still not believing this was happening, Cokie spun backward, unable to take any karate position, unable to catch hold of the small birches at her side, unable to stop her feet, still out of the tennis shoes and searching for a grip among the sand and rocks, unable to stop her feet from slipping and unable to stop her own fall.

One great blow to the head and Cokie fell, screaming and screaming and screaming, all the way to the water below.

The woods were silent. For one short moment, Cokie struggled in the quarry water. But the blow and the fact that she could not swim gave her no chance for survival.

She who had been the hunter had become the prey.

The bear stood silent, looking down at the water. Then he turned and disappeared into the woods. Cokie's body, half submerged, was still. A dragonfly stopped to rest on a bit of her scarf, still above the surface of the water. Dragonflies hung in the air above the body. The woods were still, the little breeze stopped. Time stood still.

No one found Cokie until Monday afternoon. In fact, no one missed Cokie until Monday morning when she didn't show up at Cleaver Real Estate to keep an appointment to show a house. Clipper wasn't too worried; Cokie was often late; after two hours, however, and when the anxious seller called in to ask where the buyer was, Clipper called Cokie's home number. Knowing her ways, he still had no idea something out of the ordinary might have happened, until Malcolm called to ask to talk with him about the Johnson sale, and wanted to speak with Cokie after finishing with Clipper.

"She hasn't shown up yet, and that's a bit unusual," replied Clipper. "She was at the auction. When did you last see her, Mal?"

"Sunday; we were together a while in the morning. She said she had a noon appointment. She may have just gone off to the malls to do some shopping and forgotten her Monday appointment. I'll stop by her house, if you want." Malcolm sounded a little puzzled.

"Good idea. Leave her a note if she's not home, will you? She could have mixed Monday up with Tuesday; you know Cokie. And, like I said last week, if you want to keep at it, Mal, it's OK with me. The Johnsons are fussing now about the Lyman place, and I kind of doubt it will go through. When buyers pick at the beginning it seems to collapse before closing most of the time. They'll lose their deposit, and the Lymans told me they still want you to handle it, so guess we'll just chalk it up to experience." Clipper, stroking the prima donna in Malcolm, still felt he was of worth to the firm. "Doesn't help any if you walk out, though, Mal. Got to face things in life, you know."

"You're right; I'll try again. I'll find Cokie." Malcolm rang off.

He didn't, but late that afternoon, two horseback riders from the riding club, on their way back through the woods amid the gathering dusk, decided to stop by the quarries.

Even then, they almost missed her. The body had become entangled in the stand of cattails at the south end, and it was nearly submerged. It was the scarf they saw, and then part of Cokie's face which the carp had already begun to sample.

"What's that, Betty? Right there?"

"Oh, my God, it's a body. Let's get out of here." The two women, rather portly for the size of their small mounts, rode fast through the overhanging branches in the fading daylight. They felt the need to leave this place and put as much distance as possible between themselves and what they had seen. Cokie, face half-turned upward, had not been a pleasant sight. The women reached Minister's Road and swinging their mounts to the right, galloped toward the Hill.

"Let's get to the nearest house," gasped Betty; "we need a phone. We have to call the sheriff's office."

Her companion agreed and a few minutes later they were pounding on the door of the Patterson sisters at Deer Run.

"Good heavens, what's the matter?" Mary Ellen opened the door and stepped back from the two frantic women.

"There's a body. In the quarry. Dead. We have to phone the sheriff's office." Betty spoke with an economy of words.

"Come in. Mercy, did you see who it was? The phone is to the left of the kitchen door." Mary Ellen ushered them through the house.

"No, we just wanted to get out of there. To think we dismounted and were looking for the carp. I'll never go up there again."

"Are you sure it was dead? Was it a man or a woman?" Christina, the second Patterson sister, was enthralled. In their quiet existence, the interruption was exciting.

"A woman, I think," said Betty, who kept getting a busy signal from the sheriff's office. "Kind of sideways caught in the cattails. I don't want to think about it. It was shadowy at the bottom of the quarry path, and I almost put my hand on it—her. Why don't they answer?"

Mary Ellen Patterson, a true New Englander who knew near hysteria when she saw it, reappeared in the kitchen with a bottle and two glasses.

"Look here, you're shaking. Take a sip of this and calm down. The sheriff's office will answer eventually. And whoever it is can wait. They're dead. You couldn't have done a thing nor can you now. You'll have a heart attack if you're not careful. The dead can wait."

Dot Bailey finally answered, Reed was summoned along with two members of the sheriff's department, and Betty and her companion were told to stay put until help arrived. "How long will it be before someone comes?" Betty pulled herself together enough to ask Dot before she lost contact. "Our horses are outside tied to the fence and we can't ride to the Hill in the dark. They're going to be hungry."

Dot was used to emergencies and rather prided herself that she could deal with anything. "Stay right there. Someone will bring in grain and a trailer. I'll take care of it."

She called Lee. "There's some trouble at the Pattersons' on the Hill; two women just rode in there from the quarries and it's too dark now for them to go on by road. Do you have a two-horse trailer? You're the nearest one I could think of. Could you get over there soon with some grain and hay? It's Betty Rowe and Ann Gabel and they found a body up in the quarries—Reed and some deputies are on their way up with the ambulance and the girls were told to stay right there at the Pattersons' so he can talk with them. It's real mixed up—Reed wants you to stay there too until he comes. Can you do it, Lee?"

"I'll go right over. It will take a few minutes to hitch up the trailer. You can tell them I'm on the way with feed. There used to be stalls in the Patterson barn. Dot, who is it?"

"I don't know. That Betty was real upset. But Malcolm Bandridge and Clipper Cleaver reported Cokie Adams missing this afternoon. She didn't come in to work and they looked for her but didn't find any trace. Her car isn't in her garage."

"Oh, I hope it isn't Cokie. I'll go right along." Lee took off her apron and put on a heavy sweater. With the aid of a flashlight she made the connection between her Land Rover and the parked trailer. She threw in a bale of hay and a measure of grain, thought about a water bucket and added that. She ran back to the house, petted Kate and locked the doors. There were no stars; it was a dark night, and the thought of a body, alone in the deep quarry, was not comforting.

"Please don't let it be Cokie." She heard herself saying the words aloud.

Within an hour Reed's team was working. The ambulance could not get all the way up the path, but it went in as far as possible, the stretcher team wearing headlamps to see ahead on the dark path as they climbed the hill to the quarry.

Reed had a large spotlight and the deputy another, but they did not have an easy time getting the body disentangled from the cattails and out of the water.

Dr. Burton, who arrived last, shook his head and looked at Cokie. "Look at her face, Reed. A massive blow to the head and scratches again—almost as deep as Ted's. This better stop. Someone or something is abroad and Cokie was a tough lady. I know she knew karate. She must not have had time or else she didn't fear whatever it was. Looks like it's a job now for the attorney general and the state police."

Reed nodded. "I've called. Just sent a deputy down to the car phone. How long has she been dead, Doc, do you think?"

"I'd say twenty-four hours or more. Have to have a full examination. Did you find anything else, boys?" Doctor Burton sighed. He had liked Cokie.

One deputy was fishing the water. "I can't find anything. We won't be able to drag all the spots until morning."

"The state police will take over. Let's just get her out of here and I'll go talk to the women who found her." Reed was thinking out loud.

"It's up to me now." Doctor Burton shook his head. "She was such a pretty girl, Reed. Sometimes I don't like my job."

"I don't either, Doc. Less and less. I'm heading down for the Pattersons'—there ought to be a trooper there by the time I arrive. Murder gets complicated. And this surely looks like murder." Reed's mind was churning.

Now it has to stop. I've got to find the answer. The state police will investigate and I'll put all my information with theirs, but even then how am I going to tell them some of my suspicions? Cokie must have been close to the answer—maybe she knew. So whatever this is, it looks like it's human. It knew she had to be killed, and it must know Ted could recover his memory. This can't all be Lee's development problem, and maybe Hod is closest of all to the solution. There is evil here and come to think of it, where's the B *in Cokie's death?* Scratches—Bear—Blow? *I'll call Hod in the morning.*

Reed entered the Pattersons' to the smell of coffee. A tall, lanky state trooper was getting out a pad and pencil and he welcomed Reed. In the small communities people knew each other and the division between lawmen was not as noticeable as in cities.

In the barn the horses were snug and fed. The five women sat around the kitchen table and Mary Ellen offered coffee and cookies to Reed and the trooper.

"Did you see anyone around the quarry, any sign of movement, any noise? Like someone leaving, maybe?" the trooper asked.

You mean there could have been someone there? Watching us?" Hysteria rose in Betty's voice.

Well, probably not. Cokie's been dead a while. But sometimes people come back. Nothing unusual you can think of?"

"Nothing...? I thought she just fell in...." Betty was terrified, thinking of how she had almost touched the body.

"I'm afraid not; someone killed her." Reed spoke slowly, out of turn for it was the trooper's prerogative to conduct the investigation, but Reed's friendship with Lee and the background he'd already amassed made it impossible to keep still. Slim, an old friend of Reed's, knew a little of the background, and willingly let the slip of authority pass.

Lee drew in her breath. "Reed, were there...."

And Reed, knowing the question and looking at Slim, said simply, "I'm afraid so."

Lee felt a chill. The woods, the trails, the quarries, the friendly places were friendly no longer, but places of evil. Someone or something watched and waited. Mrs. Attlebury had seen it, Lee had seen it, Jim and Ted and Cokie had seen it and two of them were dead.

Someone or something watched and waited and planned and to what end no one yet knew. Somewhere, among the oaks and the beeches and the pines death waited in the form of a bear who was not a bear.

Lee shivered and pulled her sweater close about her shoulders. The night was getting colder. The evil was near.

·23·

For the next week Cokie's death was the subject of conversation among any given group of people in Oxford County. The real estate world reiterated warnings to its members to never go anyplace alone. The state police, the sheriff's department and Reed's town police force combed the woods around the quarries for clues; they turned up Cokie's tennis shoes caught on the rocks below, and her straw bag, caught in one of the small birches that lined the quarry. Her car was found the first day, parked off the road to the Hartley house in a stand of bushes, not easily seen by passers-by.

No one knew what she had been doing there; no one even guessed.

Except Reed and Hod, who were sure that this time the bear had succeeded because he had planned to meet his prey. Cokie must have known who the bear was; therefore Cokie had to die.

As soon as the autopsy was finished, as soon as relatives from the Midwest had come to take the body back for burial (an aunt and uncle's phone number had been found in Cokie's address book), as soon as the newspapers had stopped interviewing the state police and Reed and the real estate brokers who might know anything, as soon as he had time to take a breath, Reed called Hod.

They met on Tuesday, the 18th, at Sumner and this time they were both determined to find the answer.

"How's Lee taking this?" Hod's voice was gruff as he poured coffee for Reed. "I talked with her directly I heard it, but I haven't phoned her this week yet."

"She was at the Patterson house when Slim and I got there to talk with the women who'd found Cokie. Dot had her bring over some feed for the horses and a trailer to get them back up on the Hill. She was upset, all right, but in command of herself. I guess the hardest part was her having to call Clipper and Malcolm Bandridge—Malcolm's been seeing Cokie, you know. I had to get statements from all of them—I ought to say Slim had to—I'm so used to being on the case I have to remember it's the state police's work now. You might say I'll be doing underground investigation. Anyway, Malcolm's the last one to see Cokie alive, as far as we've been able to track down. So Lee's being extra careful, but so are all the real estate people for that matter. This kind of thing really shakes them up." Reed paused and accepted a piece of bread and a slice of cheese to go with his coffee.

Hod, fanning out more bread and cheese on an old ironstone plate, listened closely.

"Well, I've gone right down the list. Tried on everyone we spoke of for size, Reed. And I can't make it fit. I know you've had detectives on this for months and I know the state police will give it everything they have now that it's murder for sure, but we're no place. We're dealing with one smart bear. I was about to give up, but I have a couple of other ideas." Hod took up a pencil and paper and the first diagram he had made.

"You know," he continued, "my old grandmother died when I was seven. I can remember an expression she used I've never heard since—'I've been hiding and haring all over the place and I can't find it'. Guess that's kinda the way I feel. Anyway, here's my ideas."

Reed leaned forward. "Let's hear them. You know I'm not supposed to be doing the investigating now that the state police are on it, but we need all the help we can get, so I'm unofficially on the case. So far, you seem to have it puzzled out better than anyone in the departments."

Hod was silent for a moment, then he sighed and began: "Well, the way I see it we're talking two different languages here. The person—or two people—or whoever's doing all this—speaks one language. Like say French. We speak another—like English. So we're judging him using our own language and set of values, and that's the wrong approach. We're not thinking the way he thinks. You want to catch a fox, you got to think like a fox. So we got to think like a bear. See what I mean?"

"Like a bear?" Reed repeated the words. "Of course, like a bear. It makes sense."

"Yup," Hod continued, "he thinks he's a bear. Guess we've pretty well established that fact. So we have to put ourselves inside his skin and think the same way."

"All right." Reed watched Hod's pencil tracing circles on the paper. "So what's your theory?"

"I think he had most things thought out in advance. Then he was tripped up with the accidents. First off, he just wanted to scare Lee. And he didn't want it to look like just one person scaring another. He had a good cover; she's stirred up a lot of antagonism with the developers and real estate people. The word in town is that Lee Heaward is antidevelopment. So the phone calls hired out were all centered around that 'get out of town stuff'." Hod paused, methodically putting a slab of cheese on a slice of his homemade bread. He chewed thoughtfully. "Helps with the vitamins."

"What?" Reed was puzzled.

"I mean the cheese. Coffee alone leaches vitamins. I read the cheese helps. Got so I'm drinking less coffee and eating more cheese. Sorry, I got off the subject."

"Could we continue?" Reed watched the pencil.

"Sure; well, he might have hired out the barn attempt, but I doubt it. I'm guessing he did that himself. And I don't think he meant to burn it, just to scare Lee. I think he really hates Lee, why I'm not sure, but I'll bet she did something she didn't even realize that set him off. Maybe turned him down; maybe something in a real estate sale. Money or jealousy or anger. Any one of those three would do it. Anyway, he starts out with scare tactics, figuring maybe she'll turn to him for help or maybe leave the area. I can't read his mind all the way."

"Lee's a strong person. She's afraid, but she's steel inside, Hod. I think he figured her wrong." Reed pushed back the lock of blond hair. He was tired. It was a long way back to last February. He was beginning to doubt his own ability, and now the state police had charge of the case.

"Now, I think, I'm almost sure, Jim Davidson's death was an accident. He saw something at the wrong place and time. Maybe Lee was intended to be a victim; only the bear could tell us. I don't think Davidson actually figures in this at all. The bear knows. And he's thinking like a bear." Hod's voice was slow and methodical; like a hound on a rabbit trail, he was worrying his way through the briars.

"You think he's insane—this bear person?" Reed leaned forward.

"Depends on what you call insane. He sure ain't playing with a full deck of cards." Hod's accent thickened.

"The poison, the valerian. Mostly women are poisoners, Hod. And the blouse, that's a nasty touch."

"Yup, thought long about that." Hod frowned. "And then, I thought, if I was this person, dressing up like a bear, sneaking around in the woods, thinking up all this stuff, I'm pretty devious. I'm going to make it look like a woman and use an herbal poison. That'll confuse them even more. I'm going to lay false trails all over the place. So I'll use valerian; now how many people would do that?"

Reed was listening closely. "And we've been over that before. Almost anyone up on the Hill has a knowledge of herbs. Ground-up valerian could make you real sick if you used too much. So the bear just kept on trying, that's the way you see it?"

"Yup," answered Hod, "and now he's getting a little angrier and a little more careless. Mrs. Bemis got sick too; I don't think he intended that. And when it came to the barbed wire, how did he know who was going to be on the first horse? Could have been Carter rather than Lee. They ride different horses at different times. I asked Lee."

Reed was making some notes himself, while Hod talked. Now he went over them briefly and came up with a question. "Ted?"

Hod shook his head. "That's a puzzler. I think he saw something, something the bear couldn't afford to let him see. So he had to be killed. This time he meant to kill, but it wasn't planned. He missed, by the grace of God, he missed. But the person must be on pins and needles thinking about whether Ted will recall anything. Then Cokie comes into it. She could have been in the wrong place at the wrong time like Ted, but I don't think so. I think she went to meet someone, leaving her car off the road in the bushes. She must have known who she was meeting. And from what Lee and you say, she was a smart lady. This time the bear-person meant to kill. And planned it, for sure. Another thing, Reed, he has to have a place to change into this bear costume. The Hartley house? A hollow tree? The tomb nearby where Ted was attacked? You just don't go dragging a bear get-up in broad daylight for anyone to see. If you have half a brain you don't go too far in the woods dressed like a bear. Notice I said 'half a brain'."

Reed stared into space. "I looked up the definition of insane once. There are so many. The two I always remember are deranged and maniacal. They scare the hell right out of me."

"Me too." Hod picked up the riding crop he was still working on—the rowan tree wood now ready for its last polish. The old scrubbed pine table made a background for his long, tapering fingers working slowly on the crop. The coffee cups, the bread and cheese plate, the small bowl of wildflowers to one side, the faces of the two men, one blond and young and tired, the other tanned and wrinkled and determined; it was a Wyeth painting. Outside the windows a hummingbird searched in the red asters and far off, down by the river, a woodpecker drummed on a dead elm tree. The world seemed far away.

Reed shifted in his seat, breaking the quiet. "Who do you figure, Hod?"

"First I thought Sam Childs. Right off the bat he came to mind. But I couldn't locate him at all the right places at the right times. He's really angry with Lee; she caused him to lose a considerable amount of money and people have canceled contracts with him, I hear. He's smart and a thinker and he could have sneaked in most anyplace, but I don't see him using valerian to poison. So I discounted Sam." Hod wiped the gleaming wood with an old cotton rag.

"He used to hunt with Ted. I've been with them a few times, myself. I thought of him, too." Reed nodded.

"Well, he's at the head of my list as far as straight-out hatred of Lee goes. But I finally crossed him off."

Reed interrupted. "I've checked out most everyone. Nobody really has any kind of an alibi because they were all doing things by themselves. If you figured Cokie was murdered sometime in the early afternoon on Sunday, well, Sam Childs was out looking at the Crossen farm land; Bunny Cleaver was out for a walk; Clipper said he was at the office checking a late contract and Malcolm spent most of his day in his garden, after he saw Cokie in the morning. Elvira took a couple of days to drive out to the coast; she'll be back tomorrow. Lee was at High Meadows most of the day Sunday."

Hod looked at Reed. "You surely don't suspect Lee of killing Cokie? Why Lee is the one being threatened."

"I know that. I'm just trying to show you that any number of people were around but none of them can exactly prove where they were at any given time. I also thought for a while Cokie could have been the one who threatened Lee. I tell you, Hod, I just don't know."

"Cokie went to meet someone she knew, Reed. She wasn't afraid to meet them. Either the person left and the bear, or pretend bear, came then, or the person *was* the bear. You know her parents were actors. She knew how to handle herself. That's what is so frightening. He has a lot of strength, that bear."

"The deranged have great strength, Hod. We both know that." Reed sighed. "You didn't consider Malcolm? Or Clipper Cleaver?"

"Yup, I did. I considered Clipper for quite a while. But he doesn't have the imagination. He's strong and he's smart, but I can't see him making a plan to impersonate a bear and follow the *B* plan. Now, Malcolm's another story. In fact, he's our perfect suspect: little theatre, skis, used to be sweet on Lee. That's the trouble. He's too pat to be the one. In the books you suspect the ones like Malcolm, but they never did it because it's logical that they did do it. So they didn't. If you follow me. Unless he's so smart that he's daring us to catch him."

"I lost you someplace along there," Reed smiled. "But I know what you mean about Malcolm. I've been thinking about him, too. He's really a pussycat. Besides, he's taking Cokie's death hard."

"Well," mused Hod, "it could be someone we haven't thought of or don't even know exists. The one thing I'm positive of is, it isn't the Attleburys!"

Reed put down his notebook and pencil. "I can't even hazard a guess."

The rowan tree crop, finished now, lay to one side of the tabletop, and Hod placed his hand upon it gently, as though willing the magic within to commence. His eyes seemed focused far away, perhaps looking into a world he summoned to help a woman he cared for deeply yet could not protect.

He thought a moment and looked at Reed. "I can't either. I don't know how we can prove anything about anyone at this moment. We may have to bait a trap and see what we catch."

Reed nodded. "I think you're right. We may have to bait a trap."

While Reed and Hod were having their meeting in Sumner, Belle Attlebury had a visit from George Morrill, who delivered to her the auction accounting and her check. He had called before coming, and he was greeted by a glass of lemonade and fresh gingerbread. They sat together in the herb garden, the auctioneer enjoying the old lady's fussing over him, and Belle contemplated her check.

"Do you want me to take you down to Paris, Mrs. Attlebury? You ought to get that right in your savings account until you've decided what investments you're going to make." George was trying to be helpful.

Belle Attlebury laughed. "Everyone is getting a little afraid to see me drive that Oldsmobile, I guess, but I can still take the corners. I appreciate your offer, George, and I'll go get ready. I can't leave the doctor alone for very long, so we can just run right down and back. As far as knowing what to do with it, it's all arranged. I know exactly what I'm going to do."

She did.

That evening, Belle Attlebury called Lee.

"Could you stop by tomorrow on your way to town? And do you have a handy buy-and-sell agreement? Or whatever you call that paper when someone wants to buy property? I'd appreciate it, Lee; I don't want to come over there. I left Frederick for a few minutes yesterday and when I got back he was walking about with only half his clothes on. It's all right if he's taking a nap, but I'd like to see you earlier than that, if it's possible."

"I'll stop about nine, Mrs. Attlebury, if that's good for you. Do you want to tell me...?"

"No." Belle Attlebury's voice was firm. "We'll talk when you get here. Thank you, Lee."

And she placed the phone back on the hook. When Belle Attlebury made up her mind she needed advice from no one.

So it was, on the morning of Wednesday, the 19th of August, that Belle Attlebury put several thousand dollars down in escrow and signed an agreement to buy the Hartley estate property at full price through Carriage Trade Realty. Within a few hours Mr.

Cameron had given his assurance by phone that the contract would be signed on his end, and that they could close within two weeks, as Mrs. Attlebury had requested as part of her offer. Title was done; money was in the bank and would be cleared by closing. There was nothing to hold up the sale, and it would go through, exactly as Belle Attlebury requested. All the furnishings and contents were included in the sale.

Belle Attlebury had one more surprise. It would come later and it would change a lot of lives in the area for years ahead. For Belle planned to give the property to a trust, to keep a green area at the edge of the Hill forever. And she made Lee Heaward head of the board of directors of the trust, for as long as Lee lived.

The planning board approved the plans for Ted and Ellen's cabin renovations the next evening, and the contractor moved in with speed to finish the job. Between the Hartley estate sale and work on the cabin, Lee found herself with little time to dwell on past events. August was drawing to a close and ahead was the month Lee loved the best of any during the year. Hod called often, came by twice and did not push her towards any decisions. He gave her the gift of the rowan tree crop and made her promise to take it with her in the woods and on her walks with Kate. He kissed her gently and told her he would be back soon. He always was.

One other thing happened during the last week in August. Elvira Campbell called Reed and asked to see him privately. On the 28th, a Friday, he met her at a picnic area on Crystal Lake.

The circle was coming closer.

AUTUMN

ANGELICA
PARSLEY
COMFREY
GARLIC CHIVES
BASIL
VALERIAN
CHIVES

• 24 •

Elvira felt brittle. What she meant to do today was something that came hard to her and her New England background.

She had to tell Reed about her brother.

Elvira had heard of Cokie's death from a newspaper in Camden. She had gone to visit old friends for a few days, before returning to the Hill and saying goodby to Malcolm for the remainder of the year. Picking up a copy of the *Portland Press Herald*, she had read the details, and she knew then that she could no longer hold her silence.

The question was which direction to follow, and she had finally decided that Reed Jamison, even though it was no longer officially his case, was her one hope. She had never thought of her promise to her mother as being so hard to keep, but now she would have to do it in a way her mother would not have dreamed of—she had to put Malcolm someplace where he would be safe.

From himself and from the bear.

The picnic area was almost full today; it was the weekend before Labor Day and families were getting in some of their last swims and sails of the summer. Children surrounded a Red Cross instructor giving the last of the season's courses; adults sunned and kept one eye out for small children playing on the water's edge. Here and there a red leaf spotted the foliage of the oak trees bending low over the water, and the first hints of autumn stirred the air.

Elvira sat at an empty picnic table on one side of the full parking lot, and waited stoically for Reed. He was late in arriving, one of the reasons being that on the drive over from Norway he had been going slower than usual, turning over in his mind the clues he had discussed with Hod, filtering them through his mind and deciding how he might have to deal with Elvira, who was a woman he knew only slightly.

He need not have worried. The slant of Elvira's jaw could have told him her character. What she had to do came hard, but she was capable of doing it.

The tradition of New Englanders is to take care of their own. Few families in the 1800's rid themselves of their weaker members; they closed ranks around them and gave them protection. The feeble-minded old aunts and uncles, the invalid daughters and sons, the ones who tended to have "spells" on the nights of the full moon, the out-and-out neurotics, seldom left the family nest. Generally a family member was designated to be their caretaker. Only in extreme cases were they placed in outside institutions. New England family life in the 1800's and early 1900's was close-knit. A family did not desert its weaker members. The obligation belonged at home.

Elvira had inherited the tradition. She was about to violate her trust.

When Reed arrived, she thanked him for coming and spoke immediately to the point, with an economy of words. Part of what she related was what Reed expected. Part was a story he had not envisioned.

It was the story of a boy who had a terrible temper that time appeared to mellow. The story of a boy who lived in a fantasy world, who took the part of different animals in his play-acting, who became as one with several of these fantasies and was hard put to reenter the real world.

It was the story of a boy who grew older to believe he might be a witch, a warlock, a Druid or worshiper at the temple of Diana of the Woods in an ancient religion, who escaped from reality at different times in his life.

It was the story of a boy who enjoyed hiding in the secret passages of a Maine house, fooling his mother and sister as to his whereabouts. A boy growing to be a man living partly in the real world, partly still in the world of fantasy, known by his mother and sister as worth keeping an eye on, as their ancestors had called it, but who, up until now, had really done no harm.

Up until now.

Elvira told Reed of Malcolm's constant need for money and that she suspected he very well could have cleaned out the locked room of the Hartley estate—she told him of her conversation with the dealer at the flea market. She had taken the name of the booth, and later Reed, through the market's owner, traced the man and received from him a detailed account of his father's experience.

Elvira told Reed of Malcolm's interest in the little theatre lighting which could have helped him in outwitting the Hartley security system. She told him of the worship of Diana in the garden at night, and of the lack of certain herbs in Malcolm's greens garden. In particular angelica—the foe of witchcraft throughout the world. And of the fact that everything within the garden was used by witches. In fact, Reed, in short order, was given what was probably one of the most concentrated and definite courses on witchcraft and herbs that had ever been given to any police chief.

It was hard to keep track of Elvira's list of what did and what didn't belong in a witch's bag of tricks. And it was even harder to sit on the picnic bench by Crystal Lake, clear and clean as its name, and believe the things Elvira was saying.

That Malcolm believed himself, in some way, to be a witch of the woods. And, possibly, a bear.

Elvira had no actual proof. In fact, at one point, Reed wondered if she was involved and if this recital was only a way to implicate someone who was already suspect. But Elvira, with the sense of timing her family was noted for, left one important clue to the last.

"I can't find the little hand cultivator, Reed. The one I gave him last Christmas; there was a set of three garden tools, English, from Smith and Hawken, that I knew he would like. They were just the right gift for Mal. He likes garden things—last year I gave him a trug basket from Sussex and he was so pleased. But the little hand cultivator, I call it a scratcher, is gone. I asked him and he couldn't find it either."

Reed looked puzzled. "I can't visualize what you mean."

"The little hand cultivator. It looks like a claw, sort of—made of metal. That's what convinced me, finally. When Lee told me about Ted and then when I heard about Cokie's face. The scratcher would make a perfect bear claw. And it's gone."

Reed looked down the lake at the boats bobbing on the sparkling water, the children swimming and, far out, the flotilla of Red Cross instructors shepherding their charges on the swim across the lake to win the coveted badges.

He shook his head. "You think the Hartley passage, if it can be found, is similar to the one that was in your house? Malcolm told people he never found a passage at Run for Cover."

"I'm sure it's the same," Elvira replied, "and we *did* have one and he did know about it, so he is simply lying. Mother had it closed off when he kept sliding in and out of it and wouldn't answer her. That was when he was still very young. I can just barely recall the incident."

"So you really think he could be pretending to be the bear?" Reed hated to go over the same ground.

Elvira smoothed her skirt thoughtfully. "Reed, I took a chance telling you all this. You might have laughed and told me I was paranoid. But I heard Lee speak of you and say she could trust you, and you are the only one I can think of to go to. He doesn't just *think* he's a bear, Reed, he *believes* he is a bear. Do you see the difference?"

Reed, looking at the pain in Elvira's eyes, saw.

He rose, placing a hand on her shoulder. He knew what this meeting had cost her. "All right. Nothing can be proven so far. If I can get the key from either Lee or Belle Attlebury, do you think you and I could find that passage in the Hartley house? With Malcolm's being busy at something else so he won't know where we are? He's been broken up over Cokie and spends most of the time in his garden, according to Clipper. What do you think? Where are you going right now? Do you think you will be safe at Run for Cover?"

"Malcolm is my brother. I feel as though I must stay and he seems off in space right now. He is broken up over Cokie, you are right, that's what makes it so puzzling. Tell me when you want to meet and I'll go with you. Don't call me at Run for Cover if you can help it." Elvira stood up and took a last look at the lake. "It doesn't seem possible, does it? I can't really believe it could be true, when I look out across that water. I'm afraid, Reed, and I'm never afraid. If it is true, can we stop it before it happens again? And not harm him?"

"I can't answer that. I'm going to think this all over and talk with someone about it—can you go up to the Hartley house on Monday? I'll meet you at High Meadows; it's just as well Malcolm doesn't see us together. About ten in the morning? If that doesn't work out, I'll call you."

Elvira nodded, they parted, and Reed drove directly back to Paris to call Hod Cole. Then he called Lee.

"I have to take another look at the Hartley place on Monday, Lee; I'd like to get the key if possible. I might take Elvira Campbell with me and before you ask me why I'm going, just don't ask me and don't mention it to anyone. Sort of an unofficial investigation. She'll come up to High Meadows around ten on Monday morning and I'll pick her up there. Hod might be around then, too. I'll explain it to you later; just trust me. I'll tell Belle Attlebury I'm looking at the house and that'll take care of your duty to the new owner. I know you like everything just so."

Lee was puzzled, but she was sure of Reed and promised the key on Monday. A chance to see Hod tempted her and she decided to stay at home that day if she could arrange it with Meg. What Elvira had to do with all of this, she could not see, but whatever it was she knew Reed would tell her later. So she went back to the business of Ellen and Ted's cabin, now fully approved by the board and very nearly ready for occupancy.

On Monday, the last day of August, Hod came early and stopped to see Mrs. Attlebury. It was a cool day for August, a small breeze was blowing, and the branches of the rowan trees, lining the Daniels Meadow, were heavy with their red berries. Woodsmoke and early apple scent filled the air; the blue gentians were just coming into flower in the meadow and the late monarch butterflies dotted the upland pastures recovering from their second cutting of hay. A haze touched the mountain peaks. Murder and intrigue seemed far away.

Belle Attlebury sat on a bench outside her kitchen door, peeling an early Lodi apple. The peeling curled gradually to the earth, without a break, and finally fell from the sweet meat of the fruit. Belle was using her old jackknife she always carried deep in a pocket of her khaki skirt, finding it handy for everything from digging dandelion greens to trimming herbs. She offered Hod a slice of apple.

They sat quietly contemplating the day.

"I'm on my way to Lee's. Taking your advice, Belle. I kind of like that woman. I'm practicing up on my courting graces, you might say."

Mrs. Attlebury smiled. "I heard you gave her a rowan tree riding crop. Are you and I thinking along the same lines, Hod? There's an evil in the woods; I can feel it more in my bones every day."

"I think we're getting closer, Belle." Hod's voice was low.

Belle Attlebury looked intently at the weathered, deeply lined and tanned face of the woodsman. Today he wore a dark plaid cotton shirt with his sleeves rolled up and an old but clean pair of khaki pants. His feet were in Indian moccasins that Belle knew could carry him between trees and through the woods without the trace of a sound.

Belle felt a glimmer of understanding. Hod Cole was hunting today. Hod was after a bear.

"I never before believed all those tales I heard about you, Hod. Why they called you 'the old poacher'. Suddenly, I see why. You're on a trail, aren't you? Is Reed in on this too?"

Hod barely nodded. "Belle, you see too much. I'm meeting Reed this morning, after I see Lee. I wouldn't be surprised if something will happen before this next month is over. Just don't say anything, will you, and take care of yourself. What I really came to say is I'm proud of you, Belle Attlebury, for what you did. The Hartley purchase, I mean. It'll be there forever or at least as long as we're on the face of the earth, for people to enjoy. Lee's the perfect head for your trust. Belle, you're one special woman."

Hod gave her a quick hug and rose to leave. "I'll be back, Belle. Be careful."

He reached High Meadows just behind Reed. They stood together on the side of the driveway, by their cars, with heads close together and Reed talking rapidly in a low voice. What he had not told Hod on the phone he filled him in on quickly—with emphasis on the fact that he and Elvira would be alone in the house and that Reed wanted Hod to stand guard in the woods outside unknown even to Elvira.

"I don't figure any trouble this morning. He's supposed to be on the Hill and it's daylight and he doesn't know we're going to be in the house. But I can't take a chance. Since Mrs. Attlebury's purchase and the transfer to the trust I don't believe he's been in the woods. He seems to have been mourning Cokie—that is, if what Elvira said is true."

"That's a big 'if'." Hod had listened without interruption. "Well, it may have shaken you when you heard her story, but I tell you, Reed, it don't me. Sounds like something out of the Golden Bough and meant to be happening in ancient Greece, but I'm betting most of Elvira's story is true."

Reed shook his head and brushed his face with his hand. "And this isn't even supposed to be my investigation. Here comes Elvira—you talk with Lee—I'll give you five minutes for conversation before I want to know you're on your way."

Hod grinned. "I'd like to see her just a minute—then I'm your backup in the woods. I'll be out there, someplace near the house, close, all the time you're inside. You need me; you yell. I'll see you pull out in the car and then I'll walk back here. We can talk better then."

Lee, inside and watching the two men through the kitchen window, saw Elvira arrive and leave with Reed. Whatever was going on she had little time to mull over as Hod came toward the door, and this was more important. Since the day in Sumner they had not spoken again of their feelings. It was as though they had packed them away in some attic trunk only to take out and delight in when the mystery was finally solved.

Just for a moment this morning, let me hear his words. Whatever is happening, I need his strength to help me survive.

Hod never wasted words. He told Lee what little he was allowed to tell, that Elvira and Reed were inspecting the house for the passageway, and that he would be keeping watch outside.

He held Lee close, brushed her hair with his lips and assured her his feelings had not changed. He patted Kate's head, cautioned her to take care of Lee, and was gone. Lee, watching him move silently through the horse paddock and disappear into the woods beyond, felt comforted but confused.

Somewhere, in the "wild wood", lies evil. She knew Hod and Reed were hunting it this morning.

What she did not know was how the hunt would end.

·25·

It took Elvira only a few minutes to open the passageway. She stood looking at the mantel, the deacon's cupboard, the dentil moulding, and the chimneypiece. She turned her mind back to the day her mother hauled a small boy out of his hiding place and vowed to close it forever. She reached her hand out twice; stopped; thought better of it and jogged her memory. And then, with great deliberation, she moved the little basket of wormwood and moonshine a bit to one side, and pressing down on the manteltop at that spot, and then pressing backwards, the second step that Hod had not known about, she opened the panel to the left of the fireplace.

There was no sound of creaking, no trace of antiquity. The hinges were well oiled, the pieces of wood and iron swinging smoothly one against the other. The wall panel that opened was large enough for a stooping man; the passageway opening led between lath and brick walls and was wide enough to allow a person to move without brushing the sides. Beyond were stairs, and two other openings that wound between rooms. The stairs descended to the kitchen and a second set descended into the cellar, connecting with the barn.

The builder had planned well; it was a regular rabbit warren, as old man Hartley had said. The passageway was clean all the way through to the cellar; no cobwebs, no dust; someone kept it tidy. And, at the bottom of the stairs, in a small alcove backing on the kitchen chimney, was the old smokeroom used for hanging hams to cure, closed off now from the main entrance and isolated from the main house.

In it, hanging on a meat hook, was a large, furry suit. It looked like a dead animal.

Elvira screamed, but Reed covered her mouth in time to stop the noise and he gripped hard on her arm to support her. He held the flashlight steady.

"It's the suit, Mrs. Campbell. The bear suit. I figured a smokeroom somewhere. The smell, you see. Hod put me on to that. Must be where it's been kept most of the time." Looking closer, Reed marveled at the construction. "He sure makes it look real. I'm going to leave it right here, and just the way we found it. Look at the head. Papier-mâché with fur glued on. Somebody's old fur coat didn't know its destiny. Maybe that's what Cokie knew."

Elvira was struggling with hysteria. Finally, facing what she had feared, she knew now how the story would end. She reached out her hand to touch the suit, but Reed stopped her.

"No, don't take it down. We'll go back now, the way we came. I want to get out of here. Mrs. Campbell, you did what you had to do. Let's get you out of here and back home."

He hurried her along, up the stairs, through the passageway, only stopping long enough to have her show him how to open the entrance from the inside. They finally stepped back into the room they had started from; the room Jim Davidson had backed out of to his death.

Reed moved fast now, ushering Elvira down the front stairs and out of the house into the car. Hod, behind bushes alongside the barn, watched them leave and then turned slowly to scan the grounds before dissolving back into the woods.

The Hartley house, its secret divulged, stood alone on the last day of August.

Reed knew how delicate was the balance. Somehow, Elvira must be dealt with and kept apart from what surely would happen. Somehow, she must let them do what they had to do.

Reed suggested she return to Camden. "Look, Mrs. Campbell, no matter what you've told us, no matter what we've found, we can't prove a thing. Sometimes, murders can't be solved even though the police are almost positive they know the killer. We have to prove assumptions and make them stick or we just are conducting an exercise in futility. I believe you, but if I have to get up in front of a jury to testify for the district attorney, I better have my proof down cold. I've got to work this out, and you'd best be out of the way. You better be thinking about a good lawyer, if it is your brother."

Elvira, tears in her eyes, nodded. "I'm going back to the house and pack and leave Malcolm a note if he's not there. Here's my number in Camden. I'll stay a week or so. I may call in and ask you what's going on. Are you sure I should leave? Would it be better just to face him and ask?"

Reed snorted. "I'm sure. Listen, Mrs. Campbell, turn it around. You are Malcolm. Your sister and the town police chief ask you—do you think you're a bear and a killer, besides? Tell me your answer—truly now."

Elvira bent her head. "I understand. I don't know if I did the right thing to tell you."

Reed, helping her into her car, suddenly leaned over and gave her a quick, fierce hug. "Elvira Bandridge Campbell, you did what you had to do."

Within a short space of time, Lee motioned from the kitchen door at High Meadows, and Hod and Reed sat down to blueberry cake and coffee. Kate sat trustingly at the older man's knee, by now used to this quiet man, and somehow knowing with a setter's instinct, that he, too, was a hunter. Hod, looking at the ceiling and pointing to a fly, diverted Lee's eyes from the fact that he was sneaking Kate a tidbit under the table.

Lee laughed. "Neither of you," she said, "is fooling me. I know what you're up to."

"I hope not." Reed drank his coffee slowly. "Because I'm going to ask you not to ask questions. Lee, when do you get that trust organized that Belle is setting up?"

Lee replied, "We close on the property on the third—that's Thursday. The trust papers are set up for transfer on the next day. I can't tell you what this means—to think that Belle Attlebury has thought this out all summer long and never told anyone. The trust will have a board of directors and I guess I'm the head for at least the beginning. I'm going to ask some real estate people to serve with me because I think it may influence some of them to finally realize what's happening in the area and what could be done. Clipper's agreed to be a director. He's beginning to see the public relations angle of backing a green area and serving on the board. Mrs. Attlebury suggested I ask Malcolm as the Bandridges are an old Hill family. If Elvira lived here I'd ask her, but as she doesn't it will be Mal. And it may help him a little getting over Cokie's death."

"Good thinking." Reed's mind was racing. Over the coffee cup his eyes met Hod's.

"Well, I have to get along." Hod put his hands on Lee's shoulders and gently ruffled her hair. "I'll be back, sweet."

So, Reed thought, *it finally happened.*

Getting into the police cruiser, Reed motioned to Hod who followed him along Minister's Road. At the Stony Brook parking area, the two cars stopped, and the men, heads together, talked quickly.

The older man's eyes narrowed as he listened to the younger police chief's story of the passageway. Hod only asked one question. "The garden cultivator; the claw Elvira mentioned. Did you see it?"

Reed shook his head. "No, it may have been in a dark corner, but I looked carefully. He may take it back and forth with him. I wouldn't be surprised if he used the tomb sometimes to hide the suit; even maybe a tree. There's a large old sugar maple, nearly dead, on a direct line to the farm. Just remembered that. Could have been in either spot. But it wasn't in the smokeroom."

Hod spoke thoughtfully. "Smokeroom made that smell probably. On the suit. Well, Reed, looks like we're at fish or cut bait time. Next week's full moon. If he moves again, it will be then. Like I said, you want to catch a bear you got to think like a bear. We need to bait the trap."

Reed answered slowly, pushing back his blond hair. "I don't like this at all, but if we don't get him soon there'll be another death—I can smell it. If you're thinking what I think you're thinking—letting Lee be set up for him to get at—we better be right close by."

"No, I don't want to ever do that. I don't want Lee anywhere near. I got to think on this a little; see what kind of a plan I can come up with. Let me call you, Reed, in a couple of days.

Somehow we've got to plan something up by the Hartley house that will trap him. We're probably going to need some help from the sheriff's department then, too. This is not an ordinary everyday bear."

Reed agreed. "I'll see what kind of plan I can come up with. Maybe if we can flush him out...."

Hod's eyes narrowed. "You forgot something. Bear season starts in September. He won't move far from the Hartley place. That's where it has to happen."

They shook hands, and drove off in opposite directions, Reed thinking of Elvira and Hod of Lee. They were both right about one thing.

The Hartley place was where the circle would finally close.

Belle Attlebury became the owner of the Hartley property on Thursday, the 3rd of September. On the following day the Hartley Trust papers were signed and the 400-acre estate became a green area in the town of Paris forevermore. Lee became head of the board of directors, a lifetime job according to the rules Belle had penciled on a small piece of scrap paper she attached to the deeds she handed to Lee.

Simple rules, for in her own lifetime Belle had tried for simplicity.

The Hartley estate not only became a land trust, but Belle asked that the house be maintained in the condition it was presently in, and with this in mind she had given the trust an additional sum of money to be placed in investments that would allow the interest to be used for this purpose. She suggested that a museum might be established but shc left this to the board's discretion.

She asked that horseback-riding trails might be maintained and that one be called the Stubbs Trail.

She asked that cross-country skiers and Boy and Girl Scouts

might be given priority as to paths on the land.

And, although she disliked snowmobiles because of their noise, she recognized their value to many of Maine's citizens, and she asked that a track for them might be maintained on the very edge of the property connecting the Mt. Rhoda road with Minister's Road.

She was not in favor of hunting on the land, which made Hod smile, as she had placed his name, along with Clipper's and Malcolm's, on the list of possibilities she had given Lee for the board.

Belle Attlebury knew the Old Poacher. She knew she had outfoxed him this time for sure.

Clipper Cleaver was delighted after he got over his first disappointment of losing out on Hartley Heights. Development took up a lot of news space in the papers, and this new land trust was almost the first in the area. The position on the board made Clipper's name known throughout New England, along with Lee's and Malcolm's, for the Boston papers picked up the story and it became news in the city. Nobody knew who Hod Cole was, and nobody much cared, but the other three were of the real estate world, and their involvement in taking a large tract of woodland away from developers was news. Clipper, with Bunny's help, spent two nights studying up on George Stubbs, and became an authority by the end of the next week.

The 6th was a Sunday, and Clipper, very eager now to get right into the middle of this, called Lee and suggested they go look at the house, the barn, the grounds, and begin to make a few plans. Lee, listening to his booming voice over the phone, and holding it away from her ear so Meg could listen, was glad for this new Clipper who was beginning to see a new direction for some of Maine's land.

"He certainly makes a lot of noise, but I'm grateful to Clipper in ways I hadn't thought I could be. He gets things done; he really wants to help and he has some good ideas. We're going to look at it Tuesday, Meg. I'll call Belle Attlebury; she may want to go, and Clipper will bring Malcolm."

Lee, at home that evening, called Hod to tell him of the board's meeting, and then she went tiredly to bed after feeding the horses and taking Kate for a short walk. Ever since the newspaper stories had broken, both Carriage Trade and Cleaver Real Estate had phones ringing all day long. There was little time to think of anything but daily routine.

Hod and Reed conferred by phone. Tuesday would be the 8th, the day following the full moon. Both were sure this could be important to their plan.

"I'll be right there all the time." Hod spoke slowly, his chair upended against his kitchen wall and his hand hefting a piece of homemade bread and cheese. "So Lee will be safe. I've been trying to figure our move, but I haven't got it quite laid out yet. Best to just go and see what develops. We know where the suit is, so if he leaves us for any length of time, we'll know where to find him. You ought to be around, outside someplace with some backup, in case he comes out. And I plan to go back to the farm with Lee afterward."

Reed answered in what he hoped was a reassuring voice. "All right, we'll be outside. I can't see him taking on you, Clipper and Lee all at once, but we'll be sure. You said ten o'clock?"

Hod's chair came to rest. "Yup, that's what Clipper told Lee. I'm picking her up at High Meadows and taking her in my car. We'll meet the others there. Ought to be there about two hours in all. First time I've ever been on a board of directors. Going to enjoy this, I think."

Reed, at the other end, smiled at this new Hod Cole, and put the phone down gently, musing on the situation. They still had no set plan; all they could do was keep a close watch on the man who thought he was a bear.

They forgot one thing. He worshiped Diana of the Woods. This time he did not intend to fail.

On Monday morning, Clipper had a call from the Lymans. They wanted to talk with Malcolm on their forthcoming closing with the Johnsons, and on their own plans to move into Senior Citizens' housing. Malcolm was their security blanket; when in doubt they called him for advice, and as they were the direct line to more listings from elderly people, Clipper knew the value of a broker who kept his clients happy, and he promised to call Malcolm and have him get back to them. The only problem was they wanted to see Malcolm on Tuesday morning, the day slated for the board to look at the Hartley property.

Real estate, like farming, entails quite a bit of holding things together, and Clipper and Malcolm knew they had to change Tuesday's date if Lee could. A phone call solved the problem; Lee would meet them right that afternoon, and would try to call Hod. Belle Attlebury had decided not to join them. The difficulty was that for the first time in years Hod's phone was out, the result of a lumber truck running into a telephone pole near his road entrance, and for several miles around there would be no electrical or phone service for hours.

Lee considered. Three out of four always wins. She would go with Clipper and Malcolm today and with Hod on Tuesday when he showed up at the prearranged time. Visualizing being alone with Hod, this plan seemed even more to her liking than the original one. Full moon or not, there seemed no threat in any of her arrangements.

By luck, she mentioned the change to Ellen, who had decided to do a thorough job of cleaning the upstairs bedrooms and was deep in curtains and rugs when Lee, changed into a light sweater and corduroy pants, came down the hallway.

"I think I'll take Kate, Ellen, and keep her out from under your feet while you're working. As long as you will be here all day, I don't have to think of her taking care of the house. Ted has enough work in the barn to keep him busy for a few hours. Do we need anything in town?"

Ellen swept curtains into a pile and shook her head. "No, don't think so. We'll be settling in this weekend and Ted is real excited. I thought if I got this done for you today then I could work on the cabin tomorrow since we'll be bringing the furniture up on Saturday."

"I'm as eager as you. It's turning out to be a comfortable little place. I don't know why we didn't think of it long ago." Lee turned to leave.

"You forgot this, Lee. It was here by the bed. I didn't know you kept it upstairs." Ellen held up the crop Hod had made from the mountain ash.

"I don't usually. I guess I was just thinking over things last night when I went to bed, and I brought it upstairs with me." Lee suddenly sat down on the bed and looked up at the younger woman. "Ellen, I'm not sure about Hod. I don't know if it could work out for us."

Ellen stood still, staring into space for a moment. Then she looked at Lee with a smile. "You'll know—all of a sudden you'll know. It's strange, isn't it, you're the one I always ask for help, and now you're asking me. If anyone can make it work, you can. That man cares about you. Not that Carter didn't. But Hod is different, somehow. Don't keep fretting about it so much, just do it."

Lee gave her a hug, called to Kate and ran down the stairs. Minutes later she was on her way to the Hartley property.

Clipper and Malcolm were already there; the new Wagoneer that Clipper had just purchased was pulled to one side of the dooryard. Early September with its palette of colors made light and shadows over the grounds; Ted on one of his good days had cut the lawn for one last time and the old flower beds were mats of purple and maroon asters. The house looked inviting, not formidable as Lee had once known it, and the three new caretakers stood together suddenly realizing that they were now in charge of this 400-acre estate.

On paper it had seemed a small chore. In reality it seemed larger.

"Let's take a good look at the interior first. I never did see the cellar thoroughly. Then let's check out the barn. Looks to me like we may have to tear that down." Clipper was eager to begin.

Lee agreed. "I have a list of the furnishings. Meg and I made it when we handled the property. We ought to decide on our long range plans—do we want to have it like a museum—like the Moses Mason house in Bethel, or do we want to just have it open at certain times? We need at least two or three more board members; we only have four counting Hod, and I'll see him tomorrow."

Malcolm disagreed. "I don't see why we need more than four. It's not all that difficult, Lee. We don't need all those opinions. We can decide ourselves. I'm really not sure the house ought to be open to the public at all."

Lee sensed a problem she had not anticipated. Always the diplomat, she tried a new tack. "All right, let's just look around today, as Clipper suggested. Then we'll have a board meeting later on in the month and decide on our strategy for this fall and winter. Clipper, you haven't seen much of the grounds. Malcolm and I know them pretty well from riding and skiing, but I don't think you do. Maybe we can walk about a bit today."

Clipper, busy hauling a pad and pencil out of his jacket pocket, agreed. Without more discussion, Lee opened the front door, turned off the security system, and they began their tour. Kate, staying close to her mistress, followed the three brokers from room to room. An older dog now, she took the heel position with little coaxing, and resignedly kept by Lee's side hoping there would yet be a chance for a run in the woods.

They were still on the first floor when Clipper discovered he'd forgotten his camera. "Damn. Left it right on the office desk. Wanted to take a picture of that lobster pot. Well...."

Malcolm waved his hands. "Why don't you skip back and get it? You won't be over twenty minutes. We have a couple of hours. Lee and I'll just walk around a bit while you're gone. Give Kate a little run. What do you say?"

Lee agreed. "Of course, go get it, Clipper. It would be nice to get some pictures today and I didn't bring my camera. Meg and I never took one of the lobster pot as you call it. Go ahead."

Clipper broke into a little trot and was off to the Wagoneer and down the roadway.

At this same moment, Ellen, shaking out rugs, heard the phone ring and almost didn't answer. Finally, at the insistent sixth ring, she went inside and picked it up. Reed's voice came to her ears.

"I'd like to speak with Lee, Ellen. Meg said she changed her day off."

"Yes, she went up to the Hartley place today; Clipper had to change the time. She's up there with the two of them."

"What two?" Reed's voice was sharp.

"Why, Malcolm and Clipper. She said she couldn't get Hod on the phone. His phone's out for some reason. She'll go up again with him tomorrow."

This time Reed's voice was even sharper. "How long ago, Ellen? How long ago did they leave?"

"Oh, maybe ten, twenty minutes. She said they'd be there for a couple of hours. Took Kate with her. What....?"

There was no answer. Reed was moving.

At the same moment that Ellen was answering Reed's call, Belle Attlebury decided to take a walk. Frederick was asleep in the borning room and if he followed his familiar pattern, his nap would last for one-and-a-half to two hours. This would give her time to walk up along the woods path and perhaps gather a few of the purple asters. Belle had a special love for these flowers and there had never been an autumn that she hadn't filled one of her mother's old pewter mugs with them and placed it on her kitchen table.

This September, of many Septembers, Belle felt her own mortality, and the need to follow a tradition she had followed for years. The grounds of the Hartley estate were filled with asters. She could walk there and back before Frederick awoke. Tucking her old jackknife in her skirt pocket, and taking an apple to eat on the way, Belle started along the path.

And, at the same moment of Ellen's call and Belle's decision to walk out, Hod drove to Paris to check with the phone company. Details were arranged, and he swung up to the town office and went in to find Reed and talk of the next day's plans.

Reed, the girl at the desk told him, had left in a mighty big hurry a few minutes before—said he was heading up to Minister's Road. Hod felt uneasy in the back of his mind, and suddenly turned and headed in the same direction.

The circle was complete. The time had come.

·26·

Malcolm and Lee walked with Kate around the outside of the house and barn. The Gordon sniffed in a brush pile for partridge, while Malcolm and Lee discussed the ridgeline of the barn, now sagging badly in the middle.

Suddenly, Malcolm, holding his stomach, said rather frantically to Lee, "I'd better leave you for a few minutes and use that outhouse. My stomach's been bothering me for the past couple of days—I think I've eaten something that wasn't right. You go ahead in the barn. I'm going to need some time by myself." He disappeared into the side door of the ell.

Lee nodded and calling Kate, stepped inside the now open big barn door. The light inside was not bright, but with the orientation of the barn, it was still bright enough to see more of the interior than she had seen before.

Up above, several of the timbers were out of their slots and balanced precariously against one another. An old block and tackle setup was secured to one beam by a worn rope ending in a tie-up on an upright on the barn floor. The mows held hay from more than forty years before when the barn had housed a few cattle; now squirrels and porcupines lived here. Lee's eyes were seeing much they had not seen on previous visits. She had about decided in earnest that this was a rather dangerous place to be when she heard the sound.

At the same moment Kate growled.

Coming at them, from the corner off the ell, was the bear. He was moving fast; time was an element to be reckoned with now, and he could not delay. In his outstretched paw was the giant claw, the missing Smith and Hawken hand cultivator.

Lee screamed and backed closer to the wall, crowding in against the old barn boards. Almost without knowing, she raised her hands to shield her face. One hand held the rowan tree riding crop.

And then the Gordon sprang. Her great, thundering, rolling roar of a bark sounded through the barn, through the dooryard, through the woods and into the swamp. A sound harking back to primeval times when dogs hunted in packs, hunted to kill to survive. Something within the setter gave her the strength she needed, and with all the power of her eighty pounds, she sank her teeth into the bear's side.

Belle Attlebury, walking slowly up the path, nearly to the asters in the dooryard and closest to the barn, heard the setter's roar.

Hod, moving fast and running low with his rifle held close, heard the setter's roar.

Reed, having met Clipper coming back with his camera, at the edge of the dooryard, heard the setter's roar.

They heard the wild, woman-like scream of the bear as it raked its claw and opened the setter's side, and they heard the agonized screams of the woman and the dog. There was almost no time left.

Belle, closest, reached the big open door first, and her eyes scanned the barn while her swift wits searched for a way to save Lee. Still sharp in her seventies, still quick to sum up a situation, Belle did the only thing she could think of to create a diversion and back the bear off.

She cut the rope. With one swift, clean stroke she cut the rope that held the old block and tackle. The little jackknife dropped to the floor and Belle screamed for help.

And, from the shadows above, with a creaking, groaning sound, the huge wooden relic of another age swung suspended for a moment and then crashed to the floor below.

It did not come down alone.

The balanced timbers, the beams out of place, the boards one upon another, caved in like a pile of jackstraws. With a resounding crash, the whole side of the old Hartley barn gave way.

And crushed the back of the huge furry animal trying to kill Lee Heaward.

Clipper, talking with Bunny later that day, said that he thought he was back in 'Nam. Dust, dirt, splinters, broken boards and blood and the screaming. Especially, the screaming.

Lee, under the bear, and still conscious, but with one arm twisted under her, cried out for Kate. The bear, still alive, although mortally injured, screamed incessantly. Kate, pinned in the wreckage but with one paw touching Lee, and in agonizing pain from the claw wound, whimpered softly. It was a bloody mess.

The three men, moving swiftly, sorted it out. Clipper pulled Kate out gently, stripping off his own shirt to staunch the flow of blood from her ragged wound. Following Reed's frantic instructions, he called on his portable radio for help from the sheriff's office, the state police, the ambulance and a veterinarian. He placed Kate gently on a bed of leaves and left Belle Attlebury to hold the shirt firmly against the setter's side until help could arrive. Then he went back in to help Reed and Hod. It took an hour or so to clear the rubble and get the bear out first. Ropes and leverage had to be used to lift one of the timbers. A rescue squad from the fire department came to help. The state police arrived and took charge. A stretcher bearer, easing the furry body up off of Lee, cried out, "Holy God, this is a man!"

And Reed, bowing his head, said softly, "Once it was."

Lee was still conscious. Hod held her hand throughout the ordeal and talked gently to her. Once they had realized that she was trapped in a cocoon-like space with no pressure upon her, they worked to keep her from becoming hysterical until they could get her out. Her only concern was Kate, and Clipper told her twice that the veterinarian, who had been on a nearby farm call and heard his radio asking for help up at the Hartley place, felt the dog would survive.

It was a dreadful three hours. When it was over, when the bear who was not a bear was in a hospital bed dying, when Lee's arm was bandaged at the emergency center, when Kate was sewn up and taken back to the farm under heavy sedation, when Reed had a chance, he called Elvira in Camden and she drove down in record time.

Reed sat with her at Malcolm's bedside. Before he died, Malcolm told Elvira what she had long suspected. And Reed, with sorrow for this woman who had such pride in family, took it all down. Outside, the newspapers had already gotten wind of the story, and reporters waited for the police chief to leave the hospital.

When he did, he shunted them off. "I'll make a statement in a few hours. You won't believe it anyway, but I'll tell you what I can. Nothing more right now, please."

That night the full moon rose over Streaked Mountain with a clarity making it seem almost within a hand's reach. A buck, browsing in the magic circle just off the bridle path on the Hartley property, raised his head and gazed at the moon. A fox, starting out on her evening rounds of the orchard, stopped with one paw raised, to watch its rise. The horses looked out of their small stall windows and saw the light overspreading the fields. Somehow, the moonlight cleansed the land that had so recently drawn blood.

Within the house at High Meadows, in front of the old fireplace, the people gathered. There had been interviews with the state police, statements taken, and now they were alone with Reed, who wanted them to hear the ending of the story, so they might finally put it from their minds, knowing that the evil was gone for good.

Ellen and Ted came in from the cabin, and Ellen helped Lee, whose arm was aching, make coffee and heat a blueberry pie from the freezer. Lee sat on the large couch close to the fire, now burning low with an ash log, and trailed her one good arm with fingers touching the head of the black and gold Gordon. Kate's tail thumped when her name was mentioned; she was encased in a partial cast, but her eyes were bright and she would recover except for a slight limp.

"Everything you puzzled out, Hod, was exactly true. He hated Lee because he loved her—does that make sense? And she did an unforgiveable thing—she didn't choose him. He felt he had powers beyond that of an ordinary mortal—she should have realized who he was. When she didn't he started out small, with threats. The phone calls. Then he tried the barn; he did that himself and nearly was caught when Kate barked; but he got away in time. He said he really didn't intend to burn it; just to threaten.

He thought, he said, that Lee would think it was developers and turn to him, Malcolm, for help. The idea that Sam Childs might be involved was good—it created a red herring. But Lee, instead of turning to him, seemed to turn to Carter. None of his plans worked, so then he tried another tack and used the valerian. Which he stole from Mrs. Bemis's storage bottle, by the way. He didn't care when she became ill too; he hated her anyway." Reed paused.

Hod leaned forward. He sat close to Lee with his arm across the rear of the sofa and behind her shoulders. He had been listening intently to Reed, who was standing by the fire. "The blouse? Did he slash it the night of the first committee meeting as I thought?"

Reed nodded. "Yes. He went upstairs to the bathroom, saw it in Lee's open closet, grabbed her nail scissors, slashed it and stuffed it back in the closet. Another way of telling her he hated her."

Lee shivered. "I thought we were friends. I knew he was angry when I wouldn't have an arrangement with him. I had no idea how deeply it went. Maybe I could have stopped it."

"No." Reed was tired. In the few years he had been chief of police he had never faced anything such as the last few months. The pure horror of what had happened in the Hartley barn had shaken him more than he wished to admit. It was still hard to conceive that one man's mind had gone to such lengths. It was harder still to believe that this man thought himself a witch within the soul of a bear driven to murder in an elaborate puzzle he had created and dared them all to solve.

"No," Reed continued, "you wouldn't have changed things. He said he didn't intend for Jim to die; that was a mistake. He'd come up through the cellar and the passageway and came out into the room after putting the bear suit on, and there was Jim just entering the room. He waved the claw and of course Jim backed right out. It was a scary outfit. The whole idea of it, in the beginning, was so he could see what you were doing, Lee. He knew the seasons, knew the woods and when he could travel safely through them. He knew when hunting season started. That's when he stayed close to the house."

"And he really knew the house." Hod interrupted. "He knew all the passageways."

"Yes; the other thing is that he was the one who cleaned out the locked room in the beginning. Elvira pieced that together." And Reed told the story of the dealer at the flea market.

"So, then," Lee spoke softly, "I suppose when we put the property up for sale, he would lose his hiding place and that made him even angrier."

"Exactly." Reed continued, "He'd use the tomb, but that was too open, and there was the hollow tree as we thought, on a direct line, but that was too easy for any horseback rider to happen upon. The house was all-important. He was more and more frustrated; he thought he and Clipper and some others might have a deal, and that didn't work, and then Belle gave it into a trust fund after she'd bought it. He was more out of control of his territory."

"And Ted, was it the way I thought?" Hod was anxious for the answer. Ted, hearing his name, listened intently.

"You had it right on the nose. He must have come out of the tomb, and when Ted saw him, he had to move fast. He meant to kill then. In fact, he thought he had. Afterward he kept track of Ted's loss of memory, and when he saw him he was sure Ted had no recollection of what had happened. Who'd believe him, anyway? Malcolm just figured he'd let that alone for a while."

The same shiver crossed Lee's spine. "Did he mean to kill me with the barbed wire?"

"That he didn't seem sure of. He said he hoped either you or

Carter would be hurt if the horses spooked. He didn't care which one of you. He said he wished it had worked."

Lee's eyes filled. "My horses. I could have killed, myself, that day if I'd known who it was." She patted Kate.

"And then, Cokie." Reed was coming to the end. "She remembered a fur coat he'd bought. And she figured it out. He said he was sure she was going to blackmail him. There was pure hatred when he spoke of Cokie. He said for a moment he thought she might roll out of his reach. He told me he thought she knew karate. Any of you know that?"

Lee nodded. "Now that you speak of it, I think she told us once her parents were actors and knew all sorts of tricks. So she might have known karate. I hate thinking of Cokie fighting him. It must have been dreadful." Lee lowered her head and thought of her own experience.

There was a long silence in the room. The old couches, the fire, the smell of food, the sense of safety warded off the thoughts of evil.

"What kind of a man would do all those things and plan them all out and think he was a bear and a witch—or is it warlock?" Ellen had been listening, letting it all pile up inside, and now she had to ask the question.

"Not a sane one." Hod answered. "That's what the trouble was from the beginning. We couldn't understand what he was doing until we began to understand his rules. Then it was almost too late."

Reed finished the story. "He ran by the full moon. So he tried to twist it around this one last time to kill Lee. If he had succeeded, he would have met Clipper coming back and told him he couldn't find Lee. And they would have found her together; no matter what Reed or Elvira suspected, nothing could have been proven. Although he was beginning to feel that Elvira suspected."

"God bless Belle Attlebury," Hod almost whispered.

"Is Elvira burying Malcolm in Maine?" Lee held Hod's hand tightly, feeling reassurance flow through her fingers.

Reed nodded. "Having him cremated. Burying the ashes in the Hill cemetery. She said she just wanted to be alone; she may sell Run for Cover. You know what his last words were, Lee, just before he died?"

"What?"

"Damn that rowan tree crop."

Epilogue

Hod and Lee stood together in the moonlight. Ellen and Ted had gone back to their cabin, and Reed had returned to town to finish writing his report and talk with the state police.

Across the valley, the light from the old Collins farm flickered, went out, came on again.

Lee gripped Hod's arm and pointed. "Look."

Hod nodded. "Deer, isn't it? Seen that before different times when they cross a direct line. How long did it take you to figure it out?"

"A while. I thought it was magic at first. Now, when I see it, it gives me a sense of place. The deer are passing, and my world is all right again. You know, the apple pickers will be here next week. It's the season."

Hod smiled and held her close, knowing that, finally, after all the sorrow and terror, they had found their answer. "Lee, I wouldn't be surprised if it's our season too."

Inside, by a fading fire, a Gordon setter thumped her tail. A coon cat curled beneath the catnip plants in the herb garden, protected by St. Fiacre. And a man and a woman found their own magic.

Deep in the waters of the quarry on the Hartley estate, a sapphire and silver pendant is guarded forever by the golden carp. The bear who was not a bear is gone from the face of the earth.

And Belle Attlebury is forever blessed by the wild, wild woods.